DEAD
AIR

OTHER CULLEN AND COBB MYSTERIES

Serpents Rising

DEAD

A CULLEN AND COBB MYSTERY

AIR

DAVID A. POULSEN

DUNDURN
TORONTO

Cover image: ©ImagineGolf/iStockphoto
Printer: Webcom

Library and Archives Canada Cataloguing in Publication

Poulsen, David A., 1946-, author
    Dead air / David A. Poulsen.

(A Cullen and Cobb mystery)
Issued in print and electronic formats.
ISBN 978-1-4597-3668-9 (paperback).--ISBN 978-1-4597-3669-6 (PDF).--
ISBN 978-1-4597-3670-2 (EPUB)

    I. Title. II. Series: Poulsen, David A., 1946- Cullen and Cobb mystery.

PS8581.O848D43 2017   C813ʾ.54   C2016-905649-X
                                              C2016-905650-3

1   2   3   4   5   21   20   19   18   17

Conseil des Arts   Canada Council   Canada   ONTARIO ARTS COUNCIL
du Canada   for the Arts   CONSEIL DES ARTS DE L'ONTARIO
                                                an Ontario government agency
                                                un organisme du gouvernement de l'Ontario

We acknowledge the support of the Canada Council for the Arts and the Ontario Arts Council for our publishing program. We also acknowledge the financial support of the Government of Ontario, through the Ontario Book Publishing Tax Credit and the Ontario Media Development Corporation, and the Government of Canada.

Care has been taken to trace the ownership of copyright material used in this book. The author and the publisher welcome any information enabling them to rectify any references or credits in subsequent editions.

— J. Kirk Howard, President

VISIT US AT

 dundurn.com | 🐦 @dundurnpress | f dundurnpress | 📷 dundurnpress

Dundurn
3 Church Street, Suite 500
Toronto, Ontario, Canada
M5E 1M2

PROLOGUE

June 1999

The shadows were deepening as darkness rolled over and around the dense, still forest. The poplars and spruce stood silent and unmoving, the moonlight peeking through clouds, but only now and then.

Black emerged from the meeting with his inner circle — the three people he trusted. One final meeting to tie up the last loose ends and make certain everything was in readiness for the departure. There could be no mistakes — not now when they'd come this far and been so successful. In every way.

Black liked the darkness. It was why he had chosen the name. They'd all chosen colours, all four members of the organizing committee — it had been his suggestion, based on his favourite movie, *Reservoir Dogs*. And for him, Mr. Black was the perfect choice — black, the colour of coal, of outer space, of night ... of death.

The rest — the attendees (he disliked the term "delegates") were numbers. Numbers, like colours — anonymous.

The week couldn't have gone better. He was absolutely certain of that. A magical time in a magical place. Not one complaint. As tough physically, mentally, and psychologically as this camp had been, the most demanding he'd ever been a part of, every single delegate was going away from here happy, energized, and full of hope for a brighter future than ever before.

That was something else he'd insisted on. It was a camp — not a *boot camp*. Black felt the latter term had a negative ring. The left painted boot camps as intense, hate-inspired brainwashing sessions. But they weren't that, not at all. This camp had been carefully designed to prepare attendees to fight long and hard, crush all opposition, and do whatever it took to win. You could only effect change by being in power. And camps like this one equipped delegates to help bring about the victory that had to happen.

As the noise from the final night's celebration filtered through the trees, he moved away from his companions to reflect, to smile, and to plan. And to do what had to be done.

The time for reflection felt good. He thought back on all the months of planning — of arranging for this place, just a few miles from Buffalo, Wyoming, with all its Old West history and only several hundred yards from the site of the Wagon Box Fight, an important part of that history. The logistics had been flawless — from the food and drink, the supplies the instructors and guest speakers needed, everything right down to the porta-potties, every detail including the intense secrecy that was the most important detail of all. And the most amazing part was knowing that a few hours after the camp was packed up and gone, there would be virtually no evidence to show that it had even taken place. Or, most importantly, who had been there.

The presenters had been even better than Black had dared hope for — inspirational and zealous without coming off so extreme as to be characterized merely as crackpots. That was important given the number of new recruits at this gathering. And it was important, too, because that was something else the left had done and continued to do — focus its attention and its attacks on the few who were unable to contain their admitted intolerance and their over-the-top fervour. One of the Fox News commentators — Carlisle, the guy from Wichita, Kansas, who spoke on Thursday night — had said it perfectly. "The public will buy anything that is packaged and presented well — they'll buy nothing that's packaged and presented badly. We have to be better salesmen than the other side."

And Black knew Carlisle was right. Now the stage was set. There would never, *could* never be another Clinton. The second president in history to be impeached was still in place. Acquitted by a liberal-dominated court. But the slut president wouldn't be there much longer; in less than two years he'd be gone. His replacement was ready and waiting. And best of all, Black knew that after this week, after this camp — *his* camp — conservative commentators and right-wing future candidates and incumbents were more prepared to go into battle than they'd ever been.

Tomorrow they'd leave, go back to their homes and home bases, ready to take the fight to the next level. Black felt his gut tighten as the excitement of knowing what these six days had been and what had been accomplished took hold of him. He managed a rare smile.

Black's walk had taken him to the back of the camp, directly behind the RVs and tents that dotted the large clearing designated Bivouac C. His walk had been delib-erate, designed to bring him to this area. One last detail to be taken care of. And he was the one who had to do it. He knew that.

He almost laughed at the gall of the infiltrator. And the stupidity. The fool actually believed he could come in here, spy on them, steal their secrets, and walk away unscathed. And what then? Print them in some poorly crafted story the left-wing media would fall over themselves to present? How arrogant and stupid journalists could be.

This one was arrogant, stupid, *and* wrong. Wrong to think he could pull it off. And just as wrong to agree to meet Black privately — *there's something I want to share with you.* And the fool had bought it, further evidence of his idiocy.

Black stopped just behind a low canopy of brush and larger pines. He slipped the backpack off and onto the ground in front of him, reached in and took out first the night goggles, then the knife. Everything he needed.

He pushed the backpack under the brush. He'd retrieve it in the morning as they were preparing to leave. All of them. Except for the one who would *not* be leaving. He would remain here — forever.

Black began moving slowly and silently through the deep, dark woods — to the place they had agreed to meet. And for the second time in as many minutes, Black was smiling.

ONE

It was the top of the fifth inning and Kyla Sawley, three weeks shy of her ninth birthday, had just lashed a vicious liner to left.

Okay, that might be overstating things. It was actually a slow roller that the opposing shortstop, intensely focused on her gum and apparently unable to multi-task, had ignored as the ball passed by a metre to her right. It didn't have enough momentum to reach the outfield but the left fielder had to run in and pick it up as the shortstop, the biggest girl on either team and apparently annoyed at the interruption, glared first at the ball, then at Kyla.

Cobb sat down next to me at that exact moment. The once green, now *splotchy* green bleacher sat behind the first baseline and was populated by parents and siblings of the girls on Kyla's team. The opposition families outnumbered us and pretty much filled the bleacher behind the third base line.

"Awright," Cobb said. "Looks like the game's going well."

I shook my head. "Unfortunately the shortstop is the only player on that team who isn't destined for a long and successful career in the majors."

"I wasn't aware girls played in the big leagues."

"These girls could," I said. "Anyway, this will be the last at bat. The ten-run rule will mercifully end the thing. But if Kyla scores, we'll avert the shutout, a huge moral victory."

Cobb stood up, cupped his hands to his mouth. "Go —" He stopped in mid-yell, looked down at me. "What are they called?"

"The Bobcats."

"Go Bobcats!" he shouted. And sat back down.

Mike Cobb, ex-cop, now private detective and friend.

"Sorry I got here so late. I drove around town for a while. It's looking pretty good."

The town was High River, devastated by flood a year before. In fact, the game was one of the first since the flood to be played in George Lane Park, which, like most of the town, had been victim to the watery nightmare of June 20, 2013.

Cobb was right. High River's residents, as well as volunteers from all over the province and beyond, had battled back after the water's ravages and were rebuilding a community that had long been the one I'd most want to live in if I didn't live in Calgary.

The batter who followed Kyla drew a walk, and with two outs we had a runner in scoring position for the first time in the game.

The third-base coach clapped her hands together and called encouragement to the Bobcats.

"Come on, girls. Be ready on the bases. Okay, Jenny, just a base hit now."

The third-base coach and manager of the team was Jill Sawley, Kyla's mom. She was also the woman I'd been seeing for about six months, going back to a time when Cobb and I had worked together on a couple of cases, one involving a runaway, drug-addicted kid and the other the search for a sociopath who had murdered my wife several years before.

Cobb did not look like a baseball parent. Even in gym pants, New Balance sneakers, and a Minnesota Vikings ball cap, he did not have the look. In fact, at a couple of inches over six feet and damn little body fat on that frame, he looked like a cop about to bust an over-exuberant baseball parent or a dishonest umpire.

We had met for lunch about once a month and a couple of times for a few beers since our association of the previous winter, but nothing that pertained to his line of work had arisen since that time. I was happy about that. Cobb had joked about us working together from time to time to thwart Calgary's criminal element, but although I had written a number of pieces on crime in my work as a freelance journalist, I had decided that I was not cut out for butting heads with bad guys and had made that quite clear to Cobb.

So when he called this morning, wondering what I was "up to on a fine Saturday," I was suspicious. Then when he suggested he stop by the game and maybe we could have a quick chat afterward, I became doubly dubious.

But first things first. The Bobcats catcher was the best hitter on the team and she was in the batter's box tapping her cleats and taking deep breaths. She stepped out of the batter's box and looked at Jill. I noticed Jill wasn't flashing signs. Apparently, trailing by a couple of converted touchdowns, the Bobcats manager wasn't thinking of having her cleanup hitter lay down a bunt.

Eventually the batter took the hint and stepped back into the box. Two pitches later she swung at a one-and-one change-up and hit a long, towering fly ball to centre field that looked sure to be over the centre fielder's head and good for a couple of face-saving runs. And, in fact, it would have been over most centre fielders' heads.

All except maybe Willie Mays ... and the girl who played centre field for the High River Flyers. She ran for what seemed like a very long time and made a spectacular over-the-shoulder catch, crashing into the fence and crumpling to the ground. Two, maybe three seconds later she bounced up, ball in hand and a big grin on her face. The 14–0 score would stand.

"I see what you mean," Cobb said. "Big leagues."

"Uh-huh."

We stood up.

"You got a few minutes?" Cobb looked at me.

I shrugged. "If this conversation is going to result in people going out of their way to kill me, probably not." Which is what had happened the last time Cobb and I had worked together.

"Nope." Cobb grinned. "Nothing dramatic this time. A little research, that's all."

We stepped down from the bleacher as Jill arrived. She looked terrific, even in her blue-and-white Bobcats T-shirt and with the downcast expression of a manager whose team had just been shellacked. She hugged Cobb and took my hand. "I'm taking the girls to the Hitchin' Post — one of the great burger-slash-ice-cream places in this part of the world. Milkshakes. You guys wanna come?"

"How about we catch up with you later? Mike thinks he might need my expertise on something."

She looked at Cobb, a smile crinkling the corners of her eyes. "I don't want my guy shot, knifed, poisoned, or in any way harmed."

Cobb laughed. "Funny, he just said the same thing. No worries, this one's pretty benign. I won't even keep him out late at night, promise."

Cobb and I adjourned to Colossi's, a funky, independent coffee place in the heart of High River's still-recovering downtown. I'd been worried, as I had with all of my favourite High River places, that this one might not reopen after the flood. Some hadn't. Colossi's did and I was glad.

Cobb sipped a caramel macchiato. I had opted for a medium house blend.

I looked at him over the rim of my cup. "Research," I said.

He nodded, drank some more coffee, set his cup down. "I've been hired by Buckley-Rand Larmer."

I whistled. "Mr. Right-Wing Radio?"

Cobb nodded. "The same. Bodyguard work. Seems he's been receiving threatening notes, emails, phone calls."

"Who would've thought that possible?"

Cobb smiled a little. "He *has* upset a few people."

"No, 'upset' is what people get when the neighbour's muffler needs replacing. What Larmer triggers is outrage. And the outraged number more than a few."

Cobb circled the rim of his cup with his index finger, licked off the caramel. "Some of his positions might seem pretty over the top but the guy's a long way from an idiot."

"Not an idiot at all." I shook my head. "Larmer's the worst kind of extremist — intelligent, persuasive, eloquent … and dangerous."

"Your paths cross at all over the years?"

I drank some coffee, dabbed a napkin to my mouth. "We've chatted a few times. We both spoke at the same event one time. A couple of years ago. I was still trying to get over Diane's death so I didn't want to do it. But they paid pretty well and I was getting short of money.

"Of course I knew who Larmer was and had exchanged hellos a couple of times, but this was the first time I'd really come face to face with the guy for longer than a few minutes."

"And your first impression was?"

"He's a hater — French Canadians, First Nations, Muslims, environmentalists, gays, liberals — and for him it's not about disagreeing or presenting alternatives; he wants to destroy all those who don't share his views. And he's pretty good at it. Buckley-Rand Larmer has carved up enough people on his RIGHT TALK 700 radio show that his enemy list should rival the Yellow Pages. So good luck."

"Sounds like the crossing of paths may have encountered a land mine or two."

"Not really. No fireworks at all. We were speaking to an audience of U of C students. The topic was 'The Influence of the Media in the Twenty-First Century — Increasing or Declining?'"

"And?"

"And I spoke on the increasing influence of the media in the twenty-first century."

"Larmer?"

"Addressed the dangers of movements like 'Idle No More.' Referred to it as *antics*."

"And that related to the topic how?"

"It didn't. But he was by far the more interesting speaker that day. Pissed off a good number of the students but was certainly remembered. I imagine most had forgotten me and my presentation before they got to their next class."

Cobb sat back in his chair and looked at me. "He has a large following. Large and loyal."

"No question. There are lots of conservative thinkers who'd sooner stick pins in their eyes than miss one of his shows. Get their daily dose of Larmer hate-spew and they're good to go."

Cobb grinned. "I'm sensing you don't like the guy."

"Nothing gets by you." I could feel myself becoming more intense than the conversation warranted and I knew it. My turn to sit back. I smiled at Cobb, couldn't quite manage a grin. "I can get a little over the top myself thinking about guys like Buckley-Rand Larmer. They're scary. I don't care what side of the political spectrum they occupy."

Cobb nodded but didn't say anything.

"So what do you think?" I asked. "Anything to the threats?"

Cobb shrugged. "He thinks so. No surprise, this isn't the first time it's happened. Says he's always laughed it off before. But this time he's spooked. Judging from his manner when I met with him, I'd say *real* spooked. Especially since Hamilton."

I thought a moment, then nodded, remembering. "Spring of 2012, wasn't it? Conservative radio talk-show host in Hamilton, Ontario, shot in the parking lot after his show … and when that didn't kill him, they came after him a second time a few months later. Finished the job. That was a weird one."

"Yeah, getting shot the first time made him an instant hero. In fact, that probably moved his various causes further and faster than ten thousand broadcasts. Overnight Facebook and Twitter rock star. And you're right — the second time the shooter made no mistake."

"Was it the same shooter both times?"

"Never caught the guy, so the cops don't know for sure, but the word is they think so, yeah."

"Any similarities between what happened to the Hamilton guy and what's going on with Larmer?"

"Hard to say. Nothing on the surface, but with them both being in the same line of work, and both good at stirring up hornet's nests …"

"I can see why your guy would be nervous."

"My guy," Cobb repeated softly, then shook his head. "Not my *guy*, Adam, my *client*."

I shrugged. "Cops?"

"They're looking into it. But Larmer isn't convinced he's safe in the meantime. That's where I come in."

"Anybody else at the station receiving threats?"

"I've talked to all the other on-air people." He consulted his notebook. "Jared Petterson, Jason T. Carver, Nava Dehl, and Terrance Peete — they're the on-air big guns, along with Larmer. All have been threatened at various times in their careers, but none recently."

"And you want what from me?"

"Whatever you can dig up. I'd like to know as much as I can about Buckley-Rand Larmer. Going back as far as you think is relevant and going as far afield as you think you need to."

"In depth."

Cobb sat forward, drank the last of his coffee, and nodded. "Uh-huh. Everything you can give me. Maybe by learning all I can about him, I might find out something about the threat maker. Or at least the kind of person who would want to threaten him."

"Like I said, it's take-a-number when it comes to people who wouldn't mind seeing Larmer get hit by a bus."

"We're only interested in those who want to be driving the bus."

"We?"

"Partners again." The grin returned to Cobb's chiselled features. "And the good news — no budget constraints. He's paying me a big dollar and I told him I may have to call on outside resources. He couldn't nod his head fast enough. Adam, the guy's scared. He's trying to macho his way through it but it's there — fear."

"How are the threats being made?"

"Some of it's the usual stuff — phone calls from untraceable cells …"

"Burners," I said.

"I wasn't sure you knew the jargon, but yeah."

"I covered the drug trade for a few years — picked up a few things."

Cobb looked sheepish. "Sorry, I should have known that."

"No harm, no foul," I said. "What else?"

"Calls from phone booths, emails, notes in the regular mail … a couple of hand-delivered letters to the station, but of course, the delivery people were paid cash, never actually saw the person wanting the package delivered. So far, whoever's making the threats has been very good at avoiding detection."

"Phone booths, snail mail, package delivery — old school."

Cobb thought for a minute. "Good point. But there were also the emails and the calls from burners."

I nodded. "So maybe the bad guy wants to confuse investigators. Or he's just eclectic."

"He. Funny how we assume the bad guys are *guys*."

"You're right," I said. "I should've learned my lesson on that the last time around. So what's Larmer being threatened with?"

"The recurring theme is agony — pretty much every one of the threats has referenced the pain that will be coming his way. 'Like the pain you've caused others, you piece of shit.' That's an exact quote by the way. A lot of stuff similar in nature. All of which will happen if Larmer doesn't get off the air and out of Calgary — immediately."

"How long's it been going on?"

"Close to six weeks," Cobb answered. "But there's more. The thing that has him really worried is the fact that someone has been in his house — disarmed the alarm, got inside, and left a couple of pointed warnings."

I rubbed a hand across my chin. "That's taking things to another level, all right. No wonder he's scared."

"And one more thing. Some of the notes have included references to things in Larmer's life, past and present, that not a lot of people would know about."

"References to what exactly?"

"Yeah, that's a bit of a problem. Larmer won't tell me that and won't even allow questions about it. In fact, I'm getting the feeling that there are a few things Larmer isn't telling me."

"So you haven't seen the notes."

"He destroyed them."

"Kind of handcuffs you, doesn't it."

"It would if he wanted me to investigate who's doing the threatening. But that's not it. In fact, he's been very specific about how that's not my role. My job is to keep his ass on the top side of the grass. Nothing more, nothing less."

"But if the identity of the person making the threats isn't determined, you could be guarding Buckley-Rand Larmer for a couple of decades."

"My thought exactly. Which is why we're having this conversation."

"Any chance he's faking it? Making the whole thing up?"

"To what end?"

"He saw what happened to the guy in Hamilton. More listeners. More sympathy. More love."

Cobb shook his head. "I think I'd know if he was conning me. Like I said, the guy looks and sounds scared. And I don't think it's an act. Besides, if he wanted to make points with listeners he'd want it all out there. And he *doesn't* want that. At least not now."

"Do you know if the guy who got killed in Hamilton — did he receive any threats before either the first or second shooting?"

"I wondered that myself. Made some calls. If he did no one seems to know about it."

I thought about that, finally leaned forward. "I'm guessing you want whatever I can come up with fast."

"The quicker the better."

"Uh-huh."

"And for now at least I'd prefer that our arrangement remain confidential."

"You worried about Larmer finding out?"

Cobb shook his head. "No, I told him I'd have someone doing some digging — I might have failed to mention the digging would be into his past. But more than that — if there is someone out there intent on doing more than threaten this guy, I'd prefer for them not to know what we're up to."

I put my finger to my lips. "These babies are sealed."

"So you're game?"

"Researching the life of a slimeball. Being sneaky. And getting well paid to do it. What's not to like?" I nodded, we stood up and shook hands, then started for the door of Colossi's. "I'll get into this and give you a call in a day or two, let you know how I'm faring."

"Perfect."

On the sidewalk outside, Cobb said, "I'll let you get back to the baseball festivities. By the way, milkshakes when they lose, what do they do when they win?"

"Hasn't been an issue so far this season."

"Long as they're having fun."

"The kids are fine," I told him. "It's the manager we may have to arrange counselling for."

Cobb laughed and started walking away, singing, "'Take Me Out to the Ball Game.'"

"Ha, ha," I said to his back.

TWO

By nine the next morning I was at my desk — actually a table-desk I had picked up at an antique store. It had come from the Bessborough Hotel in Saskatoon, sixties vintage. It was banged up and the centre drawer — the only drawer — opened only when it was in the mood. But it was the place I liked to be when I wanted to create/research/read *Calvin and Hobbes*.

The desk faced the picture window in my bachelor apartment. The view of Calgary was the biggest reason I'd rented the place a couple of years earlier. The view wasn't as good as from the North Hill or Scotchman's Hill, but it was better than average and required a significantly smaller investment than places with *the* view.

I tinkered with the volume on my CD player, finally satisfied that Martha Wainwright's *Come Home to Mama* was at just the right level to be background for my foray into the life and times of Buckley-Rand Larmer.

I had decided to start with the obvious. Googling Larmer's name netted me a few thousand references. Initially I thought I'd start with the biggest, most frequently accessed, and work my way down to the more obscure only if I needed to. I knew there would be lots of poorly spelled, badly punctuated, "Go get 'em Big Guy. You're saving the free world from all those lefty wing nuts," and on the other side, "Drop dead, you redneck asshat."

I didn't feel either of those would be particularly enlightening and figured I'd be able to ignore well over half the posts. But I changed my mind and spent the first few hours of my assignment sifting through the ultra-passionate, often semi-articulate rants, raves, and ramblings of extremists from both ends of the political spectrum.

I came to one unsettling conclusion. The amount of hate that each side harboured for the other was astonishing. It was clear that even the most appallingly inept candidates for political office were perfectly palatable to their followers as long as they kept the other side — the hated enemy — from taking a step forward. Even if that step was arguably in a direction that would benefit a large percentage of the electorate. Had it always been this way? Maybe, but it seemed to me that Larmer and others of his ilk had taken the desire to crush and eliminate all opposition and reasoned debate to a new level — a level that appeared to have as its goal the establishment of one, and only one, way of thinking.

I wasn't surprised that the volume of right-wing rhetoric was several times greater than that on the other side — not unlike the overwhelming disparity between conservative and liberal talk-radio stations in the United States and (increasingly) in Canada. News-talk radio was almost synonymous with small-c conservative ideology.

And in the world of conservative politics Buckley-Rand Larmer was a big deal, often quoted, much admired, and the subject of countless interviews. He was also the author of dozens of articles and three books; PDFs poured forth his wisdom on countless websites and blogs.

There were pictures, too, lots of them, no doubt due, in part, to Larmer's being photogenic, even handsome. Six feet two inches, maybe three, deuce and a half on the scales and a lot of it muscle — he worked out daily and told the world via his more than one hundred thousand Facebook friends. Impressive, but only half the number of his Twitter followers.

Most of his myriad supporters appeared to expend a great deal of time and effort in trying to emulate their hero. His phrases were their phrases, his ideas their ideas, and most importantly, his hate-targets were eagerly, enthusiastically, and endlessly attacked by "Larmer Nation," a not particularly original, but probably fairly accurate term to describe the men and women, mostly men, who breathlessly awaited the next Larmer pronouncement.

But beyond reinforcing the fact that he was articulate, persuasive, intelligent, and popular with the ladies, or at least a certain segment of ladies, I didn't feel that my morning had given me much of a feel for the man. I learned that Larmer was an army brat and that his parents were both fundamentalist Christian, right-wing thinkers, which accounted for their naming their son after not one but two conservative luminaries — William F. Buckley, the brilliant political commentator who founded the *National Review,* and the novelist Ayn Rand, whose philosophy of objectivism had been welcomed by early American conservatives.

I discovered, as well, that Larmer had been kicked out of the campus pseudo-Republican, pseudo–Reform Party group that he had actively worked for during his time at the University of Ottawa. He then spent several years publicly vilifying the man he felt was responsible for his ouster in a largely successful attempt to destroy the man's career and personal life. The man's name was James Leinweber and he sued Larmer after a particularly vicious attack Larmer made during a television interview in 2002. I jotted Leinweber's name in my notebook as one of those with ample reason to want to harm his persecutor, then wrote a large "NO" next to his name when a subsequent search lead me to an obituary, written in October of 2003, three days after Leinweber had taken his own life, leaving behind a wife and twin teenage daughters.

Never one to miss an opportunity, Larmer had commented on the passing of his long-time foe and got in a few more nasty shots, insinuating that Leinweber's suicide, while unfortunate, was appropriate in that it symbolized the cowardly way the man had lived his life.

Some of what I was reading I already knew; none of it surprised me. No, that's not true. There was one surprise. It came in the form of Jasper Hugg — a man the media had dubbed Huggy Bear. Hugg was Larmer's chief adviser; no mention of how the two came together, just that when Larmer made an unsuccessful bid for the school board several years earlier, Hugg had been his campaign manager.

There were interesting similarities. Like Larmer, Hugg was a big man physically, in fact, bigger, which explained, in part, the media nickname. He was also reputed to be as mean as Larmer.

But there was one important difference between the two men. Where Larmer couldn't get enough of the limelight — he'd never met a microphone or camera he didn't like — Hugg stayed strictly behind the scenes, an almost shadowy figure, always there but seldom in front of the lens. He was never quoted or the subject of interviews.

More than one reporter described him as "secretive."

I broke for lunch, inhaling a couple of chapters of Ian Rankin's latest Rebus novel to cleanse my mental palate from the vitriol of Larmer and his confederates, while working my way through a bowl of mushroom soup and a couple of slices of nearly incinerated rye toast.

I was back at my computer by one-thirty, determined to get a better handle on the man my friend had been hired to protect. It was an hour into the afternoon when I came to an article that rather neatly crystallized my thoughts on Larmer. The article contained the nuts and bolts of an interview the writer had conducted with Larmer a few weeks earlier. But what made it interesting was the inclusion of the writer's own thoughts, good and bad, *about* the interview.

The writer was a reporter from a decidedly left-leaning provincial lifestyle magazine. Her name was Patsy Bannister, and I'd read a couple of things she'd written previously and found her pretty capable.

With Larmer she'd eased into things and for a while threw him enough softballs to qualify for the slow-pitch World Series.

But a half-hour into the interview things took a turn — she recounted the moment in her article:

> I asked Mr. Larmer if he had a criminal record. His answer was one he clearly had tucked away, ready to put to use if the need arose.
>
> "Your editor is a lesbian, is that correct?"
>
> "Excuse me?"
>
> "The woman who assigned you this interview — she is a lesbian. Is that correct?"

He paused between each of the three final words, to make the accusation more forceful.

"I don't see what the sexuality of anyone at the magazine has to do with —"

"And you, are you of that particular inclination, Ms. Bannister?"

"Inclination?"

"Are you a lesbian?"

"Let me repeat my answer to your previous, equally inappropriate question —"

"No need to answer at all," he said and sat, it seemed to me, a little taller in the seat behind his desk. The better to intimidate? Perhaps.

"You see, Ms. Bannister, what people like you fail to realize in your self-interested loathing of people like me who choose to devote our lives to making the world a better place for decent families to live in and work is simply this —"

"'Decent families' being those in which no one is gay or wears a turban or is just too damned intellectual?"

"It's simply this: We offer solutions. You offer platitudes. You and your ilk say, for example, that large industries should shut down in an area because some obscure kind of bird likes to dine on an equally obscure kind of insect there. We point out the financial implications of that stance — job losses, economic hard-

ships for decent, hard-working families —
while you celebrate that the bird will be
able to continue to lay its eggs in the same
tree it always has even though it would do
just as well in a similar tree a few kilometres away."

"But, of course, it's not about that
at all, is it, Mr. Larmer? It's really about
making sure that those large industries
and their wealthy investors get still
wealthier while the environment suffers
one more setback and —"

"Are you interviewing me, Ms. Bannister, or proselytizing?"

He was right on that point. I wasn't
there to debate his views, however abhor-
rent they were to me and even though
he had initiated the debate. I apologized
though it pained me to do so. But when,
a couple of minutes later, I asked him to
explain his opposition to Quebec remaining in Confederation, he suddenly stood
up and announced our meeting was over.

And it was.

There was more to the article. Patsy Bannister summarized the meeting in careful terms — trying to appear
at least somewhat even-handed as she characterized a
man she clearly loathed.

I'd been in that position a few times myself — having
to mask my own dislike for the subject of an interview
and present a fair representation of that person and his or

her views in the subsequent story or article. It was never easy, but I hoped I'd been more successful than Patsy Bannister had been in this instance.

I moved on from her article and read for another forty-five minutes, surprised at the amount of support Larmer commanded. I reread the Bannister interview, then on a whim decided to call her, see if she had time for a late lunch or coffee and was willing to give me a little more of her insight into the man.

The guy I spoke to in the news department of the *Herald* had a drinker's/smoker's voice that I thought was perfect for the newspaper industry, or at least the newspaper industry I had once been a part of — hard-drivin', hard livin' reporters who were passionate about writing stories for readers they didn't know and seldom met.

He put me through to Patsy Bannister and the voice I heard next was nothing like the one that had preceded it. It was soprano and gentle and slow, putting together each syllable of each word more like an actor than a reporter.

"This is Patsy Bannister," the voice said.

"Hello, Patsy, my name is Adam Cullen. I'm working on something to do with Buckley-Rand Larmer. I read your article on him — congratulations by the way — and I was wondering if you might be able to spare me some time to chat a little about him."

"Adam Cullen."

"Yeah, I used to write for the *Herald* myself and I —"

"I know who you are. *And* I've read some of your stuff. I liked a lot of it."

That stopped me for a few seconds. "Well, thanks, I appreciate that. Anyway, as I was saying, I —"

"Are you writing something about Larmer?"

"Actually, no. I'm mostly just curious about the guy, hoping to get your thoughts on him."

"Curious." She said it in a way that made me think she doubted my sincerity.

"Well, it's a little more than that, I guess. I'm researching Larmer for a … project, but I don't plan on writing anything."

"I hope you'll excuse me, Mr. Cullen, but that sounds more than a little strange."

"It's Adam, and I'm thinking my request probably does sound odd, and what complicates things even more is that I'm not able to tell you why I'm gathering information on Larmer's life. But I really would like to talk to you."

"Gee, an offer like that, how can a girl refuse?"

"I know and I apologize but —"

"It's okay. I'll meet with you. Maybe I owe you something for being an early influence."

"I doubt the influence part, but I appreciate your generosity."

"I wasn't finished. I was going to say 'an early influence, however minor.'"

I laughed and she did, too, and I was reminded that she hadn't backed down from Larmer and had a toughness that I liked.

We agreed to meet at a Second Cup near her home in northwest Calgary between five and five-thirty. I was on Larmer overload and decided to shut down my computer and let Amos Garrett try to bring some sanity back into my life. Though Amos was American-born, he, like Martha Wainwright, made the cut for my Canadian-only music collection by having lived in Canada.

In fact, the world-class blues artist had lived not far from Calgary for much of his life. I'd interviewed him years before and seen him perform several times. His *Cold Club*, almost twenty years old and still as relevant as it had been in 1996, provided a solid step in the sanity-restoration direction. I followed the mellowing period with a run, then a shower, and headed off to meet Patsy Bannister.

People seldom look the way their voices tell you they're supposed to look, and Patsy Bannister was no exception. She was dark-haired, dark-eyed, and small, bordering on tiny. I'd pictured her as tall and fair. Good thing Cobb was the detective.

It was warm enough that we decided to sit at one of four tables on a small patio outside the coffee place. The view was University Drive, and the sounds and smells were a blend of traffic and nearby steak house.

I'd offered to buy; she'd accepted and opted for a chai tea latte, while I settled for an old favourite, a large mid-grade coffee. Unimaginative but satisfying.

I delivered the drinks. She smiled at me over her mug, her generous mouth also contrasting, it seemed to me, with the soft voice.

"Cheers," she said. "If it's okay with you, I won't toast Buckley-Rand Larmer."

"I'm fine with that." I smiled back at her. We sipped our drinks, looked at each other, assessing, both of us trying to convey that wasn't what we were doing. "What are you working on these days?"

"The same thing a lot of news people in this town are working on. It's the end of June. Stampede is nine days away. I'm writing a history of the various midways that have been a part of the Stampede. Did you know that the midway used to come to Calgary and to the Stampede grounds by train?"

I nodded. "I did know that, actually. Royal American Shows, I think the midway was called."

Her eyes widened. "Wow, I'm surprised. I thought it was the job of all media to hate everything about the ten days and to cast a cynical eye over everything from the rodeo to scorpion pizza."

"I know about Royal American Shows and I like the rodeo a lot, but the scorpion-pizza thing, I might give that a miss."

She shook her head. "Just one more tasty treat available to the poor, unsuspecting schmucks looking to leave their money at Stampede Park."

I did not fit the mould Patsy Bannister had described and, in fact, had as many media friends who were Stampede enthusiasts as those who couldn't wait for the ten days to end. And I was even one of those who liked the "Cowtown" nickname Calgary carried, a sentiment that had earned me a healthy dose of scorn from some of my more "enlightened" colleagues.

A few more minutes of small talk, mostly trading names of mutual acquaintances — ice-breaker conversation. Then we sat for a while, quiet, sipping our coffees and enjoying the view. I didn't want to rush into throwing questions at her. That felt pushy, and as it turned out, was unnecessary. She broke the silence.

"You want to know something? He scared me. I'm not actually afraid of that many people, but I was afraid of Larmer."

"That didn't come across in your article. I thought you stood your ground pretty well."

"Thanks, but there was a lot more I could have written and didn't."

I nodded. "I sensed that. I guess that's why I wanted to chat with you."

"His playing the gay card, I have to admit that got to me. I'm long past being intimidated by people who want to judge my sexuality. At least I thought I was. But when he went on the attack I felt like I did in the first few days after I came out. On the defensive, I guess, but more than that, he made me feel … like an enemy."

"Well, if it's any consolation he's done that with a lot of people. It's how he plays the game. And he's good at it."

She sipped again and nodded. "Very good."

"Listen, Patsy, I'm not trying to be a jerk by not telling you why I'm researching the guy. It isn't *for* me exactly, and it's not my call."

She nodded again. "It's okay. Seriously."

"I'd like to know what else you learned about Larmer, either in your research or just other impressions you formed of him during your interview."

"My overriding impression was that he uses intimidation to get what he wants."

I nodded. "He seemed pretty touchy about your 'run-ins with the law' question. Was there anything to that or were you just fishing?"

She shook her head slowly. "The strange thing about that was I don't think he's had any problems with the law — beyond two or three speeding tickets and a couple of near-miss lawsuits based on his affinity for slander. But I threw it out there, as you say, fishing. Thing is, even after my research and interviewing the guy, I feel like there's more that I don't know about him than what I do know. And it bugs me. I'm a pretty good researcher. I like to dig deep, but with Larmer it felt like there was so much I didn't get. Part of it was the tight timeline but that wasn't all of it. It seemed as if there were gaps in his life story — times that were summarized here and there in a few sentences, maybe a couple of paragraphs."

"Any particular periods of his life that felt like that?"

"Several. A lot of the stuff from his more distant past — teenage years, for example. You know, there was the 'brilliant student, terrific debater' stuff you'd expect to hear about a guy like him but nothing in depth."

"Teachers? Fellow students? School friends? Nothing on what they thought of him?"

"Bits here and there. And all of it was like it was scripted. 'Deep guy but an okay guy. Never got into any real trouble. Bit of a loner.' It felt like blah, blah, blah. Words but no meat. Right up until Jaden Reese."

I looked at her. "Jaden Reese. Don't know the name. What's the connection to Larmer?"

"It's weird. Jaden Reese was a classmate. Died of an apparent suicide a few years after high school. But while he was in *junior* high, the story is that Larmer saved the kid from an encounter with bullies."

"Bull-*ies* plural."

"Uh-huh. Apparently Larmer stepped in when Jaden was taking some grief from a group of older kids."

"Hard to see Larmer as protector of the oppressed, although he's big enough; I imagine he was a pretty big kid growing up."

She shrugged. "That's not the surprising part."

"No?"

"Jaden Reese was gay."

I sat back, digested that. Recalled something. "Now I remember the name. I'm damn sure not a member of Larmer Nation, but I tune in just often enough to remind myself how little I like the man. And I'm pretty sure I've heard the Jaden Reese reference at least a time or two. I can't say I was paying close enough attention to recall now what Larmer said. But I seem to remember it was a source of great pride."

Patsy nodded, "Oh, yeah, *great* pride. If you were a regular listener you'd have heard it often enough to recite it by heart — every detail. It's boldface on all his brochures. 'Willing to stand up for the little guy even if the little guy is a sexual deviant.'" She laughed. "Okay, I might have paraphrased a little."

"Doesn't sound like the same guy who attacked your sexuality during your interview."

"No, it doesn't."

"You think the story is bogus? That there was no Jaden Reese?"

"No, I think there's something there. What I don't know is if I have all the details quite right. Or that Larmer does. He's like a lot of his ilk — stretching the truth a little or even a lot to make a point or a better story is standard procedure."

"But you didn't ask him about Jaden Reese in the interview."

She shook her head. "I intended to but I blew it. He gave me the perfect segue into it with his lesbian rant and I was going to come back to it right after the Quebec question, which was high on my editor's priority list. But then he ended it and I never got the chance to ask him about the Reese incident. Bad interviewing."

"Easy mistake to make." I smiled at her. "But it would be interesting to find out more about the incident — if it actually happened."

"And if it happened the way I heard it did."

"What school was it?"

"Hope Christian Academy in southwest Calgary. You probably know that Larmer's father was in the military — got moved around a lot. The Larmers were at Gagetown for his formative years." She drew out the word "formative," each syllable a word of its own. "Moved to Calgary when Buckley-Rand was eleven, finishing up grade six."

"And the Christian Academy — is it still around?"

She shook her head. "Closed a few years ago."

I studied my coffee mug. "You must have done some solid digging to find out about the Jaden Reese thing." Hoping I didn't sound patronizing. "Reese's parents still around?"

"I couldn't find them if they are. If one of his parents was also in the military they could have moved on a few times since then. We're talking the eighties, so maybe they aren't even alive anymore. Anyway, I didn't dig as hard as you think. Kind of fell into it. I probably should have gone harder after it, but I had a deadline and you know what it's like."

"Yes, I know *exactly* what it's like." I'd written lots of stories that could have been ass-kickers if I'd had a little more time. "Did you learn anything about the suicide?"

"I couldn't even confirm that it *was* suicide. Obituaries all called it a 'sudden passing.' Nothing on the net. And my source didn't know for sure — used the term 'apparent.' Hardly definitive evidence."

"True. But I would like to have heard Larmer's response to the question."

"Me, too. Damn."

I studied my coffee mug and thought about what she'd said. "Hard to imagine the Larmer of today stepping in to help a gay kid who was being bullied," I said, repeating my earlier thought.

She nodded, pursed her lips. "Seems impossible … so maybe something happened along the way to turn Larmer into the despicable creep he is … or, like I said, maybe the Reese thing didn't happen at all the way I heard it."

"Or maybe it did, because Larmer saw some advantage to helping the kid."

"Already thinking about a life in the public eye?"

"Seems a bit of a stretch." I shrugged. "Your source on Jaden Reese. You have any objection to my talking to him?"

"No, not really. Except it's a *her*."

She pulled out her phone, pushed buttons, scrolled. "Ariel Mancuso. Classmate of Larmer's. She lives in Fredericton, New Brunswick, now. I talked to her on the phone and we emailed a couple of times. I tried to get her to give me more detail about the thing with Jaden Reese, but what I've told you is what I got. She says she wasn't there to see it and the kids who were involved didn't say much about it afterward. She told me that some boys, she wasn't sure if there were three or four, and one girl were harassing Jaden — she didn't use the word 'harassing,' she might have said 'picking on.' Anyway, they were giving Jaden a bad time and Larmer came along, stepped in, and made them stop."

"What kind of hard time? Was it verbal — like taunting — or did it get physical? Was it gay-related? She tell you anything about any of that?"

Patsy shook her head. "I asked. She said she didn't know. All she remembered was that one of the boys had his nose broken, she didn't know which one."

"Could you tell if she was holding back anything from you or that she actually didn't know?"

"I thought about that quite a bit after I talked to her but I can't say for sure. I do know she was glad to get rid of me."

I nodded. "It'd be hard to know what was going on with her without being face to face. Mancuso her married name?"

Patsy shook her head. "Divorced. Went back to her maiden name. That's how I found her. Read about her in one of the old school newspapers. She was on a couple of teams and was president of some club, photography club maybe. Anyway, I wrote down several kids' names from that newspaper. She was the first one I was able to track down."

"You still have that list of kids' names?"

"Probably. I don't throw out much."

"Any chance I could look at it?"

"Don't see why not. I can email it to you."

"I'd appreciate that," I said. "Anything else you can tell me about Larmer?"

She gave me the Coles Notes version of Larmer's university history. Nothing I didn't already know.

"After he graduated he came back to Alberta and straight into a gig with the Reform Party — office job, learned the ropes, wrote a few speeches for the big boys, looked like he was going to *be* one at some point. Not sure what happened. The word is he was too extreme even for the Reform cats, but that's hard to imagine. Anyway, suddenly he was out of that job and freelancing. Ran for the school board, thankfully he lost and, bingo, he's suddenly a radio whiz kid. Righties lapping up his every nasty word."

We finished our drinks at about the same time. "How exactly did that come about, the radio gig?"

"Started with him appearing as a regular guest. If you needed somebody to slag gun control, dump on the CBC, debunk climate change — give him a right-wing position, Larmer could articulate it … and defend it. And he was pretty damn good at it."

"Have gun, will travel."

"So when the former host — the two- to six-o'clock time slot — was appointed to the Senate, nudge, nudge, wink, wink, there was a job opening with Larmer's name on it."

I nodded, thought for a while.

"Two to six. Mid-afternoon plus drive home. Huge audience potential — the guy's a big hitter."

"Bats cleanup."

I smiled at the baseball analogy. "Guy like that, as outspoken as he is, he's going to make some enemies. In your research, you hear about anybody in particular, somebody he should be watching out for?"

She laughed. "Probably dozens, maybe hundreds, but no, I didn't encounter anyone I could say is a real threat. Most people were like me — wanting to stay clear of the guy. Thing is, he's got his supporters, too. Lots of them and they're diehard faithful. I heard him referred to as the Rush Limbaugh of the North."

"Nice."

"I know." She grimaced, then stood up. "I'll just be a minute — washroom break." I nodded as she turned and headed into the building.

I spent the minutes alone thinking about what I'd learned so far. Jaden Reese had taken his own life. Years later another suicide — James Leinweber. One apparently rescued by Larmer, the other a Larmer victim. A few things to look further into. Maybe there was more to one or both deaths than there appeared. Or maybe not.

And Jasper Hugg. The almost reclusive power behind the power. In the shadows. What if it wasn't by choice? What if he resented Larmer's very public persona, was tired of being in the background? Jealousy had been the motive for countless crimes throughout history. Maybe his thinking was that he could scare Larmer enough that the great man would take off for a safer place, a safer life, leaving the door open for Hugg to walk through and finally into the spotlight.

Of course, it was all speculation. I didn't know enough about either man to come to any meaningful conclusions. And I wasn't sure any of it would be of any help to Cobb.

Patsy Bannister returned from the washroom, sat back down.

"Another tea?" I asked.

She shook her head. "Have to be going soon."

"Okay, one last thing. Jasper Hugg, what's your take on him?"

She smiled but there was no humour in her expression. "Huggy Bear," she said softly. "I don't know much about him, not really. Talked to him on the phone. It was Hugg I arranged the interview with. Very self-assured and I would say competent. Cold but capable."

"Would you say he's the brains of the outfit?"

She thought for a minute. "Maybe. Organizationally for sure. Beyond that I can't say. I had to send Hugg a list of the questions I wanted to ask for him to vet. Larmer's intelligent and brilliant in front of a microphone, but whether he's smart enough to define and defend an entire ideology on his own — hard to say. Hugg is capable of that, so maybe he's the brains and Larmer's the mouth. It wouldn't be the first time that's happened in Canadian politics ... or broadcasting. But I'm just not sure. I can tell you the Larmer I interviewed that day was very sure of himself. And he wasn't looking over his shoulder for help and guidance. So either he's as smart as he wants everyone to believe or he's very well coached and rehearsed."

"Listen, Patsy, thanks for taking the time. Just to come back to that one point. If you hear any names — somebody who had more than just a differing political point of view, somebody Larmer might have reason to fear, I'd appreciate a call."

"Fair enough, but like I said, that wasn't really my focus."

"I understand." I nodded and pulled a business card out of my pocket. "My email's on there. I'll look forward to getting the names of the kids at that Christian school."

She stopped gathering her things, took the card, nodded, and leaned forward, studying me. "This is starting to sound like there might be another story here. I know you told me you couldn't reveal the reason you're delving into Larmer's life, but if there is a story down the road sometime, turnabout's fair play. Your turn to share."

I shook my head. "No story, not yet, anyway. If there is, I promise, I'll let you in on it."

She smiled. "Right after your own story appears."

I smiled back at her. "I'm sure we'll talk again."

THREE

An hour after leaving Patsy Bannister, I was back in my apartment at my computer. Jill and Kyla were at baseball practice, so I had a couple of hours to delve further into the lives and times of Buckley-Rand Larmer and friends.

With The Band and Elliott Brood providing the soundtrack for my studies, I started with Jasper Hugg. Wikipedia yielded the basics. Hugg was forty-four years old, American-born and -raised, graduated from high school in Yuma, Arizona, attended Northern Arizona University, majored in Public Administration, worked his way through a few layers of management with the City of Flagstaff, then worked for the Republican Party in Arizona for eleven years before taking his skills north, first to Lethbridge, Alberta, then to Calgary. He and Larmer first connected via the Reform Party; Hugg was then the campaign manager for Larmer's ill-fated shot at the school board, and when Larmer became a big on-air fish, he brought Hugg along as his executive assistant.

I googled for a while without learning much of significance until I came across a heading that read "Huggy Bear Not Warm and Fuzzy."

It took me to a website that called itself *The Last Truth*. It was a sanctimonious, left-leaning site that clearly took itself very seriously, though not seriously enough to have someone edit the stuff that made up the content portion of the site. Still, the insights it offered into Jasper Hugg — if they reflected the truth, "last" or otherwise — were interesting. Hugg had been in a few legal scrapes over the years, mostly due to his willingness to get physical with those who challenged him or his views. The piece detailed three instances in particular.

The first had taken place in Flagstaff, where Hugg had hospitalized a civic employee named Victor Nagy after a confrontation that started in a staff meeting, then spilled over into the staff coffee/lunch area and finally to the sidewalk outside the main administration building. The two men had been suspended, Nagy for a week, Hugg for thirty days, both without pay. Hugg left the city job, went to work for the Republican Party, for which he had been volunteering for a couple of years. He also sued the city and got back the money he hadn't been paid during his suspension, plus an unspecified amount in damages for "personal stress resulting from the city's wrongful act."

Hugg's second documented physical confrontation involved his wife of six and a half years, Anita Dekalb. It took place shortly after their move to Calgary. There were witnesses and it sounded pretty nasty, with Hugg punching his wife twice, the second blow knocking her into a nearby parked car and onto the sidewalk. Again Hugg's victim was hospitalized, but overnight this time. Nevertheless, Anita declined to press charges; the article claimed it was because of "her husband's intimination" (the reporter's spelling, not mine). The marriage ended a few months later and the article opined that Hugg was a deadbeat dad (there was one child, a boy) but offered no evidence to substantiate the statement.

The third instance of Hugg's violence really got my attention. The venue was a downtown Calgary folk and blues club that had long since closed its doors, and it involved Hugg and a second man, "a prominent Calgary political and media figure." The unnamed second man had apparently taken exception to political remarks the singer, Wilson Hall, had been making between songs. The man had shouted profanity-laced remarks back at the singer, then when club staff, including a large bouncer, asked them to leave, a brawl ensued, with Hugg and his associate keen participants. The police arrived and both Hugg and his pal were taken away by the cops, leaving behind a few thousand dollars in damages to the club and three injured people: one member of Hall's band, the bouncer, and a bartender. Hugg and his associate came out of the fracas relatively unscathed.

The article ended abruptly there and offered no follow-up as to charges laid, compensation for the damages — nothing. Frustrating.

My reading had me wondering why Larmer felt he needed a bodyguard when he clearly already had one.

I decided I'd like to talk to Hugg's victims, starting with his ex. Though I doubted she'd agree to talk to me, I pulled out my phone directory and found two A. Dekalbs, one living in Strathmore, a community a half-hour or so east of Calgary, and the other in Lake Bonavista, the city neighbourhood I'd always most wanted to live in but never had. I called both A. Dekalbs, got machines at both, and left messages stating that I was a journalist and would like to speak with Anita Dekalb, if this was her residence. I left my number and hung up thinking I'd not likely ever hear from either of them. The word *journalist* tended to set off alarm bells, especially for those who had stories they didn't particularly want made public. But I'd learned a long time before that lying or hiding who I am was, for the most part, useless ... and illegal.

Figuring I might as well extend my losing streak, I called Information in Flagstaff and got numbers for a V.R. Nagy, V. and J. Nagy, and V. Nagy. V. Nagy's line was no longer in service, a recorded message informed me that V. and J. Nagy were Victoria Nagy and her son Jake, and another machine told me V.R. Nagy would get right back to me if I left a brief, detailed message. I was brief but not all that detailed.

The only name the report on the blues club incident revealed was that of the singer, Wilson Hall. I searched the name and found several Wilson Halls: a plumber in Jacksonville, Florida; a pharmacist in Oakdale, California; a pub owner in Reading, England; a university residence building at a small Lutheran college in Nebraska; and a folk/blues singer in Halifax. It was almost eleven at night in Halifax, so that call would have to wait until morning.

By then I was sick of tapping keys on my computer and talking to disembodied voices on my phone, so I shut it down, pulled a Rolling Rock beer out of the fridge, and put a Harry Manx CD on the stereo. I sat on my couch staring out at the unfolding sunset and wondering about Canadians' willingness to elevate unsavoury clods to positions of power. I had just concluded that Canada didn't own the patent on that particular behaviour when the phone rang.

I picked up and heard my favourite voice.

"Hi, cowboy," Jill said with a pretty bad fake drawl. "Baseball practice is over and two hungry women are willing to offer you the pleasure of our company for the price of two dinners at Ye Olde Spaghetti Factory."

"I hope you aren't sweaty," I said. "I'd hate to get thrown out of the place."

"Ladies don't sweat, we perspire and —"

"*I'm* sweaty!" I heard Kyla yell. "We had bunting practice and Mom made us run like a hundred bases."

"Okay, you can wait outside while your mom and I enjoy two delicious plates of succulent, perfectly prepared —"

"You're wasting time," Jill interrupted. "Get going and we'll meet you there in twenty."

"On my way."

A half-hour later, four of us were looking at menus. Four, because of a last-minute addition when Kyla convinced her mom that having her best friend, Josie, who was the Bobcats' first baseman, come along would make for a more complete evening.

I figured "more complete" was code for *so I don't have to listen to boring adult talk the whole time.* And while Kyla's conversation was rarely either juvenile or boring, I have to admit I welcomed the chance to talk with Jill about what I had been learning about Buckley-Rand Larmer and Jasper Hugg.

The dinner turned out to be a lively three-quarters of an hour of conversation that blended nine-year-old gossip and humour with what I thought were snappy and desperately funny responses, some from Jill, but mostly from me. Although the eye rolling I detected coming from all three of my dinner companions seemed to indicate that some of my attempts at humour fell short of award-winning.

But after we'd downed wine and Shirley Temples, spaghetti and ravioli, and two mud-pie desserts, the girls had settled into a pull-out-all-the-stops duel at some game they had on their iPads, while Jill and I sipped coffees and talked about what I'd learned so far.

"Not to be flippant —" Jill shook her head after a few minutes — "but keeping this man out of harm's way isn't going to be easy. It's only day one and you've already uncovered a few stand-out candidates to pop the guy. Give it a week and you may have to replace the toner in your printer."

I nodded. "The part I don't get is how anyone can attach enough importance to himself to not care that thousands of people hate him."

Jill took a swallow of her coffee. "I guess it's offset by the fact that just as many thousands think he's amazing and says the things they wish *they* could say."

"My dad says he's an ass," Josie said without looking up, her fingers flying dervish-like over the keys.

I glanced at Jill. So much for our conversation not registering with the girls.

"There are a number of people who agree with your dad," I said. I'd seen Josie's parents at a lot of the ball games but hadn't got past the "Hey, how ya doin'?" stage. Suddenly I liked them.

"Mike has a tough job," Jill continued. "I just hope he's able to keep Larmer safe."

Kyla looked up. "Larmer — is that the radio guy?"

I looked over at Jill, then back at Kyla. "Hey guys, this isn't fair to you two. Your mom and I shouldn't be having this discussion in front of you."

Kyla glanced down, tapped a couple of keys, looked up again. "Why not?"

"Well, it's to do with something Mike and I are working on. And there's probably a need for confidentiality here."

"Confidentiality?" Josie asked.

Kyla looked at her. "Keeping secrets," she explained.

"I can keep secrets." Josie set her iPad on the table as if to emphasize the point.

"That's good," I told them. "I'd appreciate it if this was one of the secrets you kept."

"Sure." Kyla nodded.

"No problem," Josie said. "I'm totally good at it."

"Great." I smiled at her.

"Like I never told hardly anybody about Faith Unruh."

"Jo-*sie*," Kyla hissed at her.

Jill and I exchanged glances. My look said this one's in your court. She looked at Josie. "So this Faith, what happened there — she let a boy kiss her? Or maybe she shoplifted an Oh Henry! from the 7-Eleven?"

"She died. Somebody killed her."

I was taking a drink of coffee as she said it, and my near-choking reaction would have been cartoon-funny except for the seriousness of what she'd said.

"Killed her," I repeated. "Killed her how, Josie?"

"Somebody murdered her."

Jill leaned forward. "That's a very serious crime, not something you should say if you're not completely sure about it."

I set my coffee cup down.

Josie nodded. "I didn't make it up."

She didn't look like she was making it up.

"How do you know about ... Faith?" I said.

"Same as now." She shrugged. "I heard adults talking about it. Except it was my mom and dad and our neighbour, Mr. Chen."

"What ... what happened to Faith?" Jill had lowered her voice, which was unnecessary because Josie was speaking barely above a whisper. I assumed it was part of her secret-keeping protocol.

Josie shrugged again. "I didn't hear that part. It happened before we moved there. All I heard was that she was killed in the backyard of a house down the street from us when she was eleven, and the person who did it never got caught."

"When was this, Josie?" I asked.

"Before we moved into our house," she said again.

"Cold case," Kyla said, her hours of watching *CSI* clearly paying off.

The waiter who had been serving us came to the table and I asked for a refill on the coffee.

The girls returned to their game. Jill and I struggled to find a topic that would provide an appropriate shift from where we'd been. We settled on musical theatre, but somehow the impending arrival of a travelling company's production of the *Lion King* seemed remarkably unimportant stacked up against what we'd just heard about a little girl named Faith Unruh.

Sex was awkward. No, that's not right. Sex with Jill was wonderful. It was the arranging to actually *have* sex that sometimes got a little sticky. We had been dating for several months and occasionally Jill stayed at my apartment, but never all night or even most of the night because of her babysitter.

And though we sometimes made love at her place after Kyla was asleep, I never stayed the night, either, because we — actually, *I* was worried about how Kyla would react to my being there in the morning.

But a night that had already seen one major revelation come to light would see another.

When we were on our way to drop off Josie, I admit to having my head on a swivel as we drove down her street to number 1227. She pointed out the two houses — the one where Faith Unruh had lived and the one where she'd died. I watched with more than the usual attentiveness as Josie jogged up the sidewalk to her front door. Twenty minutes later we were sitting in the living room of Jill's house, Kyla in her pajamas, a tattered paperback in her hands, Jill and I with wineglasses in ours.

No one was talking. Kyla was immersed in the adventures of James and his magical peach; my thoughts and, I was pretty sure Jill's, were on the tragedy we had heard about for the first time earlier that evening.

Kyla set her book down, uncurled her body from her reading position, and looked at her mother, then at me.

"Why do you always go home at night?"

I cleared my throat, paused, and said, "Because that's … where I live." I chuckled idiotically to show her that her mother's boyfriend was one funny guy.

She shook her head. "I mean it. Why don't you stay here sometimes?"

Jill intervened before I could say something else that was as dumb as my first offering.

"How would you feel about it if Adam did stay here sometimes?" I felt her hand resting lightly on mine.

"Okay." Kyla shrugged. "I mean, it wouldn't, like, bug me. I know you and Dad aren't ever going to be together and you guys really like each other, so why not?"

I leaned forward. "Kyla, the truth is, I'd like to stay here with you and your mom, but I guess I was worried that it *would* bother you, that you'd think I was trying to take the place of your dad. Or that I was somehow coming between you and your mom."

"Something you should know, Ky," Jill said, "is that Adam and I care a lot about each other. We're more than just friends, so if he did stay here sometimes or if I were to stay at his place, it's *because* we really care."

"Do you love each other?"

Jill blushed, looked at me. I was hoping she didn't want me to jump in because I thought she was doing just fine.

"Yes, Kyla, I believe we do," Jill said softly.

"Thought so," Kyla said, and the matter settled, she jumped out of the easy chair she'd been in and headed for her room. "G'night," she called over her shoulder.

And that, I believe, perfectly illustrates what is referred to as a roller coaster of an evening.

Having received Kyla's blessing for conjugal visits, Jill and I agreed that neither of us was particularly keen for that night to be our first *all* night.

And I guessed that for Jill, at least part of the reason for feeling that way was exactly the same as it was for me — Josie's announcement that an eleven-year-old girl had died violently in a backyard only a few blocks from where we were sitting.

FOUR

Cobb and I were sitting at a window table in Mercato, an excellent pasta place on 4th Street West. He was nursing a red wine; I was halfway through a rye and Diet Coke, and we were sharing a plate of calamari. So far the conversation had focused on Derek Jeter's final season and a lively debate about which was the better movie — *How to Train Your Dragon 2* or *Dawn of the Planet of the Apes*. I had seen the former with Jill and Kyla, and Cobb had "done the apes" with his teenage son, Peter. As neither of us had seen the other's movie, we decided to call it a draw, although Cobb insisted on one last shot.

"The major difference being, there are actual apes," he said.

I gave him a thumbs-up. As I bathed a calamari in tzatziki, I figured it was time to turn our attention to the matter at hand. "So, Larmer still alive?"

"You sound like you'd be okay with my saying, 'No, somebody offed him last Tuesday.'"

I grinned. "It would save me the trouble."

"Yeah, well, he's alive."

He didn't say any more, took a slow sip of the wine, set the glass down.

I pointed at him with my fork. "By the way, how is being a bodyguard not a twenty-four-hour job?"

"It is. I have help."

"The guys I met last time we worked together?" Two of Cobb's colleagues had once shown up, guns at the ready, in what could best be described as an armed standoff.

"Them and a couple of others."

"Larmer's in good hands."

Cobb smiled. "That's the idea."

We ate more calamari, sipped more wine and whiskey. Cobb dabbed at his mouth with a napkin, leaned back in his chair. "So, any luck digging into the background of one Buckley-Rand Larmer?"

"It's early days but I found a few bits. I have a lot more to do before I can offer you much. A couple of names, though."

I told him what I'd learned about James Leinweber and Jaden Reese. When I finished he nodded.

"Two suicides, both victims connected to Larmer."

"Two that we know of. I'm really just getting started on Larmer's back story. Who knows what further skeletons, literal and figurative, might turn up in Larmer's closets?"

"I knew about Leinweber." Cobb looked off to his right, out the window that offered a view of 4th Street passersby. He was thinking, remembering. "I did a little checking of my own when Larmer first contacted me, and I read about the suicide. Made a couple of calls. The Ottawa police looked into it at the time. Legitimate suicide, no indication of foul play made to *look* like suicide. Guy with a family, it shook up a lot of people, including the cops who investigated it."

"There are those who think that Larmer drove him to it. Destroyed the guy publicly."

Cobb nodded again. "I heard that, too. Doesn't seem out of character for my client."

"I read some of the stuff Larmer put out there. Beyond vicious."

Cobb picked up his wineglass. "I didn't know about Jaden Reese. Never heard of the guy. Anything more you can tell me about him?"

I shook my head. "Like I said — early days. But Reese's suicide seems like a very different scenario, at least as it relates to Larmer. With Leinweber he verbally crucifies the guy, maybe pushes him over the edge; with Reese, Larmer's a hero and later the guy takes his own life, might have had nothing to do with Larmer."

Cobb nodded, didn't say anything.

"But I want to do a little more digging on that one," I said.

He nodded again. "Likely nothing, but won't hurt to check it out … if you can."

"Leave it with me." I paused, then, "Can I ask you something?"

Cobb looked at me from under raised eyebrows, shrugged.

I took that for an affirmative, but paused again as our waiter, who looked old enough to have served calamari on the *Titanic,* stopped by to see if we needed another round of drinks and to tell us our main courses would be out shortly. Both of us declined another drink and the waiter cleared some dishes and moved off.

"Does it bother you working for a guy like that?"

"A guy like what?"

"Oh, I don't know … How about a sleazy, bottom-feeding scumbag, or words to that effect?"

Cobb turned serious. "No, it doesn't."

"Just wondered."

"Any more than it bothers lawyers who defend accused killers and rapists and drug lords. The law says everyone is entitled to a competent defence and that's the way it should be. Same applies for keeping people, even unsavoury people, safe from those who would harm them ... or threaten to harm them."

"The paycheque enter into it at all?"

"Of course it does. This is how I earn my living."

I nodded. Had no reply at the ready.

"Adam, there's something you need to know. If people want to hire me to protect them from real or imagined dangers, I don't put them through some ideology-testing program to determine whether they're worthy."

"Convenient."

"Damn convenient." Cobb leaned forward so I could hear him without his having to raise his voice. "I've spied on sleazy husbands and I've been hired by sleazy husbands to spy on someone else. I don't differentiate."

I couldn't think of a response, and finally said, "Huh."

We drank in silence for a time, then I said, "I don't believe you."

"What do you mean?"

"I don't believe you'd do anything for money."

"I didn't say that. There are lots of things I wouldn't do for any amount of money. I won't try to help someone get away with a crime I know they committed. And I won't try to nail someone for something I know they *didn't* do. But this isn't about that." His voice had taken on a hard edge. "This is about me working for a guy you don't approve of. And the reason you don't approve of him is you don't like his politics."

I thought about that, and realized that's exactly what it was. "What about you? How are you on the politics of the extreme right?"

"Doesn't enter into it at all. I have a client who is, or believes he is, in danger. He's received threats to that effect. Not all my clients are Mother Teresa. But all of them deserve my best. And that's what Larmer will get."

I digested that for a while before replying, "You're right, and yes, you have the right to work for whomever you want. I just wish it wasn't *this* whomever."

"Look, there's lots of it I can't stomach. There's lots of *Larmer* I can't stomach. And for the record I find Fox News and white supremacy and Beck and Limbaugh just as distasteful as you do. What I'm saying is that there's a place for people who don't think the way you do or the way I do. And that they have the same right to feel the way they feel that you have to feel the way you do."

"Not if feeling the way they do comes with —"

Our ancient waiter couldn't have timed the arrival of our main dishes more perfectly if he'd been listening to our conversation via a hidden microphone. He deposited linguine *alla carbonara* before Cobb and gnocchi in front of me, ground black pepper liberally over both, and left without a word. I wondered if he sensed the tension at the table, decided he probably did.

I settled back in my chair, took a deep breath, let it out slowly. "You're right," I said finally. "They do, absolutely. And for me to feel otherwise probably makes me as bad as the most intolerant of the haters. So I apologize." I looked at Cobb. "And for what it's worth, I mean it."

"No apology necessary." He smiled. "And for what it's worth, I mean it, too."

"But just so we understand each other —" I leaned forward, took up knife and fork "— Larmer sickens me. I can't help that and it isn't going to change."

Cobb's smile faded. "Fair enough. And I can tell you that I won't be going for evening cocktails with the guy anytime soon. But he's paying me to do all I can to keep him alive and safe. And I'd like you to keep helping me by staying on the research."

I drained my rye and diet, set my glass down. "Deal," I said. "Let's come back to Larmer later — give me time to cool off. There's something else I want to ask you about. And to be honest, it's a topic that won't be any more pleasant."

Cobb's eyebrows rose again as he manoeuvred linguini onto his fork. "Both barrels, huh. Okay, hit me with your best shot."

"You ever hear of the murder of a little girl named Faith Unruh?"

The fork hovered in mid-air. "You're a real ray of sunshine today, aren't you?"

"Sorry. The topic came up unexpectedly and I thought you might be able to tell me about it. Or at least some of it."

Cobb put the forkful of linguine in his mouth, chewed slowly, and looked up at the ceiling for a minute, then back at me. Finally he nodded and said in something just more than a whisper, "One of the worst."

I told him about Josie's pronouncement from the night before. "I wasn't sure if it was real or, even if it was, if she had it right."

Cobb took a breath. "It's real and she had it right. Come to think of it, that's exactly the part of town it happened in. I'd forgotten that."

He wasn't looking at me. Not then … and not when he began to speak again.

"It was 1991. I'd only been on the force for two years and a report came in early in the morning just after I'd started my shift. I was a uniform then and worked another part of the city, but I remember it. Partly because of the horror of it, partly because we never got the killer, and partly because of what that case did to people who worked on it. A couple of people in particular."

"Josie said the girl was eleven years old," I said.

"Yeah, she had either just had a birthday or was just about to have one, I can't recall exactly. The yard she was found in wasn't her own. She'd walked home from school with a friend. The friend went into her own house and Faith continued on the final block by herself. Somehow somebody got her into the backyard of a house two doors down and across the street from where she lived, strangled her in broad daylight, and left her next to a garage with a piece of plywood over her. She was naked but hadn't been sexually assaulted.

"All of us figured this would be quick. We'd have the guy within a day or two — had to be someone who knew her or at least knew her route home and also knew that she'd be alone for that final block. There was a fair amount of blood near the body that wasn't Faith's, so we figured we'd have physical evidence, as well. And the fact that it looked like she'd fought her killer meant she might have had time to scream, too. The investigating team talked to everyone in the neighbourhood, even asked on radio and TV for anyone who might have been driving by — got several people who came forward, had to have been very close when it happened. Nobody saw or heard a goddamn thing."

Cobb stopped talking — I wasn't sure whether it was to try to recall more or just to summon what was needed to talk about something that was clearly painful.

He went on. "When she didn't arrive home from school her parents went looking for her; they called 9-1-1 when darkness fell, and she still hadn't turned up. The investigators said she must have fought like a demon to have caused that much blood loss in her assailant. Maybe that's why she wasn't raped. Or maybe he heard someone coming — we don't know."

We don't know. Speaking in the first person and the present tense. Like it had happened only days before, not twenty-three years ago.

"Anyway, the neighbour found her when he went out to his car to go to work that evening. Worked nights at some plant or something — I don't remember the name. And like I said, it looked like an easy one. No, that's not right, none of them are easy. But maybe easi-*er*. Except it wasn't … wasn't easy at all. That time of day, how could an entire neighbourhood not have seen something, someone? Even her friend — the one she'd walked home with. They'd done that countless times. Nothing that day any different from any of the other days.

"The guy was either the smartest or the luckiest bastard alive … or maybe both. Eight years later when I became a detective, it was one of the unsolveds I was assigned to look into. Several investigators had gone back at it since the murder — some damn good cops. Nothing. Same as what I came up with."

"And no other murders around that time — other little girls?" I asked.

"Serial killer? We don't think so. At least not in Calgary. Of course the guy could have left the city and done something similar somewhere else, but we never came across others that matched up."

"What about the family? The parents have any serious enemies?"

"They weren't the perfect all-Canadian family, for damn sure. The father dabbled in drugs, mostly recreational, not the heavier stuff, at least not that he admitted to or that we could learn. Didn't deal, just used. Died a few years after Faith's death — aneurysm when he was at work. He was a welder, worked over in the Manchester industrial area. Mom wasn't an angel, either — word was she was having an affair at the time Faith was murdered. So there was no shortage of suspects, but all of them had alibis — ironclad."

"'Word was'? The affair wasn't confirmed?"

"The mom's story was that there was no affair. Just a good friend who happened to be male. She married him about a year after her husband died. But we couldn't find any dirt on the guy and nobody could say for certain that there had been anything going on before Mr. Unruh made his departure. So … *word was.*"

"And no match for the blood."

"Nope, that was pre–DNA registries and the like. Of course, the DNA has since been done — a few years ago — but no match in any of the databases. Not yet."

"Cold case." I repeated Kyla's words.

"Very."

"Anybody looked at it recently?"

Cobb shrugged. "Don't know. I'm not in that loop anymore."

Neither of us spoke for a while.

I glanced at his empty wineglass. "Feel like another?" I asked.

Cobb looked at his glass, then shook his head. "You thinking there's a story there? That why you're interested?" It wasn't accusatory and, anyway, it was a valid question.

"I don't know," I said. "I hadn't been thinking of it … but maybe. Any chance writing something might trigger some clue or some witness who saw something and never thought anything of it, you know …"

"America's Most Wanted?" Cobb shook his head. "After all this time, it's damned unlikely."

"But not impossible."

"Next to."

I agreed. "Yeah. Like I said, I wasn't thinking of writing anything. It's just … ever since Josie told us the story, I can't stop thinking about it. Like most of last night. I guess maybe having Kyla almost the same age, it bothered me more than a lot of stuff would. Almost a quarter century, and nothing."

"Yeah."

"Any chance it was bad police work … one of those times when cops actually interview the killer and miss it?"

"A Paul Bernardo miss? I don't think so. When my partner and I were assigned to take another look at the case, that was one of the first things we went back at. Every interview, every potential witness, see if there was somebody who looked okay but wasn't. I found nothing. My partner found nothing. And she was good. We even went back and talked to some people who still lived in the neighbourhood. I mean, at the time we were looking at the case, it was almost ten years since Faith had been murdered. We came up empty. And believe me, I spent a lot of nights just the way you spent last night."

I nodded. "That must be the toughest part of police work."

He started a nod, but changed it to a shake of the head. "No, the toughest part is when you nail the guy and he gets off. Those are the ones that put good cops in therapy. But something like what happened to Faith Unruh, knowing the son of a bitch was still out there, that's pretty damn tough, too." He released a sigh. "I changed my mind. Let's have that drink. I'm up with Larmer tonight, but I don't start until eight."

I looked at my watch. Four-twelve.

"You driving?"

"On foot." He pointed to his wrist. "Fitbit. Eleven hundred and fifty-four steps from my office to here."

I signalled the waiter.

"You write that story, Adam, you'll have to write about the original investigating team. Two veteran guys — near as I could tell they worked their asses off. One, a guy named Lennie Hansel, was only about three years from retirement. The Faith Unruh case haunted the guy. He was dead less than a year after they gave him his watch."

"Hansel," I said.

"Yeah." Small smile. "You can guess what all his partners were called."

"I have a pretty good idea."

"This particular Gretel's real name was Tony Gaspari. Grew up in the Italian part of old Bridgeland, not far from where you live. He was as obsessed with the Faith Unruh case as Hansel. Obsessed to the point of literally losing his mind. Cost him his family and eventually his health — at least his mental health."

"He dead, too?"

Cobb shook his head. "He's in a home. Can't do much for himself. I stopped in a couple of years ago. He knew me but couldn't connect me to his past life. I'm not sure he was aware he *had* a past life. The doctor said what he has is something akin to post-traumatic stress disorder. Said some days he's pretty good. Warned me against talking about police work and especially the Unruh case."

I shook my head.

"There was a third guy. It wasn't his case but he got caught up in it. Spent all his non-work hours on it … for years. He was single, no family. The thing got weird. He became more and more immersed in the case. And then he just disappeared."

"What do you mean? Like he moved away? Trying to escape the thing, something like that?"

Cobb shrugged. "Maybe. I don't know. Thing is, nobody knows. One day he didn't come in to work and they sent a couple of guys to check on him, see if he was all right. The house was empty. Neighbours said he'd sold it. And he had because the people he sold it to moved in a couple of weeks later. But Ken was gone. Never turned up again. Kendall Mark. I didn't know him all that well, but people who did said he just lost it. Been showing signs of some mental problems for a while. And it was the Unruh case did it to him."

He paused, took a breath, let it out slowly. "Like I said, that case has caused a lot of suffering. And not just for friends and family. You might think about that if you decide to start poking around."

"Yeah. Don't imagine I'll be doing much of that. I've got a feeling that digging into Larmer's past will keep me pretty busy for the next while."

The drinks came then, and almost as if their arrival was a cue, we didn't talk anymore about Faith Unruh. Or Larmer, for that matter. And damn sure not politics. Didn't talk much at all, really. Finished up with a little back-and-forth about the Flames most recent signing, both of us trying to end it on a light note, both of us failing.

But I had one last point I wanted to make before we headed off in separate directions. "I'm going to want to talk to Larmer … and probably Hugg."

Cobb shook his head. "I don't like it, Adam," he said. "I don't want him knowing that I've got someone checking into his past."

"But you told me he'd approved money for research. This is research."

Cobb looked at me for a long time but didn't say anything. Then he shook his head. I felt like a teenager asking Dad for the car for all the right reasons and getting turned down just because he was my dad. My anger began to rise again, but this time I was determined to keep it in check.

"I think I understand," I told him. "You don't want him to know that the guy doing the research is a wild-ass lefty who hates the ground he walks on."

Cobb smiled. "Something like that, maybe."

"Okay, how about if I can do it without his knowing that I'm even involved with you?"

"And how are you going to do that?"

"People in my profession interview guys like him all the time. I set it up like I'm doing a story on him, a freelance piece. We meet, I ask questions, he answers questions. He even knows me, albeit not well, but well enough to know I'm a legit journalist."

Cobb didn't answer right away.

"Mike, I need to talk to the man to help me with looking at his life past and present."

"You said you wanted to talk to Hugg, as well. Why Hugg?"

"Same answer. They've been joined at the hip for a long time. I need to know both of them better than I do now. Which, in the case of Hugg, is not at all."

"And you want to do this when?"

"The sooner the better."

"I get that it would benefit you to have a face to face," Cobb said slowly. "Just as long as you can keep the fact that you and I are working together on this out of it. These aren't stupid people."

"I understand that."

"Or people you should underestimate."

"I get that, too."

The waiter came by one last time, but both of us shook our heads.

Cobb told me he was going to grab a couple of hours of sleep before starting his shift with Larmer. He paid the bill. "I pay it now or pay it later when you expense it. Might as well handle it now."

I grinned at him and we left the restaurant and walked to the corner, nodding our goodbyes before I turned right to cross the street and he went left — glancing at his Fitbit as he moved off. I'd parked on a side street next to a Jugo Juice. I'd never been in one so decided to give it a try. I bought something with peach in the name, then sat down to check messages on my iPhone and pass some time before driving after the two drinks.

It was maybe an hour before I climbed behind the wheel of the Accord.

I was only twenty minutes or so from my apartment even in rush-hour traffic, which was building about the time I left the juice place. But when I got home I had no desire to actually go inside. I parked on the street in front of my building as a stiff breeze was beginning to lower the temperature. I pulled a light windbreaker out of the back seat and set off on foot, I wasn't sure where.

I wanted to walk and think. There was a lot to think about. I was still in a state of — I'm not sure what, some kind of stunned horror at the tragedy that was Faith Unruh and how her murder had impacted so many lives. And unless her killer had died in the years since he'd murdered her or been jailed for something else altogether, he was still out there presumably enjoying his life. I knew that there were those instances when cold cases were solved years after the crime was committed. It didn't happen nearly as often as television would have us believe, but the arson death of my wife and what happened years later was proof that it *did* happen.

But for now I had to focus my energies on Cobb's client Larmer and what my friend needed from me to help him keep the guy alive and well.

The temperature dropped further and the wind whipped up, but I walked on — south to 1st Avenue, then east to 12A Street at the bottom of the hill that led up into Renfrew. A couple of solid old neighbourhoods, although

Bridgeland had become hip and funky in recent years. I loved living there … and walking there. I circled around 12A Street back to 1st Avenue and retraced my steps. Thinking. Thinking hard, but mostly grasping.

Connections.

I still thought there had to be a connection between what had happened in Hamilton and what was going on with Larmer. I wasn't a believer in coincidence, and despite the differences in the two situations — one man shot from behind in a parking lot, not once but twice, the second time fatally, and the other facing threats of violence — it seemed to me far-fetched to think the two weren't somehow connected.

But what *was* the connection? A left-wing nut-job deciding to even the playing field by ridding the airwaves of some of the right-wing talkers? Someone from the right generating sympathy for his side by making it look like an extremist from the other side was so filled with hate that he was wasting some of the right's on-air apologists? Or someone who just happened to hate both Larmer and the guy in Hamilton enough to settle some score with them and no one else, with the fact that both were conservative commentators having nothing to do with the two incidents?

I had a lot of trouble giving any credence at all to that last scenario.

Of course there was a fourth option — that, in fact, the two situations weren't related at all. I decided that possibility would go on the back burner for the foreseeable future and that I would focus on … what? I was finding it difficult to separate the gathering of information about Larmer, in effect the compilation of a profile, from the assembling of a group of potential suspects, which Cobb had indicated was *not* what this was about.

A profile of Buckley-Rand Larmer. I could do that. The truth was that so far I simply didn't have enough information. Which, after all, was what I was being paid to acquire. I'd always considered myself a pretty good digger and I decided that starting the next morning I'd find out just how good.

I'd arrived at a park on the corner of 9A Street and 4th Avenue. I sat on a bench and watched a couple of kids about Kyla's age tossing a Frisbee back and forth. I hoped my being there wasn't creeping them out.

The wind had let up and the late-afternoon sun had eliminated the need for the windbreaker. I took it off and laid it over the back of the bench. An errant throw brought the Frisbee close enough for me to pick up and send it back to the closest kid. He dropped it. He'd dropped quite a few, but was grinning as he yelled a thanks at me. Apparently, I wasn't creeping them out.

I felt myself reviving — a flow of energy I hadn't felt for a while. Truth was, my heart hadn't been in a job that brought me close to someone like Buckley-Rand Larmer. But I felt like I was turning a corner. The chat with Cobb had done that. There was work to do and it was the kind of thing I liked. And did well. I thought back to some of the work I had done before Donna's death. Research and writing, putting some pretty good stuff together, some of it on my own and some a collaboration with two of my favourite people in the world — Lorne Cooney and Janice Flynn.

And thinking of them triggered a thought. Lorne had written a piece about the Hamilton shooting — pretty in depth. He'd even flown down and spent some time in Hamilton, did a nice job, as I recalled.

I headed back to my apartment feeling a little better about myself and my place in the world than I had at the beginning of my walk. I was walking faster. *A man with a purpose.* A summer that had been focused almost solely on the fortunes of the Killarney Bobcats now had added meaning, maybe even importance. As long as I didn't let myself get bogged down by how much I didn't know — about Larmer, about Hugg, about anything — I'd be fine. That's what I told myself. It wasn't a terribly positive message, but it wasn't completely negative, either.

Back home I pulled a Rolling Rock out of the fridge, built myself two baloney sandwiches, and sat down to watch an episode of *Downton Abbey,* which I'd taped a few days before and not yet watched. Nothing like forty-seven minutes with early-twentieth-century British aristocracy and their servants to purge the soul of self-doubt.

Supper, such as it was, completed — I'd finished it off with a sliced banana awash in milk … fruit *and* dairy in one serving — I decided not to wait for the next morning to get started.

I washed up some dishes, then settled back at my desk, cellphone in hand. My attempt to contact Wilson Hall had so far been unsuccessful. I'd been able to get a number for him that morning, called, and got his machine, left a message. The story of my life. I dialed his number again. Machine again, didn't leave a second message.

I checked my email, hoping for good news, and got some. Patsy Bannister had forwarded the list of names of kids she'd come up with from Larmer's Christian school.

Eleven names. Those calls I'd make the next day. Maybe even learn something more about the Jaden Reese incident.

For now I wanted to call Lorne Cooney. Lorne and I had worked together, first during our *Calgary Herald* days and since then on a few freelance projects. A laughing Jamaican, Lorne Cooney was a lefty politically and willing to tell you about it every time the opportunity arose and sometimes even when it didn't. He was passionate, vocal, and wickedly funny in his verbal attacks on those who happened not to share his views.

Got him first try. First ring.

"I think it's time we had lunch," I said into the phone. "I need some Cooney wisdom and maybe a plate of … what's that crap you like at Mucho Burrito?"

"It's not crap, man; it's a little something I like to call 'chili rellenos Jamaican.'"

"Yeah, that." I said. "How about we get some and I pick that reggae-clouded mind of yours for a while?"

He laughed. "This is perfect. I work out at a gym a couple of blocks from my favourite Mucho Burrito location. I put the pounds on, I take the pounds off. What could be better?"

He gave me directions and we agreed to meet at one the next day. "After the lunch rush," Lorne reasoned.

As I hung up the phone, I felt my mood almost completely rehabilitated. Lorne Cooney often had that effect on me, which left me wondering why I didn't make a greater effort to spend more time with the guy.

I knew the answer, just hadn't allowed myself to acknowledge it. Some years before, Lorne had been the guy to relay the message that I needed to get home right away, that something was wrong. The something that was wrong was that a twisted, sadistic killer had set fire to my house, a fire that took my wife's life. I'd spent the next few years obliterating everything about that night from my mind. Including Lorne Cooney. I was shooting the messenger and I knew it. But it didn't stop me from keeping one of my best friends at arm's length for a long time.

In the last year or so, Lorne and I had resumed our friendship and I was glad of it. We never spoke of that night — we didn't have to — but I knew that Lorne, like Cobb and Jill, understood.

FIVE

After I called Lorne, I'd been able to track a copy of his story in the *Herald* online archives. I read it twice. So the next day when we met at the Mucho Burrito downtown, I had a pretty good handle on what he'd written. But with Lorne, as with Patsy Bannister, there was always stuff that hadn't made it into print, sometimes because there was just no way of knowing how accurate one's impressions and suspicions really were.

Twenty minutes after our arrival, Lorne was gazing fondly down at the glob that had had our server shaking his head sadly as he put it together, topped off with the contents of a jar of some spice Lorne had brought with him. I had opted for the chimichangas, which earned me a relieved smile from the same server.

For the first part of our lunch together, we ate, drank Mike's Hard Lemonade, and I laughed a lot while Lorne recounted the mishaps of the previous several weeks of his life. I had long been convinced that he would have been a huge success in stand-up comedy but hoped he'd never try it, because the world of journalism couldn't afford to lose many more Lorne Cooneys.

He turned his Jamaican accent off and on depending on the context of what he was saying. Heavy accent for humorous rants against the ways of a North American world he portrayed as "on the eve of destruction" (to quote the long-ago song), and almost no accent for normal conversation.

I was on the last section of my chimi when Lorne leaned back, breathed in deeply, then out, and said, "That Cooney wisdom you referred to on the phone — anything specific, or you just want me to prattle on so you can wait for a couple of gems along the way."

I patted my mouth with a napkin. "Good as that sounds, I do have something I'd like to throw at you."

"Throw, brother, throw."

"March 2012, Hamilton. Radio talk show host gets gunned down in the parking lot next to the station. Then when that doesn't do the job, he's shot a second time five months later, this time for keeps. I wondered what you might know, I mean, I read the piece you wrote, which was excellent, by the way, but I was hoping you might have a couple of things that didn't make it into print."

He tapped his temple. "The juicy bits."

"Yeah."

Lorne drained his glass, called to the tall, skinny guy who'd served us that he was switching to beer, and looked at the ceiling for a long minute.

"Dennis Monday," he said. "Big-time fake. Fake hair, fake teeth, couple of facelifts, never had an original idea in his life. The guy who shot him the first time did ol' Denny a giant favour, man. Story is, he was on his way out, low ratings that were getting lower by the week … he gets popped but survives, comes back to the station after his recovery and he's suddenly a rock star, not only on his own show but across the network that owns several of those stations."

"They never got the guy who shot him."

Lorne shook his head. "Don't know that they even got close. Monday ... oh, by the way, the name's fake, too, he's really Dennis Bratvers. Got 'Bratwurst' in school, figured that wasn't a cool name for a budding radio star, changed it to Monday.... Anyway, he never saw the shooter, remembers a car in the parking lot when he got to his, but it was dark and he couldn't describe it at all. He went to the passenger side of *his* car, which meant he had his back to the other car, opened the door, and was bent over putting some stuff into the car when *pop, pop,* he goes down, loses consciousness immediately, and remembers nothing after opening the car door."

"Shooter take anything?"

"Not from Monday's car, at least the police don't think so, and Monday didn't figure anything was missing. What the shooter *did* take were the shell casings. Monday was shot with a Smith and Wesson 380. They got the slugs out of Monday's back and shoulder, but with no casings, finding the exact gun is more difficult."

"Think it was a hit?"

Lorne shrugged. "In some ways it feels like that, but this guy was a nothing. Why waste a hit on a radio personality with almost zero listenership?"

"Sending a message?"

"What message? You suck on the radio so we've decided to shoot your ass."

I finished my drink, shook my head when our waiter arrived with Lorne's beer and glanced at me. "Do you know if he'd received any death threats before he was shot?"

"Never heard about any, and the way Monday milked the thing after he got back on the air, I figure he would've said so if there had been any."

I told Lorne about Cobb's being hired as body-guard for Buckley-Rand Larmer and the threats Larmer had received.

"So you're wondering if there's a connection?"

"The thought crossed my mind."

"Somebody out there trying to rid the world of right-wing radio talk."

"Maybe."

"Not an unworthy goal, man, that's for damn sure." Lorne grinned, then turned serious again. "I guess it's possible. But why *threaten* Larmer? Why not just pop him? The way I hear it he has more enemies than Vladimir Putin, so even if you didn't want to kill him yourself, it shouldn't be too hard to find somebody who would."

"Maybe even a pro."

"If the first Monday shooting *was* a hit, I hope whoever paid for it got their money back. If the idea was to silence Monday, exactly the opposite happened. And if the shooter was an *alleged* pro, he's probably been sent back to Triple A."

"Maybe the idea *wasn't* to kill him — just wound him, scare him off and maybe some of the other talk types at the same time. Then he comes back, is even noisier than he was before, and *boom!* second hit, this time no mistake."

Lorne drank some beer, thought about that. "Maybe," he said slowly, "but I keep coming back to the fact that the guy was a zero, so none of it makes sense."

"Do the police think the two Monday shooters were one and the same guy?"

"Can't say for certain, but what they're pretty sure of is that it's the same gun. Again the casings were gone. But they got the slug, just one this time, and this time in Monday's brain."

"Smith and Wesson 380."

"Uh-huh."

I nodded. "So unless people are passing around the gun for other people to take a turn shooting at the guy, then it's the same shooter."

"I'd bet the plantation."

"Me, too. But now I'm wondering if the Hamilton shooting is related to the Larmer threats at all. Maybe Monday got shot because he's just an all-around dickhead and it has nothing to do with Larmer."

"Except for the fact that Larmer's *also* an all-around dickhead."

We both laughed.

"Anything else I should know?"

Lorne thought for a moment, then shook his head. "You got what I got."

"Okay, thanks for this. It's appreciated."

"Anyway, enough of this crap," Lorne said. "Tell me what's going on with you besides digging into the lives of those-whose-names-cannot-be-spoken."

We spent the next half-hour catching up.

SIX

Jasper Hugg was indeed a big man. I had him at six-two or three and closer to three hundred pounds than two hundred. And whoever said he wasn't warm and fuzzy had pretty much nailed it.

Hugg had an old-style crewcut and black-rimmed glasses, giving him an early-sixties, clean-cut, studious look. A Buddy Holly head on an offensive tackle's body. His suit jacket was hanging over the back of his chair and he was wearing a stiffly starched white shirt and a Calgary Stampede 100th Anniversary tie. His sleeves were rolled up a couple of turns to expose wrists the approximate circumference of my neck.

I'd been sitting across from him for at least twenty minutes, giving him a detailed explanation of my writing experience and elaborating on points in my writing resumé, which he had insisted on seeing. I'd called early that morning, then faxed over a proposal for a feature on Larmer that I had no intention of writing. I needed to get my own feel for these two men, and as I'd told Cobb, that could only be done in person. Hugg had agreed to see me that afternoon at three o'clock. I'd arrived ten minutes early and been kept waiting for thirty-five minutes before the door to his office opened and with a nod he indicated I should enter.

What I entered was a utilitarian, no-nonsense space that looked like I thought it would — all business, all the time. On the wall behind Hugg, a couple of cheap prints flanked a copy of Hugg's degree from the University of Northern Arizona. No people pictures on the walls or the desk.

We got to the meat quickly. Almost no get-acquainted chat.

"I'm actually thinking of two pieces," I said. "One on Mr. Larmer and one on you. I really like to look at the stories behind the story, you know?"

Hugg shook his head.

"Oh, I know, you're a behind-the-scenes guy." I held my hands up and nodded understandingly. "Everyone knows that and frankly I admire that in you, but I think we could do it without invading the privacy you value or betraying secrets that you'd prefer were kept under wraps."

I was about to make myself gag and I could see that my car-salesman approach wasn't cutting it with Hugg.

"First of all, you won't be interviewing me," he said in a voice that was a cross between Southern gentleman and pissed-off bartender. More pissed-off bartender for me. I figured the smooth, Southern-gentleman voice was saved for people who mattered more to the program than I did.

"And secondly, we don't have 'secrets we'd prefer were kept under wraps.' The liberal media, of which you are a part, Mr. Cullen, may believe that, but one of the reasons Buckley-Rand Larmer is as popular as he is has to do with the transparency that his listeners can count on in every broadcast. He quite literally *tells it like it is.*"

The liberal media of which you are a part. So Hugg had checked me out in the time between my call and the start of our interview.

"I'm not sure that my career as a crime writer qualifies me as a member of the liberal media, Mr. Hugg. Your program clearly appeals to the law-and-order segment of society. My writing career has been about law and order. That said, I understand your not wanting to be the subject of an interview. I respect your wishes and while I'm disappointed that we won't be able to include what I think would be a fascinating look at your life and contributions to what is clearly one of western Canada's most successful radio programs, I do hope we can move forward with an interview with Mr. Larmer."

"I spoke to Buckley-Rand. He indicated he knows you."

I'd wondered what Larmer's associates and friends actually called the guy. Now I knew. I decided that if I really wanted to be admitted to his exalted presence, I'd better control my urge to refer him as "Buck."

"Yes, we were part of a university conference a few years ago," I said. "I think Mr. Larmer's presentation resonated with the students far more than mine did." A little self-deprecation never hurt. Especially when it was true.

"What is the focus of the piece you want to write?"

"I'd really like to let people know the man he is when he's away from the microphone. Talk about his early influences, his journey to becoming the success he is, what his life is like when he's not in the studio."

I had to tread carefully. I didn't want to give Hugg the impression that the interview and subsequent article would reveal too much of the real Buckley-Rand Larmer. Secrecy was a key element in their strategic plan and I knew that both these men had several skeletons in several closets. If there was any concern that I might accidentally stumble across one or more of those skeletons, I knew any chance I might have of talking to Larmer would disappear into the air like poplar fluff.

Hugg sat back, looking somewhere over my head. "Buckley-Rand told me he enjoyed meeting you at the conference you both spoke at, and he indicated that though much of what you said was crap — actually, I think he used a stronger word — he would be prepared to have you interview him."

"I appreciate that very much," I said. "When do you think might be convenient for a first interview?"

"First?"

"There's always the possibility of a follow-up — clearing up points, expanding on something that was said, that sort of thing."

"There will be one interview, Mr. Cullen. And that interview will only happen after you first submit your questions for him in writing. If Buckley-Rand and I are both satisfied with the tenor of the questions, we'll set a time and place for you and him to meet. I trust that is satisfactory."

Patsy Bannister had mentioned the vetting process and the questions submitted beforehand, and since my interview was bogus, anyway, I smiled and said, "Of course. I'd be happy to send the questions in the next couple of days, if that's all right."

Hugg stood up, not an action that could be described as one fluid motion. He opened the drawer of his desk, pulled a card from it, and handed it to me. "My email is on the card. I'll look forward to receiving your questions."

"Thank you," I said and turned for the door. Next to the door was a framed photograph. I hadn't seen it before because it was behind me. Four people smiled at the camera from in front of what looked like a tourist lodge at some mountain lake. I recognized three of the people in the photo. They were younger versions of Jasper Hugg, Buckley-Rand Larmer, and Preston Manning, former leader of the Reform Party of Canada and a pioneer of the Canadian right.

I turned back to Hugg. "Nice picture. Who's the guy on the far right?" (I had to fight off a smile at the thought that all of them were on the far right.)

"You don't know?"

"Thus my question," I said.

"Thank you for coming by, Mr. Cullen," Hugg said. "Again, I'll look forward to that email."

"The guy's identity is a secret?"

"The gentleman is deceased."

I look at the photo again, then back at Hugg. "When he was alive, did he have a name?"

"I have another meeting, Mr. Cullen. Thank you for taking the time to come by."

As I left his office, I was pretty sure that his reluctance to identify the guy in the photo wasn't out of the need to guard some secret so much as it was gamesmanship, plain and simple. *I know something you don't know.*

Jasper Hugg. Hard guy to like.

SEVEN

I'd been to seven or eight Calgary Stampede parades in my life, and except for one when rain began falling just after the first marching band passed by, I'd enjoyed them all. But I hadn't been since the one Donna and I had attended together just months before her death.

This year a special request from Kyla had me digging out my cowboy hat, boots, and Wrangler jeans the night before the parade. I had decided years before that if I was going to get into the Stampede spirit, I would do so in clothes that real cowboys might actually wear. No floppy, flower-covered hat for me, no bling-infested shirt that members of either sex could wear with the certain knowledge that they looked ridiculous. And no T-shirt with a stupid Save a Horse, Ride a Cowboy message emblazoned across the front.

The plan was for me to pick up Kyla and Jill at five-thirty in the morning, which was the departure time Kyla had determined would guarantee us decent seats on the parade route. I was nearing a decision on what shirt I'd be wearing the next morning when Loverboy's "Turn Me Loose" signalled an incoming call on my cell. Call display showed me it was Jill. I turned down Ian Tyson's

Cowboyography (part of the mood setting) on the stereo and hit the talk button on my phone.

"I hope this means Kyla has backed up our departure for downtown to at least six o'clock," I said, expecting to hear the laugh I loved in response.

"Adam, I'm sorry, we can't go."

I had just bent over my boots, ridding them of mud that had been caked in place since I had last worn them almost a decade before. Jill's words straightened me up in a hurry.

"What … what's wrong?"

"It's Kyla," Jill answered. "She's been fighting some kind of flu bug for the last few days and I thought she was starting to come out of it, but today she's worse again. I don't think we can go."

"But I just talked to her yesterday. She didn't say any —"

"I know. She thought, like I did, that by today or tomorrow at the latest she'd be fine, but …"

I switched gears faster than I thought I knew how to. "What do you need me to do?"

"Nothing, Adam, we're okay, really. I'm hoping that another day in bed will start to bring her around, but unfortunately that day in bed just happens to be parade day."

"If she's had this for a few days, you don't want to fool around. If you think we should run her into emergency, I can be there in twenty minutes."

"No, I think she should start feeling better tomorrow or the next day. If she doesn't I'll take her in to see our doctor."

"Are you sure? She's no wimpy kid. If she can't make the parade, maybe —"

"I *am* sure. Really. And I'll be keeping a close eye on her. It's not the first time. She's had a couple of these bouts in the last year or so. They usually last a few days, then she's back to being herself. Just bad timing this time around."

"She must be really bummed to have to miss the parade."

"She is."

"You want to put her on? Maybe she could use a dose of my endless supply of kid-humour … might cheer her up."

"Thanks, Adam, but she's in the bathroom. Hasn't been able to get far from it for the last couple of days … and especially today."

"Diarrhea?"

"Yeah. Poor kid."

"Make sure she's staying hydrated. Diarrhea can really dehydrate people."

"Thank you, Nurse Cullen. I'll be sure to heed your advice."

"Sorry," I murmured, "I guess that sounded stupid. I know you can take care of your daughter."

"Actually, it didn't sound stupid at all. It sounded like someone who's concerned about someone he cares for very much. And I appreciate it, Adam."

"The offer I made earlier still goes. If you want me to come by, it's not a problem. I can be there in —"

"I know," Jill chuckled, "twenty minutes. We're fine, really. Kyla just feels bad that she's causing us to miss the parade.'

"Tell her to forget about that or I'll hafta mosey over there and tan her britches." My drawl was pathetic but it got a small laugh from Jill. Very small — a courtesy laugh from a worried parent trying not to sound worried.

"Listen, call me in the morning," I said, "and if she's isn't showing some improvement, I think we should get her to your doctor or to emergency."

"Deal," Jill said softly. I could hear her talking to Kyla. Muffled, her hand over the receiver. She came back to me a few seconds later. "Kyla's heading off to bed. I think I'll do the same thing. But I will call you in the morning … partner. I promise."

"Okay, good night, babe. Give my girl a hug for me, okay?" I said, and we ended the call.

I sat for a few minutes looking out the window, hoping that Kyla's illness was nothing more than the flu. I didn't like the fact that it had happened before … *a couple of bouts in the last year*. And both of them going to bed just after six o'clock in the evening, which likely meant that neither had been getting a lot of sleep. It was a while before I finally decided to build a rye and diet and restore the volume on the stereo, just in time to hear Ian Tyson sing about Charlie Russell and his wife, Nancy.

After a few more minutes of sitting inert on the couch, I finally headed for my computer to continue my search into the backstory of Buckley-Rand Larmer. First I spent a half-hour drafting the questions I would send to Jasper Hugg in preparation for my Larmer interview. I had to be careful. The questions would have to be seen as non-controversial without raising Hugg's antennae and having him twig to the fact that the interview was merely a ruse to get me some face time with Larmer.

So I started with some easy ones, the kind that any journalist would ask and undoubtedly had been asked by other interviewers, including Patsy Bannister. Then I threw in a couple that Hugg could nix so that he could feel important. And make it appear that the interview was a serious attempt by a journalist wanting to look at the many facets of a complicated public figure.

> Question (5) How do you see the media's role in what appears to be more and more the federal government's strategy to wage war on individuals and organizations that critique or take issue with government policy?

> Question (7) Would you characterize the mandate or at least part of the mandate of conservative talk radio to be acting as a public-relations arm for right-wing parties and politicians?

I suspected both of those would be punted from the approved list and didn't care.

I finished off with a few more fluff questions, concluding with a query as to how Mr. Larmer viewed the ongoing discussion about a new home for the Flames. I figured the question would show my desire to allow Larmer to showcase his "everyman" side and I knew he was a big hockey buff, even considered himself somewhat expert — though I'd seen no evidence in my reading to date of Larmer's ever having played or been directly involved in the game beyond kid community hockey.

I reread, touched up, and was finally satisfied. As I fired the questions off to the email address Hugg had provided, Valdy was succeeding Ian Tyson on the stereo. I added Spirit of the West to the CD waiting compartment.

Next I made a list of "Persons of Interest" under three categories:

Larmer	Hugg	Monday (Dennis Bratvers)
James Leinweber	Victor Nagy	
Jaden Reese (Ariel Mancuso)	Anita Dekalb	
Kids from Hope Christian Academy	Wilson Hall	

It was a small list, and I had to admit to myself that it was entirely possible that none of the people on it had anything to do with the threats to Larmer. Or what had happened to Dennis Monday. Or could provide me with information that would point me in the right direction. But it was a start, and having the list gave me a sense of *doing* something.

A second list consisted of the names of the eleven students who had attended Hope Christian Academy at the same time as Larmer, Jaden Reese, and Ariel Mancuso. I looked over the list to see if any names jumped off the page at me, Hope Christian alumni who had grown up to take a place among Calgary's illuminati. I didn't recognize any of the names. Decided I'd start on them the next day.

I took my computer to the couch and set myself up more comfortably than I'd been at the kitchen table. Big mistake. I was asleep before John Mann was halfway through "Save This House."

I woke up an hour and twenty minutes later with a kink in my neck that I was convinced was irreversible. After I stretched, rubbed the source of the pain, and downed two glasses of water and an Advil, I sat back down at my computer thinking I'd have another go at one of the people on my Hope Christian list before turning in.

I was leaning toward Ariel Mancuso. There was a side of me that believed the Jaden Reese part of Larmer's backstory was a non-starter. Reese was dead and the only person Patsy Bannister had been able to track down who knew anything at all was Ariel Mancuso, who claimed she didn't know or couldn't remember much about the bullying incident. Yet there was something about the episode — the fact that it was so out of character for the homophobic Larmer to have done what he claimed to have done — that the other side of me wanted to pursue it further.

But before I could enter her number, Loverboy announced I had a call.

"Hello."

The voice on the other end of the line was male and deep, gravelly. A smoker's voice.

"Wilson Hall. You've been trying to reach me?"

If Hall was a singer, then clearly his singing voice had to differ from what I was hearing at that moment. Or maybe this *was* his singing voice, and the guy defied all odds and enchanted audiences with a sound about as gentle as a prairie snowstorm.

"Thanks for getting back to me, Mr. Hall. I'm trying to learn more about an incident you were involved in at a Calgary club a few years ago. A fight apparently broke out. A man named Jasper Hugg was involved."

"You a cop?"

"No, I'm not, Mr. Hall. I'm a writer. Doing some research. Background on Hugg and an associate of his. Trying to get some first-hand insight into what went on that night."

"First of all, man, if you're not a cop, drop the Mr. Hall shit. Nobody calls me that. Wilson will be fine."

"Great, Wilson," I said. "And I do appreciate your getting back to me. It must be pretty late where you are."

He laughed a deep-throated gurgle that ended in a coughing spasm. There was a pause, I guessed while he drank some water, or something else. Then he came back on the line.

"Eleven-thirty isn't late for a musician, man. We don't sleep like other people. Anyway, what do you want to know?"

"Just kind of what happened that night. When did you first notice Hugg and the guy with him?"

"I guess I saw them out there during my first set. A couple of big dudes. *Big* dudes. Didn't think much about it. It was a pretty good house that night, lots of people. Those two were also maybe a little older than most of the people there, but that's about it for what I noticed … or at least what I remember."

"And when did things get … unruly?"

"Unruly, that's good. It was a clusterfuck, is what it was. It was during my second set. I was doin' a cover of 'Four Dead in Ohio.'"

"Crosby, Stills, Nash, and Young."

"Right. And these two guys are suddenly up and hollerin' … basically shoutin' us down, which isn't easy to do when you're playing electric guitars and stuff, you know?"

"Yeah," I said. "What were they hollering?"

"A bunch of shit about how the people who got shot at Kent State deserved what they got and the only mistake was not takin' out a bunch more of those long-haired fags … that kind of stuff. Then they started in on Neil Young and what an embarrassment he was. About then the bouncers got in there and a couple of guys in the band, pretty big guys themselves, went down there and from then on it was chaos, man — chairs flyin' and people punchin' and kickin' the crap out of each other. A few minutes later the cops showed up. There were some guys who'd taken some serious shit. Our bass player, Percy Squires, for one. Big, tough black guy, he got his nose busted and his eye socket damaged. Took a chair across the face. Broke his hand, too — hittin' somebody or the wall or somethin'. The bigger of the two assholes that started the thing, guy with the weird name —"

"Hugg?" I said.

"Yeah, Hugg. *Hugg,* for fuck's sake. Anyway, man, he was bleedin' some and the other one I couldn't see because two cops had him wrapped up and were haulin' his ass outta there. One of the bouncers and a couple of other people were hurt, too, but not that bad.

"And that was about it, man. End of the night. End of the gig. End of the band. Percy wasn't able to play for a couple of months, lost interest after that, and two of the other guys quit — we had a girl in the band, too. She didn't want any part of bar gigs or much else after that. Now I got me a guitar player and that's it. We do a lot of small clubs, acoustic gigs in places where that kind of shit ain't gonna happen. Doin' okay, too."

"What happened after?"

"What do you mean?"

"I read there were no charges laid. Is that true? Anybody go to jail?"

"Jail. Just overnight. No charges, man. Nobody got charged with shit. I figured the club would press charges or somethin' but … nothin'. People said there were some payoffs for damages and stuff and I know a lawyer came around and talked to Percy, but he wouldn't ever say what went down. I figure he probably got greased some, too — decided to let it go. But I don't know that for sure. It all just sort of blew over and I went down a different road. Got a CD if you're interested."

"What do you call it?"

"*Empty Spaces*. I think it's pretty good, you know?"

"Where would I find it?"

"You can get it online and in a few stores — I don't know about out where you are."

"You know what, Wilson … I'm going to keep an eye out for it. I'm kind of a collector, so I wouldn't mind having it."

"Sure, man, yeah … well, I hope you like it."

He said it like he had zero belief in my ever owning a copy of *Empty Spaces*.

"Listen, thanks for this. One last thing. Do you remember the name of the other guy — the guy with Hugg?"

"I never heard it. He was a prick, though, just as mouthy as Hugg — had a lot to say."

"Yeah. Listen, thanks again, and I hope things go well for you on the music side."

"Me too, man, me too. Hey, if you ever write anything about it, make sure you say that it was Hugg and that other asshole who started the whole shiteree, okay?"

"I'll make a point of it, Wilson."

We hung up and I sat back to think about what I'd learned. It wasn't much. A little more background on the unsavoury character that was Jasper Hugg. Bully with a capital *B*. But I already knew that. There wasn't much in the conversation with Wilson Hall that moved me any closer to knowing who might be threatening Buckley-Rand Larmer. He might have been the other guy in the bar that night. Or he might not have been. The mouthy part fit, but Larmer didn't strike me as a fighter, especially a bar fighter, which takes a certain amount of raw toughness. But hey, maybe Buckley-Rand Larmer, rescuer of picked-on gay kids, was tougher than I gave him credit for.

There *was* one tidbit that had come out of my conversation with Wilson Hall, but I knew I'd have trouble confirming it. Hugg and his buddy may have been connected, may have known someone in authority who could sweep a clusterfuck under the rug.

It's hard to read people over the phone, but I didn't get the feeling that Wilson Hall was intent on ridding the world of right-wing radio types. And while the bass player may have had a legitimate beef with Hugg, it sounded like that had all gone away, courtesy of a good, old-fashioned payoff.

I sat for a while thinking about Wilson Hall and Percy Squires and how what had happened had hastened the breakup of the band. Then I dug out my wallet, retrieved my PayPal information, and ordered *Empty Spaces* from Online Vinyl — The Record Store Located Conveniently on the Information Highway. I'd used them before and despite the long, silly name, the place provided excellent service. Their claim to either have in stock or be able to get every piece of recorded music ever made wasn't far from the truth.

And while I'd bought the CD, at least partly as a gesture toward Wilson Hall, I was surprised at how much I was looking forward to hearing it.

EIGHT

The first twenty minutes of my conversation with Buckley-Rand Larmer were uneventful, in part because I wasn't really on my game.

Hugg had called that morning at eight-thirty to tell me that my appointment with Larmer was scheduled for eleven. I started to tell him what I thought of that kind of notice but decided it was probably part of the mind games people like Hugg and Larmer play all the time, and graciously thanked him for getting me in so quickly.

Jill called about fifteen minutes later to give me an update on Kyla. No change. The call was brief, almost terse, which wasn't Jill. Again I offered to come over to help in whatever way I could.

"Adam, I know you want to help and I appreciate it, but right now we're okay. And she hasn't said it directly, but I get the feeling that for now Kyla wants it to be just her and me dealing with … whatever we're dealing with. I hope you're okay with that."

"Of course I'm okay with it and I don't blame her a bit for wanting this to be a mother-daughter thing."

"I'm so glad to hear you say that." Jill sounded relieved. "You know she's crazy about you, but this —"

"No need to say any more," I interrupted her. "Just get that kid back on her feet fast. I feel a night at Chuck E. Cheese's coming on."

"Now *I'm* feeling sick," Jill said and I could hear the attempt at a smile in her voice. "I better go. Call you when I know something."

Two cups of coffee and a couple of pieces of toast with peanut butter hadn't exactly energized me, also contributing to the slow start to the interview. Larmer was all courtesy and co-operation for the first while as we chatted about the university conference we had been a part of, and Calgary's recovery from the flood (lots of criticism of the provincial government there).

And to be fair, Larmer's second-floor office wasn't helping me to be as sharp as I needed to be. For starters, it was seniors-residence hot. There was an air conditioner in the window, but it wasn't running. It was either out of order or it, too, was part of the game, the "make the interviewer as uncomfortable as possible" game.

I decided I wouldn't give Larmer the satisfaction of even one wipe of the forehead.

It wasn't what I had anticipated for the office of a guy who, love him or hate him, was fast becoming one of radio's most recognizable voices. It was small and, like Hugg's, sterile and almost completely lacking personal touches. The desk was wooden, blond, and spotless, one lone piece of eight-and-a-half-by-eleven paper on its surface. I guessed the list of questions I had submitted to Hugg were on that paper.

A radio sat on a small table in the far corner of the office and I could hear the low drone of, I guessed, one of Larmer's colleagues waxing eloquent on the virtues of fracking or shouting down a caller who dared to suggest that the phrase "politically correct" is not a bad thing.

And there was a smell, not altogether unpleasant but a bit pervasive; it was a mix of floral and freshly turned dirt, both being smells that remind me of spring and the outdoors. Except that I couldn't see a plant or a container of topsoil in the room.

I considered all this as my host delivered a long-winded recommendation of a book written by an Australian economist who, according to Larmer, had solved once and for all every economic difficulty the world was facing or, indeed, would ever face. I promised to read the book at my first opportunity and decided to get into some meatier stuff before I was suddenly informed that the interview had been scheduled for thirty minutes and that "we'd better wrap it up, thanks for coming."

"I mentioned to Mr. Hugg," I began, anyway, "that I'd like to provide readers with a glimpse of the private Buckley-Rand Larmer. I'm sure with the tremendous listenership you have, there are a great many people who know and admire your public persona, but I feel that the time is right for a look at the man behind the man." I inwardly congratulated myself for the catchy turn of phrase that I hoped would resonate with Larmer as much as it had with me.

"You seem to be suggesting," Larmer retorted, "that there's a significant difference between the private and public person when, in fact, there is not." His eyes narrowed as if to emphasize the veracity of his statement. "The person the listeners hear and that audiences see is the genuine article, Mr. Cullen. I haven't found it necessary, as some have, to be a different person on air than the person I am in my home or in my car driving down the highway."

Which, of course, was bullshit. But I didn't think pointing that out would assist in the bonding process, so instead, I said, "I understand and while that's true, I know that when I listen to someone, I want to know at least some of the details that make up that person. What does he or she have on the walls at their home? What music do they listen to as they're are driving that car down the highway? That kind of thing is exactly what I'd like to focus on."

"Trivialities, Mr. Cullen, and not the kind of information anyone would be interested in, I'm sure. But to satisfy your curiosity, it's awards and plaques on the walls — indicators that what I'm doing is working and that it's appreciated. And I don't generally listen to music in the car. I'm usually dialed into my own station —" he gestured in the direction of the radio in the corner "— or I'm listening to books on tape that have to do with subjects that interest me. The Beach Boys and Nickelback do not."

I wondered about a man who displayed awards and plaques in his home and not in his office. I let my eyes glance at the wall behind Larmer. A couple of framed photos; one, I was sure, was the same one I'd seen on my way out of Hugg's office — the identity of the fourth person in the photo still a mystery to me. No plaques; of course not, those were at home.

"Those were simply examples," I pointed out, knowing that he was being deliberately obtuse, "and I'm sure that if those areas are not of particular interest, there are other elements of the private Larmer that would be. What my readers have always found interesting in the people I've profiled in the past is the person's background — the journey that brought that individual to where he or she is now, the hills and valleys of that journey."

"Again, Mr. Cullen, I don't see that as productive." Larmer's mouth formed a smile that lacked humour or warmth. "The last thing we would want to do is bore your readers, and I can assure you that my growing up was uneventful, duller than a ten-watt light bulb."

"Well, of course, you would be the better judge of that, although I have found that modest people often under-estimate the importance of their own lives and of moments in those lives."

Larmer lowered his head and smiled. Humility per-sonified.

"Mr. Cullen, I'm happy to talk to you about what is wrong and what is right in our city, in our province, and in our country. The journey, as you call it, that has brought me to the positions I hold, and share with other like-minded and equally dedicated people, is irrelevant."

This was going nowhere and I was tiring of trying to get past the wall of secrecy around him. Time to change gears. "Yet you often refer, for example, to the incident from your youth when you stepped in to rescue a young man — I understand he was gay — from a group of bullies."

Larmer sat up a little straighter and pulled his shoulders back, both indications, I was fairly sure, that I had struck a nerve and that the session was likely near-ing its completion. "I use that example, not as some kind of boast or self-tribute but as a metaphor for some of the things that are happening today, most notably the desire to paint the right as a group of twisted haters with an agenda that is based on narrow, paternalistic intolerance and —"

He stopped in mid-sentence, picked up the piece of paper on his desk, glanced at it. "You have not so far put forward a single question from the list you submitted."

"No, I haven't," I admitted. "In fact, a request for a list like that is something I would expect from a politician, not from another member of the media. Would you allow yourself to be controlled to that extent by someone you were planning to interview?"

"Those I interview have never felt the need to vet me prior to my conducting the interview. Perhaps that's where we differ."

"That would be one of several differences between you and me, Mr. Larmer. And their not imposing a pre-interview vetting process on you says more about their courtesy than it does about your abilities."

He looked at his watch. "Well, as pleasant and stimulating as this has been, I'm afraid I have another appointment and will have to bring this to a conclusion."

"Of course," I said. I put the notebook I had set on my lap at the beginning of the interview back in my briefcase — there was not a word on it — and stood up. "Thank you for your time."

He didn't stand or respond beyond a small nod and I showed myself out, opening the door just as Hugg was coming through from the other side. I wondered if Larmer had some device on or under his desk to summon his burly assistant when he felt the need.

Neither Hugg nor I spoke as we passed one another.

Right behind Hugg and walking slowly but purposefully through the outer office waiting area was Mike

Cobb. He glanced at me, then walked past and trailed Hugg into Larmer's office. I heard the door close behind me. I made for the stairs and the exit.

Once outside I stood for a few minutes in the parking lot with a new appreciation for the term "fresh air." I was surprised to note that my legs were actually shaking. There was an all-metal park bench to my left near the corner of the building and I decided to sit for a couple of minutes before driving. It was probably more like ten minutes before I felt myself come down from wherever I had been after talking to Larmer. I watched the driver of a baby-blue Firebird talk on his cellphone while parallel parking. Nifty. I finally felt as normal as I was going to feel after a half-hour with Larmer, climbed into the Accord, and rolled out into light 17th Avenue traffic.

I felt like I needed a cleansing procedure but settled for a visit to a nearby gym I sometimes frequented. Spent a half-hour on the treadmill and pushed a few weights, but my heart wasn't in it. The post-workout shower was the best thing that came out of my stop there. As soon as I was dressed I pulled out my phone and called Jill. I got her machine at the house, then dialed her cell, which went straight to voice-mail. Unusual, but I told myself it wasn't worrisome … yet.

Next I called Cobb.

He answered with, "So, did your meeting come up to your expectations?"

"Pretty much but only because they weren't great expectations."

"Great expectations. Catchy."

"So when do you get off? I'll buy you a beer."

"Couple of hours. I've got one of the boys coming in to take over. I'm running a little behind on sleep."

"Maybe the beer's a bad idea," I said.

"No, the beer's a good idea. How about the Ship and Anchor? Decent food, has a patio. We catch some rays, get some refreshment."

"You had me at food. What time?"

"I can be there about four."

"See you then."

I called Jill again, still no answer at either phone. Told myself again that everything was fine. Wasn't sure I believed me.

I looked at my watch — almost one-thirty. I decided to head for the Britannia Shopping Plaza on Elbow Drive. I wanted to load up on groceries, the kind I hoped Jill would like and Kyla could tolerate. And maybe stop in at Owl's Nest Books, pick up something for Kyla. I'd come to know the folks at Owl's Nest during the short-lived run of my own kids' book, *The Spoofaloof Rally*. The store held the record for most sales anywhere of my one and only book. Unfortunately that record was six, leaving me a few thousand short of a bestseller.

I cranked the Accord's stereo, and twenty-five minutes into Amelia Curran's *Spectators*, I parked my car and spent the next twenty-five wandering the aisles of Sunterra Market squeezing rutabagas and examining asparagus and stuffed veal. I loaded a couple of bags into the car, walked up the street to Owl's Nest, and grabbed a copy of Marty Chan's *The Mystery of the Frozen Brains* for Kyla. It sounded like something she'd like.

Feeling more human at last, I spotted the Starbucks across the street and figured I had time for an iced caramel Frappuccino. I'd finished almost half of Kyla's book before it was time to head back to 17th Avenue and my meeting with Cobb. At the end of every chapter I called Jill's number. Nothing.

Cobb was sitting at a patio table near the sidewalk when I arrived. He was working on a beer, and as I sat he pointed at his beer and raised his eyebrows.

"As soon as possible," I told him.

The bar had Dos Equis on tap and Feist on the outdoor stereo. "You chose well," I said.

Cobb grinned. "Learn anything in your meeting with Larmer?"

"It wasn't a meeting; it was an interview."

"Tomato, to-*mah*-to. How was your interview?"

"About as I expected. I didn't learn much more about the guy. He's tough, he's smart, and he has no time for people who don't think he's pretty special. All of which I knew or at least suspected."

Cobb drank from his beer glass. "And how does that help with your research?"

"I'm not sure it does," I admitted. "Still, I'm glad I met with him. Bottom line — this is a guy who's driven by a desire to elevate a particular ideology and is both calculating and ruthless in his dealings with those from the other side. That's a formula for making enemies and I'm guessing Larmer has made plenty over the years. Discovering which one is angry enough to threaten him or even do him harm isn't going to be easy."

"What was it you said before, take a number?"

"Something like that, yeah."

I recounted my conversation with Lorne Cooney.

"I'd be stunned if there wasn't something connecting the Monday shootings in Hamilton and what's happening with Larmer."

"Certainly a possibility."

Cobb looked at his beer glass, then at me. "So what's next?"

"For me? I keep digging. The guy has a past, what appears to be a *shadowy* past. I want to get behind the curtain that seems to block out so much of who he is and how he came to be that person. That's where I think I should be concentrating my efforts — where I think I can do you the most good. The trick is to not get sidetracked by focusing on one person or one incident."

"Difficult not to do."

"Damn difficult."

Next I told him about my chat with Wilson Hall. Hearing it out loud, I realized it wasn't all that relevant to the Larmer threats case unless Larmer was the other guy in the bar with Hugg the night of the brawl. And that I didn't know. I paused at that point in the story.

"Any chance you could get a look at the police report on that incident and find out who the other guy was?"

He made a note in his pad. "I'll see what I can do."

I nodded and finished relating Wilson Hall's commentary about that night and what happened, and didn't happen, after.

"This is the kind of stuff I'm talking about," I said. "It's too easy to get diverted onto something that isn't what you're paying me for." It sounded like an apology and I guess it was.

When I completed my recap, Cobb said, "Interesting stuff, though, and maybe even helpful in that it gives us a look at one of Larmer's key associates. And don't think what you're doing is a waste of time. When I was a cop I learned very quickly that in every investigation there were going to be countless conversations, threads, encounters that would take me nowhere. And in a murder investigation the chances of solving a murder become less and less with the passage of time. But it has to be done. And every once in a while that conversation that you were sure was going to be a complete waste of effort turns out to be important."

"Thanks, Coach, that's what I needed."

Cobb smiled. "No worries." A beat, then two. "Besides, this isn't a murder investigation. Time is important but not critical. Take the time you need and trust your instincts. I do."

"Again … thanks." I was staring at my beer glass.

"But there's something else, isn't there? Something that's bothering you."

I looked at him. "You know what? You're good at this. And yes, there is something else."

He looked for a second like he thought I was going to launch into another rant about the evils of the right and how despicable it was for him to work for someone like Larmer. But that wasn't it. Not this time.

"It's Kyla. And Jill. Both of them, I guess."

"What about them? If this is one of those rough-patches-in-a-relationship moments, I can tell you that Jill's nuts about —"

I held up my hands to stop him. "It's not that. At least I don't think it is." I told him about Kyla's illness. "I'm worried about her and I'm worried about her mother and I'm bothered that I'm not part of what's going on. It seems … deliberate."

"Maybe it seems deliberate because it *is* deliberate," Cobb said slowly. "You've got a kid with an ugly case of the flu or something like it, and you've got a mom who's justifiably worried. You're probably not on the radar for a couple of days, that's all."

"I know you're probably right, and I also know I sound like a jerk making this about me. I just want to be there for both of them and it sucks that I can't be."

"You know what? I think I know Jill pretty well, and I'm guessing she knows how much you care and appreciates it more than you know. But this just isn't the right time for you to be there. Who knows how physically sick Kyla is — vomiting, diarrhea, all of it. To a kid that stuff's yucky and embarrassing and they turn pretty private, even though what they want most of all is a hug and a smile. You'll get your chance and when you do, don't forget the hug or the smile."

Sometimes I forgot that Cobb was a husband and a dad. And from what I'd seen and been able to gather, he was pretty good on both counts. I sat for a minute, then nodded. "For a gumshoe you're a pretty smart guy."

"Now there's a term you don't hear nearly enough." He grinned.

"I can't decide whether I like gumshoe or shamus better. You have a preference?"

He laughed and shook his head. "I'm okay with either one."

"And for the record, you're a damn good friend, too."

The grin remained. "Yeah, don't forget that when, because of me, some very bad people are trying to shoot your ass."

"You said that wasn't going to happen."

"I said it wasn't going to happen *right now*."

Both of us laughed and clinked our beer glasses.

That night I made a couple more calls to Jill. Got the machine both times. Stopped calling because I didn't want to wake her or Kyla if they were finally getting some sleep. I read for a while, fell asleep on the couch, woke up at two in the morning and stumbled into bed, fuzzy-headed and grumpy.

NINE

I slept badly, rose early, and with the first morning coffee in hand, reclaimed my spot on the deck recliner to do what I enjoyed most about mornings and my apartment — watch the city, at least my part of the city, come to life for the day.

After a half-hour of tranquility I stepped back inside and headed for the shower. I emerged a few minutes later and saw that I'd missed a call from Jill. Called her back, got the machine. So much for tranquility. I called again fifteen minutes later — machine again. I decided the only way to deal with my worry over Jill and Kyla was to put it aside for a while and turn my attention one hundred percent to Buckley-Rand Larmer.

I promised myself that I'd know more about Larmer by the end of this day than I did at its beginning. I just had to figure out how I was going to get that done.

The computer hadn't offered up much so far, but as I worked on a second cup of coffee I dialed up my Larmer file and stared at my pathetic list of "persons of interest," realizing again how insignificant my efforts had been to date.

I spent an hour looking for numbers for the eleven former Hope Christian Academy students, came up with four possibles. I hated making cold calls, always had, dating back to my earliest days at the *Herald*. *"Hi there, you don't know me but I'm hoping that you'll tell me everything you know about a topic that is probably very painful for you and maybe even give me the clue to breaking the case wide open thus sending me on my way to a Pulitzer Prize."* Yeah, I hated making those calls and procrastinated my way into putting these four off until later in the day.

I decided to get out of the apartment, hit the streets, do a little actual physical research. And I even had an idea where to start. A guy I'd known in high school, pretty good athlete, became a teacher after university; he taught in traditional schools for a time, then became the principal at a charter school — not a Christian school exactly but a school with family values as one of its important tenets. If there was anybody who could point me in the right direction to discover what I could about Larmer's alma mater, Hope Christian Academy, it was Richard Deckard.

Richard Deckard. The guy took a lot of grief in high school because of the name — *Blade Runner* had come out some years before, but it stayed popular with enough of us that Richard "Don't call me Rick" Deckard came to hate the name, the movie, Harrison Ford, and a bunch of us who tortured him with questions about his "replicant" upbringing.

I found R. Deckard in the phone directory, called his house, and listened to a voice I hadn't heard in a couple of decades. Deckard remembered me and had read about me during the excitement (his word) of the previous winter. He agreed to meet me later that morning at the school — Hillcrest Academy — where he would be working on some things for the next school year.

"So much for summer holidays," I said, hoping I sounded suitably sympathetic.

"It's not so bad," Deckard replied. "It's amazing how much I can get done when there are no teachers or students around the place."

We rang off and I grabbed jeans and a Houston Texans hoodie, topped it off with a Willow Park Golf Course ball cap, and headed for northwest Calgary. I took a longer route out of habit. 4th Street Northwest wasn't the most direct way to where I was going, but because it housed Queen's Park Cemetery, it was a road I had frequented in recent years. As I'd done hundreds of times since Donna's death, I slowed and turned left into the gentle, tree-lined lanes that led eventually to the resting place of the woman to whom I'd been married for seven amazing years. My stops varied in length — sometimes just a few minutes, often longer. Occasionally I took a bag lunch with me and sat on the grass, eating a sandwich and staring at her name on the headstone.

Today would be a short visit, but I knew that after the stop I'd feel better about the day and about … pretty much everything. The first minutes were always the same, fighting back tears, often unsuccessfully, as I grieved Donna's being gone. Then as I stood before where she lay, eventually the peace would engulf me. I wasn't one to talk to the person I was visiting as I knew some people did, except as I was leaving when I whispered, "Bye, babe, I love you," and walked slowly back to my car. I did that every time and I did it this time.

On the way out of Queen's Park, I performed a second ritual. I lifted my ball cap, something else I always did, as I passed the spot where Donnie Goss lay. He was six years old when he was assaulted and murdered at the Calgary Zoo sixty-seven years before. I had written about it several years ago and would be forever touched by the way the small city that was Calgary back then poured out its sympathy and love for the boy's family and its loathing for the man who took a child's life. Just weeks after the murder, a Calgary movie theatre interrupted that evening's film to announce to the crowd that there had been an arrest in the Donnie Goss murder investigation. Several kilometres away a similar scene played out at a baseball game at Calgary's Buffalo Stadium. Both crowds applauded the news. The killer, who had previously taken the life of another boy in Vancouver, that one eleven years old, was executed a few months later in Lethbridge, alongside four German prisoners of war in the largest public hanging in Canadian history.

This time as I drove past Donnie Goss's gravesite, I was reminded of the murder of another child, Faith Unruh, a murder still unsolved, the victim's killer likely still on the streets.

Out there. Somewhere.

After leaving the cemetery, I continued north on 4th Street to McKnight Boulevard, where I rolled west into North Haven, an unpretentious middle- to upper-middle-class neighbourhood that housed Hillcrest Academy. Like several of the city's charter schools, this one made its home in a building that had been a public school until it was decommissioned by the school board and purchased by the people behind Hillcrest.

The building was long and low, its one-storey, brick-and-mortar, nondescript exterior sitting across from a strip mall and kitty-corner to a Baptist church.

My last encounter with a private-school principal had not gone well, and for a few minutes I sat in the Accord, not moving, looking across the street to the school, working at pushing unpleasant memories from my head. Eventually I switched off the ignition, opened the car door, and stepped out into the warming, soon-to-be-hot July day.

The main entrance into the school was locked, but Deckard must have been listening for me, because seconds after I banged on the door, he opened it, grinning and extending a hand.

"Hello, Adam, good to see you, it's been a long time."

"A very long time." I shook the offered hand and as he stepped back, I moved into the cooler air of what appeared to be an important intersection in the school. Halls from three directions met where we were standing.

"Thanks for taking the time to see me, Richard," I said. "I'll try not to keep you from your work any longer than necessary."

"No worries." He grinned again. "It *is* summer holidays, as you pointed out. Come on, I put on some coffee in the staff room. You drink coffee, I hope."

"Only because taking it intravenously is frowned upon."

"A man after my own heart."

He led the way down a hallway with walls still plastered with the previous term's student art, some of it very good. Of course, given my own utter lack of artistic skill, I've always found anything recognizable impressive. But even my untrained eye could note the talent of several of the Hillcrest kids.

Like hospitals, schools have their own distinctive smell. Unlike hospitals, that smell is something I don't mind, though it's hard to analyze. The combination of books, floor wax, sneakers, and young energy is not unpleasant, though in July the sneakers and energy were missing, the school a reflection of the emptiness of its halls and classrooms.

The staff room was large and had a friendly, comfortable feel to it, but not comfortable enough for teachers to hang out for more than recess, lunchtime, and maybe the odd spare.

"Grab a seat, Adam. How do you take your coffee?"

"Just milk if you have it." I took a chair at the table that sat in the centre of the room and watched him pour the coffee. Not a big guy but still fit-looking, with thinning hair and a ruddy complexion. Sweatsuit and expensive-looking sneakers for off-hours at the school.

He brought the coffee and we sat in awkward silence for a few moments, sipping and looking up at the ceiling like it was the Sistine Chapel. I'd noticed it before — what had happened the year before with Cobb and me and Donna's killer had been pretty big in the media at the time. And ever since, people had trouble making small talk with me. *"Hey, Adam, ol' buddy, what's been happening with you?"* or *"So, Cullen, long time no see, you stayin' out of trouble?"* were conversation killers. Which was okay. I'd never been a big fan of small talk.

That being the case, I figured it was up to me to get the ball rolling. "Richard, I'm hoping you can help me with something. I'm looking for information about Hope Christian Academy, a charter school that was around for quite a while but closed a few years ago."

He was nodding before I finished the sentence. Then the nod shifted to head shaking. "Hope Christian Academy," he said slowly. "Came to be known as Hopeless High. Of course, it wasn't a high school, but apparently whoever coined the phrase was big on alliteration. The sad part is, there was some truth to it. Too bad really, there were some good people there, especially early on. But academically there were problems. The staff and principal at the school were pretty fundamentalist, and they butted heads with Alberta Ed right from the beginning. Teaching creationism, circumventing most of modern science, minimal attention paid to the arts — pretty much what you'd expect. Then later there were some what you might call irregularities on the financial side. Some of the parent group and at least one of the administrators, a guy named Coyle — can't recall his first name — were accused of misappropriating funds, maybe even skimming some for themselves.

"Anyway, it all came crashing down. Coyle disappeared and so did some of the school's more prominent families. Moved away en masse. I don't think anyone was ever charged with anything, but it was a pretty dark time for the charter-school movement in this part of the world."

"You know anybody who worked there … teachers, administrators, anybody I could talk to?"

He thought for a minute, picked up his coffee cup, but didn't take a drink.

"Yeah, a couple of people. Teachers. I didn't know any of the administrators except for Coyle, and that was only through the media. Let's see … Moira Chadwick, I met her a few times at conferences. Seemed like a pretty good gal. I tried to hire her a couple of years ago, but she was back in the public system, happy and doing well. Didn't want to leave. Then there was a phys. ed. guy. I didn't know him very well. Cooper something. Cooper Webb maybe or something like that, I'm not sure."

"He still around Calgary?"

"I think so.… Weir, that was it, Cooper Weir. I don't think he's teaching anymore, but last I heard he was still around, doing something, I'm not sure what. I imagine a person could find him, though."

"What about Moira Chadwick? Any idea where I might find her?"

"Last time I talked to her — when I was trying to get her to come here — she was teaching at Langevin."

Langevin Junior High School. About six blocks from my apartment. Trouble was, she would be away from the school for July and August.

"Any idea where she might live?"

Deckard's brow knitted as he thought. At last he shook his head. "Sorry, Adam, I don't think I ever knew that."

"You didn't happen to keep her number around — after she declined the job offer?"

Another head shake. "Sorry again. I really had no reason to hang on to it."

"No problem. Listen, you've been very helpful and I appreciate it. One last thing. Buckley-Rand Larmer was a student there."

"Mr. Right-Wing Radio? I didn't know that."

"Yeah. So you probably didn't hear anything about him as a student."

"Can't recall anything. I don't think I heard of him at all until he got big on the radio."

I swallowed the last of my coffee and stood up. "Sorry, I have to run, but I've got a couple of appointments and, besides, you've got stuff I'm keeping you from doing." Again I said, "I appreciate this, Richard."

"Hey, no problem, wish I could have been more helpful. And … uh … you can call me Rick. I got over that whole thing with the movie once I got through school."

I smiled and nodded. As I started toward the door, Deckard moved ahead of me to show me the way out. "So why the interest in Larmer? He do something dastardly as a student?"

"Not that I'm aware of. I'm researching a possible story, but he's a hard guy to get a read on."

"Yeah. Listening to the guy, he sounds like someone who might've set fire to cats when he was a kid."

I gave Deckard my noncommittal smile.

He suddenly looked aghast. "Damn, I shouldn't have said that! I mean, you might be a fan or something. I didn't mean to —"

I held up my hands.

"It's okay, I'm not a fan. Trust me."

"Okay … uh, listen, Adam. There's something I've been wanting to say. I … uh … I want you to know how sorry I was to hear about what happened to your wife. That must have been awful for you."

"It was pretty tough."

"Good that you got the person who set that fire. Hard to figure why someone —"

I held out my hand. "Thanks again, Rick. Have a great summer and take care."

We shook hands and I headed out the door into a day that seemed that much hotter set against the air-conditioned building I'd just left.

I slid into the Accord and pulled out my phone. Dialed up the Calgary phone book and stared at twenty-one Chadwicks, none of them Moira.

"Hell, if this being a detective was easy, everybody'd be doing it," I said out loud.

It turned out to be easier than I'd anticipated. Sixth call, this one to G. and M. Chadwick, I struck gold. When I asked for Moira Chadwick, the pleasant-voiced woman who'd answered the phone said, "This is Moira. How can I help you?"

I told her who I was and that I was hoping she might have a few minutes to talk about Hope Christian Academy to help me with some research I was doing for a possible story for the *Calgary Herald*. I'd found that throwing the *Herald*'s name out there often helped break the ice when I was cold-calling people.

Except that Moira Chadwick *did* know me … or at least she said she knew *of* me. Which is maybe why she agreed to meet me at a Second Cup not far from her home. It was in Cedarbrae, a long but pretty easy drive from North Haven.

We ended the call and I dialed Jill's number and again got her machine. I thought about just dropping in — it was more or less on the way, or at least I could make it on the way, but I remembered what Jill had said about Kyla's being embarrassed by the manifestations of whatever it was she had and decided against dropping by. I set the phone down and pulled out into next-to-no-traffic, planning to retrace my steps as far as McKnight to Crowchild and head south from there.

I glanced at my rearview mirror as I moved away from the school, watched a small, dark-blue car — a Jetta — pull away from the curb maybe half a block back and fall in behind me. What was it someone said? Just because you're paranoid doesn't mean someone isn't after you … or words to that effect. Except there was no reason on earth for someone to be after me. I hadn't dug up anything remotely meaty in my investigation of Larmer; in fact, "floundering" might best describe my efforts to date. So I turned my attention to Calgary's all-sports radio station and drove on.

At some point I realized my stomach and I were seriously at odds and decided to stop for a bagel. I exited Crowchild at 33rd Avenue and found a promising place in Marda Loop. The stop took three or four minutes at the most and I was back on the road, New York bagel and orange juice making their way toward the abused party.

It was when I was pulling back onto Crowchild that I again noticed the Jetta. Pretty sure it was the same car, three vehicles behind me and one lane over. I set the bagel down and decided to see if I could determine if I was being followed. Hoping that my time with Cobb had taught me something, I eased my way into the right lane heading off onto Glenmore, connected to 14th Street West, and watched my rearview mirror. The Jetta moved one lane to the right but was still one over from me. I sped up, then braked hard, and made a sharp right turn into the entrance to Heritage Park. The Jetta sped by and I saw the driver's head bobbing to music, only a shirt collar and toque visible. I was fairly sure it was a man, and he seemed to pay no attention to me.

I tried to be the kind of observer Cobb had instructed me to be, but all I saw was a blue Jetta with a male driver. Not much. I decided I was paranoia personified and rolled slowly back out onto 14th Street and completed my journey to the rendezvous point for my meeting with Moira Chadwick.

Another coffee place, my third of the day, and it was just past noon. And next to no food so far. Half my bagel had found its way to the floor of the car, face down, courtesy of my evasive action to escape the following — or not following — Jetta. If I kept up my current caffeine-to-food ratio, I'd soon be reduced to a ninety-pound mass of vibrating urinary disease.

She was already there when I walked in. She apparently recognized me — another byproduct of all that had happened the year before — and waved to me from a table near the back of the customer area. I waved back and, seeing she was already working on a drink, I headed for the counter, ordered a caffè latte and three butter tarts. I knew three tarts was saying to Moira, *You can have one but I'm eating the other two, damn it*, but I thought if I smiled a lot she might not recognize my urgent need for calories—a lot of calories.

I joined her with the tarts in hand and waited to hear my name to announce the drink was ready. We shook hands and I thanked her for taking the time to chat with me.

I liked her right off. She was mid-forties, with short brown hair, kind of a medium-plus build — unlike some, it seemed, she actually did take time to eat from time to time — and soft, friendly features that broke into a warm smile at the slightest provocation.

"You're doing me a favour." She chuckled. "The first two weeks after school ends I usually park myself in front of the television, eat potato chips, and watch bad TV. So this is, as the kids like to say, epic."

I'd explained on the phone that I wanted to talk about Hope Christian Academy and she was apparently up for the task.

"So what exactly did you want to know about Hopeless?" She chuckled again.

"I just learned today about the nickname. How did it become known as Hopeless High?"

"Just so many things went wrong, some of them stupid things. One year a teacher lost all of her class's final math exams. Never, ever found them. Then there was the time we had two boys break their arms in the same basketball game. Even the same arm. Do you know what the odds are for that happening?"

"Probably even higher than for a whole set of exams going AWOL."

She nodded and was about to continue when we heard my name called. I stood up. "Did you want anything else?"

She shook her head. I retrieved my drink and settled back down opposite Moira.

"Tart?" I asked, hoping the insincerity of my offer wasn't too apparent.

"Thank you," she said and took what appeared to be the smallest of the three. I liked her even better at that moment.

After one bite, she dabbed at her mouth with a napkin and said, "We had a flood one year — broken pipes — and the furnace quit the next year. It was like the school was jinxed. But, of course, there were other more serious things that happened, which is why Hope Christian Academy is no more."

"How long were you there?"

"Eleven years. I came in the second year of the school's operating and was there to the bitter end. And 'bitter' is the operative word in describing the end of the school's life."

"Administrative issues?"

"You heard about that." She nodded, then sipped what I guessed was a tea of some kind.

"There was a parents' council, which was not unlike the parent-teacher groups in public schools. Except that this parents' council had tremendous power — essentially ran the school, hired the principal and even some of the teachers, controlled all the finances. Things were okay for a while, actually for a number of years. Then a guy named Coyle, Milton Coyle, rose to the top of the parents' council and things went sideways pretty fast. He had two kids in the school and he was an architect, or so he said. Not long after he took over the leadership, things began to go badly, lots of cutbacks, then paycheques were late, then still later, and we all knew it was just a matter of time."

Her cellphone buzzed. She pulled it out of her purse, looked at it, hit a button, and dropped it back in.

"Sorry. Anyway, we stumbled our way through the last few months until June 2003. I think most of us knew it was over. And it was. They announced the school would be closing and everybody just scattered to the four winds. Some, like me, got other teaching jobs; some left education, went down different roads, and some I have no idea because they just disappeared. Including the charming Mr. Coyle and his family. I heard they went to Europe, but some people said Texas. If I were a gambler I'd bet Texas — Milton seemed a lot more Texan than European. And that's it. Sorry if I rambled, but get me started about Hope Christian and it's hard to get me stopped."

I let her catch her breath and take a couple of sips of tea. "I appreciate the overview," I said after a couple of minutes. "That helps me. I'm wondering if you recall Buckley-Rand Larmer when he attended Hope."

"Ah, the famous voice. Of course I remember him. Is that why you wanted to talk to me?"

"It is," I admitted. "Are you okay with that?"

She paused. "I think so." She nodded with a half smile. "But you're going to be disappointed."

"In what way?"

"If a journalist is asking about a celebrity's student life, then clearly you're hoping for something good, maybe juicy. I'm afraid I don't have much of that for you. Nothing salacious … or even all that interesting, really."

"Did you teach him?"

She nodded. "Uh-huh. Had him for English one year and social the next. And you're going to ask if I remember anything remarkable about him, and I'm afraid my answer's no."

"What *do* you remember about him?"

"Before I answer that, maybe you should tell me what exactly it is you want this information for."

I nodded. "Fair enough. You said you know me, so you may also know I'm a writer … a journalist. Freelance mostly. I'm thinking of writing a piece on Larmer and I'd like it to be in depth. A look at the past, the present, maybe even the future — will it be politics, a big TV gig on Fox News, who knows? The man is not without certain talents."

I hated lying to her, but I justified it by telling myself it was not inconceivable that sometime I actually *could* write something about Larmer.

She pursed her lips and the corners of her eyes wrinkled a little as she thought. Took a long minute before she responded. "I guess the easy answer is that he didn't show any of that in school. Or at least not much. But you have to remember this was junior high. Lots of kids don't really start to come out of themselves until high school. But if I look back at it, I suppose there was the odd sign that this was a young man who kind of had a plan. You remember Alex Keaton in *Family Ties*, the Republican kid?"

"The Michael J. Fox character?"

"Right. There was some of that in Buckley-Rand. Even the name itself. He insisted on being called Buckley-Rand. Buckley didn't cut it. The teachers complied; I'm not sure about the students. And I remember him wearing ties, even a blazer or a suit once in a while. I mean, there were lots of times he was in sweatshirt, jeans, and sneakers like the other kids, but every now and then, maybe one day every couple of weeks, there he'd be, looking like he was leaving for a funeral — or a business meeting — partway through the day."

"Anything besides the clothes?"

She looked disappointed that I hadn't thought the attire was significant. Actually I did, but clearly I hadn't shown it.

"I don't think I ever heard anything about his being politically active, you know, making speeches in the hall, handing out pamphlets to the other kids, or anything, but again, this was junior high."

"What about his reading? Anything significant there?"

"You mean, what kind of reading did he do?"

I nodded.

"I remember him *being* a reader. Lots of junior-high boys aren't. But Buckley-Rand always seemed to have a book with him. I can't say I recall what kinds of things he read, though. My guess is he'd have been more of a non-fiction reader than YA novels and so on, but I really can't say that for certain."

"What about his grades? Was he a pretty good student?"

"Pretty good is the perfect description. He was one of those kids who got the 'Buckley-Rand isn't reaching his potential' note on his report card. He made just enough effort to get decent grades — grades that would keep the school and his parents off his back. But he was a smart kid, that was obvious. A smart, bored kid."

"How about trouble?"

"I don't know of any. It's strange — he didn't give the teachers any problems that I know of, or any of the kids for that matter. Yet he wasn't well-liked. By anybody. He was a loner and I suspect it was by choice. Not shyness so much as he maybe thought none of the other kids were worthy of his company. But again, that's a perception, not a fact, so please take it as such."

"Not well-liked by the other kids," I repeated. "What about Jaden Reese? After Larmer rescued him from a pack of bullies, surely he thought the guy was all right."

Again she paused, this time a little longer. I started to wonder if she'd heard of Reese and Larmer's intervention. "Oh God. Jaden Reese. It's been so long, I'd almost forgotten …" She paused, then added, "That whole thing was weird."

"Weird as in …?"

"I don't know. Usually something like that happens, it's all over the school. There were whispers, but that was it. And what you asked about … I never saw Jaden Reese and Buckley-Rand Larmer talk to each before or after that day."

"Almost like it hadn't happened."

"Almost, yes."

"Which is, as you say, weird. You'd think Jaden, out of gratitude, might have wanted to at least talk to the guy who saved him."

"And I'm not saying that didn't happen. I'm just saying I didn't *see* it happen."

"How likely is it that you would have seen it, if it did happen?"

"One of the things I did like about Hope — there was a policy that teachers didn't just sit at their desks. During class changes and before and after school, we were expected to be in the halls, talking to kids as they went by, interacting. It wasn't a security thing, either; the administration just wanted us to be visible, show the kids we cared enough to get out of our classrooms, smile at them, say hi, that sort of thing."

"So you saw Larmer during some of those times."

"No more than any of the other kids, but, yes, I saw him."

"But never talking to Jaden Reese?"

"Never. And I remember that because I did think it was strange. If the little rumblings we heard were true and Buckley-Rand had saved Jaden from a beating, then you'd think … I don't know, it was just strange."

"Were you aware that Reese was gay?"

She paused, then nodded. "Again, it wasn't something that was talked about among staff and admin. Hope was a Christian School — conservative family values, yada, yada. We knew, but that was it."

"Anybody disciplined because of the fight?"

She shook her head. "I don't think so. At least if there was any disciplinary action, I didn't hear about it. The fight was off the school grounds, but even so there could have been repercussions for those involved, but with nobody saying much, it probably would have been hard to do a whole lot."

"One kid apparently had his nose broken. Did you hear anything about that?"

She paused, thinking, then shook her head. "I didn't. And I don't recall seeing anyone in the hall with a bandaged face or anything. Of course, it's possible he went to a different school. Or didn't go to school at all."

I looked down for a minute, then back up at her. "How about we share that last tart?"

"Thanks, but one's my limit. I think you better have it."

"Oh, all right then," I said and we both laughed.

I hate it when women see right through me.

Back in the car I cranked my head around, scanning the street for a dark-blue Jetta. Saw nothing. I phoned Jill. This time she answered the phone, but sounded like she might have been sleeping. At two-forty in the afternoon.

"I'm sorry if I woke you," I said.

"It's okay," she murmured. "I was going to call you. I was just grabbing a nap. I've kind of been sleeping when Kyla sleeps and last night that wasn't a whole lot."

"So our girl isn't getting better?"

"I honestly don't know, Adam. Sometimes I think, okay, she's over it, and then bang, suddenly she's got bad cramps and she's back in the bathroom again."

"Both of you must be going through hell right now."

"Yeah, I guess … some anyway. I talked to the doctor twice today and I went out and got some meds he prescribed, so I'm hoping that will get things back to normal. Now all we need is some sleep and everything will be perfect."

"And you're finally getting some and I phone and wake you up. I'm sorry."

"Hey, hey, none of that, okay? You couldn't have known and I know you've been trying to reach me. I should have called back but I thought I'd just lie down for five minutes and —"

"Hey, hey, none of that, okay?" I mimicked, got a small laugh. "Look, I'm going to hang up, you go back to sleep, and if you call me later that's great and if you don't that's okay, too. Just take care of yourself and your daughter and remember I love both of you."

"I could never forget that. Thanks, Adam. We'll talk later, okay?"

"Of course it's okay. Now get back to sleep."

I heard a half-hearted attempt at a chuckle as we both rang off. I sat unmoving for a long time, worry about Jill and Kyla interspersed with questions about the growing-up years of Buckley-Rand Larmer — questions I couldn't answer. I wondered if there was anyone other than Larmer himself who could.

I reached into the CD case and pulled out Diana Krall's *Glad Rag Doll*. I figured with a cut like "I'm a Little Mixed Up" on the album, it was pretty damned appropriate. The rest of my day was spent phoning people I'd already phoned and listening to their voice messages again, a brief stay on the computer, a TV dinner, a couple of Rolling Rocks with a lacklustre Blue Jays–Mariners game in the background, Fred Stenson's latest novel in the foreground, and sleep, some on the couch, some in bed. Not much further ahead on Larmer. I was glad when the day came to an end.

TEN

My sleep was punctuated by weird dreams; the only one I recalled was me as a kid in grade school encountering two classmates, one boy and one girl, arguing over a swing. I stepped in to break it up and the boy suddenly was a mafia enforcer about to blow my head off when the phone, never more incongruous than at the moment of a mafia hit, played Blue Rodeo's "5 Days in May."

I reached across to the table next to my bed and glanced at the caller ID. I picked up to hear my favourite voice in the world speaking to me. But the voice, as it had the last few times I'd heard it, had an edge to it, maybe more so this time. Concern evident even in the "Adam, I hope I'm not bothering you this early."

"You could never bother me," I told Jill as I shot a glance at my bedside clock: 7:53 a.m. "I should have been up an hour ago. Everything okay?"

Pause. "Not really. I'm taking Kyla into emergency. She's not getting any better even with the meds the doctor prescribed and I'm worried."

"Where are you going? I'll meet you there."

"You don't have to do that, we can man —"

"No argument. I'll be there. Where?"

"Foothills. We're leaving right now."

"I'll see you there."

It took me five minutes to change, wash my face, brush my teeth, and pull on jeans, hoodie, and runners. I was in the car and headed for Foothills Hospital, had just turned west on Memorial Drive when my cellphone rang. Cursing myself for not having taken the car in to get hands free installed, I ignored the call, instead pressing a little harder on the accelerator.

Traffic was decent and despite a bit of a jam up at Memorial and 10th Street — an intersection etched forever in my memory courtesy of the previous winter's re-examination of the death of my wife, I made good time. My haste and stress cost me time at the parking machine as I fumbled around long enough to have the guy behind me honking his horn and holding his hands up in the universal "What the fuck?" gesture.

I considered responding with a gesture of my own, then thought, *What if the guy is as stressed as I am and for a similar reason?* and decided to give him a free pass this time around. I finally received the ticket, parked the car, and ran to the emergency entrance, slowing to a fast walk as I entered the packed waiting area.

Jill and I spotted each other at almost the same moment and after a hurried hug we sat. She held my hand, squeezing hard. No sign of Kyla.

"Where's our girl — they have her in one of the examination rooms?"

Jill shook her head and I noticed the tension in the muscles of her face. Her mouth was taut, her eyes narrow and tight.

"She's in the bathroom." Her voice caught. "Adam, she's in the bathroom all the time. Something has to be wrong."

I nodded and leaned in to her, brushing my lips against her cheek. It would be stupid to say it was nothing when both us knew it was *not* nothing.

"Let's just see what the doctors have to say," I murmured.

"I'm really worried. She's so not herself. We've got a game tonight. Playoffs. And tomorrow Josie's mom was planning to take Josie and Kyla and a couple of other girls to the Stampede midway. This morning Kyla said to me, 'Mom, I don't think I can play tonight or go to the Stampede tomorrow. I don't want to do the rides right now.' That's just not my daughter."

I nodded again. "I know. But let's not panic. You did the right thing bringing her here — we let the doctors do what they do and we'll go from there." I looked around. "Have they said how long they think this is going to be?"

"Who knows? I hope it's not long."

"Yeah," I said, but inside I was thinking this could be a *real* long time. I looked around at the people in the waiting room, doing my own visual assessment of how sick or injured they were. I figured half of them probably didn't need to be there at all, but that conclusion might have been my own anxiety at work.

I was still working my way around the room when Kyla returned from the bathroom.

She wasn't a big kid at the best of times, but I had to work at not letting the shock of what she looked like now register on my face. She was thin and pale ... and sick. Of course diarrhea can do that, but I was instantly aware that whatever was causing this wasn't some minor tummy upset.

I smiled at her, touched her hair, and said, "Hey, kid, not feeling so hot, huh?"

She shook her head, sat next to her mom, and curled herself up against Jill's side. Jill was right. This was not Kyla.

"You want anything, sweetheart, a drink or something, maybe some water?"

She shook her head again and closed her eyes. I imagined that the endless trips to the bathroom had played hell with her sleep, which was likely exacerbating whatever it was that had hit her so hard.

"How about you?" I said to Jill. "You want something?"

"Do you think you could get me a coffee? I'd love that."

"On it," I said, and headed out into the hall and in the direction of the hospital's main foyer. As I walked I was reminded of how much I disliked hospitals. Shook it off, trying to drive negative thoughts out of my head.

I was at the coffee machine fumbling for coins when my cellphone rang again. It was Cobb. I decided to take the call. "Hi, what's up?"

"The game's changed, big time."

I was used to Cobb's often cryptic communications, but this one told me nothing.

"What do you mean?" I jammed a toonie into the machine.

"I called you earlier."

"Yeah, sorry, I was driving."

"Hugg is dead."

"What?" The news actually forced me to take a step back from the coffee machine. "What the hell happened?"

"He's been murdered."

"Jesus," I said. "Where? When?"

"Last night sometime. Or early this morning. I don't know much yet. I'm at the crime scene. His body was found in the parking lot behind the station. If you've got time, you might want to get over here and —"

"I can't," I cut him off. "I'm at the hospital. There's something up with Kyla, and Jill brought her in to emergency."

A beat, then, "Forget this call. You take care of things there. I'll keep you posted."

He ended the call without waiting for my reply and I slipped my cell back in my pocket. I was moving in slow motion now, my mind overloaded with the morning's events. *Hugg is dead … murdered.* That made no sense.

I pushed buttons on the machine and watched a cup fill with medium-blend, one milk, one sugar, realizing as I did that I didn't actually know how Jill took her coffee. I stuffed more coins in the machine and got one for myself. Then I stepped to the adjoining machine and bought a bottle of water for Kyla, just in case she was up to drinking something.

When I got back to the waiting room, neither Jill nor Kyla was there. I wondered for a second if they'd gone back to the bathroom, but as I sat down in the seat I'd been in before, an angular, red-headed woman with bad teeth and a bandage wrapped around the fingers of her right hand leaned toward me and said, "They've gone in. Over there." She pointed. "Your wife asked me to tell you."

I nodded thanks without explaining that Jill wasn't my wife and thought about whether I should head off down the hall in the direction the woman had pointed or just sit tight. I decided on the latter course of action, painfully aware again that I was not Kyla's father and had no business being in the examination room with her and her mother.

I sipped coffee and looked at the woman seated next to me, pointed at her hand. "Bad cut?" I asked.

She grimaced and nodded, then shook her head. "Not a cut," she said. "My son slammed the car door on my hand."

I winced. "Ouch. When are they going to see you?"

She looked over at the triage station and shrugged. "They don't tell you much."

"Would you like this coffee? I got one for … uh … it looks like it might be wasted."

"Well … thanks, I'd love it, but are you sure it's okay? I mean, I —"

"Trust me, it's fine. If Jill comes back, I'll get her another." I handed her the paper cup.

We sat for a while, silently nursing our coffees. As much as the smell of hospitals bothered me, sitting in a waiting room — *any* waiting room — bothered me more. I stood up.

"Think I'll test your theory." I smiled at the woman, trying to keep my eyes off her injured hand, and strode over to the desk. A nurse who looked like she was in the last hour of a twelve-hour shift raised tired eyes to look at me.

"Yes?"

"My … uh … girlfriend and I brought her daughter in — bad flu symptoms. Apparently she's in with the doctor. I was wondering —"

"Sorry, only immediate family permitted during the examination," the nurse informed me. "You'll be able to see her after they've had a chance to look her over."

"Yeah, I'm aware of that. I was just wondering if you knew anything, you know, if it is the flu, it's been going on for quite —"

"Sorry, we won't know anything until the doctor has completed his examination."

"Right," I said. "Of course. Thanks."

I walked slowly back to the chair, sat down.

"And?" said the woman with the injured hand.

"You nailed it."

Fifteen minutes later the tired-looking nurse called, "Olivia Paxton?"

The woman next to me waved her good arm and stood up. "That's me."

She started toward the nursing station, then stopped and turned back to me. "Thank you again for the coffee. I hope everything is okay with your daughter."

I smiled and nodded. "And with you, as well."

She walked off then, leaving me to think about waiting rooms and the people in them. Twenty more minutes passed and Jill appeared from the hallway to the right and crossed to where I was. She sat down and looked at me, working at smiling and not succeeding.

"They're going to keep her in here for a day or two," she said. "A specialist will be coming in later this afternoon."

"What kind of specialist?"

"Gastrointestinal. The doctor thinks it would be a good idea to check out Kyla's *gut,* as he called it. They might have to do a colonoscopy."

"I've heard of that," I told her. "But I thought it was something that only older people have."

Jill shook her head. "I guess not."

"So we don't really know much more."

Another head shake. "Not until they run some tests … and decide if she needs the colonoscopy."

"How's she feeling?"

"They gave her something to reduce the diarrhea and they've got her on an IV to get some fluids into her. Even though I had her drinking what I thought was lots of water, she's quite dehydrated."

"Can I see her?"

"You can, but you'd only be watching her sleep. She was so exhausted from getting up to the bathroom all the time for the last few days, even a little relief, and she was ready to sleep.

"Good," I said. "That's good."

Neither of us spoke for a few minutes. Finally Jill turned to me.

"There was a radio on in the examination room."

I looked at her.

"Jasper Hugg is dead," she said softly.

I nodded.

"I suspected you already knew that."

"Cobb called me a while ago. He wanted me to come to the crime scene."

She frowned. "Crime scene?"

"Cobb said Hugg was murdered. I'm surprised it's already been on the radio. Usually the cops don't release victim's names until next of kin have been notified."

"I'm not sure they did. The bulletin said an unnamed source had stated that a body was found in the parking lot of RIGHT TALK 700. And that the source believed the body was that of Jasper Hugg. The report said the police had declined comment for the moment."

"Probably somebody who hated the bastard and couldn't wait to get the word out."

Jill didn't speak for a time. "I know you didn't like him, but this is so …"

I nodded. "I was one of those who couldn't stand the man. But I'm not glad he's dead. And not like that."

"I know," Jill murmured. "Why does Mike want you there?"

"I'm not sure."

"Maybe you should go. It must be important."

"It might be," I conceded, "but this is more important."

Jill smiled and took hold of my hand, brought it to her lips. "Have I mentioned lately that I totally love you?"

"You might have, but I'm okay with hearing it again."

"I love you, Adam Cullen."

"And I love you." I wanted to kiss her but wasn't sure if that was considered acceptable waiting-room behaviour.

We sat for a while, holding hands and looking at the floor. "I … I've been really worried."

Jill nodded. "I know you have."

"No … I mean I was worried that you were keeping me at arm's length … that there was something wrong … between us."

She looked up and for a second I thought she was angry but her face softened. "I know that had to be hard for you, and I so wanted you there, but Kyla … *didn't*. Being sick like she was, Adam, it was pretty bad. No, *really* bad. There are things that happen, embarrassing things. For a little girl who wants her mom's guy to think she's amazing, when she isn't feeling very amazing … she just didn't want you to see her like that."

I sat for a long minute. "Damn," I said loudly enough for a few people to turn to look at me. "There I was focused on me, feeling sorry for myself, and the whole time this kid that I'm crazy about is going through hell. God, I'm a jerk."

"You're not a jerk, Adam. I know you wanted to be there for her, for both of us, and you had to wonder when I kept shutting you out. You're here now and that's what matters."

"Listen, Jill, I've never been a dad and there are going to be times when I'm not very good at this, and …" I ran out of words, but it didn't matter. I think Jill knew what I was trying to say.

"Listen, why don't you go and find out why Mike wanted you there," she said. "If there's any news here, I'll call you right away, I promise."

"But I'd like to be here when she wakes up."

She nodded gently. "I know, and I also know that Kyla will want to see you when she wakes up, but that might not be for several hours. So I think you should do what you need to do and I'll call you."

"Are you sure?"

"I'm sure, but you tell Mike Cobb that if he puts the man I love in danger of anything more than a cat scratch, he'll answer to me."

"I think you already told him that."

"Then remind him."

I smiled at her. "I'll remind him."

"I'm going to go back and sit with her."

A brief hug later, Jill was on her way back to her daughter's bedside and I was heading for the hospital's exit, dialing Cobb's number as I walked.

He answered after three rings. His first words: "How's Kyla?"

"She's sleeping. Jill's with her. They're going to do some tests. You still want me to come over there?"

He paused. "Yeah, I don't think it's a bad idea, but only if you're okay with not being at the hospital. There have been some developments that it would be good for you to be on the ground floor for."

"Kyla's going to be sleeping for a while and Jill's with her. I'm on my way."

"When you get here, ask for Sergeant Kirschoff. You'll need to show ID and he'll bring you to where I am."

Thirty-five minutes later I was approaching the station from the 17th Avenue side. I was two blocks away and could already see the flashing lights of several cop cars, an ambulance, and even a fire engine. Overhead a helicopter hovered in place. I figured at first it was maybe STARS Air Ambulance, but as I got closer I realized it was a news chopper from a rival talk station — only slightly less right wing in its stance than the place it was now covering.

Irony.

I parked a block away and walked the last few hundred yards, reminded of the only other time in my life I'd ever encountered a scene like this one — the day my wife's life had been taken by a maniacally cruel arsonist.

I shivered on a morning when the temperature had already reached at least 20 degrees Celsius. I asked a uniform and was directed to a guy who was carrying on two simultaneous conversations — one into a cellphone, the other into the sending unit of a two-way radio. I waited for both conversations to end and moved into his sightline.

I held up my media ID. Sergeant Kirschoff didn't appear to be happy to see me. "You guys are supposed to be behind that ring of patrol cars over there. There'll be a briefing in an hour or so. So move it."

"Adam Cullen," I said. "Mike Cobb said you'd direct me to where he is."

"Cobb, oh yeah, the private investigator." He said the last two words with the same inflection that I use when saying "prostate examination," but he pointed in the opposite direction from where the media were to gather — and closer to the station.

"Thanks," I said, and started toward the building's parking lot.

"Hold it," Kirschoff barked and I turned back to him. "You'll need this." He held out an ID card in plastic and attached to the end of a blue-and-white lanyard.

I took it, pulled it over my head, and resumed my search for Cobb. I could see that a small tent-like structure had been erected, I assumed over the body of Jasper Hugg.

I found Cobb a couple of minutes later. Like Kirschoff, he was on his phone, but he spotted me and held up one finger to indicate he was almost done.

I worked my way over to him and leaned on the fender of an ambulance. The rumble of its engine and the flashing lights quickly convinced me that a migraine headache was in my immediate future.

Cobb ended his call and gestured for me to follow him. We walked through the open back door of the station. There were several people whom I took for RIGHT TALK 700 employees milling around, some looking stressed, others looking terrified. Several were hugging, a few were crying.

Cobb ducked around a corner and into a room that housed a photocopier, a fax machine, and several shelves stacked high with stationery supplies and dozens, maybe hundreds of tape cases all labelled with dates and times. I assumed they contained the various programs.

"Thanks for doing this." He held out his hand and we shook, something we often did, always initiated by Cobb, when we hadn't seen one another in a while.

"So do you know what happened?"

Cobb nodded. "Some. The police investigators have put together a few things. Hugg came in early — by early, I mean a little after four in the morning. It looks like he was the only one in the building."

"No security?"

"They don't have cameras, but the building is locked at all times," Cobb answered. "Entry is restricted to people who have a photo ID card. It has a bar code on it that unlocks the door."

"Not exactly Fort Knox."

"No," Cobb agreed, "but they don't keep gold here."

"I just thought after Hamilton …"

"Good point." Cobb pulled out the notebook he carried with him all the time, flipped some pages, and made a notation. "Think I'll ask about that."

"Anyway," I said, "Sorry to interrupt."

Cobb waved it off and continued telling me the story of what happened to Jasper Hugg.

"Sometime between six and six-thirty, three people arrived together — the host of the show that starts at 7 a.m., the producer of that show, and a news guy. They pulled into the parking lot and parked next to Hugg's car, a Lexus. They commented about his being here that early, but no one seemed to think it was any big deal. Except that when they got out of the car, one of them — the news guy, his name is Todd Hippel — saw what looked like someone lying on the ground at the far corner of the building. There's some grass there and a park bench, and they initially figured it was a drunk or druggie sleeping it off. The guy was half on the grass and half on the pavement of the parking area. They were about to ignore whoever it was and head into the building when Hippel noticed that the person on the ground was big, as in *real* big.

"That got Hippel thinking — Hugg's car and a big guy on the ground. So he decided to head over there to make sure it wasn't Hugg and that he hadn't had a heart attack or something."

Cobb must have thought of something else because he suddenly stopped talking, pulled out the notebook, and made another notation before slipping it back into his blazer pocket.

"Another question I need to ask," he explained. "Anyway, the person on the ground turned out to be the very dead Jasper Hugg, and it was obvious that he hadn't died of natural causes. Hippel called it in and a patrol car was here in minutes, confirmed that it was clearly a homicide. That's when detectives and a woman from the ME's office were called to the scene. That's where we're at now."

"What *did* he die of?"

"Stab wounds. Several of them. At least one to the heart, five or six to the upper torso, and a couple to the neck and head area. According to the nurse, from the Medical Examiner's office, at least three or four of the wounds would have been fatal by themselves."

I glanced at my watch. It was 9:39 a.m. Hugg had been dead for at least three hours, maybe longer. I looked back at Cobb.

"I'm not sure why I'm here."

"There are a couple of things I want you to see." Cobb began moving out of the building and back toward the parking lot.

Once outside he walked quickly toward the area that seemed the most frenzied. We reached the yellow crime-scene tape and out of habit I stopped. This was where my fairly extensive experience as a crime writer had taught me I belonged. On the outside of the tape, and later, coffee in hand, at the scene of the media briefing where we would be told what the police wanted us to know and nothing more.

Cobb lifted the tape. "You're okay to follow me. We just can't get too close."

I stepped under the upraised yellow plastic and moved up alongside Cobb. "At some point," I told him, "you're going to have to tell —"

I stopped in mid-sentence as just a few metres directly in front of me, one side of the tent structure was open. And there was the body of the man I had talked with in his office just a couple of days before. He was lying next to the park bench I had sat on after my interview with Larmer.

Jasper Hugg lay face up, his right arm directly out to the side, the other, awkwardly beneath him, or at least it appeared so from where I stood. He was wearing a black-and-yellow track suit, and I wondered if, after putting in a few early hours at the office, he had been on his way for a morning workout or a jog when his assailant attacked him. Much of his head and face were covered in blood, and I wasn't sure I'd have recognized him if I didn't already know who it was. The top half of the track suit was stained bright red from the neck down, almost to where the sweatshirt stopped and the sweatpants began.

I turned to Cobb, partly to address him and partly because I was finding looking at Hugg very difficult. "Do the police have any idea who killed him?"

Cobb didn't look at me, focusing instead on the body I would have preferred not to see. "More on that later. Look over there."

I looked in the direction Cobb had indicated and two people, a man and a woman, stood close to the body, the man making notes or drawing something in a notebook, the woman speaking intently to someone in what looked like hospital garb. From time to time one or the other of them would point at Hugg. I couldn't tell if they were arguing or merely animated in their discussion.

A photographer was snapping pictures, a second was videotaping the scene, and three or four other people, as near as I could tell, were gathering bits of what I guessed was possible evidence from the ground around Hugg's body. I couldn't tell what they were finding, but whatever it was was placed in plastic bags and carefully labelled. I spotted Lynn Cannizaro, a registered nurse from the Office of the Chief Medical Examiner whom I'd met previously while covering violent crimes in my freelance work. She was closest to the body and occasionally speaking into some kind of recording device.

"The good news," Cobb relayed in a voice barely above a whisper, "is that the lead detectives are good, very good." He nodded at the woman, who was just wrapping up the conversation she had been engaged in.

"Yvette Landry. Been on the force twelve years. Was RCMP before that. Damn good cop, but I recommend you don't piss her off. She's tougher than truck-stop meat loaf and doesn't give a damn about whose feelings get hurt during an investigation."

Cobb pronounced her name "Laundry," with a slightly French intonation, and I was reminded once again that he was fluently bilingual, an ability that surprised me every time I thought of it.

Cobb moved his gaze in the direction of the male cop. "Andrew Chisholm. He's not quite as good as Landry, but he's good. Easy to underestimate because he's soft-spoken and smiles a lot. Drinks a bit, too, but as far as I know it doesn't get in the way of his doing his job."

I looked over the blood-soaked body again. "Weird," I said.

"What is?" Cobb looked at me.

"Hugg was a big man. Presumably strong. You don't just walk up to a guy like him and stick a knife in him without a fight or resistance or … any way of knowing if …"

Cobb shook his head. "I didn't get much from the detectives, but they did say it didn't look like Hugg struggled much until at least the first knife thrust, and maybe not much then depending on how badly he was injured. So either he knew his killer and was lured over here, or someone snuck up on him."

"In either case he didn't realize he was in any danger."

Cobb shrugged. Noncommittal. "It seems a plausible scenario. The other thing that seems likely is that the killer was big, or at least tall. Hugg has several wounds on the upper parts of his body. A small guy, a) would have had trouble overpowering a guy like Hugg who wasn't just big but also tough, and b), would have had difficulty inflicting wounds to Hugg's face and head in particular, unless he was as tall as or almost as tall as his victim."

"Maybe some of the damage was done after Hugg was on the ground."

Cobb nodded. "A possibility for sure. But at least some of the nastier cuts, the ones that would have brought Hugg down, had to happen when he was still on his feet."

I turned away from the body. I wasn't good at the kind of gruesome clinical discussion we were having about someone who, a few hours earlier, had been a living, breathing human being. I wanted to get away from there. I *needed* to get away from there.

"All of this is bloody fascinating," I said, immediately regretting my choice of words, "but I'm not sure why you're telling me any of it. I don't expect to write a novel based on your working for Buckley-Rand Larmer, and while the murder of his associate is unfortunate, certainly, it has no particular bearing on me and —"

"That's just it," Cobb interrupted.

"What?" I turned to look at him. "What's just it?"

"I know you're not comfortable with this, and I won't keep you here any longer than necessary, but the truth is, Hugg's death will very likely have a direct bearing on both of us, at least for the foreseeable future."

I raised an eyebrow at him but didn't interrupt.

"The police have taken Larmer into custody for questioning and it's very likely they'll be formally charging him with the murder of Jasper Hugg."

Several seconds passed before I was able to manage a response.

"Goddamn."

"Yeah."

"I didn't think those things happened this fast. Hugg hasn't been dead that long and already they've detained a suspect."

Cobb nodded. "It doesn't often happen this fast, but it can in the right set of circumstances."

"Was there a witness?"

"I'm not sure. They've got something they think is solid, but I don't know what that is. The cops don't see me as a need-to-know person."

"But why? What the hell motive would Larmer have for killing someone he relies on so heavily?"

"They did tell me that. They're convinced that Hugg was planning some kind of palace coup either to take over the show himself or to bring in someone he could control a little more. According to the cops, Hugg and Larmer hadn't been seeing eye to eye on things for quite a while."

"Is this a theory or do they have some evidence of this?"

Cobb shrugged. "Don't know that, but I doubt they'd take him in for questioning without something concrete as to motive."

"And even if Larmer and Hugg were adversaries in the workplace, why not just fire the guy? You don't usually kill somebody over philosophical differences."

Cobb remained silent, looked deep in thought.

I thought back to my meetings with both men, scanned my memory for any hint of a rift. If there was one, I hadn't seen it.

"So I guess that would address a couple of points — the one about Hugg knowing his attacker and the fact that the attacker was a big man. Larmer works on both counts."

Cobb nodded. "It appears that Hugg had gone out to the parking lot, either to get something or to go for a run. He heads over this way, maybe to start his run, or maybe in response to someone."

"The killer."

"That seems likely."

"Larmer."

"Not Larmer."

"But I thought you said —"

Cobb held up his hands, palms facing away.

"The cops are wrong. Larmer didn't kill Hugg."

"And you know this because?"

"Because he told me."

"Larmer told you he didn't kill Jasper Hugg?"

"Yes."

"When? It seems like this is all moving very fast."

"He called me, told me to get here fast. I was here when the police read him his rights, slapped on the cuffs, and led him away. I had a chance to exchange a few words with him before they hauled him off. He told me he didn't do it. I believe him."

"End of story?" I said.

"End of story."

"Oh, well, that settles it then. A guy who makes a living by playing games with the truth and is a candidate for the Jerk Hall of Fame tells you he didn't kill a guy who the police, who are actually investigating the crime, say he did. And, as you just noted, they presumably have gathered evidence in support of the charge they are getting ready to lay but you've decided on the basis of him saying, "Well gee, Mike, I really didn't kill the guy, you know what I mean?' to which you say, 'Yeah, Buck, I absolutely know what you mean' — based on that conversation you've decided that Larmer is innocent."

"Actually, sarcasm aside, you're not far off on that."

I looked back at where the body lay. I heard Yvette Landry say "We're good here." She was speaking to Lynn

Cannizaro, who in turn signalled a couple of attendants, who moved into position to remove Hugg's body, first to the body removal vehicle and then to the morgue.

"Any idea when you'll be scheduling the autopsy?" Landry asked.

Cannizaro shook her head. "Obviously, this will be a priority. If we can, later today maybe. Call me this afternoon. By then I'll have talked to Grey and should have an idea."

"Grey" was Grey Bruce, Calgary's Chief Medical Examiner, at least five years past retirement age and possessing more energy than most of the staff who worked for him, most of whom were thirty or forty years his junior. For all his vitality, however, Bruce was more than a little erratic and extremely resistant to pressure from outside forces, including the police.

Landry nodded and Andrew Chisholm added another notation to his little notebook. I turned back to Cobb.

"Sorry, I know I sound like an ass. This …" I waved my arm to take in the crime scene, "this is way out of my league, Mike. I want you to know that."

"I get that, and I'm sorry I asked you to come here, but I'm going to need your help and —"

"I need to get back to the hospital." I started to leave, stopped and look back at Cobb. "Why? Why do you need my help? How does this change what I was already doing?"

Mike took hold of my arm. His eyes narrowed.

"He's hired me."

"Hired you."

"Yeah. To prove his innocence … in the event he's charged, and I think he will be. He's got a lawyer, of course, but he wants me on the team."

The light finally went on. "And you brought me here because you want me on the team as well and figured I should be in on the ground floor."

Cobb nodded.

I paused, thinking. "Do you have any idea how much of me wants to rejoice that Larmer could be sent away for thirty or forty years? There is nothing about the man that I don't find repugnant. Even if he and I shared the same world view, which I thank God we do not, I couldn't stand to be around the creep for longer than five minutes. This is the guy you want me to help get off."

"No, not help get him off," Cobb said. "Help prove his innocence. That's not the same thing."

There was a big part of me that wanted to tell Cobb to shove it.

Instead I said. "I have to think about it. I'll call you."

I cast one last look back at where Hugg was being lifted into the back of the body transport van. I didn't look at Cobb as I started toward my car. "I'm going to have to think damn hard about this."

I didn't know if he heard me.

I called Jill.

When she picked up, I said, "Hey, it's me. I'm finished up here for the moment and headed your way. You need anything?"

"Don't need anything, but you might want to delay your arrival here. They gave Kyla something to help her sleep and she's just dozed off. It might be two or three hours before she wakes up. I'm going to hang out for a while so I'm here when she wakes up but if you have stuff to do, maybe you should. How did it go?"

"Bad enough that I don't want to talk about it on the phone," I replied. "I'll tell you about it when I see you. And yeah, I could use a little time right now. I'll come up to the hospital in a couple of hours."

"You okay?"

"I'm fine," I said. "Just a little stressed. Murder isn't nearly as much fun as it was when Columbo and Jessica Fletcher were on the job."

"I imagine not."

"We'll talk when I see you."

We rang off and I started the Accord.

Ever since I was old enough to go places by myself, my favourite place to go has been the public library. For me the library had always been more than a place to find books. Long before there was an internet it was the greatest information source out there. It was a place I could go to read the latest copy of *Sports Illustrated*, *Alfred Hitchcock Mystery Magazine* (the publication that sparked my interest in journalism and, in particular, the crime beat), and *The New Yorker*.

But more than merely the place I went to replenish my reading supply and learn about the Hindenburg disaster, the library was my refuge, the place I wanted to be when no other place would work — a place to think. I needed that place now and stopped at the Louise Riley Branch on the North Hill.

I found a table and settled in with my notebook, a sharp pencil, and the calm that being there brought. I made notes on everything I knew about Buckley-Rand Larmer and Jasper Hugg. I started with my first meeting with Larmer when we were presenters at the university and continued right up to my conversation with Patsy Bannister and my own ill-fated meeting with Larmer. I wanted everything I knew about him, including my online research notes (I rewrote those as a review tactic) in that notebook. Then I duplicated the process with Jasper Hugg.

I read and reread, cross-referenced, underlined, crossed out, and doodled in margins. And after almost three hours I was no closer to a decision on whether I would work with Cobb to prove Larmer innocent.

I packed up my notes, exchanged smiles with a pleasant-looking librarian and stepped out into the beginnings of a lovely Calgary evening. I'd been longer than I intended, but on my way back to the hospital, I stopped at a florist and bought an arrangement after telling the woman this needed to be the cheeriest bouquet ever designed. When she'd finished I had to admit she'd created something amazing. Even after a day that had included seeing a dead body up close — a lot closer than I cared for — receiving an offer I wanted to refuse, and getting mediocre news or no news about Kyla's condition, the flowers and the other elements in the arrangement were almost able to make me forget the past several hours.

When I arrived at emergency, a nurse you'd like to have for your sister informed me that Kyla had been moved to a ward, gave me explicit directions for getting there, and complimented me on the floral arrangement.

When I got to the room on the seventh floor, the door was pulled to and I tapped softly. Jill's voice, sounding a lot better than it had earlier, invited me in. Kyla was sitting up, looking less pale but still a long way from chipper. She had an intravenous hooked onto her left arm and a glass of what looked like apple juice in her other hand. She managed a smile in my direction, and the smile got bigger when she saw the flowers.

Jill rose, kissed me on the cheek, and said, "Adam, those are beautiful." She made room on the wide windowsill for the vase and its contents.

"Picked 'em myself," I handed the arrangement to Jill and winked at Kyla. "Okay if I sit here?" I pointed to the edge of the bed.

"Uh-huh." She nodded seriously. "What I have isn't supposed to be catching."

"Actually," Jill added, sitting in a chair near the window, "we don't know what she's got, but they're moving forward with finding out."

"Well, that's good news." I looked at Kyla. "Isn't it?"

"Not exactly," she said with an unhappy shake of her head. "Tell him," she instructed her mother.

"Well, unfortunately" — I could tell that Jill was trying to make her voice sound cheerful — "the preparation for a colonoscopy requires that you completely clean out your system."

"Clean out as in …?"

"Uh-huh. You have to drink stuff that will … well, clean out your system."

I felt bad for Kyla. Somebody who'd spent all that time in the bathroom for the last several days was now going to have to take stuff that would put her back in the bathroom. "The good news is," Jill added, "she doesn't have to go through that until tomorrow. First they want to get her built back up a little."

"But I can't eat anything." Kyla frowned. "Except Jell-O, which I hate, juice, which is okay, and tea with no milk or sugar."

"And popsicles." Jill smiled. "Don't forget the popsicles."

"Which would be okay if they had more than one flavour — orange. How many orange popsicles can you eat?"

"Yikes!" I said and turned to Jill. "Do they actually think she's got anything left in her to clean out?"

"Hah!" Kyla nodded violently. "That's what I said."

"Unfortunately that doesn't seem to be how it works." Jill reached over and patted her daughter's leg in condolence. "The doctor says she can go home after she comes out of the anaesthetic for the colonoscopy and she'll be able to eat pretty close to normally."

It seemed to me that Jill was working pretty hard at finding positives to focus on and that Kyla wasn't totally buying it.

I looked at her. "Think you could spare your mom for fifteen minutes or so?"

"As long as you're not taking her for a nice dinner."

I laughed. "Nothing but coffee and orange popsicles, I promise."

Kyla giggled, which I took as a good sign. Jill bent over the bed and kissed her. "We won't be long."

As we got to the door, Kyla said, "Adam."

I turned back to her.

"Thanks for the flowers. I totally love them."

"You're welcome, sweetheart."

Jill didn't say anything until we were in the elevator. "How did you know that the thing I wanted most in the world was a coffee?"

"Hell, I wasn't thinking of you. I wanted one for myself."

She punched my arm and managed a smile that created more lines around the eyes than usual. The past few days had taken a toll.

The elevator door opened and we made our way to the cafeteria, which was populated by a few nurses, a couple of doctors, and a group of school kids a year or two older than Kyla who looked like they were about to perform for some of the patients, maybe a school choir. Or maybe they'd already performed and were grabbing snacks and drinks before leaving the hospital.

I pointed to a table and Jill nodded and headed off in that direction while I got the coffees.

I set one down in front of her, sat down, and took one of her hands in mine. "Okay, what are the doctors saying?"

She shook her head. "They really aren't sure. They'll know more once they have the results of the colonoscopy."

"But what's a colonoscopy for? What's it supposed to find?"

"A specialist stopped by for a few minutes and said they wanted to check for inflammatory bowel disease — colitis or Crohn's disease. That's a possibility, but we won't know until after the test."

"And if it's one of those?" I'd heard the terms before but knew almost nothing about either.

"I'd already done some reading even before the specialist talked to us. Lots of times colitis or Crohn's is worse in kids. But usually it can be controlled with diet and medication. Sometimes there are surgeries to remove the diseased part of the small bowel or colon. But they try to avoid that if they can."

Diet. Medication. Surgeries. Not happy words.

"Damn," I said.

"Let's not get ahead of ourselves. There's a process here. The colonoscopy is the first step. Once we know what's causing her problem, then we can start figuring out how to deal with it."

I nodded and forced a smile. "Yeah ... but damn."

"I know. Now why don't you tell me what happened with Jasper Hugg."

I released her hand and took a long swallow of the coffee. It wasn't bad.

"Multiple stab wounds. Pretty awful."

Jill muttered something under her breath that could've been a curse. Aloud she said, "Do they have any idea who might have ..."

I nodded. "The police have someone in custody."

Maybe it was the look on my face or maybe it was her intuition, but she set her coffee cup down. "Larmer?"

I nodded again.

"But why? Why would he ...?"

"That's where it gets tricky."

"Oh? Tricky how?"

"The cops have arrested Larmer and are going to charge him with murder. Cobb says he's innocent and wants us to prove it."

"That doesn't sound easy. Why does Cobb think Larmer didn't do it?"

"Because ... Larmer told him he didn't do it."

We sat for a while, neither of us saying anything.

Finally Jill spoke. "You said 'us.'"

"What?"

"You said Mike wants *us* to prove it. *Us* as in him ... and you."

"Yeah, that's pretty much it."

"Which puts you smack in the middle of a murder investigation. Again."

"It would," I said. "Except that I haven't agreed yet."

"You haven't?"

I waited, wanting to find words that would adequately explain what I was feeling. I picked up my coffee, then set it down again. "Jill, I find Buckley-Rand Larmer one of the most appalling people I've ever come across. For me he has no redeeming qualities. He's something that has come out from under a rock, and the best thing that can happen is for him to slither back under. Or be forced back there and kept there for a really long time, like, say, forever."

"So it's safe to say you don't like him, then."

I saw the crinkle at the corners of her mouth that was always a giveaway that she was teasing me.

I realized I'd made much the same speech to Cobb and grinned. "Gee, I thought I'd done a pretty good job of disguising how I felt about the man."

She laughed. "You might need to work on that a little."

She looked at her watch and drank down the last of her coffee. "I should be getting back. But let me ask you something first. What if Mike is right and Larmer didn't kill Jasper Hugg? And say, just for the sake of argument, that Larmer wasn't a bottom feeder and you did like the guy, or didn't really know him well enough to like or dislike him. Would that change how you'd react to Mike's request for help?"

"Jill, I'm not a cop and I'm not a private investigator. And I don't want to be. What I saw today was beyond horrible. This isn't my world and —"

She held up a hand. "That isn't what I asked you."

I shook my head. "If it was somebody else other than Larmer? I don't know, but it doesn't really matter. It *is* Larmer, and he is who he is, and who he is makes me sick."

"And what if he's innocent?"

"Are you telling me you want me to do this?" I stared at her, more than a little surprised by what I was hearing. "This is a murder investigation, Jill. That means if it isn't Larmer, then the killer is out there somewhere and it's just possible that he's killed not one but at least two people, a Larmer-like lizard in Hamilton and now Jasper Hugg. I thought you and I were pretty much on the same page on the idea of keeping me out of murder investigations."

She shook her head. "No, I've never said that. I don't want you in *dangerous* situations because I love you and I don't want anything to happen to you. That's not the same thing."

"But this could be dangerous."

That was lame and I knew it and Jill saw through it right away.

"Adam Cullen, don't put this on me. I'm just asking the question — would you be okay with it if Mike is right and Larmer's innocent but is convicted, anyway. And you weren't there to help because the guy's a jerk. That's all."

She stood up then and I drained the last of my coffee and stood up with her.

"I have to get back to Kyla." She reached out and touched my face.

"I'll come up and say goodbye."

Neither of us spoke as we rode up the elevator and strode down the hall to Kyla's room. But when we stepped in, she was asleep. We stood and watched her sleep for a few minutes.

I stepped to her bedside and gently patted her shoulder. Jill came up beside me and took my hand. "You know I'm on your side, right? And whatever you decide —"

I put my fingers on her mouth and said, "Don't say any more."

She looked up at me, her eyes searching my face.

I said, "I just have some thinking I need to do."

She nodded and stepped around to the other side of Kyla's bed to sit where she'd been before.

"Promise me one thing." I said.

"What's that?"

"Promise me you'll get some sleep."

"I promise." She smiled.

"Tonight," I added.

She smiled again, gave a tiny nod.

"I'll call you in the morning."

With that I headed out of the room, this time taking the stairs down to the main floor.

I was still restless and a long way from sleepy, so I drove and walked the streets of downtown Calgary, then moved over to Kensington and walked some more. Interesting area, Kensington. It's actually just a street. You could argue one of the coolest streets in the city, but it is *one* street in an area known as Hillhurst-Sunnyside. Good marketing or maybe good luck has led to the whole neighbourhood being called Kensington. I finally settled into a bar I liked a lot — Molly Malone's Irish Pub — where I drank a Guinness and watched the last two innings of the Blue Jays game in Anaheim.

When the game ended I sat for a while nursing the Guinness and liking the noise, the energy, the pub smells. I stayed maybe an hour. Back on the street I stopped on my way to the Accord and called Cobb's cell, got his machine.

"If you've got time in the morning we need to have breakfast — how about the Blue Star Diner, maybe ten. I'll buy and put it on the expense account you're going to get. And we can get started on proving Larmer's innocence. Now there's a goddamn phrase that doesn't exactly roll off my tongue. Call me if that time doesn't work for you; otherwise, I'll see you in the morning."

I climbed into the car and started for home.

ELEVEN

I was sitting at a table with orange juice poured at both of our places when Cobb entered the Blue Star. He hadn't called me after I'd left the message on his machine the night before so I knew he'd be coming. I was looking at my phone and didn't see him until he pulled out the chair opposite me.

He was wearing a light tan blazer over a Gold's Gym T-shirt and dressy jeans. Cobb was one of the few forty-something guys I knew who didn't look ridiculous dressing like a twenty-something. He provided a nice contrast to my no-name grey T-shirt, ratty jeans, and Arizona Cardinals ball cap on backward. Going for the homeless twenty-something look.

I pointed at the juice. "I'm not sucking up. I figured it was the least I could do for dragging you across town to a place that's just a few blocks from my house."

"Didn't cross my mind." He grinned. "But thanks. Besides, I've brought the family to this place before and we love it. Even Peter, who is a pizza for breakfast, lunch, and dinner kind of guy."

"He never gets tired of it?"

"Occasionally. That's when he switches to pizza pops."

I smiled and nodded. "I don't think I've asked for a while and I should have. How is your family?" I knew Cobb was crazy about his wife after almost twenty years together and lived for his kids, though Peter was a challenging sixteen-year-old and daughter Kennedy was entering puberty at full gallop — and with attitude.

"Everybody's good. Lindsay said there was minimal bloodshed over the choice of movie last night, and since I wasn't there to referee, I'm happy for that. School went well last year. We'll see how things unfold this fall. Every year they get older, I get more nervous. But so far it's all good. What about you? How's Kyla?"

The waitress, young and full of far too much energy for that early in the day, brought two menus and a coffee pot. Cobb ordered the eggs Benedict and I ordered two fried eggs, chicken sausage, hash browns, and toast.

When the waitress moved off and Cobb and I had doctored our coffee, I gave him the abridged summary of the day before.

"Colonoscopy." He shook his head. "Had my first one a couple of years ago. The crap they make you drink before the thing is the worst part of the whole deal. I feel for the kid."

"Yeah, me too."

"Adam, if there's anything I can do … I know people say that all the time, but I mean it. Anything at all … anytime."

"Thanks, I appreciate it. Jill will, too."

We both sipped coffee before Cobb said, "I'm glad you're on board for this, Adam. Speaking of help, I wasn't kidding — I'm going to need yours."

"Have you talked to Larmer yet today?"

"No, but I talked to Detective Landry. Buckley-Rand Larmer has been formally charged with first-degree murder in the death of Jasper Hugg." Cobb took a sip of coffee. "He spent the night in jail and was transported to the Calgary Remand Centre this morning. We're meeting this afternoon — one o'clock."

"We?" I repeated.

"Larmer, his lawyer, a guy named Shulsky, me ... and you if you want to be there."

"Do you want me there?"

"It wouldn't be a bad idea, but it's your —"

"Count me in."

"Good."

I leaned forward, aware of the need to keep my voice down. "Look," I said, "I get that you believe Larmer didn't stab Jasper Hugg, and next to Jill and Kyla, you're the person I trust most in the world. But I'd like you to lay out for me why you think Larmer's in the clear on this."

"Sure."

That was as far as he got as our server bounced to our table with our food. Crazy fast service. For a few minutes we were busy adding condiments and getting ready to move in on food that smelled as good as it's possible for food to smell.

We each sampled a couple of bites and the taste matched the aroma. As I chewed I realized I was nodding and when I looked at Cobb I saw he was doing the same thing. I came up for air, drank some coffee, and set my fork down — the way the etiquette books say you're supposed to. I was pretty sure the people who wrote those etiquette books had never eaten at the Blue Star.

"You ever read *Calvin and Hobbes*?"

Cobb failed to set his fork down but he did straighten and pause. "Used to. Hasn't been around for a while. Didn't the guy retire?"

"Watterson. Yeah, sort of. But I still go online and read them from time to time. I found one this morning that couldn't be more appropriate. Calvin says he's thinking of starting his own radio talk show. He tells Hobbes how he's going to spout simplistic solutions for hours, ridicule people who disagree with him, and generally foster cynicism, divisiveness, and a lower level of public dialogue. Hobbes tells him he was born for the job."

Cobb chuckled. "Funny. And timely."

"And damn close to the truth," I added. "And that, by the way, is the last editorial comment I will make for the rest of this breakfast."

We again devoted several minutes to the enjoyment of the food. Eventually we slowed, took more breaks, drank more juice and coffee.

"Okay," Cobb said during one of the respites. "Here are some of the reasons I think Larmer didn't do it. First of all, motive. I think it's flimsy at best to think Larmer was worried about Hugg taking over the show. Especially given Hugg's aversion to the public eye … but if he was, even if he had another on-air personality in mind and assuming that Larmer actually knew something was going on, why kill the guy? Why not just fire his ass? Which is pretty much what you said."

I nodded. "Yeah, I recall saying that."

"Secondly, there're the threats and that killing of the talk show guy in Hamilton. I'm thinking there's a connection, and I've already checked it out and Larmer has an unsinkable alibi for both times the Hamilton radio guy was shot."

"Unless he hired somebody."

Cobb nodded. "Unless that. Which I also asked him in the few minutes I had with him yesterday and which he also denied." He paused in mid-point as our waitress returned, this time with the coffee pot. She eyed our rapidly emptying plates.

"How's the breakfast, guys?"

"We're hating every bite," I told her.

"We get that a lot." She laughed, filled our cups, and moved off.

"I've got another question for you," I said.

"Shoot." Cobb looked at me intently.

"Let's go back to the motive thing for a second. What if Larmer found out or at least suspected that Hugg *was* behind the threats? Isn't it possible that he could have offed Hugg almost in self-defence? Or as a first-strike action?"

"Simple answer, yes, it's possible he could have done that. As a matter of fact, I'm betting the cops and the Crown prosecutor are very interested in going down that road."

"But let me guess — Larmer says he didn't even consider Hugg as the person behind the threats."

"Actually I didn't get a chance to ask him that yet. I will in the meeting this afternoon."

"Okay," I said, "this could go on for a while because as you know nothing would tickle me more than for Larmer to be convicted of murder and spend the next twenty-five years or so hosting all-night radio at the crowbar hotel. However, my debating the merits of the case would be counterproductive in that I am being contracted to help you prove that Larmer didn't kill Jasper Hugg. So where do you want me to start?"

Cobb reached into his blazer pocket and pulled out a sheet of paper, unfolded it. "Names and phone numbers of everybody on staff at the station. Not counting Larmer and Hugg, there are fourteen people. How would you like to talk to a few of them? I don't expect interrogation — just do your journalist thing and see if anybody is of interest. If there is we go back at him or her a second time and see what's shaking."

The waitress arrived to remove plates, which made my hesitation look less deliberate. When she left I said, "I don't know. Research is one thing. Questioning potential suspects is a little out of my line. I'd hate to mess up and we miss the killer because I thought she looked like somebody I'd like to take home to meet the parents."

Cobb shook his head. "You've interviewed hundreds of people. And you've got great instincts. Bottom line here is we need to move fairly quickly, and if I have to talk to all fourteen, that could tie up two, three days. I'd like to be doing other things as fast as I can get to them. But this is important. One of these fourteen could be the killer and we need to talk to them all. But here's what we'll do — you interview four or five and if you're not confident with how it went after you've talked to them, I'll take a run at them."

I paused, then nodded. "Okay, when do you want to get started?"

"Right after the meeting at the lawyer's office."

I had just fired up the Accord when my phone signalled an incoming call. I didn't recognize the number but took the call, anyway.

"Hello."

"Looks like things are heating up big time on the Larmer front."

I hate it when people launch into a conversation without identifying themselves.

"Who is this?"

"Sorry. It's Patsy Bannister. I thought you'd see it on caller ID."

"No problem. All I got was the number."

"Sorry," she said again. "Did I catch you at a bad time?"

"No, not really."

"I've been reading and watching … Jesus."

"Yeah," I said. I'd already decided to say as little as possible to anyone asking about the case, but I was aware that Patsy might have to be an exception. She'd been pretty forthcoming with information going the other way and would undoubtedly expect a little quid pro quo.

"I can't believe Larmer would whack the guy that was such a huge part of his getting where he is. It doesn't make sense unless he just lost it and —"

"It's too soon to say that Larmer killed Hugg. The police obviously have evidence sufficient to bring about an arrest, but Larmer claims he didn't do it." I decided to leave Cobb's name out of it.

"He told you that."

"Yeah," I lied.

"Well, no surprise there. So where are you in all this?"

This was the part I wasn't sure I wanted to share.

"What do you mean?"

"Well, a few days ago you were researching the life and times of Buckley-Rand Larmer. Now that includes a murder charge. Just seemed unlikely to me that you wouldn't be, at the very least, interested."

"Fair enough. I'm interested."

"Any chance you can keep me in the loop on this?"

"I can't promise that, Patsy. First of all, I'm not sure how 'in the loop' I'll be myself." Another lie, but what I didn't need was to be seen as a potential source of information by a media person I liked but didn't know well. Certainly not well enough to trust. "But I'll tell you what I will do. I know I owe you one. If it looks like something is breaking one way or the other, I'll make sure you get a shot at it. Obviously I can't speak for the cops, but we both know how that will go."

"Yeah, media briefings. Bare minimum. Ask for the public's help. A couple of teasers and that's it."

"Yeah, about like that. And even if I am involved, it won't be my call to give you what I know. But like I said —"

"Yeah, I know," she interrupted. "I'm in the queue. Okay, thanks."

She ended the call and I knew she wasn't happy, and in her shoes I'd have felt the same way. But I also knew there'd be damn little I'd be able to give her that she couldn't get from other sources. That was how it worked. If we were lucky enough find the killer — assuming it wasn't Larmer — then I'd be happy to give her a head start on the rest of the pack. But I didn't want to promise that. And there were a lot of things that had to fall into place before that happened.

I decided I had time to get home, take a run, shower, and get to the meeting with Larmer and his lawyer.

Which started as badly as it is possible for a meeting to start.

Larmer's arraignment was scheduled for the next morning, which meant that if there was to be bail, it would happen then. Thus the meeting took place at the Calgary Remand Centre.

The room was small, spare, and hot. It smelled faintly of onion rings and long-worn socks. The socks I understood, the onion rings not so much. An incongruous painting of what looked like a Hawaiian beach hung on one wall. Justice system humour?

I shut down my phone as I took a seat on the opposite side of a heavy rectangular metal table from the defendant and his team. I'd just wrapped up a call to Jill and had learned that the colonoscopy was scheduled for two-forty-five. Jill said the procedure should take about an hour, but that Kyla wouldn't be fully back from the anesthesia for another couple of hours after that. The good news was she'd be able to go home then. I told Jill I'd check in later and we ended the call.

I looked across the table, but Larmer was looking away and didn't notice me.

Shulsky had brought along a couple of assistants, but before he could complete the introductions, Larmer did notice me. He pointed across the table and screamed, "Get that bullshit bastard out of this place right goddamn now!"

Quite a different communicator as the accused in a murder investigation than he'd been during our meeting at the station. I was willing to cut him a little slack on that. As I was the bullshit bastard in question, I thought it best to keep my mouth shut and let Cobb and Shulsky sort out whether I would remain in the meeting or not. Shulsky looked at Cobb, eyebrows raised, waiting for an explanation. Cobb chose to direct his comments to Larmer and leaned forward, arms on the table.

"Something you need to be aware of. You have a lawyer and he may or may not be able to get you out of the mess you're in. And make no mistake, whether you killed Jasper Hugg or not, you are in a very large mess. You seemed to realize that in the hours immediately after the murder and the minutes after your arrest, which is when you asked me to stay in your employ, albeit in a different capacity — as an investigator rather than a bodyguard."

Larmer opened his mouth but Cobb raised his hands in a no-nonsense "I'm not finished" gesture, and Larmer, to his credit, closed his mouth and listened in doleful silence.

"That was a good decision on your part," Cobb continued, "because I'm very good at what I do and will be useful to both you and Mr. Shulsky here in the unfolding of this case. So, if you're smart, you *want* me, Mr. Larmer, and let me make this very clear, you will get me only if Mr. Cullen works the case with me. And I'd appreciate it if you'd decide on that fairly quickly, because I have a busy schedule and will want to be moving along if I'm not needed here."

I was pretty sure Buckley-Rand Larmer wasn't accustomed to being spoken to in the way Cobb had just spoken to him. And I was once again beyond surprised at the different faces of Mike Cobb. The often pleasant, almost gentle guy, especially around family and friends, became a pitbull on steroids when in his investigator persona.

The simple truth was that neither of us knew just how much of an asset I'd be. And, of course, there was another way of going about this, which was to keep me in the background beavering away without Larmer's knowledge.

But that wasn't how Mike Cobb worked. He wanted me there and he wasn't about to go about having me on his team in some surreptitious way.

And I knew two things for certain. He was neither afraid of nor intimidated by Larmer … and he wasn't bluffing. Larmer would back down or Cobb and I would be enjoying beer and something Italian at a nearby dining establishment within the hour.

For a few seconds I wasn't sure which way it would go. But only for a few seconds. Larmer glanced at his lawyer, who opted to remain silent and stare at his hands. The corner of Larmer's thin mouth twitched once … twice.

"He stays," Larmer said in a voice that, had there been even the slightest background noise in the room, wouldn't have been heard. But he wasn't finished.

His next words were at normal volume. "But I want both of you to know that I don't like being played and I don't like being bullshitted." He turned his gaze to me. "And that phony interview you staged with me was bullshit."

Again I said nothing. Cobb was still leaning forward staring at Larmer. "Are you finished?"

"I'm finished." Larmer ran a hand over his face, a face that had grown considerably redder in that past couple of minutes. "And I will guarantee you one thing. You'll both be finished for good if you pull any more shit."

"Right, then let's get to it. There's a lot of work to be done here." Cobb leaned back. "Mr. Shulsky, I know there are things you'll want to discuss with your client that don't involve Mr. Cullen and me. So why don't we take a little time to look at the things that are of interest to all of us? What can you tell us about what the cops have to work with?"

"What we've got so far is sketchy," Shulsky said, his voice at least an octave lower than his body said it should be. "We'll get more in the next twenty-four to forty-eight hours. The police received an anonymous tip that said someone was seen lying in the parking lot area of RIGHT TALK 700, that this person was covered in blood and appeared to be either badly hurt or dead, and that a gold Lincoln Navigator was seen leaving the area at a high rate of speed."

Cobb looked over at me. "Mr. Larmer drives a gold Lincoln Navigator." He looked back at Shulsky. "I'm assuming the police have taken custody of the vehicle."

Shulsky nodded, then went on. "The tenor of the questions the police investigators asked my client would indicate they are basing much of their arrest and charge on four things — that phone call, physical evidence found in my client's SUV, the lack of a corroborated alibi for Mr. Larmer, and the alleged existence of a feud between my client and the deceased."

Cobb looked at Larmer. "The uncorroborated alibi being?"

"I was doing what most people do at that hour of the morning — sleeping." Larmer's words were clipped, showing his continued unhappiness with my being there.

Cobb returned his gaze to Shulsky. "Are we closer to an exact time of death?"

"What I've got so far is between 5:00 and 7:00 a.m. Give or take thirty minutes either way."

"What time was the tip called in?"

"Six-forty-eight."

Back to Larmer. "What time do you usually get to the station?"

"Shortly after nine," Larmer said. "And in anticipation of your next question, my alarm goes off at 6:30 a.m. on days I'm on air. I get up and am out the door twenty to thirty minutes later en route to the gym near my home, where I work out, shower, and have breakfast. I leave there around 8:30 to 8:45, which puts me in my office by 9:15."

"And that's what you did the morning Hugg was murdered?"

Larmer paused, looked at his lawyer again, then shook his head.

Cobb said, "Is that no, I won't answer the question, or no, I didn't follow my normal morning routine on the day Hugg was killed?"

"The latter," Larmer said slowly. "I wasn't feeling well that morning and slept late. I woke up a couple of times but I went back to sleep. The second time, I think it was about 7:30, I got up, took a couple of Tylenol, and slept a while longer."

"And you were alone that night?"

Larmer started to say something, settled for a nod.

"Thus the uncorroborated alibi."

"Yes," Shulsky answered.

Cobb stopped then, sat back in his chair, thought for a while. When he spoke again, he was addressing Larmer. "So you slept later than usual, then got up, and what came next? Shower, breakfast, drive to work?"

"Partly."

"Partly," Cobb repeated. "What part?"

"The part about getting up, showering, and having breakfast. I didn't drive to work — it was a nice day, so I walked. Thought it might help bring me out of the fog I was feeling from whatever was wrong with me that morning."

"How long is the walk?"

"Half an hour maybe. Or a bit more. Forty minutes, tops."

"Had you parked the Navigator in the garage?

"Yes."

"When?'

"The previous afternoon when I arrived home from the station."

"And I'm guessing you didn't happen to see or hear anyone taking it out of the garage yesterday morning or the night before?"

"No, I did not."

"And you didn't happen to look in the garage that morning before you left for work?"

"No, I did not."

Cobb had his little notebook out on the table in front of him. Now he pulled a pen from an inside jacket pocket and made a couple of notes.

He aimed the pen at Larmer as he said, "What was the source of the feud between you and Hugg?"

"No source because there was no feud."

"Dispute, then."

"No dispute, no feud, no disagreement. The show is getting better ratings than it ever has. Advertising revenues are at an all-time high. We're living —" He stopped, checked himself, looked genuinely upset for a couple of seconds. "We *were* living the broadcasters' dream. There was nothing for us to disagree about."

"Broadcaster's dream," Cobb repeated, "turned nightmare. Who do you think did this?"

Larmer shook his head. "I honestly don't know. I've thought about nothing else since … this happened. And I just don't know. The easy answer is some left-wing psycho-job, but I realize that *is* the easy answer. And maybe not the right answer."

"Wouldn't a lefty psycho who was unhappy with something that was said or done on the show be more inclined to exact his or her revenge on the host of the show rather than on the producer?"

"I would have thought that, yes."

"What about enemies? We know Hugg could get physical at times when things weren't going the way he liked them."

"That happened rarely, Mr. Cobb," Larmer pointed out.

"Maybe," Cobb replied, "and maybe not. But we know it happened. What's your answer to my question?"

"Enemies?" Larmer smiled, but it was a smile without warmth. "I'm not sure I can help you there, Jasper, and all of us in this radio format, have people who don't like what we stand for and who we stand up against. Maybe sometimes they dislike the messenger, too. But I'm not sure I'd class those people as enemies."

"Somebody killed him. One assumes there was a reason. And at least one person in the world disliked him enough to want him dead. Often we refer to those people as enemies."

Larmer shrugged. "Point taken."

"Whether it happened rarely or not, you are aware of Hugg's propensity for violence?"

"I'm not sure what you're referring to." Larmer frowned.

"Hugg had been in trouble a few times for hitting people," Cobb said.

"Including his wife," I added. It was my first contribution to the discussion, and judging from the look on Larmer's face — it went from a frown to disgust — my effort wasn't particularly welcome.

"I suggest you talk with his alleged victims." Larmer sat back in his chair, directing his comment to Cobb and ignoring me. "I never saw Jasper display the behaviour you're describing and to my knowledge he was never convicted of anything approaching an assault charge. In fact, I doubt very much he was ever charged." He continued to look hard at Cobb as he said, "You might want to have your trusted assistant do some real research for you. Something more fact-based and less reliant on rumour and innuendo."

Shulsky cleared his throat. "If we can wrap this up, gentlemen, my client and I have a number of things to discuss."

If Cobb heard that, it didn't appear to register. His eyes rested on Larmer. "On your way to the station the morning Hugg was killed, you make any stops? Starbucks? Timmy's?"

"What is the purpose of that question, Mr. Cobb?" Shulsky said.

"Might be helpful in terms of establishing credibility for our client's story."

"That would be my job, Mr. Cobb. Now, as I said, Mr. Larmer and I have work to do and the time to do it is not limitless."

"You didn't answer my question," Cobb said to Larmer.

"The answer is no."

"Last question," Cobb said. "Did it cross your mind that Jasper Hugg might have been the person making the threats against you?"

The reply was quick and succinct. "Not for a second."

Cobb stood up and I followed suit.

"Thanks for your time," Cobb said. "We'll be chatting again." He turned to Shulsky. "I'll see you at the arraignment."

"Your presence won't be needed there."

"Mr. Shulsky. I remind you that we are both after the same result here — that is establishing the innocence of your client. In my book that doesn't make us adversaries. In fact, that puts us on the same team."

"You'll forgive me, Mr. Cobb. My experience with private detectives has been … unpleasant in the past." Shulsky shifted his gaze to me. "I would say the same thing applies to my previous dealing with journalists. So if we stay with your team analogy, let's think of it this way. You are the offence and I am the defence. And in football the two are not on the field at the same time. In other words, you do what you do and I'll do what I do. And occasionally and if absolutely necessary we can meet for a chat on the sidelines."

Several suitable responses formed in my mind, but I figured none of them, even with the expletives deleted, would advance the teamwork concept Cobb had alluded to, so I settled for what I thought was a stern look.

Cobb said, "I'm betting you never played football, Mr. Shulsky. "I'll see you at the arraignment."

No one answered, so we made our way to the door and knocked. We were let out by a uniformed guy the size of a motorhome. I was tempted to ask if he'd played offence or defence.

Cobb and I split up after the meeting with Larmer and Shulsky. He didn't tell me what he was going to be doing and I didn't ask.

I called Jill and was heartened by the life that seemed to have returned to her voice. "We're just leaving the hospital. Should be home in a half-hour or so. I might spring for a coffee if you stop by."

"Good news?"

"Not really," she said. "But not *bad* news. We meet with a specialist Monday and should know what's happening then. In the meantime, I have a daughter who is hungry for the first time in over a week and has requested that I provide barbecued ribs and baked potatoes as a special treat. We're both hoping you'll join us."

I said, "Are you kidding? Barbecued ribs, baked potatoes, and my two favourite babes on the planet? You'd have to lock me in the trunk of my car to keep me away."

"How are things going in the investigation?"

"Slow and so far not much to show for it. But we'll keep slugging. Which reminds me, I have a few calls to make, then I'm on my way. Anything you need me to bring?"

"Just you and maybe a few mega-hugs."

"I can do that," I said. "See you soon."

I wanted to go home and change — my time at the remand centre in the presence of Larmer, Shulsky, et al. had left me feeling the need for a vigorous shower. I rolled through Bridgeland, and as I always did when I crossed First Avenue heading east, I felt something good move through my body. It was as if my neighbourhood was a harbour from those parts of the city I knew were out there like rough waters, dark and silent and cold.

When I got home I opted instead for a bath and while the water was running made three of the four calls I needed to make — four being the number of people working at the radio station that Cobb wanted to me to interview.

The four I had drawn included a news/sportscaster named Lance Knight, ad copywriter Helen Burgquist, a show researcher named Bernie McCready, and the newest member of RIGHT TALK 700, Shawn Beamer, who was in promotions and handled their social media, as well. I had time to reach the first three and made appointments for the next morning. Helen Burgquist was the only one who'd needed persuading.

"I've already spoken to the police," she told me in a voice that I figured had a lot to do with why she wasn't on air. "Junior-high whiny" might best describe her tone. "I can't see any need to talk to anyone else. Especially someone unofficial."

I could've enunciated a fairly lengthy sentence in the time it took Ms. Burgquist to say the word "unofficial."

"Yes, ma'am, I understand that, but I'm working with a private detective who has been retained by Buckley-Rand Larmer, and I know you'd want to do anything you can to help clear Mr. Larmer's name."

"Only if he didn't kill Mr. Hugg."

That caught me by surprise and I was a few seconds coming up with a response. "Absolutely, I … uh … quite understand and would not want to try to influence you in any way. We'd just like to ask you a few routine questions that I'm sure you've already answered for the police. It would be very helpful if you could spare the time."

"As long as it's not too much time."

"I promise to keep it as brief as I can. Shall we say 10:15 a.m. tomorrow?"

"There's a Second Cup across the street. I don't want to do this in the station."

"That's just fine, Ms. Burgquist, I'll see you then. Uh … just one thing."

"Yes?"

"What you said earlier. Do you have some doubt as to Mr. Larmer's innocence?"

"I have no opinion one way or the other. I just want Mr. Hugg's killer to be arrested as soon as possible. No matter who that person is."

For that last statement she applied the same inflection as she had to the word "official." Helen Burgquist was not a woman without opinions and I expected at least one of my interviews the next day to be, at the very least, interesting.

A bath and a shave later, and after I was dressed and ready to head out the door, I called the last of my four subjects. Shawn Beamer agreed to meet me at 10:45 a.m., which meant my interviews were each roughly a half-hour, one after the other. I was hoping I'd given myself enough time with each, but truth was, I wasn't sure I had enough questions for more than five minutes apiece.

I raced out the door, had to come back twice, once for my wallet and once for my phone, but finally was on my way.

I'd taken to altering my route slightly on my way to Jill's house in order to drive down the street and by the house where Faith Unruh's body had been found. I'd even crawled slowly down the back alley a couple of times to get a look at the garage beside which her body had been found. I had no way of knowing, of course, if it was the same garage that had been there at the time of the girl's murder, although it didn't look new, so I guessed it was the same building.

I'm not sure what my reason for doing that was. It wasn't like driving by the house and garage was suddenly going to provide me with the answer to the long-unsolved crime. And I didn't think it was simple ghoulish curiosity.

A book or an article? I doubted that unless there was a chance it might trigger some memory, some long-forgotten something that had seemed like nothing at the time, but now, so many years later, seemed somehow wrong. Maybe then I'd write something. But even that wasn't why I went by there.

So what, then? Part of it, I suppose, was a desire to preserve Faith Unruh's memory, at least in my own consciousness. After all, what happened with cases like hers after the family and the investigators, even the killer, were all gone? Would anyone remember?

It was possible, in the same way I remembered little Donnie Goss, that there might be the odd person who would recall, however hazily, the murder of the eleven-year-old girl who was on her way home from school.

That night as I drove down the street Faith had lived and died on, I tried to picture in my mind that day. What had the weather been like? I wasn't even sure of the exact date. What were the girls thinking about on that walk home from school? What had they talked about? School? Their plans for the summer? Boys? Faith's birthday?

I knew so little. But I decided that I wanted to know more. I wasn't sure how I'd make that happen, but maybe for whatever I might one day write, I was determined to learn all I could about that long-ago horror.

But now was not the time for that process to begin. I turned my car and my attention in the direction of the woman I was surer than ever I was in love with and her daughter, who I hoped was on the way to recovering from her illness.

They met me at the door before I could ring the bell and I hugged them both. And instantly received a rebuke.

"I won't break if you give me a real hug, you know," Kyla told me, stepping back and regarding me with a critical eye.

I moved forward and gave her what I hoped qualified as a real hug and we both laughed. I was happy to be laughing and, most of all, I was happy *she* was laughing.

The evening was given over to barbecued ribs and a hard-fought game of Scrabble. I was reminded yet again that a wordsmith should have been a lot better at Scrabble than I was — and for the first time in days, things felt close to normal.

Kyla headed off to bed with a book in tow, and Jill and I sat over a couple of glasses of wine. Neither of us felt like talking, but there was a lot of looking at each other and soft smiles back and forth.

"I was just thinking ..." Jill said at last.

"Thinking," I said.

"About how it would be nice if you didn't have to make that long, arduous drive home tonight."

"Long *and* arduous," I agreed, the smile on my face and in my voice.

"Yes," she said.

I nodded. "I think maybe you're right."

TWELVE

My first interview was with Lance Knight, surely one of the stupidest on-air names ever — knight ... lance, yeah, I get it. He had been the station's news director since September 2007, and because sports were given minimal attention and importance at RIGHT TALK 700, the job of sports director was lumped in with that of news director. That meant Knight or one of the two other news voices reeled off a few of the previous day's scores at the tail end of a few of the day's newscasts.

Knight was short, maybe five-six, but must have weighed well over two hundred pounds, making him the approximate shape of a round bale. He was wearing a tan blazer over what looked like a T-shirt and jeans, a decent ensemble that would have been almost stylish on a less rotund frame.

But the man had a radio voice, deep and resonant, and he used it well. We'd agreed to meet in the station's coffee area, which was actually a room that would have made a terrific broom closet. A card table, with three wooden chairs, provided the only flat surface for cups and plates. I remembered Helen Burgquist's suggestion that we meet at the coffee place across the street. Wise woman.

I'd gotten there first and had taken the liberty of making myself a cup of Keurig coffee. I'd found a small container of one percent milk in a fridge the size of a microwave that sat next to a microwave the size of a toaster. I was sitting at the table, my notebook and four-colour pen — the only kind I ever used — resting next to my coffee cup.

"Mr. Cullen, I'm guessing," Knight said with a glance in my direction as he took the two strides required to get from the doorway to the coffee machine. Two more strides would have taken him through the wall.

I would soon learn that Knight did not merely *say* things, he boomed them. "I see you found the coffee," he boomed over his shoulder. As it was obvious he'd seen my cup already, I didn't think the comment required a reply. He didn't use milk but added two cubes of sugar from a glass container perched precariously on the postage stamp–size counter.

When he sat, he took a swallow of coffee from the ceramic cup he'd brought with him, then gave a satisfied "ahh" and nodded at me. I took that to mean he was ready for questions.

"Thanks for taking the time to meet with me," I began.

He nodded again. He was cradling the cup in both of his beefy hands. The cup had a picture of Niagara Falls on it.

"How well did you know Buckley-Rand Larmer?" I asked him.

"Well, let's see … I was already here, been here maybe a year or so before he came to the station. Hell of a coup, getting that guy,"

"Oh? How so?"

"Have you heard the guy?"

"I have, yes."

"Then you'll have to agree that there aren't many — not even the big gunslingers down in the States — who are better than him. Dynamic on-air presence, charismatic, articulates conservative positions as well as anyone. That's what I'm talkin' about."

"I see."

"Gives us something else, too. A lot of conservative format stations don't do well with female listeners. We do just fine in that department, and the reason is Buckley-Rand Larmer. That voice, that presence, that intelligence, and he's easy on the female eye, if you know what I mean. Our demographic includes more female listeners than virtually any news-talk station in the country."

He put his hand to his mouth and lowered his voice. "Of course, he needs to remember to keep it in his pants ... if you know what I mean."

"As in he likes the ladies as much as they like him," I said.

Knight winked. "You could say that."

"Has that ever presented problems that you're aware of?"

"Nothing that couldn't be looked after." His volume returned.

"Payoffs?"

Knight shrugged and looked concerned, like he was afraid he'd said too much.

"Anyway, to answer your question, I started here in oh-six and, like I said, Buckley-Rand came on board about a year after that. I've known him a long time and I would say pretty well, too — maybe as well as anybody here. Except for Hugg, of course."

"Would you say Mr. Larmer was well-liked around the station?"

"Hell, yes. Not liked as in huggy-kissy, and he doesn't

go to the bar with the gang for TGIF drinks, stuff like that, but sure he was liked. And more than that, he was respected. That's the word I would use. Buckley-Rand Larmer was respected."

"Anybody *not* like him?"

"Here at the station? No, I don't think so. Nobody I'm aware of, at least."

"Any of his … extracurricular activity involve people who work here?"

Knight shook his head vigorously. "Listen, I don't want you to take what I said earlier too seriously. Boys will be boys, right? It's no big deal and I don't want you to think …"

Backpedalling big time.

"And what about Jasper Hugg? People like him as well as they like Mr. Larmer?"

Knight paused and pursed his lips before answering. "'Like' might not be the best choice of words to describe how people felt about Jasper. I would say people coexisted with him. I wouldn't say they *dis*liked him. But Jasper Hugg wasn't a man who instilled that … friendly feeling in people, you know?"

"Not a warm, fuzzy guy."

"Neither warm nor fuzzy."

I nodded, made a note in my notebook, mostly so it would look like what he was telling me was important enough to warrant my writing it down. It was a technique I'd often used in the interviews I conducted, the idea being to give people the feeling that they mattered. That sometimes led to them being a little more willing to part with information they might not otherwise have shared.

"Knowing the two men as well as you did, what do you think of the murder charge laid against Buckley-Rand Larmer?"

Knight considered his answer for several seconds, then shook his head. "I think it's nuts. There needs to be a reason for someone to kill someone else. A motive. These two men had worked together and worked hard to make Buckley-Rand's show and all the programming on the station appeal to a large audience. And they accomplished that. The show's numbers have been growing almost every month and it's because of the work of those two men. No, I can't see Buckley-Rand as the killer here. Makes no sense."

I was beginning to think I'd misread Lance Knight. My first impression of him had been that he was just an obese version of the buffoonish Ted Baxter character in the old *Mary Tyler Moore* TV show. (Baxter was played by an actor named Knight — interesting coincidence.) But I was wrong. This man was articulate and far from stupid. I was surprised to find myself almost liking the guy.

"Anyone else at the station who might have had issues with either man?"

Again he paused. "I really don't think so. I mean, nothing that was, you know, a blow-up or anything. People disagreed, sometimes voices were raised, but really, there was nothing that would precipitate fisticuffs, let alone a murder."

"Anything unusual happen in recent weeks around the station?"

"What do you mean by 'unusual'?"

"I'm not sure I know myself what I mean. Someone behaving differently, something that wasn't quite the same as it had been in the past. You know, those little things that just don't feel right — arguments, bad blood, somebody threatening someone else ... anything along any of those lines?"

This time no pause. Instant answer accompanied by vigorous head shake. "No, I can't say I saw or heard anything like that. Nothing at all."

"Do you have any idea who might have had a reason to want Jasper Hugg dead?"

"I'm sorry, I can't honestly say I do. *Groups* of people maybe, such as the libs that don't like us for our politics. Lots of them. But as to one individual who could've done this, no. I can't point to anyone and say, maybe that's the one right over there. Sorry, I wish I could."

"One last question, and I know you've already answered this for the police, but where were you the morning Jasper Hugg was killed?"

A small smile formed on Knight's puffy features. "You're right, I was asked that and the answer is 'At home.' My first broadcast that day wasn't until noon so I was planning to have a fairly late breakfast with my wife and cut the grass before I headed into work. We had breakfast, Bea and I, but before I could get to the lawn I got the call from the office that, uh, Jasper was ... deceased."

"Who called you?"

"Al. Alonzo Diaz. He's one of our news guys — mostly a reader as opposed to on-the-street reporting. He was pretty shook up when he called. So was I ... I mean, after he told me what had happened."

I swallowed the last of my coffee, pulled out a business card I'd had made up a couple of days before, and handed it to him. He took it, then read it aloud. "Adam Cullen, Freelance Investigations." He looked at me. "Your name's familiar.... Hey, wait a minute. Aren't you the guy ... yeah,

I talked about you in a couple of newscasts. Your wife was killed in a fire set by that crazy —"

"Yeah, that was me." I stood up. "I appreciate your taking the time to do this, Mr. Knight. And if you think of something else, anything at all that you think might be helpful, just call me or shoot me an email."

"Listen, I was just thinking, I mean, this just came into my head … how would you feel about coming on air and talking about what happened with your wife? I mean it would be a moving story and we could take the opportunity to reinforce the importance of effective law-enforcement legislation, you know?"

I'd stopped liking Knight now and wanted to end the conversation quickly. "Yeah, I won't be doing that. Thanks for your time."

He shoved the card in his pocket, stood up, and held out his hand. "Sure, sure, I understand. Listen, good luck, you know … with everything, I mean it. I hope you guys and the cops find whoever did this and get Buckley-Rand back here ay-sap, you know?"

"We'll do our best."

The questions and the answers with Helen Burgquist were almost a copy-paste of my conversation with Lance Knight. Right up until I asked her if she could think of anyone who might want Jasper Hugg dead.

A small woman, she straightened in her chair and stared at me for several seconds before she answered. Like she was deciding if I was worthy of hearing her response.

Decided I was. "Well, you could start with me. I'd have cheerfully choked the man."

I drank coffee while I tried to come up with a suitable response.

"I see," I said. "Is there a particular reason for your feeling that way or is that more of a general feeling about Mr. Hugg?"

She smiled. "Actually that was probably said more for effect. I've had challenging bosses before, but there were times when Jasper Hugg was more than challenging — more like exasperating. But no, I'm not capable of killing someone — not even Jasper Hugg."

"Exasperating how?"

"He was the second-most arrogant man I've ever known, right behind Buckley-Rand Larmer." The smile was gone. "And a meaner pair never walked the earth."

So much for the accuracy of Lance Knight's assessment of intra-station relationships.

I thought back to my phone conversation with Helen Burgquist. "You told me that you hoped the killer would be found as soon as possible — I think that's the phrase you used."

"Mr. Cullen, I just told you that there's not much about Jasper Hugg that I liked, other than that he was very good at his job, and maybe even less that I like about Buckley-Rand Larmer." Her eyes narrowed. "But I can guarantee you as sure as I'm sitting here that the man you are representing did not kill Mr. Hugg."

"What makes you so sure?"

"Yin and yang," she said. "One force passive and negative — that's Hugg. The other active and positive — that's Buckley-Rand. They were inseparable, and more than that, I think both men were fully aware that they needed each other to be successful. One was the behind-the-scenes string-puller, putting it all together, and the other was the public face of what they both believed — out there, forceful, persuasive. They were the perfect match."

I sat back to think about what she'd said, but she wasn't finished. "Which doesn't mean they got along all the time. My God, the two of them were often at each other's throats. Figuratively," she added quickly. "But then they'd get it sorted out and turn their attention to whatever the next threat to what they believed in was, and they'd put together a plan of attack. And 'attack' is the operative word, Mr. Cullen."

"Were there others who felt about them the way you do, Ms. Burgquist?"

"Helen, please."

"Sorry … Helen."

"Have you ever heard the show? The callers? The hate? We have to run a seven-second delay so a technician can cut out the foul language, the nastiest of the threats, and so on."

"Would you say there was anything to those threats?"

She shrugged. "Who can say? You naturally want to think it's all just idle talk, but there have been other incidents, haven't there."

"You mean the Monday shooting in Hamilton — although the killer apparently had to take two cracks at it."

She shook her head. "Yes, but there were others. That explosion in Fresno, California — station with a similar format to ours. Of course, they said it was a gas leak or something, but Buckley-Rand claimed it was deliberate, even said so on the air, which I thought was a bit brazen, but of course he was a man who could …" She paused.

"Make things sound true because he said them," I finished for her.

"Something like that, yes." She nodded. "But I don't think he was doing that with the explosion thing. He really believed there was something fishy about that. And then there was the woman in Dallas … or Houston … anyway, somewhere in Texas — I think she was a columnist for a paper down there, but she did some guest things on a couple of conservative television talk shows. She was gorgeous and the story was she was about to get a regular spot on Fox News, but then she had a heart attack or something in the middle of her morning workout at a gym. Buckley-Rand was sure it was foul play. Though he didn't go on the air with that one as far as I know."

In thirty seconds Helen Burgquist had given me a whole lot to think about. I remembered hearing of the Fresno explosion but hadn't really followed the story — certainly didn't make a connection with either this case or what had happened in Ontario.

Until now. As I worked at remembering, I recalled that there had been one fatality and a couple of people injured, maybe three.

But the woman in Texas was brand-new information to me — another suspicious death and again the victim was a right-wing media personality.

I wondered if Larmer had ever mentioned either of the two incidents to Cobb. You'd think he would have if, as Helen Burgquist contended, he thought there was something suspicious about both the woman's death and the Fresno explosion, that they were both part of a great conspiracy to silence the most vocal of the right-wingers. I'd ask Cobb later.

"Do you recall when those two incidents took place?"

"Not exactly. Two or three years ago maybe. I think the explosion in California was sometime around Christmas, but I'm not sure which Christmas."

"Was there anyone at the station who had a more volatile relationship with either Hugg or Larmer? I know you've indicated there may have been people who didn't like one or both, but …"

"Are you asking me if I think someone at the station might have murdered Jasper Hugg?"

"Yes, I guess that's what I'm asking you."

She sipped coffee, her eyes never leaving my face. ""I suppose I'd have to say it's possible. But I know what your next question is going to be, and no, I can't point to anyone as a likely suspect. I'm sorry."

I ended the interview by asking her where she'd been at the time of the murder, then spent ten minutes on my phone after she'd gone back to the station. Helen Burgquist's alibi was easily verifiable and, once verified, airtight; she'd had an early medical appointment and had stayed at her daughter's home that night as it was closer to her doctor's office. I spoke with the daughter — Helen had been okay with my doing that and had provided the daughter's phone number. And while it could be argued that people were asleep and might be unaware that someone slipped out of the house, stabbed Jasper Hugg, cleaned herself up afterward, and snuck back into the house undetected, it seemed at the very least far-fetched. Surely if you planned to murder someone you wouldn't choose to do so while a guest in someone else's home. That, and the fact that Helen Burgquist was too small to have inflicted the kind of damage I'd seen on the body of Jasper Hugg, had me eliminating her from the list of people we should be looking at.

That done, I had time to think about what she'd told me about the other incidents. I wished I had time to hit my computer for even a few minutes, but that would have to wait. I dialed Cobb, got his machine, decided not to leave a message.

Next up was Bernie McCready, a man who could have been part of a beer commercial featuring the most *un*interesting man in the world. He and Shawn Beamer, my final interview, had both agreed to meet me at the Second Cup, sparing all of us the agony of the station's pathetic coffee room.

Medium height, medium weight. From his clothes, which I suspected came from a closet known lovingly as Fifty Shades of Grey, to a facial expression that defined bland, to a voice that was Midwestern nasal, the man was an all-natural cure for insomnia.

And, in fact, I found myself desperately wanting to yawn five minutes into our time together. He was short on facts and long on pontification.

"One of the finest men I've ever known," McCready told me when I asked him about Larmer. "People love that man — they're willing to follow that man. He's a leader of men, plain and simple."

"A leader of men," I repeated, finding my voice drifting toward the same monotone McCready had perfected. "What about women?" I said it mostly to point out that there were two sexes, something I often wondered if right-wing radio was aware of.

"Ah, the ladies." McCready got a weird look on his face. I think he was trying for suggestive; mostly he looked, well … silly. "He could lead them, too."

That got my attention, particularly after what Lance

Knight had said about the trouble Larmer apparently had "keeping it in his pants."

"What are you saying, Mr. McCready?"

"No surprise, I suppose," he said. "Good-looking man, great voice, intelligent — has everything women want. And he knows it. Uses it well."

"So you're telling me that Mr. Larmer was a ladies' man?"

"Ladies' man, philanderer, seducer, pick your descriptor."

I was a little surprised — there was something akin to emotion in McCready's voice. And a look on his face that wasn't as admiring as it had been a moment before. In fact, I wasn't sure what it was — disapproving, disappointed, like a parent whose kid has been caught shoplifting a CD from the record store.

But it didn't last long. Once we moved off the topic of Larmer's facility with the opposite sex, a talent I suspected McCready did not share and may have been envious of, his voice returned to the dull drone of earlier.

Thankfully, McCready had nothing more to contribute and I was happy to excuse him, but not before he launched into a lengthy oration on the long-term benefits of having church-based charities, rather than government, doing most of the heavy lifting when it came to welfare distribution.

His alibi — I dove in while he was taking a breath during his dissertation — was that it had been his turn to drive his kids to school after spending the early morning getting them ready. He was between school and the station when he heard the first report of an "incident involving an individual with potentially life-threatening injuries."

I prayed the alibi was solid because I'd sooner have garroted myself than have had to do a follow-up interview with Bernie McCready.

But before I bid him a fond farewell, I asked him if he'd ever been to Texas or California — a question I'd decided to add since my chat with Helen Burguist. McCready had been to both, although his California trip had been to Disneyland with his parents when he was nine years old and his Texas excursion was a college thing that had happened years before the death of the reporter.

That left only Shawn Beamer, handler of social media. For a long time I had tended to think of social-media types as techno-geeks — soft, awkward, very *Big Bang Theory*. Happily, I had discarded that unfortunate characterization some years before.

Shawn Beamer would have dispelled all remaining vestiges of that flawed judgment had there been any. He was neither soft nor wimp-like. Tall and lean, he had a firm handshake, a ready smile, and a steady gaze that regarded me with something between curiosity and anticipation. I guessed he was mid- to late-twenties.

We both got coffee, my third since the interviews had started, and sat in a couple of comfortable easy chairs I'd been eyeing since I'd first arrived at the Second Cup. They'd finally become available just before Beamer's arrival.

He stretched out, crossed one long leg over the other, and tested the coffee temperature as he waited for me to start.

"How long have you been at RIGHT TALK 700?" I began.

"Right to it, huh? No small talk."

"Sorry," I said. "This is my fourth interview in a couple of hours and I'm probably getting a little punchy. I apologize if that came across as rude. How 'bout them Stampeders?" Trying for humour.

He smiled, shook his head. "No need to apologize,

and I understand that you'd want to move things along. Besides, I saw McCready on his way back to the office. If you just interviewed him, you might want to pop a couple of energy drinks to keep from lapsing into a coma."

I laughed. "Glad I'm not the only one he has that effect on."

"I think it's pretty well universal. Anyway, I came here in September of last year. Moved here from Oshawa, Ontario. Had a somewhat unexpected breakup with my girlfriend — that's code for 'She dumped me.'" He smiled ruefully. "Figured it was time to check out new challenges in new places. And here I am." He spread his hands, palms up.

"Like it?"

"Calgary? I love Calgary. The job? It's okay. I can take it or leave it, I guess."

"Why's that? Not a believer?"

He shrugged. "Not a believer, not a disbeliever. Guess I'm sort of apolitical. I mean, I care what's going on in the world around me, but I don't exactly share the passion of the people at the station."

I wondered how that attitude would sit with the Larmers and Huggs of the world. "You get much pressure to fall in line? Become more passionate?"

Another shrug. "Actually, less than you'd think. Of course I'm careful not to wear my 'I Don't Give a Shit' T-shirt, but as long as I do my job, they pretty much leave me alone."

"How does someone become the go-to person on social media, anyway? Are there courses? Or are you self-taught?"

"A little of each. I've been into computers since junior high. Social media is just the latest leg of the journey, I suppose. I had a blog in high school, but once I was out of high school I got too busy to keep it up so I started tweeting. That whole 140-characters thing has its appeal, especially when you've got deadlines and stuff coming up but you think you should be out there talking about something."

He paused, drank some coffee before continuing. "Then I figured I better get some formal training, especially if I wanted to make a career out of communications. So I got a diploma in Applied Arts from Humber College in Toronto and four months later I'm wearing a cowboy hat and living ninety minutes from great skiing."

"Do you actually write the posts that go out on the station's social media, or are you only responsible for getting them up and out there?"

"The latter. I get the messages from management or the on-air people, then I post them and monitor the responses."

"Who writes the majority of what you post?"

"A lot of it comes from Buckley-Rand. A couple of the other on-air types send me stuff fairly regularly, as well."

"How about Hugg? You get much from him?"

Beamer shook his head. "Almost nothing. Once in a while in a meeting he'd say we should get this or that up on Facebook or Twitter or on one of the blogs, but then somebody else would write it."

"How did you get along with Hugg?"

"Same as everybody else. Carefully."

"Hard guy to work with?"

Beamer considered this. "Not if you did your job and met his expectations. Oh, and didn't disagree with him — that was never a good idea. I didn't really have any reason to disagree with him so I'd say we were okay, at least I thought so."

"Anybody at the station who wasn't okay with him?"

He paused, took a sip of the coffee. "There were lots of disagreements around the place and occasionally there were lost tempers, but I'm guessing what you want to know is if I thought the disagreements were the kind that could end up with somebody killing somebody. I'd say a definite no to that."

"Does that include Larmer?"

He took longer this time before answering. His words were accompanied by a slight nod. "I think so, yes. Buckley-Rand is a different kind of guy — volatile, mean, maybe even ruthless when it comes to advancing the conservative agenda. And he and Hugg were two of the loudest voices sometimes. But no matter how big or loud their disagreements, I never once thought, *Shit, one of those guys is going to smoke the other one.* It just wasn't like that, you know?"

"So in your mind, it's unlikely that Larmer murdered Jasper Hugg."

"I guess anything's possible. But probably not that."

"And there's no one else at the station you think the police ought to be looking at?"

"As a suspect? I really don't think so."

"How about outside the station? You hear anything about somebody — a sponsor, a listener, somebody Larmer or the other on-air people eviscerated? Anybody maybe pissed off enough to do something like this?"

He paused again. "Sorry, I wish I could point you at somebody … I mean, only if there was something to it, you know, but the truth is, this is a puzzler. It's damn sad and it's a total puzzler."

"The responses you monitored online, especially the ones where people disagreed, did you get many where you kind of thought, *Whoa, there's some serious hate going on here?*"

He nodded, smiling. "Hell, yeah, lots. But to be honest, the real scary randos were the ones who agreed with the stuff the station put out there."

"Randos?"

"Sorry. Web-speak. Randos are the odd, the socially inappropriate, basically the losers."

"Got it."

"Anyway, some of those posts made Buckley-Rand and the rest of them look like Joe Clark."

Joe Clark. Interesting choice for his comment, especially from a guy who was likely still in day care when Joe Clark was a prominent political figure. I got the impression that Shawn Beamer had done some reading and some thinking.

"And the morning of the murder, you were …?"

"Oh, my alibi. That's a bit problematic. I went to the gym early, got there right around six, but for the first while I was by myself. Nobody in the place except Champ Carroll, the guy who runs the place, and he went out for a while, told me to keep an eye on the place."

"He do that very often?"

Beamer shook his head. "Never before that morning. Said he had a meeting with his investment person."

"So how long were you by yourself?"

He shrugged. "I don't know. Forty-five minutes, maybe an hour. I finished my workout and had my shower and when I came out, Champ was back."

"Where's the gym?"

"Downtown. On Fourth. Right next to the Westin."

Which meant that Beamer could have had time to leave the gym, get to the station, kill Hugg, and be back in the time the manager of the place was out. So he had the opportunity. Of course, I had no idea about motive or any of the other factors that figured in a murder case. Still, I thought Cobb might want to do a follow-up with the young man. Thing is, I kind of liked the guy, but I'd already learned in my brief acquaintance with crime investigation that liking or not liking a potential suspect had zero bearing on anything.

"What's the gym called?"

"Champ's. Not very original, but a good facility. And the guy knows his stuff."

"Got a number for the place?"

"I don't think so, but it should be in the book."

"Book? As in phone book. Does anybody use those anymore?"

Beamer grinned and shrugged.

"And how old are you?"

"Twenty-nine. I hit the big three-O in a couple of weeks."

I shook my head. "I hate to have to tell you — it's all downhill from there."

He laughed. "So I've heard."

"Well, thanks, Shawn, this is really appreciated. Oh, one last thing. You do much travelling?"

He looked surprised by the question, but after a second shook his head. "I want to, for sure. Already got a pretty big bucket list. But with school and everything, not much so far — unless you call a couple of spring-break-ski-and-drink-till-you-puke trips travelling."

"So no trips to Texas or California in recent years."

He shook his head. "Can't say either of those is on the bucket list. Only American stop for me was in Wyoming. Laramie. I did a summer course in screen-writing, if you can believe it. Thought I might want to write for television or the movies." He grinned and held up both hands. "So far I haven't created anything screen-worthy."

"Laramie," I repeated. "University of Wyoming. Played them in baseball. I went to Oklahoma State. Both teams were called the Cowboys. Played hell with the fans and cheerleaders."

Beamer laughed. "You played baseball?"

"A little. When were you there?"

"Summer of 2011."

"Yeah, my college career was over a long time before that." I stood up, drained the last of my coffee, and extended a hand. "Thanks for your time."

"No problem." He got to his feet, too. "If there's anything else you need from me — I don't know that I'll be any more help than I was today, but I'd be happy to try. And good luck, I hope you or the cops — somebody — gets the bastard who did this, you know?"

"Yeah, I know."

He left first and I got the number for Champ's and called. Champ himself answered the phone. Maybe a one-person operation. I told him who I was.

"I was just talking with one of your clients," I said, "in connection with an incident you may have heard about — the murder of Jasper Hugg in the parking lot of RIGHT TALK 700."

"Yeah, I heard about that."

"The client is Shawn Beamer. He's indicated he was working out at your gym that morning and that you were gone for a while."

"Yeah, I opened up, but then I had a meeting. I'm the only guy here, so if I have to step out I sometimes ask somebody to keep an eye on things, answer the phone. I usually like for it to be a woman — they're more, ah, responsible, but that morning Shawn was the only one here. It's like that during Stampede, so I got him to do it. He's a good kid."

"Do you recall how long you were out?"

"I'd say an hour maybe. Give or take."

"And Shawn was there when you left and when you got back?"

"Yes and yes. The kid a suspect?"

"Everybody's a suspect, Mr. Carroll."

"Even me? Shit, I was the one who was out of the gym that morning. Maybe you better be checking me out. I wouldn't mind being a murder suspect. Be good publicity for the gym." I heard a chuckle.

"Did you know Jasper Hugg, Mr. Carroll?"

"No, but I've listened a few times to that other asshole — Buckingham whatever. Besides, I thought the police charged him with the murder."

"They did."

"So I guess that means I'm not a suspect."

"Sorry to disappoint you, Mr. Carroll."

He chuckled again. "It's okay. Could've used the publicity though. I mostly rely on word of mouth, you know? Speaking of which, you wanna drop in some time — the first workout's on me."

"Thanks, I'll keep that in mind. One last thing. Did you happen to mention to Shawn beforehand, the day before or something, that you'd need him to watch the place that morning?"

There was a pause at the other end of the line, then a phlegmy cough before Champ answered. "Can't recall for sure. I probably mentioned it to somebody, kind of hoping they might be available to watch the place. But did I mention it to Shawn? I might've … or I might not've. My guess is I didn't. Sorry, I just don't remember."

"Thanks again, Champ."

"Sure. And don't forget — first workout's on me."

"Got it."

I rang off and made a quick stop at the washroom before heading out into the sunshine. I stopped at the curb while my eyes adjusted to the July sun and was about to cross the street to the Accord when I caught sight of a small, dark-blue car — maybe a Jetta, but too far away to say for certain — pulling away from the curb a few cars ahead of where I'd parked the Honda. It sped away and quickly merged into traffic, although I was able to pull out my phone and take a desperation shot as it moved off. I looked at the photo but it told me nothing conclusive. Blue car, roughly the size and shape of the Jetta; that was it. But it gave me an idea.

I changed directions slightly and stepped into the front reception area of RIGHT TALK 700. I smiled at the receptionist I'd met earlier that morning when I'd arrived to interview Lance Knight. A nameplate I hadn't seen the first time I'd met her indicated she was Jocelyn Ohlhauser. She was pretty in a down-to-business way and she returned the smile

"Where would I find Shawn Beamer?" I asked her.

"His office is upstairs — down the hallway to the right." She pointed.

I thanked her and climbed the stairs two at a time, then turned right as directed. I popped my head into the first office I came to. The door was open but no one was there. I surveyed the top of the desk hoping to see a nameplate identifying the occupant. But first my attention was caught by a photo of a striking woman. I'd have put her at fortyish, but she could have starred in one of those mother-daughter commercials where you can't tell which one's which. Next to the photo was the name of the office's resident — Bernie McCready. And the beautiful woman in the picture? Wife? Sister? Girlfriend?

I looked around and leaned in far enough to get a look at what had been written across the bottom of the photo: *To my Bernie. Love you, Sugar. Tammy.*

There was a heart next to Tammy's name. The photo and inscription surprised me. No, I'll be truthful, they *shocked* me.

McCready may have been duller than a three-day rain, but he clearly had something, God knows what, going for him that was below the surface. *Way* below the surface. And clearly I had once again misjudged someone.

I was still dealing with the incongruity of the Mr. and Mrs. McCready situation as I moved down the hall to the next office. A woman I didn't know but who I guessed was one of Cobb's interviewees was at a computer typing faster than I can talk. She saw me and looked up, showing some irritation at the interruption but doing a decent job of disguising it.

"Sorry to bother you," I said. "I wonder if you could tell me where I'd find Shawn Beamer."

"Right behind you." She gestured and was back at her typing before I got turned around.

And right behind me is exactly where Shawn Beamer was. I supposed he'd had to make his own washroom stop.

"I do have one more question," I told him. "You have an office or a workspace somewhere where we could talk for a second?"

"Sure," he said. "You're almost there." He led the way past one more office to the last one down that hall, and as it turned out, the smallest one — barely bigger than the main-floor coffee room. He pointed to a chair, squeezed past me, and sat behind the desk.

"Something else you wanted to ask me?" He looked a little embarrassed that I'd seen his office and I decided to be quick.

"Are you into cars at all, Shawn?"

He shook his head. "Not really … I never was. I mean I've always had a car since I was legal, but I guess computers are more my thing."

"Right. Listen, I need a favour."

"Sure, like I said, anything I can do …"

"There might be," I told him. "Is there some way you could find out what the people who work here drive? And maybe let me know as soon as you can?"

He thought for a few seconds, then nodded. "Sure, I guess so. Is it okay if I just ask people or do you want me … undercover?" He hunkered down, looked around, and laughed.

I laughed with him. "If that's your best spy impression, I think we better keep it out in the open. But I wouldn't mind knowing sooner than later."

"Okay, leave it with me."

I wasn't sure if Cobb would approve of my asking someone with a less-than-airtight alibi to help me gather information, but I didn't have a lot of other ideas. Besides, I figured if Beamer *was* someone to keep an eye on, this would give me the opportunity. I gave him my email address and we parted company for the second time in minutes.

After one more look around for a small, dark-blue foreign car and drawing a blank, I climbed into the Accord, rolled down 17th Avenue to 4th Street West, and turned south. I parked directly opposite the Purple Perk, crossed the street, and got the last empty table in the place. I couldn't have swallowed any more coffee to save my life, but the place had a meat loaf sandwich that I would've walked barefoot on broken glass to get to.

I ordered the sandwich and a hot chocolate, then, as I sat at a back corner table, I pulled out my phone and called Cobb again.

"Nice timing," I heard him say. "You caught me between interviews."

"I didn't know you were interviewing, as well. I just wrapped up. I hope you're not stuck in that miniscule coffee room."

"Hell, no. I set up shop at a tavern just down the street."

"Why didn't I think of that? I settled for a coffee place."

"And that, my friend, is why I'm the detective and you are just the lowly assistant."

I laughed, took delivery of my sandwich and hot chocolate, and licked some whipped cream off the top of the mug.

"How'd the arraignment go?" I asked him.

"Short but not so sweet. No bail, at least not for the moment, though the judge did tell Shulsky he could file a follow-up request and he'd consider it. Shulsky huffed and puffed and I could see Larmer was having a hell of a time not blowing up completely, but he kept it together."

"Humbling experience, jail," I said.

"I don't know, lots of superstars have done a little time here and there and seemed to get through it, ego still intact. Can you say Conrad Black?"

"True enough."

"What've you got?"

"Well, one item that may be interesting. Monday getting shot in Hamilton and now Hugg might not have been the only attacks on right-wing media personalities." I told him what Helen Burgquist had said about the explosion in California and the death of the woman journalist in Texas." Waited ten or fifteen seconds for a response.

"You still there?"

"Stupid, stupid, stupid," he hissed into the phone.

"Sorry," I said, a little angry, "I thought it was something —"

"No, no, not you," Cobb cut me off. "Me. I remember the California thing — it was a big deal at the time, but as far as I know there was never any evidence of criminal intent proven. Guess I just put it out of my mind. Shouldn't have. I didn't know about the Texas death. Where in Texas?"

"Don't know. I'll look into that. Should be easy."

"That and when."

"Right. Helen said the two incidents were fairly close together, but I'll check that out."

"Good. They may or may not be related, but they're definitely worth a look."

"Sure, I'll get on both right away," I said.

"How about your interviews? Anybody jump out at you as capable of being the killer?"

"Not right off," I told him. "But I've got a couple of things to check out. There's one guy, a fairly young guy, you might want to follow up with. But let me put something together on that for you, too."

"Good, thanks. A couple of things for you to be aware of. I talked to Detective Landry and she was fairly forthcoming. The attack on Hugg was frontal, meaning head-on — I'd already figured that, but now we've got it officially, and since we're not going to be privy to the results of the autopsy, this is helpful. She also told me that given the kind of wounds that were inflicted, it's almost certain that the killer was splattered with blood, probably a fair amount of it. And again, based on the entry pattern of the wounds, the killer was very likely right-handed."

"With all that blood on him, it would certainly have drawn attention if anybody'd seen him."

"Yeah, I've thought about that. The police did a pretty thorough canvass, no witnesses so far. Or at least no one who's come forward. Sometimes someone sees something strange and it doesn't register until they hear that there was an incident that might have been related to what they saw. I'm betting the police will have a news conference and ask for the public's help. The other possibility is that the killer had a car and got into it quickly and left the scene. Somehow got washed up and changed without anybody seeing him covered in blood."

"The car in question being a Lincoln Navigator?"

"That seems a possibility."

"Meaning that either Larmer murdered Hugg or someone took the car that morning and returned it to the garage after committing the murder."

"I think it's fair to say that the police are leaning toward the former."

"If there is a media briefing, you want me to attend?"

I could hear Cobb breathing as he thought about it. "Might be a good idea. Could be a waste of your time, but you never know. There might be something useful that we don't already know. I'll see if I can find out if there is one and if so, when and where."

"Right, oh and by the way, the word is that Larmer was something of a ladies' man. I got that from a couple of my interviewees. Might have caused a few problems for the station."

"No real surprise but interesting nevertheless. Could have something to do with threats but doesn't explain Hugg getting wasted."

"Pissed-off husband setting him up?"

"Wow, that's some kind of pissed off. Wouldn't it be easier to just push the guy who's screwing your wife into traffic? Still let's keep that thought in the background. I don't like to rule out anything until we're sure."

"Got it."

"As for my interviews," Cobb continued, "I'd say I'm drawing blanks here. About fifty-fifty between those who thought Hugg was the second coming and those who thought he was the devil incarnate. About the same breakdown on Larmer. Anyway, I've got another one coming up — probably the second-biggest star in the station's on-air stable. Better go."

He rang off and I started in on my sandwich, glancing out the window that looked out on 4th Street from time to time, checking for the blue Jetta. I didn't see anything.

THIRTEEN

Tom Cochrane and the rest of Red Rider were just finishing up "Lunatic Fringe," with Elliott Brood on deck on my embarrassingly inadequate stereo. Great music collection. Below-average technology for conveying that music to the listener. I promised myself for the fortieth time I would do something about that. Soon. Really.

I was rewriting my notes from the interviews. They were brief. I summarized the conversations with the four RIGHT TALK 700 employees and refrained from adding comments. I knew I was biased and the best way for me not to taint what I passed on to Cobb was to keep my opinions to myself. I knew he'd ask me again if I thought any of the four people I'd interviewed was capable of killing Jasper Hugg. When he did, I'd tell him that I thought three of the four were *capable* (I'd leave researcher Bernie McCready out of that conversation, unless boring people to death could be considered a capital offence), but I would likely add that despite Shawn Beamer's flimsy alibi, I didn't really like any of them for the attacker and it didn't appear that any of them had been in a position to be implicated in the Hamilton, California, or Texas incidents — though I knew I'd have to check further into that before confirming my non-suspicions.

I finished the notes as Elliot Brood was wrapping up the *Days into Years* DVD. As I looked them over, I realized they were far from my best work — sketchy, not comprehensive, and not particularly illuminating ... and I knew why. I was distracted — at least some of my focus was on the blue Jetta. In our previous collaboration, Cobb and I had been followed on at least a couple of occasions and one came close to a disastrous conclusion for us. Maybe that explained my being somewhat hung up on the possibility that once again I was being tailed.

Pushing those thoughts aside and wanting to keep moving forward with the case, I went to my laptop and searched "explosion radio station Fresno." Wikipedia gave me this:

> On November 3, 2011, at 2:48 p.m., an explosion shook the Malahattan Building in downtown Fresno, just blocks from Cal State University, Fresno. The building, which housed radio station KKMR at the time, was severely damaged and one station employee lost his life while four others sustained injuries ranging from minor to severe, and in one case life-threatening, although the injured party survived. The deceased was Michael Morrissey, station manager, a veteran of the radio business who had been with KKMR for eleven years; the most seriously injured was Kirby Heibert, who was a student at the nearby university on a basketball scholarship

and was working part-time carrying out miscellaneous tasks at the station. He wasn't normally at the station at that time of the day but had a class cancelled that afternoon and had gone into work to catch up on some office cleanup. Sixty-four-year-old Ned Waterhouse, a writer in the promotion department, was just months from retirement. Waterhouse's injuries from the blast were minimal, but he suffered a massive heart attack thought to be brought on by the shock and stress of the explosion and was hospitalized for seven weeks while recovering from the incident.

Two station employees suffered less serious injuries. Assistant Program Director Dewey Hutsell, who had been with the station for just under four years, returned to work two months after the explosion on a part-time basis. Radio-show host Jackson T. was on the air at the time of the explosion and was in his sixth year with the station; he sustained non-life-threatening injuries. He never returned to radio and is now a counsellor at Mississippi Valley State University. All of the remaining staff returned to work at the station as their health allowed.

The explosion took place one day after a Just Energy Natural Gas crew had completed work on a line test and change of the meter at the Malahattan Building. Investigators into the cause of the explosion stated that the cause was a gas leak due to improper installation of the meter, but months later there were those who felt that the explosion was deliberate — triggered by a device set at or near the newly installed meter.

While a number of station and gas-company employees were questioned at length by FPD fire investigators and homicide detectives, no arrests were ever made and no charges were laid. The station reopened six weeks to the day after the explosion and the first day of broadcasting was dedicated to the employees who were casualties of the explosion.

I summarized that report and a few others, all of which gave similar accounts of what happened that November day in 2011.

Next I searched "Texas female journalist heart attack gym." Up came a December 19, 2011, story about the sudden and unexpected death of Jasmine Swales, a forty-two-year-old journalist who had been working out at a gym in downtown San Antonio, Texas. I noted that her death took place forty-six days after the Fresno explosion:

Ms. Swales was nearing the end of her workout when suddenly she clutched at her throat and fell to the floor. Her trainer, Rudy Lopez, a skilled paramedic who had worked for two years as an Assistant Trainer with the San Antonio Spurs of the NBA, immediately called 9-1-1, then worked over the fallen woman until an ambulance arrived. Ms. Swales was pronounced dead on arrival at the nearby Christus Santa Rosa Hospital.

While the cause of death was at first thought to be either a heart attack or an aneurysm, an autopsy was inconclusive and referred to the presence in the victim's bloodstream of a potentially fatal dosage of aconite, an alkaloid toxin that comes from the deadly root of the aconite plant. Traces of tincture of aconite were found in the victim's bloodstream, as well as in a bottle from which Ms. Swales had been drinking a commercial sports drink. A criminal investigation followed and concluded that Ms. Swales's death was homicide, but no charges were ever laid in connection with the incident.

Jasmine Swales was, in the words of the reporter, "flamboyant and provocative, a gifted writer and orator who was kept busy travelling from one end of the United States to the other, speaking here, fundraising there — she was the darling of the Republican Party and conservative talk-show hosts, and reviled by Democrats and the left."

I made more notes. And while there was nothing in the accounts I read to connect either incident to the murders of Jasper Hugg or Dennis Monday, it was clear that recent years had taken a heavy toll on right-wing media personalities.

It occurred to me that my time could be best spent by a) looking into where people on our suspect list had been during the San Antonio, Fresno, and Hamilton killings and b) trying to learn if there was any connection between the victims in the four violent episodes we were now aware of.

I checked my email and was surprised to see a message from Shawn Beamer and even more surprised that there was an attachment listing the staff at RIGHT TALK 700 and the cars they drove. It appeared Beamer had been both fast and thorough. In the cases of those who owned two cars, he had listed both. And he'd provided years, makes, colours, and licence-plate numbers, as well. He'd also included a note to me.

"I figured it would be faster if I just asked everybody. Hope that's okay. There were a few who told me to bugger off — I got their stuff by spending a little time in the parking lot. Cloak and dagger after all, ha ha."

I took a second to note that Beamer himself drove a black 1997 Chevy Blazer. Larmer, I already knew, made do with a gold 2012 Lincoln Navigator. I glanced down the rest of the page — Helen Burgquist drove a 2013 Toyota Corolla, Lance Knight owned a Silverado pickup, and Bernie McCready's ride was a 2006 Ford Focus station wagon. No surprise there.

No Jettas on the list, dark blue or otherwise.

I wasn't surprised by Beamer's news. I'd been 90 percent certain that the Jetta threat was in my mind only, a remnant of the shock of the events of a few months previous. And if someone was following me, the chance that it was someone from the station seemed remote at best.

My notes completed, I spent the next hour doing what I had been doing more and more in recent days — searching for information pertaining to the death of Faith Unruh. As was the case all the other times, I found nothing new or interesting. More news reports almost word for word with those I'd already read. I checked sites listing unsolved mysteries in Calgary, then Alberta, and finally Canada. Nothing.

I googled the names of her parents, again learned nothing I didn't already know. I finally shut down, saddened and a little angered that there was so little record of a child's life that had ended so early and so horribly.

I poured myself a rye and diet and took up the spot on my couch that afforded me the best view of the city skyline. I thought again about Buckley-Rand Larmer and was surprised to realize that I was actually beginning to want him to be innocent of the Hugg murder and all the other killings that may or may not have been related.

I thought about why that was. I knew at least part of my changing feelings had to do with Cobb and his belief in Larmer. If Cobb felt Larmer was innocent, I was willing, or at least I was *becoming* willing, to set aside my personal loathing for Larmer in favour of not seeing a man convicted of something he hadn't done.

I thought again about the four attacks on right-wing media and, as I had before, looked for connections. Four violent incidents — I was, for the moment, and for the sake of argument categorizing the death of Jasmine Swales as a violent act. Was there some connection between the victims or were the attacks random? And why multiple victims in Fresno, not just a single victim? Why were four very different methods of killing used — a shooting, a stabbing, an explosion, and a lethal dose of a poisonous substance?

And then there was the fifth case — Larmer himself — first threatened, then set up. A different kind of death? Maybe, but why? If he was connected to the others by something more than just being on the right side of the political spectrum, then why hadn't he been killed?

And if there *was* a connection, what could it be? These were very different people in many respects, from different parts of two countries, from superstars — Swales and Larmer — to apparatchiks — Hugg and Monday. As I thought about it until my head began to throb, I kept coming back to their political stance: not merely right wing, but insofar as I could gather, the *extreme* right. Did that make them more susceptible to fatal attacks?

If so, had some nut from the "socialist left," a favourite Larmer phrase, finally snapped and decided to exact revenge on the hated opposite side by killing its team favourites? Except that this wasn't someone losing it and going on a rampage. This was a carefully crafted and, at least so far, well-executed plan.

And as Cobb had told me a few times, the question in criminal investigations involving violence was why. Figure out the *why* and the *who* will often follow.

I decided I'd done enough navel gazing and wanted to swing into action, thinking I'd tackle first some unfinished business — the names of the four former Hope Christian Academy students I'd been able to track numbers for. One of them was Ariel Mancuso.

I'd start with her only because it was a name I'd actually heard before — in connection with the Jaden Reese bullying incident.

She'd told Patsy Bannister she didn't know the details of the fight other than that there were either three or four boys and one girl picking on Jaden Reese, who was gay. Larmer had stepped in to rescue the kid and somebody may have suffered a broken nose. Ariel hadn't been one hundred percent sure on that point.

Before I could punch numbers, "American Woman," courtesy of Burton Cummings and the rest of the Guess Who, indicated I had a call. It was Jill.

"Any news?" I barked at the phone.

"Here in the civilized world it's customary to begin phone calls with 'Hello.'"

"I'm sorry," I mumbled. "I guess I just wanted —"

"I know." She laughed. "News, you wanted news, and I have some. There's a new cupcake place on Richmond Road — why don't you stop by there and pick some up and we can talk over dinner."

"Sure … that's … but can you tell me anything? Good news, bad news?"

"Neither, really — just news. And as with any news, it depends on how positive or negative people are in receiving that news. Kyla and I have decided we're going to be very positive."

Hearing her voice and what she had to say calmed me down some. "Sounds like a damn good plan," I said. "Any preferences as to cupcake flavours?"

"We're pretty easy on that, although chocolate is never a bad bet. And after the orange popsicle debacle, I might avoid anything involving orange."

"I'll be there — with a positive outlook and positively nothing orange."

She laughed and I could hear Kyla in the background laughing, too. Good sign.

I had a couple of hours and decided to spend at least some of that time tracking former Hope Christian Academy students. Back to Ariel Mancuso. I knew two things. She'd taken her original name after a failed marriage and she was living in Fredericton. I dialed information, explained that I had nothing more than the name.

"No one by that name," the voice on the other end of the line said.

"How are you spelling the name?" I asked. "I'm thinking it's m-a-n-c-u-s-o." That was met with several seconds of silence, then a cheery "Hold for the number."

I wrote it down, then pressed 1 to be connected. Five rings later I figured I was about to be connected to her voice mail when a female voice came on the line.

"Hello. I'd like to speak to Ariel Mancuso," I said.

"This is Ariel."

I decided I had nothing to gain by easing into the thing. "Ariel, my name is Adam Cullen. I'm a journalist in Calgary and I'm currently working on a murder case involving someone I believe you knew when you were attending Hope Christian Academy. His name is Buckley-Rand Larmer. Am I right in saying you knew him?"

There was a lengthy silence on the line before her voice, quieter now, said, "Randy Larmer? Is that who you're talking about?"

"I only know him as Buckley-Rand Larmer. The kids at school called him Randy?"

"Yeah. He didn't like it, which is maybe why they called him that."

"Not well-liked, then?"

She paused again before answering. "You could say that. Boy, this is weird. You're the second person who's called me about him in the last few weeks."

"I know. Actually I got your name from Patsy Bannister, the reporter who talked to you before."

"But she didn't say anything about a murder case."

"That's happened since she talked to you. She probably told you Larmer's a radio talk-show host out here in Calgary," I said. "Maybe you saw something about the case in the newspaper or on the television news."

"I don't follow the news very much. Which I guess sounds dumb especially since I was the photographer for the Hope school newspaper. But it wasn't much of a paper, really. Just school gossip mostly, and we covered the sports teams, threw in a few jokes and a schedule of what was coming up at the school. We put the thing together in an afternoon once every two weeks. I always had a photo or two in there. Like I said, it wasn't much."

Her voice had been tentative and soft at first. Like she was shy or not trusting of me. One of the reasons I hated cold calls. But it was getting a little stronger now.

"Ariel, Mr. Larmer is accused of murdering a colleague at the radio station. I'm working with a private detective to try to prove his innocence and we want to learn as much as we can about him, including his life as a young person."

Yet another pause. "I didn't know him very well at all. To tell the truth I didn't like him enough to want to hang out with him or anything."

"Were you in the same grade?"

"No. He was a year older than me. I was only at Hope for one year. Then we moved out here. My dad got transferred. I guess I haven't thought much about the school or the kids that went to Hope since we moved away from Calgary."

"There was one incident in particular I wanted to chat with you about. Involving another student — Jaden Reese."

This time I got the feeling Ariel was choosing her words carefully. "That other reporter who called — Patsy something — she asked me about that, too."

"Yeah, the story is Larmer jumped in when some other kids were bullying Jaden, and I guess he more or less got it stopped. Rescued the kid who was being bullied, I guess you could say."

"Yeah."

"Is that about the way you heard it happened?"

"I wasn't there."

"No, I wasn't suggesting you were. But you mentioned your paper printed school gossip. I thought you might have heard something."

"We didn't print anything in the paper about it."

"I understand." I was getting frustrated with her evasiveness and wished I could be face to face with her. See the body language, the facial expressions. "But Patsy indicated you knew at least a little about what happened that day."

"All I know is what I told her. There were some kids picking on Jaden Reese and Randy came along and made them stop. Not much more to it than that."

"Except that Jaden was gay. Is that why the kids were bullying him?"

"Um … I don't really know."

"You told Patsy there were three or four boys involved and there was a girl there, too. Do you know any of the names of those kids?"

"No, I really never heard the names. Or if I did I don't remember them. It was a long time ago." No pause this time.

"Was there much talk about the incident around the school? You know, kids just talking about stuff?"

"I don't think so, no."

I figured I'd gotten about as much from the conversation as I was going to. Or at least as much as she was going to give me. Which I was having trouble figuring out. Over the years I'd talked to lots of people about their former days as students and most had loved talking about anything even slightly juicy. Unless …

"Ariel, just one last question. Is there any chance you were the girl who was there the day Jaden Reese was bullied?"

"No, I told you — I just heard about it. Look, I have to go. Please don't call me again."

"Sure, and I'm sorry if this is unpleasant. If you think of anything that might be —"

The buzz on the line told me she'd ended the call.

I stared at the phone for a while before clicking off, wondering if she had just got tired of talking to me or if I had actually struck a nerve. I decided to try the other three names on my list of former students of Hope Christian Academy. All three were boys, all living in Alberta, two of them in Calgary. The good news is I reached all three first time. The bad news is they had less than nothing to give me. One kid had never heard of Larmer (apparently he, like Ariel Mancuso, did not watch, read, or listen to the news). The other two knew of Larmer from school, though not well, and were surprised that he was now charged with murder. Neither offered any insights into the student version of Buckley-Rand Larmer. One knew the name Jaden Reese but hadn't heard about a bullying incident involving Larmer or Reese. Like I said, less than nothing.

I had a couple of hours before I'd be making my cupcake run on the way to Jill's house. I sent a series of emails to the four RIGHT TALK 700 staff members I'd interviewed, asking them for names of people with whom I could verify their alibis for the dates of the attacks in Hamilton, San Antonio, and Fresno. I figured that should get the steadfast Helen Burgquist on the warpath for sure.

Spinning my wheels. It felt like I'd been doing a lot of that. I wanted to be busy — for two reasons. First, I wanted to contribute something to Cobb's investigation, and so far I didn't feel I'd done much of that. And second, I needed to keep my mind off whatever was wrong with Kyla, at least until I heard it first-hand in a few hours.

Kyla and I have decided we're going to be very positive about the news.

What did that mean? Did that make it automatically bad or at least unpleasant news? Otherwise, why would you have to make an effort to adopt a positive attitude toward it?

I forced my mind back to Cobb's case. Funny that I still thought of it as Cobb's case and not *our* case. Was that because of my continuing dislike of Larmer or because I just hadn't been able to really take hold, grab something meaningful, and run with it?

I put Glass Tiger in the CD player and reread all my notes, adding to them a summary of my brief conversation with Ariel Mancuso. Again I wondered as I did so if I'd struck a nerve when I asked her if she'd actually been there when the bullying of Jaden Reese was happening. I wasn't sure it mattered — other than to cut off one more possible source of information about Larmer's back story.

I reviewed my lists of names — the students from Hope Christian Academy, the staff at RIGHT TALK 700, the victims of the four incidents involving right-wing luminaries. And after an hour, I knew no more than I had an hour before.

I was spared further self-pity by my phone. It was Cobb.

"You got beer?'

"Of course. Where are you?"

"On the sidewalk in front of your building."

"Come on in."

I buzzed the downstairs door open and had two Rolling Rocks open and sitting on the table by the time he got to my apartment door.

We exchanged greetings that weren't much more than grunts and took up seats, Cobb on the couch, me on my recliner.

"I hope this visit means you've solved the case," I said, "because I got nothin'."

He laughed and shook his head. "The case isn't solved," he said. "There's a lot of slow-dancing associated with detective work," he said. "Or pouring molasses, if you like that analogy better. Have patience — there will be better, more productive days."

"Good to know," I said. "You want a sandwich or anything?"

He shook his head. "Had one, thanks. I just came by to give you an update. Got the autopsy results, or at least a summary of the autopsy results." He pulled out his notebook. "Seven stab wounds in all — one to the head, one to the face, two to the neck, and three to shoulder and arm. Neck wounds, arm and shoulder wounds all to the victim's left side, again indicating his assailant was right-handed."

Cobb paused and I thought about what he'd said.

"Seven stab wounds," I repeated slowly. "What does that say about the killer? I wonder if there isn't some kind of hate motivating the killer here. Didn't you say that one of the wounds to the head or the neck would have been sufficient to kill him?"

"That was the Medical Examiner's initial opinion at the scene, yes."

"Is there any way of knowing if any of the wounds were inflicted after Hugg was dead? Or at least helpless?"

"Your thinking being?"

"Well, again I'm just wondering if the killer was acting out of rage, at least in part, inflicting maximum damage even after the death of the victim wasn't in doubt."

"Interesting thought. Might speak to motive to some extent, as well. Rage … revenge. I want to think about that some more, but for now it's going in my notebook." He flipped a page and made the note.

I drank some beer. "Are we assuming that the killer drove to and from the murder scene in the gold Lincoln Navigator? Because if we are, that narrows the possibilities: one, that someone took the vehicle from Larmer's garage, returning it afterward; or two, that Larmer is the killer and it was him in the Navigator."

"Yeah, that's about how I see it. I guess the third possibility is that there are two gold Navigators — the killer just happened to have the exact same vehicle as Larmer."

"Yeah, good luck selling that one."

Cobb nodded. "Yeah. We'll know the results of the forensics on Larmer's vehicle in the next day or two at the latest."

"What's your best guess?"

"On the Navigator? I'm betting the police will find traces of Hugg's blood in the car. Which will prove that the killer drove that vehicle at least away from the crime scene. What it doesn't prove is that Larmer was the driver ... or the killer. But their case is stronger with that evidence than without it. Which means we have work to do, my friend."

"If the killer was able to get into the garage and remove the Navigator and get it back into the garage with traces of Hugg's blood conveniently in place, I wonder if this guy might have planted other physical evidence."

"The murder weapon?"

"Maybe."

"Or maybe he realizes that doing that might be a little over the top, a little too convenient. The cops aren't stupid — they'd twig to something too obvious. Besides, I'm sure they've gone over Larmer's house thoroughly, and if there was a knife, Shulsky would know about it."

I nodded. "But how about more blood? On a piece of clothing or even a strategically placed drip here and there? We know that someone was in Larmer's apartment previously. Maybe the killer got in there again."

Cobb's eyes narrowed. "I've thought about that. And you're right, it's possible."

Neither of us spoke for a couple of minutes, the sound of Broken Social Scene's *Forgiveness Rock Record* low in the background.

I held up my beer and looked at Cobb. "Another one?"

Cobb shook his near-empty can, then shook his head.

I said, "Doesn't it seem a little convenient that Larmer says he walked to work that day? Which is why he didn't notice his car was gone?"

"Unrelated," Cobb said. "The killer will have known Larmer's normal departure time for work. I'm guessing the Navigator was already back in the garage right where he'd left it."

"Smart killer."

"Lots of them are. And if this one had already killed three people prior to Hugg, that speaks to his or her intelligence."

"Her?"

"You never know."

"This has 'male' written all over it."

"I think so, too, but I'm not going to rule anything out."

"How much of Larmer's story do you believe?"

"I'm not sure. I know he's capable of lying. But saying that he walked to work later than usual isn't a very helpful lie. So I'm guessing it's true. I'm sure the prosecution will point out that Hugg was killed between five and six and that it would have been possible for Larmer to be the killer. He could've driven to the scene, killed Hugg, returned home, cleaned up, as you say, and then walked back to work."

I drank the last of my beer. "Okay, but let's look at it another way. If I'm Larmer and I just killed somebody and that person's blood was all over me, I'm not likely jumping into my car. The man would absolutely know that he'd put the victim's blood in his car and unless he's stupid, which he's not, he'd know that one of the first places the cops would look is the car — right after they searched his home. Doesn't that speak to your earlier point — that the physical evidence is too obvious to be credible?"

"I'm hoping the investigators will see it that way." Cobb didn't look overly optimistic.

"And to be honest," I added, "the more I think about it the less I see Larmer as a stabber. If he was to off someone — and I'm not saying he did — I could see him poisoning the woman in Texas and I could see him blowing somebody up like the California thing. In both those you're not face to face with the victim when he or she is dying. And I could even see him shooting someone à la Dennis Monday. But this kind of viciousness seems way too out of control for Larmer."

"Right. Do me a favour and don't repeat that particular analysis to anyone else, okay? All we need is some Facebook post saying that one of the people representing Buckley-Rand Larmer says the man is capable of murder using methods other than stabbing."

"I wasn't planning to use it in my next media interview."

Cobb laughed. "Good. Just making sure. How's Kyla?"

"I don't know. We're having a dinner meeting tonight to talk it over. I was just on my way to get the cupcakes."

"Cupcakes."

"Can't let just anybody pick cupcakes."

Cobb grinned. "Right, I won't keep you. Just wanted to give you the lowdown on the autopsy."

"Thanks, I appreciate that."

He set his empty beer can on the table as I gathered keys, wallet, glasses, and cellphone. We left together. I locked my apartment door and we trotted down the stairs and out into the late-day sunshine. Cobb waved, climbed into his Jeep Cherokee, and was gone. Out of a newly developed habit I glanced up and down the road before heading for the Accord. No Jetta or suspicious cars of any make or model.

The dinner (including the brilliant selection of cupcakes), the conversation, and the laughter were all good. But they were just a precursor to our sitting down to talk about what was up with Kyla, and what came next.

When the time came for the serious part of the evening, Jill and I were on the couch with coffees. Kyla was sitting on the floor facing us, taking a very long time to down a third chocolate cupcake.

Jill got right to it. "Kyla has Crohn's disease." She said it matter-of-factly, no emotion in her voice or in her eyes. I looked at Kyla, who had never, it seemed to me, been more like her mom than she was at that moment. Resolute. Serious but not scared. Which meant that the only one who was a psychological mess was me.

"What does that mean, exactly? I looked it up when you first mentioned it was a possibility, and I know it's an inflammation of the inner walls of the gastrointestinal tract and there's no known cause. And that's about the extent of my knowledge."

Jill nodded and Kyla set her plate down, and hugged her knees as she listened.

"That's right," Jill said. "And there's no cure, either, although there's been a lot of progress in controlling the symptoms. There can be a fair amount of pain, diarrhea, sometimes vomiting, and often weight loss."

I fought the urge to glance at Kyla to see how much the latter symptom had affected her. I knew she'd lost weight; it seemed to me quite a lot of weight, and I wondered if she'd gain some of it back, lose more, or what. I waited for the answer and it came quickly.

"That's kind of the bad news," Jill went on. "The good news is that we can do a lot ourselves — plenty of exercise, proper diet, hydration, sleep — just a healthy lifestyle generally. Plus there are medications that can help keep things under control."

I looked at Kyla. "Exercise. So baseball is still okay?"

She grinned at me. "Uh-huh. But I might have to quit smoking."

She had me for a second and the look on my face must have given me away because both she and her mother burst out laughing.

"Okay, you two, ha-ha. But what I want to know is what I can do. Besides not buying cigarettes."

"Can I answer that, Mom?"

Jill looked at her daughter and nodded. Kyla turned serious. "Mom and I already talked about this. There are going to be times when I feel kind of crappy like I did last week. When that happens I know it's not going to be fun, but there are going to be lots of times when I feel good, too."

"I read about that," I told her. "That it's kind of up and down with periods of flare-ups and then remission. The idea is to keep the flare-up times short and the remission times long."

"Right, but the one thing I don't want is to be treated like a sick person. I want to be as normal as I can and for everybody to treat me that way."

She fixed me with a look.

227

I nodded. "Fair enough." I knew that acting as if everything was fine would be the hard part for me, but I would do my damnedest to comply with her wishes.

"So that means when we go to Chuck E. Cheese's I can still whip you at every game in the place."

"You wish." She laughed.

No one spoke again for a few moments and finally Kyla stood up. "Think I'll go to bed and read for a while, okay?"

"Of course it's okay," Jill said. "I'll come in a few minutes to give you a hug."

"I'd like mine now," I said, and she gave me a strong squeeze before heading off down the hall.

Jill and I drank our coffee without saying anything. At last I looked at her. "How are you doing?" I said.

And for the first time that I'd seen, tears formed and slipped slowly down the face I loved. I put my coffee down, moved closer, and held her.

"Adam, I was so scared."

"Yeah," I said. "I know. But really, this isn't so bad, is it?"

I was saying it to her but I was also saying it, at least partly, *for* me.

"The worst part was not knowing," she said. "Now that we do know and there are things we can do, we'll be okay. It might take a little while, but we'll be okay. She's amazing. All I have to do is be half as strong as she is."

"Me too," I said. "And I will be. *We* will be."

FOURTEEN

The drive home was slow and circuitous. It felt good just to drive, watch night fall over the city, and listen to Joni Mitchell. Finally I swung into Bridgeland and rolled around behind my building to the house a couple of doors down where I a rented parking space. I didn't always use it, but there wasn't room on the street, so this time I did.

Maybe it was the pleasant evening air or maybe it was that my mind was still focused on Kyla and how the months ahead would unfold, but whatever it was, I never saw or heard the guy. The first I knew he was there was the cold metal pressed hard against the back of my neck. And though I'd never had a gun barrel jammed against me before, there was no doubt in my mind that's what it was.

"You make one goddamn sound, you son of a bitch, and it's the last one you'll ever make," a voice I didn't know growled into my ear.

I could feel his breath as he spoke.

I tried for calm, with limited success. "Wallet, back left pants pocket," I said. "Take it and I don't turn around until you're gone."

The words were greeted with a derisive laugh. "I don't want your fuckin' money, you piece of shit. On your stomach."

I was aware how quiet everything was. Even his voice, vicious in its rage, was hushed.

"What do you —"

"On your stomach," the voice hissed.

I dropped to my knees, leaned forward, my arms in pushup position, hands pressed into the gravel surface of the lane. I felt his knee press the middle of my back, hurting like hell, squeezing the air out of me.

"It's been a long time," the voice said, "a long, long time. But your time's up, asshole."

I was trying to think, to force my mind off the pain in my back and make sense of what he was saying. I told myself if this was the person who killed Hugg, I'd probably already be dead. Who, then?

"Look, whatever it is you want, why don't you just tell me and —"

"The first thing I want is for you to shut up! You got nothin' to say that I wanna hear. But I got a few things to say to you."

I didn't answer, thought it best to listen.

"You thought you had it made after all this time." The knee pressed still harder and I groaned. He paid no attention. "That nobody was even looking for you. Wrong again, low-life fuck, wrong again. Just like you were wrong checking back in at the old haunt, stopping by to reminisce about what you did, thinking who the hell would be around to see or care after all this time. Well, that's where you fucked up. There's one guy still watching, waiting for you to come back. And here you are. And here I am."

My mind was racing, trying to think of something I'd written that could have brought on this level of anger.

Some story that involved my damaging someone's reputation. Doing enough harm to bring about *this*? I tried to make sense of his words, which was made all the more difficult by the fact that I was having trouble breathing, and the pain of his knee pressing down on my back was beyond excruciating. *That nobody was even looking for you.*

"What are you … talking about?"

The blow was fast and hard, his fist striking just above my ear. "I told you I didn't want to hear you talk," the voice snarled. "Do it again and this gun butt will leave a dent in the side of your skull."

The only good thing was that his shift in weight, made in order to be able to hit me, eased for the moment the pressure on my back. I gulped air and tried not to think about the pain in my back and now my head. I had to concentrate, had to get some kind of read on why this was happening.

"How old are you, asshole?"

"What … I'm thirty-eight."

He didn't say anything for a minute, then, "Makes you fifteen then."

Fifteen. What, fifteen years old? Fifteen when I did what? I tried to think. *Okay fifteen, I was fifteen in 1991.*

If I could get him to tell me his name, maybe I could make some sense of what was happening, And why. But I knew asking would likely get me another blow to the head, this time with the pistol. I had a crazy thought — or maybe not so crazy. What he'd said … well, there was one thing, one case he could be talking about. If I was wrong … I tried to push that thought out of my head.

I tried to turn my face toward him. He grabbed my hair and pulled back hard. This was only going to get worse. I had to do something.

"Kendall Mark." My words weren't much more than a whisper as I fought the pain of my head being pulled back.

There was a pause; maybe he even let up just a little.

"What? What did you say?"

"Kendall Mark. Are you Kendall?"

He let go of my hair and kneeled harder on me again, his face close to my ear.

"Where'd you get that name, asshole?"

"If this is about the Faith Unruh case, I know you worked on it, maybe you still are. I am too. Mike Cobb and me. You know Mike Cobb."

If I was wrong and this wasn't Mark, or even if it was and he was too far gone to remember Cobb or to get past his wanting to get revenge on the killer, even if he had the wrong guy, then …

"Cobb."

"Yeah, Mike Cobb."

"What were you doing there?"

"At the house she was found?"

"Yeah, the house she was found. I've seen you drive by there a few times. In the alley, too."

"I told you. Cobb and I work together on a few things. I'd heard about the murder of Faith Unruh and Cobb and I talked about it — that's where I heard your name. Look, if you ease off on my back a little I can tell you exactly what I was doing there."

"That's not how it works, prick. You tell me first. If I believe you, then I ease off. And if I don't …"

He didn't finish, but I felt the pressure lessen again, just a little, but it helped. At least I could breathe and talk a little easier.

"You're right," I said. "I have driven by her house and the house where her body was found. My girlfriend and her daughter live not far from there, and when I'm heading over there for a visit, I'll sometimes go by the places where Faith ..." As I was saying it I realized that what I was telling him might not make sense to him. I wasn't even sure it made sense to me.

"I ... I just wanted to get the feel of the place, where she lived ... where she died. I'm not sure why. I guess I thought maybe doing that would help me to understand what happened, maybe get some kind of idea about the kind of person who murdered her. I don't know if that sounds weird, but —"

"Sit up." I felt him move off me.

"What?"

"Sit up. Slow, then turn around and face me. Stay sitting."

I moved slowly, partly because I didn't want to do anything to set him off again. And partly because I was hurting in several places. I pulled myself up, turned, and stayed sitting on the gravel, looking at the man I thought was Kendall Mark.

He was standing, but when I turned to face him, he sat down opposite me. If I hadn't been so damn sore and still more than a little scared, I might have laughed at the bizarre scene — two men sitting in the dirt and gravel of a back alley in the semi-dark of a moonlit night.

What wasn't funny is that the man opposite me was holding a gun, and that gun, while it was no longer pressed against my neck, was aimed at my chest.

Kendall Mark, if that's who he was, was black. Cobb hadn't mentioned that, but there would have no particular reason that he would. This man was big, even sitting cross-legged on the ground. I guessed over six feet tall and well over two hundred pounds. Not much of it looked like fat and his face lacked the fullness of guys who were just beefy.

"Start talking again," he said. "Tell me more about you and Cobb and we'll see if I believe you. You better hope I do."

I took a breath and nodded that I understood the meaning of what he'd just said. "I got to know Mike Cobb a few years ago when I hired him to try to find the person who killed my wife; it was arson. Then we worked together again last winter on a different case, but along with it we found the arsonist. There was a car wreck and she was killed."

"The arsonist was a 'she?'"

"Yeah."

He nodded and I took another breath, still struggling to breathe normally after having a very large guy kneeling on my back for what seemed like forever.

"Then a couple of weeks ago, Mike recruited me to help with another case. A media guy was stabbed and we're working to clear the guy who was charged with it."

"That just happened a few days ago. You said a couple of weeks. I told you not to lie to me." He raised the gun and pointed it at me. "Big mistake."

I put my hands up. "Hold on a second. "It *was* a couple of weeks ago. We were already working with the accused. Mike had been hired as a bodyguard for a radio talk-show host named Buckley-Rand Larmer and asked me to check out some stuff on Larmer. While that was going on, the other guy was murdered and the cops arrested and charged Larmer."

He lowered the gun, but not much.

"And what does that have to do with Faith Unruh? And this part better be damn believable."

"I heard about Faith's murder not that long ago. I talked to Cobb about it, figuring he might know something. I guess the thing just bothered me a lot, maybe because the woman I'm seeing has a daughter just about Faith's age. Or maybe it was just the horror of what happened. And like I said, I don't know why I've been going by there. I know it's next to impossible that I'll figure anything out, but I can't get it out of my mind. I'm drawn to it, I guess, maybe in the same way you are."

"Drawn to it," he repeated.

"I don't know if that's the best choice of words, but —"

He cut me off. "You don't look like a cop, private or otherwise. Rent-a-cop maybe. Give you a uniform and you could guard warehouses and shit. That's the job you look like you could do."

I shook my head. "I'm not a cop at all. My name's Adam Cullen. I'm a journalist. It just turns out that Cobb has needed some of the things I'm able to do to help him with a couple of cases."

"Journalist. You think there's a story in the Faith Unruh murder?"

I wasn't sure what the right answer to that question was. I decided to go for candor … and hope I was right.

"I don't know. Maybe, if I thought it might help after all this time to get people thinking about it again. But I don't really know."

He looked hard at me. I figured he was making up his mind about me. And I thought again about what Cobb had said about Kendall Mark's pretty much losing it after trying unsuccessfully to find Faith Unruh's killer. This man didn't look out of control. He looked determined and he looked angry, maybe even troubled. But he didn't look like he was about to freak out and shoot me just because I was there. At least, that's what I wanted to believe.

"You didn't answer my question," I said, rubbing my left hand over the fully formed lump where he'd hit me.

"What question?"

"Your name. I asked you if you were Kendall Mark."

A scowl that looked pretty much permanent creased his features, but his head moved up and down a degree or two. "I don't use it anymore."

"The name?"

Another small nod. "Yeah. Changed it to Marlon Kennedy a few years ago. Not legally — just changed enough things to make me Marlon Kennedy and for Kendall Mark to go away."

"You must be watching Faith's house and the other house almost all the time to know I've been there."

He lowered the gun a little. "I can give you exact times you arrived and when you left, whether you drove or were on foot, what you were wearing. I've got it all."

"How can you be watching all the time?"

"Surveillance. I've been watching those two places for almost twenty years. Got cameras on both places, and I'm watching a lot of the time. Figured the killer would come back there someday … to look around or gloat or just see what it looked like after all this time. And when he did, I'd be ready. I wanted you to be that bastard. I wanted that bad."

I nodded. "I understand." What I didn't understand was what could bring someone to watch a place all that time.

"How are you able to do that? I mean how do you live?"

"You mean a job? Part-time. I mow the grass and tend the flowers at a couple of parks not far from there. Nobody pays attention to a guy looking after a park. I've seen a couple of people over the years who might have known me if they'd actually looked at me. I work mornings seven to noon. Gives me the rest of the day and night … to check my tapes. And watch."

"When do you sleep?"

"When I can. Bought a house across the street from the Unruh house. Got a good view of the backyard where they found her from my back bedroom window. And I can see the Unruh house from my living-room window. I drink a lot of coffee and I watch."

"Jesus."

"Yeah."

We sat in silence for a couple of minutes.

"Let me see your wallet," he said.

"What?"

"Your wallet. Let me see it."

I pulled it out and tossed it to him. He looked at my driver's licence, leafed through it for a minute or so, I figured to verify I was who I said I was. Then he tossed it back to me.

"So what now?" I said.

"I keep watching."

"Listen, Marlon … Is that what I call you? Marlon?"

He shrugged. "Don't matter."

"I was thinking that if we could talk sometime, maybe share information, not that I have a lot, but maybe in talking we might think of something that's been missed or overlooked."

"That isn't very likely."

"No," I agreed, deciding not to push it.

"But maybe we'll talk sometime. Give me your phone number. "

I found a receipt in my wallet and a pen in my pants pocket, then wrote out my cellphone number and passed it to him."

"If I want to talk, I'll call you."

"Sure. Can I ask you one question?"

He looked at me.

"What do you drive?"

"Why you asking?"

"Someone's been following me. I wondered if it was you."

"You see what this individual who's been following you was driving?"

"A dark-blue Jetta," I said.

The smallest hint of a smile formed around Kendall Mark's mouth. "Well, ain't that the goddamnedest coincidence," he said.

FIFTEEN

I don't have a particular routine I like to follow after a confrontation with an armed guy in a back alley. When I finally got into my apartment, I didn't turn on lights or music and I didn't phone Cobb or Jill. I did nothing. Not at first. I sat on the couch looking out the window and thought about what had happened to me on this night.

And I thought about how little I knew about what went on in the city I had grown up in and loved. Like every city this one had a dark side. Killers and victims. Violence and terror. Hard streets that most of us never travelled and often didn't know about. And on those streets were unknown people — some like Kendall Mark, others like the man who killed Faith Unruh. They were out there. Unseen and anonymous.

But not Faith herself. She was not anonymous. Not as long as Kendall Mark lived and waited and watched.

Mark was not crazy. There was no trace of slathering, wild-eyed, out-of-control madman in the person who'd held me at gunpoint, at least not that I saw. A crazy person would likely have killed me before I could have offered an explanation. No, what I had seen was an obsessed former cop whose desire to avenge a horrible crime had taken over his life. Some might argue that maybe that *was* a form of insanity or at least a manifestation of it. Perhaps.

I meant what I'd said to him. If Cobb and I ever found anything that might be useful I'd let him know, despite the very real risk that he might do something I wouldn't condone.

Of course, all this was likely moot, anyway. After years of trying, Mark wasn't any closer to finding Faith's killer and was now reduced to watching the crime scene, live and on tape, hoping that old adage about the perpetrator returning to the scene of the crime bore truth.

I poured a stouter version of rye and diet than usual, put Colleen Brown on the stereo, and sat down to let her take me away from where I was. I had a couple of her CDs but opted this time for one of her earlier works, *A Peculiar Thing*. But halfway through the drink and the third cut on the CD, appropriately called "A Mystery," I couldn't sit still any longer and grabbed my cellphone to call Cobb.

"Whaddaya got?" he growled into the phone. "My wife and I are watching a chick flick and I hate to miss a single minute."

Normally I would have laughed, but on this night humour wasn't working for me.

"I encountered an old friend of yours. Or at least a former colleague."

"Who?"

"Marlon Kennedy."

There was silence for a few seconds. "How am I supposed to know this guy?"

"It's a new name. Used to be known as Kendall Mark."

Silence again, not as long this time, then softly, "Damn."

"Yeah. It wasn't a real cordial meeting. At least not at first. He took me down in the alley behind my place, held a gun to my head. He'd seen me driving by and stopping around Faith Unruh's house. He's been watching the place for years. Thought I was the killer coming back to reminisce. When I convinced him I wasn't, we chatted for a while."

"You okay?"

"Physically, not bad. Mentally and emotionally not so hot. How is it that working with you is a can't-miss formula for having people come at me with various forms of weaponry?"

"Sorry, pal, you can't lay that one at my door. You did this on your own. I didn't even know you were going anywhere near the Unruh murder scene. Which leads me to the question, Why *are* you doing that?"

"Yeah, that was Mark's question, too. I told him I didn't know, and that's the truth. I *don't* know. Anyway, how about I tell you all about it in the morning? I don't want you to miss any more of the movie."

"You sure you're okay?"

"I'm fine."

"And Mark is gone? You're safe?"

"I'm safe. I'll talk to you in the morning."

I ended the call and sipped my drink. Talking to Cobb, even briefly, had calmed me down some. And Colleen Brown's amazing voice was working its magic.

I fell asleep on the couch, woke just after 2:00 a.m., and rolled into bed to dream of an empty house on a deserted street. But where the front windows should have been was a pair of eyes. They were unblinking and showed no emotion, gave no sense of life as they watched and watched. And waited. It was the only house on that side of the street and sat directly opposite the house Donna and I had lived in. The house that had been set ablaze by someone consumed with rage and hate. Enough to kill the only person in the house at the time of the fire.

Donna.

I awoke with a dry mouth, a headache, and the overwhelming sadness I still felt whenever I thought of Donna.

My feet weren't yet on the floor when there was a knock at the door, gentle at first, then, as I made no move to answer it, louder and more persistent. I padded across the floor, rested my forehead against the door.

"If your name isn't Mike or Jill, bugger off," I said.

"Wow, that was close. I'm not Jill, so that left me only one chance. Lucky me."

"Do you have coffee with you?"

"Don't I always?" Cobb said, and I heard a chuckle follow the words.

"You didn't yesterday. Just mooched my beer." I opened the door and he crossed in front of me and set a Starbucks Coffee Traveler on the table — ninety-six ounces of Pike Place. Apparently Cobb figured the discussion of my previous evening would require the ingesting of an insane amount of caffeine. There were also doughnuts from Tim Hortons — he had been busy.

"Call it even." He grinned but I could see he was looking at me, studying me to check for any lingering ill effects from my adventure.

"Why don't you have a seat and enjoy several cups of coffee while I grab a shower." I glanced at the Traveler carton.

"Didn't want us to run short." He grinned again.

"We should be okay."

He crossed the room to my record collection, a series of boxes, shelves, albums, and CDs that covered a third of the living space in my already too-small apartment.

"You got any Melanie Doane?"

I was surprised. I didn't really know Cobb's taste in music, but I hadn't thought it would include a Canadian Maritimes singer, even one as good as Melanie Doane. "It's more or less alphabetical," I told him. "The *D*s should start about there."

I pointed, then turned and headed for the bathroom.

When I returned ten minutes later, rubbing a towel over my wet hair and kicking a pair of socks along the floor in front of me, Melanie and Ron Sexsmith were workin' it on the stereo — something from her *A Thousand Nights* album — and Cobb was staring at his iPad.

He looked up at me. "Been looking back. Kendall Mark disappeared three years to the day after Faith Unruh died. Cleaned out his bank account, took the easy-to-carry stuff from his apartment, and not much of that, and walked off into the sunset. As near as I can tell nobody's seen him since."

"Until last night."

"Until last night." Cobb nodded. "Of course, there was lots of talk when it happened. Everybody assumed he'd left town. A couple of his friends, guys he'd worked with — pretty capable cops — tried to find him. Nothing. How does a guy disappear in his own town and not be seen by someone in all that time?"

"Damned if I know. He changed his name. Maybe he changed the way he looked, too. I've never seen the guy before, so maybe he had plastic surgery, altered himself somehow. You didn't tell me he was black."

Cobb's face jerked up and he stared at me. "What?"

"I said you didn't mention he … Oh, crap, let me guess. Kendall Mark was white."

"As vanilla." Cobb shook his head in disbelief.

Neither of us spoke for a while. At last I said, "Is there any chance the guy who jumped me wasn't Kendall Mark? And if he wasn't who the hell was he?"

"Take me through it."

It took a while. I went slowly, not wanting to miss any details. Cobb stopped me only a couple of times to ask a question.

When I finished, Cobb said slowly, "So the guy takes you down, is ready to kill you, but backs off when you tell him you know me and that you're fascinated by the Faith Unruh murder. When he's finally convinced of that he lets you go."

I nodded. "That's about it, yeah."

"Except that the guy's black and Kendall Mark is white."

"Yeah. And let's not forget he also changed his name."

Cobb stood up, topped up his coffee, and pointed to my cup. I shook my head and he sat back down.

"As strange as it feels that Kendall Mark, now black, suddenly surfaces after all this time, it feels even weirder to think that the guy you met up with last night could be anybody *but* him."

"Maybe it's like that book we all read in high school, what was it … *Black Like Me*," I said. "You know, the one where the guy changes his skin colour to try to know what it's like to be black."

Cobb remained silent … thinking. "But why?" he said finally, shaking his head again. "I get going off to try to mount your own investigation. You're obsessed. You can't let it go. You want to be left alone so nobody can interfere. I get all that. But why change your appearance so radically? You wouldn't have to do that."

"Maybe you would," I countered. "If you really wanted to disappear, leave your career, your friends, the life you've known and, most of all, not be found, what better way?"

"Maybe," Cobb sounded dubious.

"And what if you thought it possible that you'd already met the killer, maybe even questioned him as part of the initial investigation or one of the follow-ups. You start hanging around the neighbourhood, and if the killer does happen to be one of the locals and sees you, he's likely to go far away, fast. And the one thing you want, if you really believe that the killer is someday going to return to the place he did his killing, is for him to think he's okay, that there's no one around to bother him while he thinks back or relives it or does whatever killers returning to the crime scene do. And if he sees some black dude that's moved into the neighbourhood, he thinks nothing of it."

Again Cobb stayed silent. Deep in thought. Finally he nodded. "You know, that could be it. And when you think about it, maybe it's not that crazy, after all."

"The guy I saw last night was pretty damn scary, but he was a long way from whacko."

Cobb took a swallow of coffee and said, "I want to hear it again, including the blue Jetta."

I started by telling him of my own growing obsession with the case and of my recent visits, both by car and on foot, to the house where Faith Unruh lived and the yard in which she died. I went back though the various times I'd seen the blue Jetta. Then I recounted everything that had happened the night before one more time.

By the time I finished we had both refilled again, actually making progress on the coffee. Cobb said nothing at first, then, "He's living there. Somewhere close by."

I nodded. "Down the street a few doors."

"Okay, we're going to find him and at the very least warn him about putting a gun to people's heads. If you hadn't guessed who he was and mentioned my name for corroboration, you might be dead."

"Maybe." I nodded. "I'm not sure he's interested in seeing the killer go through the justice system."

"And that's not good. If he goes rogue vigilante with someone he thinks is the killer and he's wrong … yeah, we need to talk to Kendall Mark."

I nodded agreement. "Something else. I don't think he's been sitting there watching the area all day every day all these years. He's got cameras to do at least some of that. I think he's been investigating, talking to people, trying to find new information. He says he hasn't found anything new, but I'm not sure he would have shared it with me if he had."

"Another reason for us to talk to him. But I think we better leave that for now and get back to our own case."

"Larmer," I said, sounding like I was reminding myself what case he was talking about.

He glanced at me, then reached into a briefcase he'd brought with him. He pulled out four white, letter-size sheets of paper, and after moving the coffee cups to one side, set them on the table. I noticed that at the top of each sheet was the name of one of the murdered victims.

And below that was a profile of each. Personal information — height, weight, age, education, how long they'd been in the conservative media, and other points Cobb clearly felt were pertinent.

After he had them spread out on the table he looked up at me.

"I think the key to this thing is right here." He tapped the table. "These killings don't feel random to me. I think there's a connection. The killer is somehow connected to each of the victims. Or the victims may be connected to one another. And if they are and we can find that connection, I think we might be able to find the killer, or at the very least prove that Larmer isn't that guy."

"Find the why and you'll often find the who," I said.

He looked up at me with a half-smile, mouthed the word "motive," then took a swallow of his coffee and stared at the four pieces of paper.

"Well, there's the obvious," I said. "Each was a right-wing media personality."

He nodded. "True, but I think there's more than that. If that's all there was, then it would be random. But I don't think the killer is content with taking out just anybody who happens to be on the right politically and earns a living by being in the media. I think each of these people were murdered for another reason besides their politics — maybe the same reason in all four killings."

I looked again at the sheets of paper, then shook my head.

"Well, what are you thinking?" I looked at him. "You put this stuff together; you must have some thoughts about this other motive."

He studied the pages for a few seconds and nodded. "Yeah, I have. Nothing definitive, more like questions really. Their ages, for example, all in their early to late forties. Maybe not significant, except that it makes them contemporaries."

"True enough. None real old, none real young. So what does that mean?"

He shook his head. "Maybe something, maybe nothing. The other thing they have in common is right here. I looked over the stuff you dug up on them and it looks like all of them have been part of the political right for a pretty long time. No newbies. So if they've all been around for a while and all are in the same age bracket and are pretty well-known within their own circle of conservatism, doesn't it make sense that they might have known each other?"

I wasn't so sure. "Maybe. It's likely they knew *of* each other, but did they know each other personally? Hard to say."

"Okay, let's look at it another way. You're in the media; you've been a journalist for some time. Let's take some of your colleagues in Vancouver, Toronto, Halifax. How likely is it that you know them?"

"Same answer. It's possible, maybe even probable, that I've heard of them or their work. And I may have met some of them."

"And if you did meet them, how would that have happened?"

I thought for a minute before answering. "I don't know. Conferences, workshops, awards events, or maybe when I'm travelling I stop in and say hello. That last one I admit doesn't happen all that often unless I already know the person."

Cobb was nodding, more animated now. "My thoughts exactly. It's the same with cops. Conferences, workshops on forensics, new technologies, that kind of thing."

It was my turn to nod. "Yeah, that might make a starting point … see if we can draw some lines that connect these four people."

Cobb stood up. "Right. If you're okay to work on that stuff, I'd like you to get started. I have to meet with Larmer. The good news is it's just him and me. No Shulsky this time."

"He might be able to help with the question of conferences and other meetings where the four victims could have met."

Cobb nodded. "Good idea. I'll throw it at him."

"Meanwhile, I'll talk to people I know in the business and see what I can find out. Trouble is, if the conferences were put on by right-wing think tanks or the like, most of my colleagues wouldn't have been there and probably wouldn't have even known about them. But that said, it won't hurt to try. And, of course, there's my ever-present friend — Google."

Cobb nodded and stood up.

"Where the hell do you think you're going?" I said. "We've still got several gallons of coffee to drink."

"I'll have to leave you to it. I'm already wired and having to piss every three, four minutes. By the way, the cops have scheduled a media briefing for 10 a.m. Friday morning."

I didn't bother to look at my calendar. "I'll be there," I said.

I was about to ask what he thought they might want to tell the waiting world, but my cellphone offered the first notes of "Takin' Care of Business." I looked at the screen. "Jill," I said.

"Right, I'm out of here." Cobb started for the door. "Tell her hi for me."

I waved and answered the call.

"Hey, how are you guys?" It was more than a throw-away greeting. Since Kyla's recent medical issues, when I said "How are you?" I really wanted to know how they were.

"Kyla went back to arts summer school today and she was pretty pumped when she left here. She'd signed up for it weeks ago, but has only gone twice since the summer started. Then she got sick. But this morning her colour was better, she ate a pretty good breakfast, and she was smiling. I'd say we're doing pretty well."

"That's great," I said. "And how about you?"

"I'm smiling, too. My daughter's feeling better, I have a terrific guy in my life, and it's a gorgeous day outside. I'd say things are pretty good."

"It's good hearing the life back in your voice," I told her.

"So what do you say we celebrate all the good stuff that's happening to us with a barbecue tonight?"

"Love it. Your deck or my balcony?"

"I was thinking here," she said. "How about ribs? You bring red wine and I might let you join us."

"I have a better idea. How about I bring the wine and the ribs and I do the barbecuing. You and your daughter sit back, look lovely, and admire my technique on the barbecue."

"You have technique?"

"I'm more than just a cupcake guy, you know."

Adam, you don't have to —"

"No argument. I'm doing the cooking. Need anything else?"

"Just you, mister. See you around six."

We rang off and I headed for the computer once again, this time to search out the kind of conferences right-wing media might want to attend.

An hour and a half later I had a list of a half-dozen annual events that could fit the profile, as well as a couple of one-offs. Now I just had to figure out how to make the information useful. I started by emailing organizers, telling them I was a freelancer and interested in attending their upcoming event and asking for the list of conference-goers for the last few years. I batted .333 on the recurring conferences, which I thought was okay. Two told me they'd get them out to me in the next couple of days, one more said it didn't keep records of previous attendees, which I knew was bullshit because you'd want to invite and encourage past delegates to come again next time around; two replied that they respected the privacy of those who attended their events and wouldn't be sending me any information. One did not respond at all, at least not right away.

I realized at that point that I'd made a tactical error. I couldn't blame the conferences that were reluctant to share delegate information with just anybody.

So I picked up the phone and called the first conference organization to give me a straight refusal. It was called the Organization of American Unity, was based in Kansas City, and it staged an annual conference called Freedom Calls. When a woman answered I asked for the name I'd seen identified as the secretary manager of the OAU, someone named Denton Jarvie.

Jarvie came on the line, his voice a deep, smooth drawl with special attention paid to diction. When he identified himself and greeted me, I got right to it.

"Mr. Jarvie, my name is Adam Cullen. I'm afraid I have to confess something to you. I sent you an email a couple of hours ago that said I was thinking about attending the conference this fall and hoped you might provide the names of previous conference delegates."

"I recall the email." Jarvie's voice turned icy.

"I'm sorry to say that was a deception. It's true that I'd like to have access to the lists of attendees for the past few years, but the reason for my wanting to see them is not what I indicated in the email."

"I see ... and what would be the reason, then? The *real* reason?" Still frosty.

"I'm calling from Calgary, Alberta, Canada, and I'm part of a team representing a man who is charged with a murder." I paused to let that sink in. "It's a murder we don't believe he committed. His name is Buckley-Rand Larmer and the victim was a colleague of Mr. Larmer's — Jasper Hugg. Mr. Larmer is a tireless worker for the conservative cause. You may know him at least by reputation and you may have heard about the case."

There was a generous pause on the other end of the line.

"I am aware of the case, of course, Mr. Cullen. Mr. Larmer is a great champion of the right and many of us are watching and monitoring the situation with concern."

"I understand," I said. "Mr. Jarvie, there's something you might be able to do that would help us and in turn be useful to Larmer's case."

"I'm sure the OAU would be more than willing to do what we can as long as what we are asked to do is legal and ... uh ... appropriate."

"I'm certain that what we're asking fits both of your criteria." I was having trouble dealing with the silky smooth delivery of Jarvie's every word. I figured I better speed things up before I explained to him how annoying he was.

"We?" Jarvie said.

"What?"

"You said 'we.' Who else is working with you on this?"

"Mr. Larmer's attorney, Stanley Shulsky, an investigator named Mike Cobb, and me."

"Thank you. Go on."

"We're hoping you might be able to provide those lists of delegates to past conferences going back maybe five years, even a little farther if it's possible."

"I'm curious as to how that might assist Mr. Larmer."

"We're looking at other attacks on conservative-media people to see if there are any connections between the victims. Connections that might help to establish a pattern and maybe get us closer to the killer or killers."

"Ah, well, there you are, then," Jarvie said. "You see, I know about the attacks on high-profile conservative spokespersons and have always felt that there was something that would tie the victims of these attacks together. Everyone, well almost everyone, laughed at my assertion. Now it appears there might be vindication at last because, you see, I couldn't regard these as simply random acts and —"

"Can you help us, Mr. Jarvie? I'm sorry to interrupt, but there's a bit of a time crunch here."

He hesitated, no doubt disappointed that I hadn't wanted to hear his entire dissertation. "I'll go to work on it right away and email the lists."

I gave him my email address, then added, "And I want to apologize again for the deception earlier."

"I'll send the lists," he repeated and hung up without accepting or acknowledging my apology.

My next call was to an organization calling itself the Association for Conservative Broadcast Values, which staged an annual event called "Let's Make It Right" that moved from venue to venue each year; recent locations for their conference included New Orleans, Oklahoma City, Denver, and Houston. This time my confession fell on the ears of Wanda Lucksinger, a no-nonsense woman whose voice indicated that either she gargled with gravel or she was 130 years old. She would not discuss my request until I forwarded my credentials, along with Cobb's and a letter from Larmer (whom she had heard of) authorizing me to receive information from the association on his behalf.

I put in a call to Cobb thinking he might be at the remand centre and could get Larmer to draft a letter for Wanda Lucksinger. There was no answer and I figured he had, at the very least, been required to shut off the phone, or it had been taken from him to be returned after his visit was complete.

I tried two more conference contact people but got no answer, left messages. I decided not to pursue the one-off events just yet because I felt that the odds were better that the victims met at an annual event. I decided to at least wait until I received the lists that were coming and to pursue the two groups I hadn't been able to reach.

My phone rang. It was Cobb.

"I got your message and ran back inside. Larmer had a good idea — he suggested we get Shulsky to write the letter. It'll be on legal letterhead and might pack a bit more of a wallop."

I thought about Wanda Lucksinger. "Yeah, that might be the better way to go," I agreed.

"And Larmer's putting together a list of conferences, meetings, and the like that he's aware of. He'll get it to us in the next couple of days."

And that was it. I didn't ask about the meeting with Larmer. I knew Cobb would tell me what I needed to know when I needed to know it. And I had a sense he was in a hurry, so we ended the call.

I resumed my post at the computer and discovered that Denton Jarvie's promptness was every bit as reliable as his pompousness. The lists were already in my inbox and I spent the next ninety minutes poring over them while first Buffy St. Marie, then Bruce Cockburn filled the room with magic.

I learned that Jasmine Swales had twice been to the Freedom Calls event — 2007 and again in 2009. I also discovered that Dennis Monday had attended the event once, in 2011, and that none of the victims of the Fresno explosion had ever attended the Freedom Calls conference.

Nor had Jasper Hugg, although I did notice that Larmer had attended once — in 2008. No surprise, but not much help in terms of connecting the dots.

I scratched the Organization of American Unity off my list of possible connections.

While I was waiting for lists from a couple of the other groups I had approached, I had an idea. It still bothered me that Kyla had missed the Stampede Parade. The Stampede was moving into its final weekend and I decided to try to make up for her disappointment.

I called a long-time friend — Mac Grantham — who worked in the Promotion Department of the Stampede.

Over the years I'd done him a couple of favours —
pounding out stories on the joys of deep-fried butter on
a stick or the undeniable talent of the World Champion
hoop dancer. I wasn't surprised when I didn't get Mac
first try. Things might be just a little hectic during the
ten days of the Stampede. I left a message telling him
that I was hoping he could wrangle up three tickets to
the infield for the rodeo the next day. I was happy to
pay for the tickets, but I knew that this late the chances
of getting decent seats anywhere in the grandstand were
slim, and in the infield almost zero without some inside
help. I refrained from reminding him of my near Pulitzer
Prize–winning deep-fried butter piece.

I'd seen the rodeo from the infield only once in my
life — Donna had sprung tickets on me as a surprise
gift "for being a great guy" and I remembered that there
was nothing quite like being a few feet from where the
cowboys were warming up and resining equipment while
broncs and bulls stomped and snorted.

It was a long shot, but if my contact came through I
was fairly certain Kyla might join the hordes of women,
young and old, who thought of me as "a great guy." Or
at least a guy who could score cool stuff now and again.

I hoped I'd know before I left for Jill's house and
the barbecue. I checked my in-box and found an email
from one of the organizations that had agreed to send
me their delegates list, without my ill-conceived bullshit
story. This one was called the Coalition of Conservative
Cooperation, the CCC. Their lists only went back four
years, and I didn't find any victims' names on those lists.

I was nearing the end of my perusal of names when
the phone rang.

I reached over, took her hand. "Jill, there's nothing you can't say to me. Well, except for 'Get lost, buddy.' Maybe not that."

"Yes, well this isn't that."

I started to say something that might or might not have been funny, but I stopped. Something told me this wasn't the time for kidding around.

"Adam," Jill began, "a couple of days ago, Kyla asked me if someday we'd live together. 'Like a family' is how she worded it."

I paused before responding. "What did you say to her?"

"I told her I didn't know. I said we hadn't been together that long yet and didn't want to rush into it. She looked kind of disappointed."

I took a sip of wine and looked at her for a long time before answering. "Jill, I'd be lying if I said I haven't thought about it. There's no two people I care about more than you and Kyla. And I visualize in my mind the three of us living together and that's a wonderful visual. Like a family. That pretty well summarizes how I picture it."

"Why am I feeling there's a *but* coming?"

"No *but*, not really. Maybe a *not yet*. I guess I'm still working out a few things —"

She held up a hand to stop me. "It's okay. You don't have to explain. I get it, I really do. I guess because I'm having some of those same things happening for me, too."

She didn't look angry or upset and I was relieved at that. We sat for a few minutes, silent and still. Then she set her wineglass down, reached over, and took my hand.

Her voice was soft, the words slow and gentle. "When you get married you think it's going to be forever. I was so in love and things were really good for a long time.

"Hey, Adam, Mac here."

"Knife, how ya doing? Been a long time."

"The Knife" was a nickname that had been hung on him several years before, most likely after several rounds of drinks, which is when ideas like Mac the Knife seem almost divinely inspired.

"It has. But hell, when the author of some of the Stampede's greatest writing *ever* calls, I drop trivial shit like impending visits from heads of state and return the freaking call."

"And that's as it should be."

We both laughed. Then Mac turned serious.

"Hey, listen, Adam, I don't check in with you nearly as often as I should, and that's crap. How've you been doing?"

I knew that he was referring to how I'd been doing in the years since Donna's death. Mac was one of the people who knew I hadn't been very good for a long time.

"I'm okay, Knife, I'm okay." *As long as I don't think about it.*

"Good, I'm glad to hear it. And good news, I got some tickets for you. Four rows up, dead centre. They're sponsor tickets and they can't use them."

"You're the best. What do I owe you?"

"This one's on the house. Just make sure you stop in here some time. Be nice to catch up. We can split a Scorpion Pizza."

"Yeah, can't wait."

We both laughed at that.

"Tickets will be at Will Call in front of the grandstand. Have a great time."

"Guaranteed. And, Knife? Thanks, I appreciate it."

I hung up and when there were no more replies from conferences with lists for me to check, I decided to put the Larmer case out of my mind for a while and go for a run. Along the way I checked over my shoulder several times for the dark-blue Jetta, but Kendall Mark was apparently at his post near the Faith Unruh murder scene. And probably saw no reason to follow me now that he knew I wasn't connected to the girl's death.

At least I hoped that was his thinking.

The evening was close to perfect. For my drive across town I had Paul Brandt's *Risk* at a decibel level that I'm sure is what they warn you against. I arrived at Jill's just after six, a bottle of Amarone in one hand, Sunterra Market ribs and a Marianas Trench CD for Kyla in the other. I didn't really know her taste in music, but I figured I might as well start the Canadian music indoctrination process. I knew there was one direction I wouldn't be going after hearing her say a few days before that Justin Bieber was "talented but just too immature," a sentiment I shared. Of course there was always Nickelback and their love 'em or hate 'em camps (I'm in the former), but I figured I'd better clear that one with her mother before I invested in a CD.

The ribs were beyond wonderful; the weather was deck-perfect, and not a single mosquito ventured onto our turf.

After dinner, Kyla asked if she could go to her room to listen to her "awesome new CD."

When she'd gone, I topped up the wineglasses and looked at Jill.

"Is she really a fan of that band or is she looking excited because she knows I want her to be? And did she really want to hear it right this minute or is this part of a plot to give us some alone time?"

"Yes, yes, and yes. Yes, she does like Marianas Trench; we even saw them a couple of years ago. I mean, she's not like some nine-year-old girls who want to marry one of them, but she does like their music. And yes, if it turned out that she hated them, she would pretend to be excited so you wouldn't feel bad. And yes, she wanted us to be alone on the deck in the moonlight with the wine and each other because … well, because that's the kind of person she is."

I thought about that. "She is a very special girl. Like her mother."

"And there's a fourth reason she wanted to go."

I looked at her, trying to read her face. She looked serious but not angry or upset. "And what is that?"

"She knows that there's something I wanted to talk to you about. To ask you about."

"You can ask me anything, you know that."

She shook her head, smiling. "No, it's not one of those probing your past, learning your secrets kind of things."

"Phew," I said, trying to mask the fact that I actually *was* relieved, not because I had any interesting secrets, but because I hated those you-tell-me-yours, I'll-tell-you-mine moments in life. I was glad this wasn't one of those.

"I've been thinking about something," Jill said slowly, her voice lingering on each word. "Something Kyla and I have talked about."

"Now you've made me curious."

"Well, I …" Jill stopped and sipped her wine.

"If I didn't know better, I'd say you were nervous."

"And you'd be right."

Then Kyla came along and something I didn't think could possibly get any better … suddenly did. And then three or four years later things started to unravel. First little things, then bigger stuff. Things were said that I wouldn't have thought either of us were capable of saying.

"And one day I realized I didn't love the man I was married to … and that he didn't love me. In fact, we didn't really even like each other anymore. One night we were sitting on the deck … on this deck … and I said, 'This really isn't working, is it?' and he looked almost relieved that he hadn't had to say it. He was gone in a few days. Of course it wasn't until several months later that I found out about Judith and that they'd been seeing each other for over a year before we split. Guess I was the stereotypical *last one to find out* wife."

There was a solitary tear on her cheek and I wanted to brush it away but wasn't sure she'd want me to do that.

After a minute she went on. "I told myself I could maybe fall in love again but that I'd never ever trust again, at least not like I did with Keith. And now here I am and I have fallen in love again — but the thing is, I do want to trust you. That's the thing I'm working my way through."

I nodded, lifted her hand to my lips, and kissed it. "I know there's nothing I can say that will make that better for you. I hope one day you'll feel you can believe in me as much as you believed in him. And if that's going to take some time, that's okay with me."

There was a hint of a smile on her face as she said, "I love you, mister … so much."

I took another sip of wine. "I guess there are two things I'm dealing with. One is guilt, the thing about why was it her and not me — survivor guilt. Stupid, I know, after all this time, and I know Donna would want me to be with someone that I care about. But I'm still troubled by that, I guess."

Jill nodded but didn't say anything.

"And the other thing is straight-up fear," I told her. "Just as dumb, in a way, but when you've had someone you loved so much taken from you the way Donna was taken from me, there's this fear, this … what if I love someone that much again and it happens again? What then?"

"Adam, all of us have to live with that every day. People have horrible car accidents, they get sick; there are a lot of things that can happen. But I don't think we should live our lives as if something terrible could be just around the corner. I know I shouldn't be saying this because I haven't been through what happened to you. But it just seems sad to live with that fear every day. I hope you'll be able to get past that."

"I'm working on it, Jill, I really am. But I guess we both need a little more time, at least that's how it seems to me."

She nodded, her head moving gently in the growing shadows. "That's how it seems to me, too."

"Does your husband … does Keith know about Kyla's Crohn's?"

Jill nodded again. "Yes, he does. Kyla usually spends a month with him and Judith in Toronto every summer. I called him a couple of days ago to tell him that because of what's going on with her health, we'd have to shorten it up, maybe a week in August if she's doing okay."

"How was he with that?"

"He was fine, though angry that I hadn't let him know sooner, which I should have. But he was fine with Kyla coming for a shorter visit this year. He really is a pretty good guy when it comes to being a dad — just not quite as good at being a husband. But maybe he's better at that, too, with his new wife."

I reached for the bottle of Amarone and poured a little more into each of our glasses. I help up my glass for a toast. "Here's to both of us working out the things we need to."

We clinked glasses and she said, "Cheers to that. And to … *like a family*."

I liked that and we smiled at each other, then she kissed me slow and warm.

I pulled back. "Oh my God," I said.

"I hope you mean that in a good way," Jill said. "That isn't exactly the reaction I was hoping for."

"No … no," I stammered. "It wasn't the kiss. I just remembered something. Don't move."

I jumped up, ran partway down the hall, and called, "Kyla, can you come out here, please?"

I looked back at Jill, who was shaking her head in a way that said she was saddened by the fact that I had just lost my mind.

When Kyla didn't appear I called again. Nothing.

"She's probably got headphones on so she can listen to her new CD without disturbing us. She won't be able to hear you."

"Right." I nodded. I walked down the hallway and rapped on Kyla's door, gently at first, then harder. The door opened and Kyla blinked at me as she pulled her headphones off.

"Did you knock?" she asked.

"I did, yes," I told her. "High-level meeting in the living room. I have something to tell you and your mom. Sort of a surprise."

"A good surprise?"

"I think so."

She flipped the headphones onto her bed and followed me to the living room. She looked at her mom but got only a shrug by way of response.

As Kyla sat down next to Jill, I stepped dramatically to the centre of the room and said, "I hope neither of you ladies has a commitment tomorrow, because I have tickets for the Stampede rodeo. The three of us are going to be sitting in the infield grandstand, about twenty feet from the cowboys."

Blood-curdling would best describe Kyla's scream as she launched herself at me, throwing her arms around me in a hug that was just this side of a Michael Ferland bodycheck.

Jill beamed at me from the couch.

As Kyla released me, I sat back down and said, "So let me see if I've got this right. All I have to do to get on the good side of you two is get you close to a big bunch of cowboy hunks."

"Uh-huh." Kyla giggled.

"Works for me, too," Jill said as she and her daughter high-fived each other, then me. As she leaned in to wrap her arms around my neck, she whispered, "Like a family."

SIXTEEN

It was halfway through the steer wrestling — bulldogging in rodeo parlance — when I happened to glance up at the infield press box, off to my right. Lorne Cooney was sitting in the front row. His head bobbed up and down as his focus jumped back and forth from the action in the arena to his almost frenzied note-taking. My thought was: *I'm looking at the only Jamaican rodeo reporter in the world.*

The steer wrestling ended and there was a break in the action as a presentation was being made onstage. I told Jill and Kyla I'd be right back and strolled over in the direction of the press box. Lorne happened to look down and I waved and shrugged — my way of saying, *What the hell are you doing here?*

Lorne grinned — his default facial expression — and pointed to the beer garden behind the press box. Five minutes later we were enjoying a beer on a 28-plus Celsius day.

"What do you know about rodeo?" I laughed and took a swallow of cold brew. "Be like sending me to cover a conference on teenage dating rituals."

"Too late," Lorne said with a chuckle. "I did that one last year."

He took a long pull on his beer and said, 'You know what it's like at the *Herald*, Adam, very few full-time writers and none of them wanted this gig. Then the guy they did hire could only work the first seven days. When I heard they needed somebody for the last three days, I bought a cowboy hat, read a couple of media guides, and watched *Junior Bonner* three times and *bingo!* here I am."

I looked at him. "Steve McQueen."

"Not a bad movie, actually."

"Well, I hope you didn't pay much for the hat."

"Are you kidding me? Woman up there —" he jabbed a thumb in the direction of the press box — "she told me I looked just like John Wayne."

I nodded. "Yeah, I can see that. Besides, I heard the Duke was heavy into reggae."

"Yep, pilgrim," he said, and we both laughed.

I pointed at him with my beer. "The funny thing is, I was going to call you. Wanted to pick your brain about something."

"The Larmer thing?"

I nodded. "We don't have to talk about this right now."

"No, I'm good right now. Lay it on me. And I appreciate that you didn't say anything rude about the brain you're wanting to pick."

"Yeah, like I'd do that." I grinned. "So, here's the thing. I'm working on looking at other right-wing victims of violent, usually fatal attacks. I told him about the Fresno and Texas incidents and he nodded thoughtfully, knew about them in general terms.

"I wondered if you had any ideas on conservative-themed conferences, conventions, and the like that the victims might have attended. I've checked out a few but so far haven't found any that had all of them in attendance at the same time."

He nodded approvingly. "Not a bad idea if you're looking for connections."

"Maybe. Guess I'll see if anything comes of it. Like I said, nada so far."

"Don't forget the less orthodox gatherings — those might be interesting, too."

"What do you mean *less orthodox*?"

"I've heard rumblings, rumours that there were some pretty shadowy kind of underground gatherings of right-wing media, spokespersons, potential candidates, those kinds of people. Some of them run by quasi-Republican types. Pretty extreme, and very secretive. I never got close enough to get names or even places and dates of the events. But the word is, they're a reality. And still taking place. The kind of people you're talking about just might have gone to an event or two of that kind."

I drained my beer. "Interesting thought. I have to get going — Jill and Kyla are up in the stands. Any chance you could send me what you've got on this stuff?"

"Sure, it's not much, but if it'll help, I'm happy to send it along. Anything new from your end on the Larmer thing?"

"Not a lot but we'll keep plugging."

Lorne chuckled. "A lot of people are hoping Larmer did it. And that he goes away for a long time. Your boy isn't well-liked."

"Who would've believed it. Anyway, better get back to your perch. Saddle bronc riding's about to start."

"Um …" Lorne said, " help me out here, Adam. How's this differ from what we saw earlier? Guys riding horses that buck, right?"

"The bareback riding, you mean? Pretty simple really. This one's called saddle bronc riding because there's a saddle. Bareback riding, no saddle. Duh. You better get back there and watch."

Lorne grinned, nodded sagely, and headed for the press box. I bought three sandwiches and three bottles of water and headed for our seats. When I'd distributed lunch, Jill said, "Was that Lorne I saw you talking to?"

Jill had met Lorne a couple of times and just as almost everyone did, liked him instantly.

"Yeah, he's covering the rodeo for the *Herald*."

"Lorne Cooney, rodeo writer?" She was as incredulous as I had been.

"Not many people realize that all the best rodeo writers are from Jamaica."

We both laughed and I turned to see that Kyla, who had been loving every minute of the rodeo, seemed even more focused as the younger steer riders were gathering behind the chutes in preparation for their event, which would follow the bronc riding. I looked down behind the chutes and noted, as Kyla no doubt already had, that this event featured cowboys not much older than she was.

All in all, a pretty good day.

I change the ring tone on my phone every few days so I won't get bored. I had downloaded "At the Hundredth Meridian" the night before. What had seemed like an inspired idea at eleven-thirty the previous evening felt much less so at six-twenty in the morning, as The Hip started my day. I pried an eye open and glared first at the clock, then at the phone.

I considered not answering, but as emotional maturity returned I realized that early-morning phone calls are often purveyors of news, usually, though not always, bad. And I remembered that the daughter of the woman I love was still recovering from a bout of a serious illness.

I didn't take the time to check caller ID and spoke as normally as I could into the phone. "Hello."

I didn't recognize the caller's voice. Female, pleasant — didn't sound like a bill collector or a Revenue Canada operator. I'd never actually spoken to one of the latter but I had always imagined a voice somewhere between Jack Nicholson in *A Few Good Men* and Fran Drescher. This voice was neither.

"I hope I didn't awaken you, Mr. Cullen."

I did my best "Hell, I've been up for hours" impersonation.

"No problem. Something I can do for you this morning?"

"This is Anita Dekalb. I'm returning your call. I just arrived back in the country and am on my way from the airport to my home. Returning calls."

"Sure," I said, my mind scrambling to process the name. I was about to give in and ask her to refresh my memory when it hit me. Jasper Hugg's ex.

"I … uh … appreciate your getting back to me, Ms. Dekalb, and I'm sorry for your loss."

"Okay, first of all, I didn't suffer any loss," she said, her tone surprisingly matter-of-fact. "I'll never celebrate anyone's dying, especially the way I've heard Jasper's life ended. But I hated the bastard. I didn't come back for his funeral or whatever they're doing for him. This was my planned return from a vacation in Britain and it just happens to be right after my former husband was stabbed to death. You can feel bad for Jasper if you care to, but don't feel bad for me. I haven't lost a goddamned thing."

There was a part of me that wanted to say, *Don't hold back, Anita, baby, tell us how you really feel.* But I had a feeling that living with Jasper Hugg involved challenges I wouldn't have a clue about.

"Besides, your call to me was from before somebody stuck a blade into Jasper. So this isn't about that."

"Well, I guess in a sense it is. I'm part of a team that is representing Buckley-Rand Larmer. But you're right. We were already involved with Larmer on another matter before your hus … *ex*-husband's death. Now, of course, things have taken a —"

"Buckley-Rand and Jasper. Now there's a couple of pricks for you. Now one's dead and the other one's in the can. That's enough to send a girl to the Red Mile for an evening of celebrating."

"I realize the timing is kind of bad with you just having returned from a trip, but I was hoping I might be able to talk with you in person. There are a few things you might be able to shed some light on."

"Are you one of them?"

"Sorry, Ms. Dekalb, one of what?"

"Jasper Hugg and Buckley-Rand Larmer both define the word 'asshole.' Are *you* one?

"I'd like to believe I'm very different in the way I think from either Larmer or your late husband. But I will admit there are those who probably think I qualify for asshole-dom in other ways. You may have to decide for yourself."

She didn't laugh. "I'm going home to bed for a few hours. Then I want to unpack everything. You can call me between four and five this afternoon. Is my number on your call display?"

"Yes, it is. I —"

"Then I'll hear from you later."

The call ended and I finally sat up in bed. One thing the straight-from-the-hip, straight-from-the-lip Anita Dekalb had done was to bring me to a state of full consciousness.

I was suddenly looking forward to my chat with her. I crossed the floor to the stereo and put the first White Horse CD on, then climbed back into bed. Getting the rest of this day rolling was going to take a little time.

The next time I looked at my clock, it read eight-thirteen. I'd gone back to sleep and would forever be grateful to Luke and Melissa for making that possible.

The Calgary Police Service briefing got underway at eleven in the morning. Deputy Police Chief Darnell Edmunds was first to the podium, welcoming the media, then introducing the police service members on hand, finally turning the microphone over to "Yvette Landry, the lead detective in the ongoing investigation."

Landry was a confident, no-nonsense woman. Her summation of the charge against Buckley-Rand Larmer and the evidence against him was delivered succinctly and directly. It was a no-frills presentation and the police service had chosen wisely. She came across as credible and competent, just as Cobb had described her.

She touched briefly on some of the points Shulsky had indicated would be part of the Crown's case if and when it came to trial. She emphasized the opportunity and motive elements of the case, noting that "in Mr. Larmer's own words, he walked to work later on the morning of the attack on Mr. Hugg. The time of the attack suggests that the accused had ample opportunity and time to drive to his place of employment, commit the crime, return the crime vehicle to the garage, clean it up, and set off for work a second time, this time on foot."

A couple of reporters' hands went up, but Landry shook her head. "There will be time for questions at the end."

She glanced at her notes before looking up and continuing with what I thought was the most important, though not unexpected, information conveyed. "Our forensic team completed its examination of Mr. Larmer's vehicle, a 2012 Lincoln Navigator SUV, and has confirmed that traces of blood were found on the front seat and floor of the vehicle. The samples are undergoing DNA testing and we will clearly know more once we are able to confirm whose blood it is. Some effort had been made to remove the blood from the vehicle, but that effort was not entirely successful and, as I have noted, significant samples of someone's blood were discovered in and recovered from the vehicle. If it is found that the blood is that of the victim, Jasper Hugg, that would establish with some certainty that this is the vehicle the perpetrator drove after committing the crime that resulted in Mr. Hugg's death."

My head snapped up at that. I wondered if a good lawyer would have much difficulty in dissecting that statement if it were made in court.

Having completed her statement, Landry nodded and stepped back from the podium. Clifford Frobisher, a police lieutenant in the information services department, took her place and opened the floor to questions. This was often the time when interesting discoveries were made — areas where the police case was lacking or points within the investigation that had not been addressed. Today, however, there were no fireworks and nothing was asked that Detective Landry couldn't manage with relative ease. I'm not sure if that was because the police case was rock solid (I didn't think it was) or because the media in attendance were either uninterested or poorly prepared or both. I couldn't believe there wasn't major interest in the media given that a member of that fraternity was the accused in a spectacular and gruesome murder.

I decided to refrain from asking any questions, though I had a couple. I felt that with Cobb and I working for the accused it might be best to maintain a low profile. On my way out of the building Neil Misener, a *Calgary Sun* writer I'd known for a long time and had disliked for almost as long, sidled up alongside me.

"Looks to me like Larmer's fucked," he said matter-of-factly.

"You don't sound heartbroken, Neil," I said. "Is that your personal reaction to Larmer's being charged or is that the *Sun*'s stance, as well?"

The *Sun* occupied a place on the conservative side of the political spectrum. It was to print what RIGHT TALK 700 was to broadcast. I remembered that Larmer had penned some columns for the paper over the years. And one thing I knew for sure was that Larmer didn't pick his spots. Though he was as far to the right as it was possible to be, he'd been known to eviscerate other conservative writers, thinkers, and pundits when their views didn't align with his or weren't extreme enough to suit him.

"Come on, Adam, I'm not celebrating and I'm not heartbroken. You know and I know the guy's a dick."

"That may be, Neil, but you know and I know that this isn't about that."

"Yeah, see you around, Adam." He slouched off toward a coffee machine as I headed out the front door into the welcome sunshine, somewhat dismayed that I had just defended, sort of, a man I loathed to a man who was ostensibly on his team. Weird world sometimes.

I called Anita Dekalb just after four and she agreed to meet me right away, which meant a hasty trip across town to the Dekalb condo in McKenzie Towne. I buzzed her intercom at exactly ten minutes to five.

Once we had shaken hands and I was welcomed into the living room, she asked me if I'd like coffee and I said I would if it wasn't too much trouble. She smiled by way of answer and disappeared into the kitchen, which is when I took stock of the art that graced the room's feature wall. While I know very little about what differentiates good and not-so-good art, my guess was that several of these pieces were worth serious money if they were originals. And my first, very brief impression was that this was not a woman who collected prints.

I turned away from the art to examine the rest of the room. What I saw confirmed my initial impression. These were not hard times for Anita Dekalb. The room was spacious, bright, and expensively furnished. What it was not was comfortable. It was a little too formal, too courtly for me. Maybe it was the art that gave the space its … I guess the word would be "dignity." It was nice, but not a room in which I could ever bring myself to kick off my shoes, stretch out on the all-white leather sofa, and enjoy a bag of tortilla chips and the latest Giles Blunt novel.

I tried to determine whether Anita Dekalb lived here alone or there was a new man in her life. If there was, I could see no obvious evidence of him.

When she returned to the living room I studied her with considerably more diligence than I had applied to the artworks. Anita Dekalb is a movie-star name if ever there was one. And Ms. Dekalb lived up to her billing. In fact, she was something of a work of art herself. Think Kim Basinger with shorter, less … um … buoyant hair. And I quickly concluded that Anita Dekalb was very much aware of how delightful men found her.

She was wearing blue capris and a sleeveless blingy top that reminded me of the old song "Accentuate the Positive."

I quickly learned that the room didn't affect the condo's inhabitant the same way it had me. After handing me my coffee — in a mug not a cup — she pointed to the sofa, and when I was seated, stretched out on a love seat that I guessed cost more than my car, lit a cigarette, and said, "You wanted to ask me about Jasper."

The coffee was take-your-breath-away hot, so I set it aside to cool and regarded Jasper Hugg's ex-wife.

"How long were you and Mr. Hugg married?" I started with an easy one.

"Fourteen years, seven months."

"Precise," I said.

"When people are in prison, in a war, or in hell, they tend to know exactly the duration of their time there."

"Would you say your time with Mr. Hugg falls into one of those categories?"

"I would say my time with Jasper falls into all those categories, Mr. Cullen."

"Then I'm guessing this wasn't one of those 'we've grown apart but we'll always be friends' situations?"

"In the same way I know how long the marriage went on, I also recall exactly what I'd had to endure. My husband was physically abusive toward me exactly — she drew out the word — forty-four times. Mostly punching or slapping but a couple of times he kicked me. He seldom used objects to hit me, not out of a reluctance to inflict the kind of damage a golf club, for example, might do, but because he was aware that a five iron might leave rather damning evidence. So he mostly stuck to what he could accomplish with his fists, which was considerable. I didn't keep track of mental or psychological abuse because they were ongoing."

I wasn't sure how far I wanted this to go, especially since the abuse issue hadn't been on my list of questions. As I listened to her, I realized it should have been. I was getting a side of Hugg I hadn't known about. And I didn't want to shut her down if she wanted to tell me more.

"Did you and Mr. Hugg have children?"

She shook her head. "I have a daughter from an earlier relationship, but no, thankfully Jasper and I never had children. And please don't call him Mr. Hugg. I find that distasteful. Call him Jasper or Hugg or something, but I can do without the mister."

I nodded and offered a smile. "Violent people often make enemies, Ms. Dekalb. I'm wondering if you are aware of anyone in particular who might have wanted to seek revenge on your husband."

"Apart from myself, you mean?" She smiled humourlessly.

I could only nod.

As Anita Dekalb considered this, I took up my coffee again and tried a sip. This time my lips escaped relatively scald-free.

"My guess is that Jasper had lots of enemies, people who aren't exactly overcome with grief at his passing, however gruesome. But if you're asking me if we were ever threatened while we were walking along the street or if we received threatening phone calls, no, I'm not aware of any of that happening."

"What about Buckley-Rand Larmer, Ms. Dekalb? What do you know of his relationship with your former husband? Cordial, professional, strained? How would you characterize it?"

"Mr. Cullen, I hope you'll forgive my being vulgar, but if you put two assholes together, the shit's going to fly. And that's the way it was with Jasper and Buckley-Rand. Both are brilliant, ruthless, driven men; both will stop at nothing to win whatever battle they're fighting. But if I may return to my earlier analogy — sometimes their shit flew toward each other. That said, Mr. Cullen, I can tell you that Buckley-Rand Larmer did not kill Jasper Hugg."

"I'm sorry, but you know this how?"

"There are two things you need to know about Buckley-Rand Larmer and Jasper Hugg. First, they needed each other more than any two people I've seen. I mean that in a professional sense. It was almost as if Jasper was inoperative when Buckley-Rand wasn't there."

I nodded and started to respond but I sensed she wasn't finished.

"They tried a couple of times to part and go in different directions and couldn't do it. They'd flop around like fish on the bottom of a boat, Jasper the worse of the two. Because Buckley-Rand still had his raison d'être. Jasper did not. Buckley-Rand Larmer was completely dedicated to the right, and Jasper was completely dedicated to Buckley-Rand."

I drank coffee again while I thought about what she'd said.

"And the second thing I need to know?"

"It's even more compelling than the first. However, I will share it with you only if I have your assurance that it remains absolutely confidential. Not even Buckley-Rand can know I've told you this."

"Fair enough, but I'm not working alone on this case. I have a partner, and actually I'm working *for* him. If this is significant in terms of helping us prove Larmer didn't kill Hugg, he's going to need to know."

She nodded slowly. "But that's where it stops."

"But if it's significant —"

She held up a hand. "That's my condition, Mr. Cullen. I'll tell you because it will prove Buckley-Rand Larmer is innocent. And I'll agree that you can tell your partner. But it ends there."

I waited another minute and knew she wasn't budging.

"All right. Guaranteed confidential."

"Oh, and for the record," she smiled, "it is significant. Buckley-Rand was with me that night and into the morning. If you tell that to the police, I'll deny it."

I sat back and looked at Anita Dekalb for a long time, trying to decide how to respond. I finally concluded there really was only one answer.

"A minute ago you asked me to forgive your vulgarity. I hope now you will forgive my rudeness. You are lying."

"Am I?'

"Hard to be in bed with someone in Calgary and be in London at the same time."

She took a long drag on her cigarette and smiled. She was enjoying her performance much more than I was. "Difficult, yes, Mr. Cullen, but not impossible."

Since I had nothing to say to that, I waited.

"Skype is a wonderful technological innovation, Mr. Cullen. And used creatively it can also offer many of the same sensual joys as having that person in bed with you can."

I've conducted hundreds of interviews over the years and in all that time I can count on the fingers of one hand how many times I have genuinely been gobsmacked by what I've been told. Anita Dekalb just used up one more finger.

I drank coffee, several sips, while I tried to gather myself and come up with an appropriate response or follow-up question.

"If you like I can offer details as to just how —"

I held up a hand. "Not necessary. But there are a couple of points I'll need to clarify."

"Of course there are."

Anita Dekalb was able to take fairly ordinary words and make them sound like dirty talk.

I bought myself a little time by pulling out my notebook and pen and taking a sip of coffee.

"How long were you and Mr. Larmer … uh … on Skype?"

"Quite a long time."

"Can you be more specific?"

"Well, of course, there's the time difference — it was seven hours later for me and it was about noon in London when we started, so I guess that made it about five in the morning over here."

"And it went on for …?"

"Oh, two hours or so, with breaks, of course to … catch our breath. I mean, I wasn't really checking the clock at that exact moment. It had been a … very good night."

Yeah, more information than I need on that score, thanks.

"The time thing is kind of important — do you have even a general idea as to when you and Larmer ended the session?"

She didn't hurry her answer. "I want to say sevenish in Canada."

"Do you know if he was going directly to the station at that point?"

"He didn't say."

"Right, so we have the perfect alibi and we can't use it."

"That's right."

"Can you tell me why the need for the secrecy?"

"No, I can't."

I paused, trying to think. "Okay," I said, "in the time since I arrived here, you have referred to Larmer as an asshole and a prick."

"That's true. And believe me, he is both."

"And yet you were … intimate with him."

"I hope you're not from that old school of thinking that sex must go hand in hand with love. Because I assure you, Mr. Cullen, that is not the case with me. In fact, I would suggest that sex need not be accompanied by even a liking of the partner. Particularly, as is the case with Buckley-Rand, if there is a quite remarkable libido that comes into play."

"Did Mr. … did your … did Jasper Hugg know of your … uh … relationship with Larmer?"

"No, he did not."

"You're sure of that."

"Absolutely certain."

"Right." I nodded. "So now that we're back at square one, I'm wondering if you have any suggestion as to who we might look at as a potential suspect. What about others at the station? Anyone there that Hugg had run-ins with that you're aware of?"

"Don't forget, Mr. Cullen, Jasper and I haven't been together for just over two years. But in the time we were together I wasn't aware of anyone at his workplace who would have wanted him dead. Were there disputes? Arguments? Differences of opinion? Of course, but I never heard my ex-husband — and this is one of the few good things you'll hear me say about him — I never heard him badmouth those he worked with … with the exception of Buckley-Rand, and we've already been over that."

"One last question, Ms. Dekalb. I'm not sure you are aware, but there have been other killings of conservative broadcasters, writers, and so on. We're trying to establish whether there is a connection between those other deaths and that of Jasper Hugg. Would you have any kind of record of conferences, large-gathering sorts of meetings he might have attended in the last few years?"

"I'm afraid I don't. I wasn't all that interested in his comings and goings even when we were together. When he was out of town, I knew I wasn't going to be hit or knocked down or screamed at. As far as I was concerned, he wasn't away nearly enough. That said, I do remember one thing that may be helpful. Jasper's day planners were his bible. He preferred them to a smartphone calendar and he hung on to all of them, going back a decade or more. If you could get those, perhaps you could track his travel for past years."

"Any idea where those old day planners might be?"

"No, but I expect they're somewhere in his home. He always had an office at home; I'm sure he still does. If the police don't already have them, it might be worth pursuing."

I stood up. "You've been very helpful. I appreciate it."

She slowly eased herself off the love seat and rose to her feet, her every move highly sensual. I was again reminded she was very aware of that.

What I wanted to ask her was how a creep like Hugg could ever attract and marry a woman like her, but I decided against it. We shook hands and she smiled at me. It was, it seemed to me, a genuine smile.

"I hope you find the person who did this to my ex-husband, Mr. Cullen. It's true that by the end of our time together I loathed the man, but that doesn't stop me from wanting to see a killer brought to justice."

"Of course."

"And an innocent man set free," she added with a final smile.

"Uh, one last question. I know I said that a minute ago, but your … uh … liaison with Larmer, was it going on while you were still married to Hugg?"

She shook her head. "No, and if you'll allow me to anticipate your *next* last question, I have been with Buckley-Rand three previous times. All three times were here and all three times he stayed the night, showered, and went to the station. At least that's where he told me he was going."

"Over what span of time?"

"All within the last year or so. And now if you'll forgive me I have an evening engagement to get ready for and would like to bring this to an end. Good luck with your investigation, Mr. Cullen."

"We're going to do all we can, Ms. Dekalb."

As I said the words I was studying her and trying to decide if she was capable of hiring someone — either on her own or with Larmer — to kill Jasper Hugg. My gut told me she hadn't played a role in his death, but Anita Dekalb was a woman full of surprises. I couldn't rule out that she had one more tucked away.

I called Cobb after my meeting with Anita Dekalb.

"Mike, we need to meet. I've got a couple of things for you. And they're more than over-the-phone items."

"Okay, but it's got to be fast. I've got a meeting with Larmer at the Remand Centre this afternoon."

"Where are you?" I asked him.

"Canada Olympic Park. Peter's attending a seminar up there, back-country hiking. I just dropped him off."

"Okay, how about Kensington? Half an hour?"

We agreed to meet at a coffee spot called Higher Grounds. Twenty-five minutes later I dropped the double bomb on Cobb. "Larmer has the perfect alibi and we can't use it."

I recounted the conversation I had with Anita Dekalb. Cobb was much less gobsmacked than I was, although I think my news surprised him at least a little.

He gazed into his coffee cup for a while before answering. "Okay, assuming that she didn't make up the whole thing, it just confirms what we already knew — Larmer didn't kill Hugg. But if we can't use the information, we've still got work to do."

"A sidebar here. Can Skype sessions be checked? Are there records? Can they be deleted?"

Cobb shrugged. "No idea, but I'm not sure it matters, especially if we can't use what she told you anyway."

"I don't get it. Even though she thinks the guy's an ass-hole — and that's a direct quote — she's attracted to him enough to sleep with him three different times ... and do the other thing on another occasion. Why wouldn't she go to the cops with the alibi that lets him go free?"

"I'm guessing that either she or Larmer or both of them have relationships with other people, relationships that might take a serious hit if word got out that they've been less than faithful. And you have to remember that Larmer thinks he's going to walk, that it's just a matter of time until the cops or you and me or Shulsky come up with something, other than the Dekalb alibi, that will get him off. Why put her in a bad spot if you don't need to?"

I thought about that. "If it was me I'd want to be out of jail as fast as possible and I'd use whatever it took to get me out."

"But you're not Larmer. Right now he's being gallant for the lady. And probably enjoying playing that role." He paused and I thought back to my conversation with the deadly dull Bernie McCready. It was looking like his contention that Larmer was a ladies' man of considerable skill was accurate.

Cobb went on. "Or there's another possibility. Maybe he thinks that sleeping with Hugg's ex might actually be seen as a motive for the murder. Hugg found out about it, threatened him, maybe confronted him, and Larmer decided to kill him. I can see the cops putting that kind of spin on it. Maybe Larmer's thinking the same way."

I was liking Larmer less all the time, but I didn't bother mentioning that. Instead I told Cobb about the day-planning calendars.

Cobb nodded. "I'll talk to the detectives handling the case, see if they have them and if they'll let us take a peek. I'd better get moving. I'd hate to keep our client waiting." He glanced at his watch. "And oh joy, this time it's with his lawyer. Want to come along?"

"Think I'll pass on this one."

He chuckled. "I thought that might be your reaction."

SEVENTEEN

I find middle-of-the-night phone calls even more alarm-ing than early-morning calls.

I guess there's always a chance that the Pulitzer Prize committee makes all their congratulatory calls at three in the morning, and maybe there are wild women out there who randomly dial sleeping guys to lure them out for a night of wicked frivolity. I have never received either of those calls.

The few times I have been roused, mid-sleep, from my slumber have either been bad-news calls or in more recent times calls from Cobb, who is apparently unaware of the difference between day and night, light and dark, a.m. and p.m.

This call — I pried an eye open just enough to note that the exact time was 3:54 a.m. — established an entirely new category. This call fell into the *Seriously?* category.

The voice was familiar although it was different this time. Perhaps, like me, Ariel Mancuso didn't do late-night calls well. Except this wasn't a late-night call for Ariel Mancuso. Because she lived in Fredericton, this was an early-morning call.

Whatever the reason, her voice was hesitant, halting, like a teenager calling someone of the opposite sex for the first time.

"Adam? Adam Cullen?"

"Hello, Ariel," I said, my voice not likely much better than hers.

"How did you … Oh, right, call display."

"That's it. What can I do for you, Ariel? Last time we talked I had a sense we didn't part well."

"Yeah, well, that's kind of what I wanted to talk to you about."

"Kind of," I repeated.

"Yeah. I've been thinking a little more about that day—you know, the day Randy and those other kids …" She hesitated.

"And what have you been thinking?"

"I called up one of the boys who was there that day. His name is Logan Branksome."

There were fairly lengthy pauses between each of her statements, like she wanted me to prompt her each time. I decided to wait it out this time.

"Yeah, so anyway," she said finally, "it didn't turn out quite the way everybody thinks."

I sat up, reached for the pen and pad I keep beside my bed, and for the next several minutes I took notes. A lot of very interesting notes.

Basia Bulat was amazing me as she did every time I listened to *Tall Tall Shadow*. I was working a coffee and three slices of toast and strawberry jam when Blue Rodeo's "Cynthia" emanated from my cellphone. The ringtone clashed with Basia, probably the first less-than-amazing sound the group had ever issued.

I hit speaker phone so I wouldn't have to hold the phone — my laziness stunned even me. "Hey, good-looking!"

"You better have call display, mister, or you will be in a great deal of pain next time I see you." I could hear the smile in Jill's voice.

"Naw, I figured there's a ninety percent chance it's a chick and eighty percent that she's good-looking. You gotta play the odds."

"The odds of your ever getting anywhere near this chick in any meaningful way just diminished a great deal."

"You say that now, but you and I both know you can't resist my dazzling charms."

We both laughed.

"I think I liked you better as the shy stumblebum you were when we first met," she said.

Another laugh.

"Actually," I said, "the truth is, you are the second woman to call me today and the first call was very interesting indeed."

"Tell all."

"I think I'll save this one for when I see you. Anyway, how's my girl?"

"Actually that's why I'm calling."

My frame of mind did a one-eighty. "What's wrong?"

"I'm sorry, I shouldn't have said it like that. No, nothing at all to worry about. In fact, Kyla's feeling really well. And looking so much better, too."

"Wow, scared me there."

"I know, and I'm so sorry. But maybe I can make it up to you. Kyla's been invited to a sleepover at Josie's house.

That means we have the evening to ourselves and —"

"Is she well enough to be away from home overnight?" I interrupted.

Jill laughed. "I love you so much for how much you care about Kyla. But yes, she's still on prednisone and some other things and she's feeling really well. I don't want to start taking normal things away from her if she's up to it."

"Yeah, you're right. I just … you know …"

"Yes, I do know. You're wonderful."

"So, does this evening to ourselves include dinner at a great place, a couple of glasses of a nice dry red, and maybe a little smooching after?"

"I'll have to think about the smooching, but I'm sure we can manage the dinner and wine. I made a reservation for tonight at Caesar's. Sound good?"

"Are you kidding? One of my favourite places in the northern hemisphere. Yes, it sounds good."

"Perfect. Kyla's heading over to Josie's around five. How about you come by about six?"

"In my best bib and tucker."

We rang off and I looked at my watch. Lots of time to get work done. And I knew exactly where I planned to start.

A shower, a shave, and then Gordon Lightfoot and I were enjoying the drive across town when Cuddy, Keelor, and the boys announced an incoming call.

"I've got the planners," Cobb announced.

"And a pleasant good morning to you, too," I said.

"Sorry. I've got a lot happening. But I think we need to take a look at these a-s-a-p. What's your morning look like?"

I had a few things I wanted to check out, but I agreed with Cobb that a couple of hours examining Jasper Hugg's day planners could be time well spent.

"Where are you?" I asked.

"Shulsky's office. Sixteenth Avenue, close to Foothills Hospital."

"Perfect. Ten minutes at the most. Starbucks next to Earl's on Sixteenth at Tenth. That work for you?"

"On my way."

Fifteen minutes later Cobb was sitting opposite me sipping a vanilla steamer that looked beyond bland while I worked a Pike. The day planners, twelve in all, sat stacked on the table.

I nodded admiringly. "Still got pull with the boys in blue, I see."

"Actually that was Shulsky's work. I think he's getting worried that his client might be in a little deeper than he thought. Seems to want to co-operate a bit more."

"Can't hurt to have a smarmy lawyer in our corner."

Cobb shrugged.

"You get anything from Larmer yesterday?"

Cobb reached into the breast pocket of his blazer and extracted a couple of sheets of note paper. "I think Mr. Larmer is maybe getting the bad vibe from his lawyer. A little less cocky, a little more 'what do you need from me.'"

"Humility. Not a quality that exactly oozes from the guy."

"It's amazing how the prospect of a long association with the federal penal system can change one's attitude." He unfolded and spread the sheet between us. "He gave me a list of conferences and events where folks of his ilk meet and mingle. Said he couldn't remember all the names of the events or the organizers, but gave us as much as he had."

"And if I cross-reference that list with what I can dig out of Hugg's planners, who knows what evil lurks in the hearts of men?"

Cobb smiled. "Did the Shadow ever fail to solve a case?"

"Never. And we're right there with him." I grinned.

"Yeah, we're two for two."

"Exactly," I said.

Cobb stood up. "I'll leave all this with you. If you lose any of it, Shulsky and I will break your kneecaps."

"Can't have that. I'll guard the stuff with my life."

"Okay, I'll see you later."

Once Cobb was gone, I stepped to the counter for a refill, one eye on my table the whole time. Once I had the coffee in hand I decided to change locations. A table in a back corner had become available and I wasn't keen on having people glancing over my shoulder as I worked.

Once in my new spot I settled in for a couple of hours of eye abuse, going from Larmer's handwritten notes to specific dates in the various day planners ... and back again.

Much of it was mind-numbing, but there were a few *aha* moments. I listed those in my own notebook. There were six that piqued my interest. All of them were on Larmer's list and were also noted in Hugg's planners. Two were conferences that had taken place in Los Angeles, four years apart, 2004 and 2008; one was in New York in 2001, just three months before 9/11; another was in Toronto, also in 2004; and yet another was in 2003 in a small Wyoming community called Buffalo, which I learned was located about a hundred miles from Casper. The sixth event that had made both lists was the Kansas City Conference of the Organization of American Unity — the 2007 Freedom Calls event I'd checked out earlier. I stroked it off the list.

Now the real work could begin. Larmer had been able to provide names of organizers for three of the events — the two in Los Angeles and the Dallas event. The Wyoming conference sounded a bit odd. It was titled "America: Right to Be Proud, Proud to Be Right."

Who thinks of these goddamn names?

Larmer had actually been one of the guest presenters but hadn't been able to name the organizers. My first thought was that he had to know who'd hired him. But in fairness, I knew Larmer was much in demand as a speaker and with a large number of engagements, it was certainly possible he might forget a name.

Once again I would have to go through the process of tracking someone who could give me lists of delegates. I didn't like my chances with an event that had taken place many years earlier — such as the 2001 New York event. And since it was one for which neither Larmer's notes nor Hugg's calendar entries had offered names of organizers, I decided to put that one aside for later.

I went out to the car, deposited all the day planners in the trunk, took my computer from the back seat, and returned to my spot in the Starbucks after ordering a caramel macchiato and a chocolate-chunk cookie — I didn't want to be one of those people who sit in a coffee place for four hours and nurse one grande the whole time. And there was also the fact that I really liked chocolate-chunk cookies.

An hour and a half later, I had consumed both the drink and the cookie and had got almost nowhere. Google offered little on three of the conferences and nothing on a couple — the Toronto and the Wyoming events.

Cobb had said criminal investigations were often a slow dance. But every once in a while things sped up just a little. And when I searched Buckley-Rand Larmer and

Buffalo, Wyoming, together, we went from waltzing to jiving in seconds.

Well, that's not exactly accurate. The first attempt didn't yield much. But when I made it Buckley-Rand Larmer, Guest Speaker, Buffalo, Wyoming, I got lucky. I found a link to an interview Larmer had done with a reporter from the *Buffalo Bulletin*.

The interview was pre-conference and loaded with Larmer crap — and next to no information about the conference or what he planned to talk about during his presentation. What it did give me was the name of the reporter — Martin Gathers.

I placed a call to the *Bulletin* office and was told by a woman who sounded more like she was from Buffalo, New York, that she had worked at the paper four years and had never heard of Martin Gathers.

That took me to Facebook where I learned that there were five Martin Gathers, but the one that interested me was the guy who was the city editor at the *Omaha World-Herald*. I called the newsroom at the *World-Herald* and after surprisingly pleasant conversations with a receptionist and a writer, got through to the city editor's desk.

"Gathers," said a voice that sounded younger than Gathers could possibly be.

"Mr. Gathers, my name is Adam Cullen. I'm a journalist up here in Canada — Calgary, Alberta. I'm working with a private detective on behalf of a client who has been charged with murder. His name is Buckley-Rand Larmer." I paused to catch my breath and maybe get a feel for whether he was with me so far.

"What'd you say your name was?"

"Adam Cullen," I answered. "I just finished reading an interview you did with Larmer back in 2003 when you were still out in Buffalo, Wyoming. Have I got the right Martin Gathers?"

There was a long pause and finally, "Son of a bitch."

I wasn't sure how I should respond to that so I didn't.

"I remember that guy. Even read a couple of things about him. He's up there in Canada, too, isn't he?"

"Yes, he is. Here in Calgary. Kind of a big deal on a conservative talk-radio station."

"Big deal, huh? How about self-righteous prick?"

I was suddenly liking the hell out of Martin Gathers. "So you do know the gentleman. And yes, there are those who definitely see him in that light."

"You one of those who see him in that light?"

"Mr. Larmer and I are not close."

Laughter on the line. "Nicely put. What can I do for you, Mr. Cullen?"

"Adam. I understand Larmer was one of the guest speakers at some kind of conference that was taking place in Buffalo. I'm having trouble finding out much about it."

"Well, no shit. I was right there and I couldn't find out *any*thing about it. Very secretive. To hear Larmer tell it, everybody who was anybody from the political right was going to be there, but, of course, he wasn't able to name names."

"So you interviewed him before the conference got underway."

"Yeah, I ran into him in a bar in town. Just up the street from the old Occidental Hotel — you must have heard of the place."

"Sorry, can't say I have."

"Owen Wister's *The Virginian*. You familiar with the book?"

"Know it and read it."

"Well, that's the place he wrote about in the novel where the big shoot-em-up takes place at the end. Anyway, none of that matters shit. I see this guy in the bar and he's a stranger in town so I get to talking to him. He gets just drunk enough to get me interested in this big event he's going to be part of but not drunk enough to tell me anything useful. Mostly spiels about his view of the world. He didn't even tell me where the thing was taking place. I talked to everybody in town. If people knew anything, and I think maybe some of them did, they got paid to keep their mouths shut. I even drove around the countryside some to see if I could see something that looked like it might be them. Never found a damn thing."

"I notice you didn't run a picture with the piece."

"Nope, he wouldn't let me. Said we could talk but no photo."

"Larmer didn't happen to mention any names of people involved in organizing the thing, did he?'

"Nope, sorry. It was like everything was this big secret, you know?"

"Did he tell you anything else about the conference or even that it *was* a conference?"

"You read my article; what I got, you got."

"And nothing after the fact, once they were gone — nobody got a little chattier about anything?"

"Uh-uh, not a damn thing. So did he kill somebody?"

"We don't think so."

"Too bad."

"We think the murder he's accused of carrying out could be part of a series of killings of right-wing media luminaries. You ever hear anything about that?"

"Nope. We've got one of those stations here — I guess every place bigger than Buffalo has one, but I haven't heard about a conspiracy to waste the talent. Of course, I don't listen to that crap so maybe that's why."

I was disappointed that Gathers hadn't given me more, but I couldn't think of anything else to ask that might get us any further along.

"Listen, Martin, how about I give you my phone number and if you think of anything else, I'd appreciate a call."

He took the number and we disconnected. I sat back and stared at my computer for a few minutes, then read Martin Gathers's article a second time. Same result. Nothing there that could help me find out what the hell had been going on in Buffalo, Wyoming.

My phone rang. I picked up.

"Yeah, Adam, there *is* something I forgot." It was Martin Gathers calling back. "I should have thought of it when you mentioned the photo that wasn't. The morning after I talked to Larmer, I was in town heading to a restaurant for breakfast. I got just inside the door and I saw your guy, Larmer, sitting at a table with another guy. Working for a small-town paper, I never stepped out of my house without my camera so I just kind of got myself into a good spot where they weren't likely to see me and banged off a roll of film. I never used any of them in the paper, I'm not sure why; I'm not even sure why I took them other than the guy pissed me off with all the cloak-and-dagger stuff."

"And you don't know who the guy with Larmer was?"

"No, but I can tell you he wasn't from Buffalo or anywhere close by, so I'm guessing he was attending the conference."

"I don't suppose you have any of those photos in some packing carton in your basement or somewhere?"

"Yeah, that's the good news; I'm pretty sure I do. Might take a little doing to actually find them, but I'm happy to do what I can. Not sure how it'll fit into your murder investigation, though."

"Neither am I, Martin. We're just looking for information right now and probably grasping at straws a little, too."

"Been there a few times myself. Why don't you leave it with me? Give me your email address and if I can track them down I'll scan them and send you what I've got."

"I'd appreciate that a lot."

"There's something you can do for me, too," Gathers added.

I hesitated. "What's that, Martin?"

"I want the story before it hits the wire. People down here, a lot of them have heard of Larmer."

"That can only happen if we get it figured out before the cops do."

"Fair enough. I just don't want to find out every paper west of the Mississippi has the story before I do."

"I'll do my best, Martin, that's all I can promise."

We exchanged email addresses and rang off for the second time.

I checked my email and found that another of the conferences I'd contacted earlier had sent its list of conference attendees for the past six years. This one was called "Make a Right Turn." Catchy. The conference was an annual event in Philadelphia except for 2009 when for some reason it moved to Newark, New Jersey. It took me an hour and a half to cross-reference my victim list against the delegates and found that only two had ever made the right turn. Dennis Monday had attended the 2005 edition of the conference and Jasmine Swales had been to the Newark event.

Larmer had been twice, once as a delegate and once as a speaker. His topic was noted in parentheses next to his name: Buckley-Rand Larmer (Why Political Correctness Is So Hopelessly — and Dangerously — Incorrect).

I set my notes to one side just as a beep from my computer told me I'd received another email. This one was from Martin Gathers. Attached were two photos, the same two guys in each, taken from slightly different angles. I stared at the images for a long time. The second man, the one sitting opposite Larmer, was dark, tall, and unsmiling — serious-looking.

And I'd seen him before.

It took a minute but I was able to recall where that was. It had been in another photo — he was the fourth man in the picture I'd seen on the wall of Jasper Hugg's office.

I picked up the phone.

"I want to talk face to face with Larmer," I told Cobb.

"Change of heart? I thought you didn't enjoy up close encounters with our client."

"There's a few things I want to ask him about and I'd like it to be face to face."

"What've you got?"

"You've been in Hugg's office?"

"Several times — a few times when he was alive, a few more since his death."

"Right. Do you remember the large framed photograph near the door of his office — looks like some guys at a hunting or fishing lodge in the mountains?"

"I've seen it. Can't say I paid a lot of attention."

"There are four people in the photo: Larmer, Hugg, Preston Manning, and a fourth man. I asked Hugg who it was when I met with him and all he'd tell me was that the guy was dead. Wouldn't give me his name. Played a little cat-and-mouse with me."

"And?"

"And I've come across another photo of the same guy and Larmer sitting in a restaurant in a place called Buffalo, Wyoming. The photo was taken at the time of one of the conferences Larmer had on his list. Maybe 'conference' is the wrong word for whatever this was. But the event was also listed in Hugg's day planner. It could be that both Hugg and Larmer were at that conference."

"And the mystery man in the photograph?"

"Maybe. Can't say for sure. But the guy must have been a big deal to be fishing or whatever with the likes of Preston Manning. And he just happens to be in the area at the time of a very shadowy gathering of right-wing hotshots in the Bighorn Mountains in Wyoming."

I told Cobb about my chat with Martin Gathers and his unsuccessful attempts to find out anything about the event or even exactly where it was held.

"I'm going to be tied up for a couple of hours," Cobb said. "Why don't you meet me in the parking lot of the Jubilee Auditorium at three o'clock. We can leave your car and run up to the remand centre. I'll call Shulsky and make sure everything's cleared for us to talk to Larmer when we get there."

"Will do," I said, and we rang off.

There was something gnawing away at my memory — something I was missing. I decided to get into gym clothes and go for a run in the hope that maybe the air and the exercise would lift the veil from whatever it was that was swirling around the edges of my memory.

It worked. Three miles into my four-mile run, I realized that I had seen the man in the two photos somewhere else. In yet another photo. And by the time I got back to my apartment I was fairly sure where.

Delaying my shower for the moment, I raced to my computer and pulled up the stories of the other right-wing murder victims.

And there it was. Among the images of the victims of the Fresno, California, explosion that all but destroyed radio station KKMR was station manager Michael Morrisey. Morrisey was also the man in the photo on Hugg's wall and in the two pictures Martin Gathers had sent me.

I wasn't ready to start high-fiving people just yet. I told myself it could be important or it could be insignificant. A lot would depend on what Larmer told us when Cobb and I sat down with him. With that thought in mind, I headed for the shower.

The same thought was there as I looked across the table at the half-smirk half-scowl that occupied the face of Buckley-Rand Larmer whenever I was in the room.

I laid the photo of him and Morrissey from the restaurant in Buffalo, Wyoming, on the table in front of him.

"Who is he?" I asked.

Cobb had suggested during the drive to the remand centre that I lead the questioning of Larmer, at least initially. I was happy to oblige.

Larmer shrugged. "Probably a fan. I have lots of them. Sometimes I take the time to visit with them. I'm very generous that way."

"Yeah, you're a real peach," I said. "The guy is Michael Morrissey — make that *was* Michael Morrissey."

"If you already knew who he was, why'd you ask me? I hate it when people waste my time."

I made a show of looking around the room. "Yeah, I can see you have a lot on the go."

"Fuck you."

I glanced at Cobb. The look on his face said, *Not the right place, not the right time.*

I looked back at Larmer. "We know that Morrissey was the station manager at KKMR in Fresno, California, at the time somebody blew the place up — killed him and injured several others. The picture you're looking at was taken at one of the events you listed in your note for Cobb. This is the one at Buffalo, Wyoming, 2003. What I'd like to know is what role Morrissey had in the camp … boot camp … conference, whatever name they give those things. You were one of the speakers. Was he?"

"Well, aren't you Mr. Research. Who would have guessed?"

"What part did Morrissey play at the Buffalo event?" I repeated.

Larmer shrugged.

"Maybe I could intervene here just a little." Cobb leaned forward, his grill almost nose to nose with

Larmer. "We've been working very hard —" he gestured at me — "both of us, to try to find evidence that might just get you out of here and maybe even result in having the charges against you dropped — charges that the police feel strongly will hold up very well in court. So what we need to know, and we need to know it *now*, is whether you feel like helping us do our work or if you'd rather play your little games. Which is it going to be?"

Larmer matched Cobb glare for glare. But finally he sat up a little straighter in his chair and looked at me.

"I don't know what Morrissey did, only that he was a part of it. To be honest, that was one of the strangest three days of my life. I gave one presentation and led one workshop, was there for three days. Don't misunderstand me, there was a lot about the event that was excellent, an energy to the thing that was exciting. But without a doubt it was the most secretive conference I'd ever been a part of."

"How did you get paid?"

"Cash. Delivered by courier in advance. First time that ever happened to me, as well."

Now that Larmer was rolling, I could tell he was enjoying relating the story.

"Something else," he said. "People didn't use their names. The organizing committee were colours."

"Colours," Cobb repeated.

Larmer nodded. "Morrissey was Mr. Black. There were four or five of them, I think. Hugg was Mr. Pink, I remember that, but I don't remember the other colours."

"Quentin Tarantino would have been so proud."

Larmer ignored me. "Everyone else was a number."

"Even the guest presenters?"

Larmer nodded.

"What number were you?" Cobb asked.

"You seriously expect me to remember that? It was 2003."

"So you don't know what number you were assigned?" I went at him again.

"I told you I don't remember. The whole thing was a little too Batman and Robin. They gave us poker chips with our numbers on them. Childish, if you ask me. I threw the damn thing away right after it was over."

"How many delegates were there?"

"Not sure. It was well attended, I remember that."

"By well attended, do you mean twenty, several hundred, several thousand?"

"This is only a guess, but I'd say a hundred or more."

"What kind of people were there — the delegates, I mean. Were they media, political types, academics ... what?"

"All of the above," Larmer answered, his voice conveying the contempt he felt for me and my questions. "I remember there were supposed to be some big names there. It was a big selling point for the conference. But I can't say I saw any what I would call superstars. In fairness, I wasn't there for the whole event. As I said, three days and then I was off to another gig."

"So Hugg and Morrissey were on the organizing committee. Who else?"

"I can't remember. To tell you the truth I'm not sure I ever knew. Like I said, very hush-hush."

I glanced at Cobb. He nodded at me to keep going. "Why was that? Was there stuff talked about at this camp that was somehow subversive? More subversive than usual?"

"Subversive. Ah, the word choice of the pathetic left."

"Was it?"

"Subversive? No, I would say it was a unique experience designed to prepare all of us for important tasks ahead."

"What sort of tasks?"

"I'll bet if you spent a little time thinking about it, you might be able to answer that all by yourself. Being a crackerjack researcher and all."

"The poker chip. Any identifying marks — casino name?"

"Something else that falls in the category of 'I don't remember.' Are we finished here?" He stifled a yawn.

I looked at Cobb. He raised his eyebrows about a millimetre. My call.

"Not quite." I ran through the names of the victims of the various attacks. "You see any of those people at the event?"

Apparently Larmer thought that question was worthy of some effort. He thought for a long moment, then shook his head. "I honestly don't remember. It was a long time ago and I attend several conferences a year. I seem to recall Dennis Monday was there, but I can't swear to it."

I looked at Cobb again. I wondered if he was thinking what I was thinking. Hugg, Morrissey and maybe Monday. All dead and all perhaps at the event in Wyoming.

Cobb was looking at Larmer. "Think hard. It might be important. *Did* you see Dennis Monday there?"

Apparently Cobb was thinking exactly as I was. Larmer furrowed his brow, either trying hard to remember or *looking like* he was trying hard to remember.

"Listen, I wish I could help on this," he said at last, "but I just can't be sure. I may have seen Monday there, but that's all I can give you."

Cobb nodded and stood up. I followed his lead.

"Thanks," he told Larmer. "You think of anything else that might help us, get in touch."

I nodded grudgingly in Larmer's direction. The guard who'd been in the room with us opened the door and I followed Cobb into the hallway.

Neither of us spoke until we were outside, and even then not until we had both taken several deep breaths. There was an atmosphere in the remand centre. It wasn't a prison, but the air, the walls, the people — all of it was stifling. And for just a few seconds I was able to muster a little sympathy for Larmer at having to be in there.

"I need a coffee and I need it to be somewhere a long way from here," Cobb said as we climbed into his Jeep. Neither of us spoke during the drive and not even until we were sitting at an outdoor table at Weeds, a café/cappuccino bar on 20th Avenue.

"So what's next?' I asked as I lifted my cup for a first swallow.

"Hard to say," Cobb admitted. "What luck have you had with the other conferences? Any others that had more than one or two of the victims in attendance?"

I shook my head. "Not so far, but I haven't heard back from all of them yet."

"I guess that leaves us with two choices. Do we narrow our focus, at least for a while, and concentrate on this one?"

"'This one' being the gathering in Wyoming?"

Cobb nodded. "Yeah. The danger is we could waste a lot of time on it and have it amount to nothing."

"I wish Larmer had been more certain about whether Monday was there. That would be three out of four of the victims confirmed at this event. That becomes pretty significant."

"Okay, so we've got two for sures and one maybe. Is that enough to go after Wyoming full out for a while?"

I shrugged. "Your call. I mean, I get that it's tough for him to remember that far back."

"Maybe." Cobb studied his coffee. "Or maybe not."

"What do you mean?"

"Larmer's a pretty good actor. Great smile, smooth talker, but honesty isn't his best policy."

"You think he knows more than he's saying about the thing in Wyoming? Hell, I don't even know what to call it. Was it a camp, a conference? What?"

Cobb smiled. "The 'Wyoming thing' works as well as anything. Here's what bothers me. Larmer and Hugg were joined at the hip. Does it make sense to you that Larmer is as much in the dark as he says he is about an event that his bosom pal helped organize?"

I thought about that. "Good point. So you're thinking that Larmer isn't being totally honest. For what reason? What's he got to gain by being secretive with his own people?" I hated thinking of myself as one of Larmer's people.

"Hard to say. All I know is that as much as he wants us to clear his ass, he can't bring himself to co-operate with us."

"I think it's me he really can't stand. I wonder if I'm something of a stumbling block in the investigation."

"Okay, first of all, get that thought out of your head. Whether Larmer realizes it or not, you're critical to this thing. And that's not going to change."

I thought about that, then nodded. "All right, so what's next?"

Cobb studied the ceiling for several seconds. "I say we take a run at this. I might be wrong, and if I am we waste a bunch of time. But this thing doesn't pass the smell test. Besides, it's not like we've got a lot of other hot leads to follow up on."

"Can't argue that," I agreed.

"Okay, then let's do this. I'd like to know more about what went on in Wyoming. You think you can do a little more digging?"

I shrugged. "I can dig. I just can't promise I'll turn up anything. Like Larmer said, it was awfully damn hush-hush. But let me see what I can do. Let me go back at my friend Martin Gathers."

"Good. I'll give Larmer a day to think about it, then I'll have another chat with him. He might want to be more forthcoming once the results of the examination of his car are released, and that's supposed to be later today. That came, by the way, from Shulsky, who suddenly has become very co-operative."

"Maybe he sees you as the lesser of two evils." I set my hands as if I was weighing two things. "Larmer … Cobb … Larmer … Cobb."

Cobb grinned. "That could be it. Or maybe he's starting to see that whoever set up his client did a pretty good job." He pushed back his chair. "Okay, let's go to work. Set everything else aside and see if you can find out anything more about Wyoming."

"Got it," I said and downed the last of my coffee.

"How's Kyla?"

"Pretty good, I think. Jill says she's okay to go to a sleepover tonight. Which means it's date night for me and my lady fair. Caesar's no less."

"Nice." Cobb nodded approvingly. "Have a lovely time. Just make sure you solve the case before morning."

"I somehow think that won't happen."

"I thought as much." Cobb grinned again. "Have a nice evening, anyway. Let's go get your car."

EIGHTEEN

That's exactly what Jill and I were doing a few hours later in the pleasantly plush downtown location of Caesar's Steakhouse. We'd already shared an order of escargots and a gladiator salad and were halfway through a bottle of Amarone while waiting for our New York strips to arrive.

We'd talked about Kyla and I'd brought Jill up to speed on the Larmer case, including the fact that Cobb and I were going to concentrate our efforts on the Right to Be Proud, Proud to Be Right conference, at least for now.

"You're kidding, aren't you?" she said.

"About what?"

"The name. You're making that up."

"Truth is stranger than fiction, baby. That was the name."

"I don't think I can eat."

I laughed. "Hey, that stuff resonates with the Larmers of the world. Get used to it. And anyway, I can eat both steaks."

"What are you going to do to learn more about what went on there?"

"I've got a couple of ideas. I'll call Martin Gathers in the morning and see if he's got anything else for me. Now that we've ID'd Morrissey as the guy with Larmer in those pictures, maybe that'll shake something loose in his memory."

The steaks arrived, and for the next half-hour we didn't discuss murders. Our conversation focused on the food and how much we were enjoying it; and then, as the Amarone disappeared, the topic became what might happen once we got back to Jill's childless-for-a-night home.

I was enjoying that part of the discussion when suddenly Jill turned serious.

"Adam, I don't like it."

"Damn, I don't even have my shoes off yet and —"

"No, I mean it." She shook her head. "This whole thing is starting to scare me. Think about it. What we have here is a serial killer who doesn't mind a little collateral damage if that's what it takes to eliminate a target. What makes you think this person will just stand idly by if you and Mike get even remotely close?"

I wanted to do what tough private eyes have been doing in books and movies since Dashiell Hammett was a tyke. Reassure the lady that everything was under control and there was nothing to worry about. But I couldn't, because the simple truth was that nothing was under control. Both Cobb and I were struggling to make sense of a series of crimes that we simply didn't have enough information about. And Jill was right. There was a very good chance that someone ruthless enough to have killed several people was out there and just might know more about us than we knew about him. Or her.

"I don't know what to tell you, babe, except that I plan to be as careful as I can."

"And we both know that might not be enough."

"Yes, we do. But I can't walk away now and leave Cobb to do this on his own."

"I know. And I'd never ask you to. I just want you to know that this is scaring me and I don't like the feeling that something could happen to the man I love."

"How about we just focus on the last four words of that statement?"

She nodded and smiled and for the rest of the evening gave it her best brave face. But our lovemaking later that night, in addition to being a little more uninhibited than usual, was also more urgent.

I reached Gathers at his office. It was just after nine in the morning Omaha time and I could hear him alternately chewing and drinking something as we spoke.

"Sorry to bother you again, Martin, but there have been a few more developments in the case and I wondered if you'd thought any more about the conference that Larmer attended near Buffalo."

"Yes, I've thought about it, but no, I haven't remembered anything else about that whole thing since I talked to you last. Sorry."

"Nothing to apologize for," I told him. "I just thought I'd check in one more time."

"I understand and I wish I could help more than I have."

"Actually you've been a tremendous help. We identified the man in the pictures you sent. Name is Michael Morrissey. He was one of the conference organizers and used the name Mr. Black for the conference. The organizers all used colours as sort of *noms de plumes* for that event."

"Colours." Gathers repeated. "Like in *Reservoir Dogs*?"

"Exactly. Either of those names mean anything to you? Morrissey or Black?"

He didn't answer right away. "No, I got nothin'. You try talking to the guy?"

"Yeah, not possible. He's dead."

A long pause.

"How did he die?"

"He was the victim of an explosion at a conservative-format radio station in Fresno, California, back in 2010. The other employees all survived. When we talked before I told you that we think there is or was a conspiracy to kill a number of right-wing media types. It looks very much like Morrissey was one of the targets."

"Damn."

"Yeah."

"No, I mean, I thought maybe we'd finally found out who John Bones was."

"John Bones?"

"Yeah. That's what everybody called it. A body they found four or five miles out of town, out near where the Wagon Box Fight took place — that's a battle that happened back in 1867. Anyway, a partially buried skeleton or at least part of a skeleton was found by some hunters out near there. At first people thought it must be one of the people who fought in the Wagon Box Fight. But the skeleton was much more recent — been there maybe a few years at the most.

"The forensics people weren't able to identify the guy, but they did determine that he was a murder victim — he'd been stabbed more than thirty times, a real vicious attack. But without knowing who the victim was, the investigation petered out fairly quickly and it became a cold case. After a while everybody pretty much forgot about it."

"And this body was found after the conference — after 2003?"

"Oh, yeah. In fact, I remember it wasn't long before I came out here to Nebraska, and that was December 2008. So it was a few months before that. Late summer maybe."

"Who investigated the murder?"

"Well, let's see. The local sheriff was a guy named Crombeen, Jud Crombeen. He's retired now. State cops were involved, I remember that. And an FBI agent from Cheyenne came by, took a look around, but didn't stay long. After a few weeks everybody left. Crombeen stayed with it but was never able to find out anything. So John Bones remains a mystery."

"Crombeen still live in the area?"

"I seem to recall he retired to Sheridan, about a half-hour north of Buffalo."

"Okay, thanks for this, Martin."

"Remember our deal — you find something, I'm in on it."

It was like a mantra with media, an eye for an eye and a scoop for a scoop.

"Like I told you, Martin, I'll do my best."

Tracking Jud Crombeen was easier than I thought it would be. Call information. Call Jud. A male voice answered on the third ring. This detective work was a piece of cake. I decided I wouldn't share that sentiment with Cobb.

Crombeen's voice was deep and resonant. He could have made it big in FM radio. I explained who I was and gave him the Coles Notes recounting of Larmer, the possibly related killings of conservative media people, and told him I'd like to ask him about John Bones.

"What could he have to do with your case?"

It was a good question and I was honest with him. "Likely nothing. But there was a gathering of right-wing political types in that area in 2003. Very secretive. I think it's a long shot, but I wondered if Bones might somehow have been connected to that event. Did that conference take place while you were sheriff?"

"Hell, yes, I was sheriff for thirty-two years."

"What do you know about that gathering, Mr. Crombeen?"

A pause. "Not much. They were in and out before I really even knew they were there. In fact, I never actually knew just where the thing took place. Or how long it lasted."

"How's that possible?"

"What do you mean?"

"I just wondered how it was possible that a hundred or more people could come into the area that you have jurisdiction over and you didn't know anything about it."

Crombeen's voice got deeper and louder. "What exactly are you saying?"

I realized I had nothing to gain by alienating the guy. "I apologize. That didn't come out right. What I meant was that this group must have been very secretive indeed to escape the notice of an experienced and capable lawman."

"That wouldn't have been possible."

"Excuse me?"

"If I'd been there I'd have found about them … checked the whole thing out. But I wasn't there. I was on vacation at the time. Left a young deputy in charge, a kid named Williston. He didn't know a damn thing about it until he read something in the *Bulletin* about it after it was over and everybody had cleared out. When I got back,

I checked around, but the trail was cold by then. And other than breaking a couple of camping and large-group regulations, I couldn't see that whoever it was had caused any real trouble. There wasn't much point in pursuing it. And I remember there were some big-time drug problems at the high school that kept me busy after I got back from vacation. That was my priority."

I thought for a minute about what Crombeen was telling me. And I thought about the way he was telling it. Like a prepared statement. But maybe I was being overly suspicious for no good reason.

"Okay, about John Bones. Anything at all you can tell me about him?"

"Not a lot. We couldn't identify the remains. The skull was gone — some of the other bones, too. Probably carried off by animals, or possibly the killer or killers. Without an ID, it made investigating further damn near impossible."

"What were you able to find out?"

"I just told you."

"Yes, sir, I understand. But I notice he's called *John* not *Joan* Bones. So the forensics people were able to determine the skeleton was male."

"Right. Okay, let me think. Male, between the ages of thirty and forty. White, fairly big guy — at least tall. They did a DNA check, found no matches in any databases. We did the Missing Persons checks. Nothing. And that's about it."

"I'd like to go back to the 2003 gathering. You said you didn't know where it took place at the time. How about afterward? Were you able to determine where it took place after the fact?"

Pause. "Yeah, roughly."

"How roughly? I'm just wondering — John Bones's remains were located near the site of the Wagon Box Fight. I guess I'm curious as to how close that was to the site of the 2003 conference."

Another pause, longer this time. I guessed he was deciding whether to speak further with me. In maybe thirty seconds he'd made his decision.

"I don't think you and I have anything more to talk about."

"Listen, Sheriff, I don't want —"

The click and buzz on the line told me I was talking to myself.

Cobb stirred his drink for the third or fourth time, then looked up.

"So what do you think?'

"I don't know. We've got a body, well, a skeleton, that was found a few years after a right-wing conference that had two, maybe three of our victims in attendance. And we've got a sheriff who investigated and doesn't want to talk about it. So let's think about the possibilities. John Bones could be another victim of the person killing off conservative media types"

I nodded, sipped my rye and diet. "Or maybe he's an unrelated death altogether."

"Except that he didn't just die out there. He was the victim of a savage murder. Seems a bit of a coincidence, doesn't it?"

"And neither of us are big believers in coincidence."

"I wish that sheriff had been a little more forthcoming."

"Me too," I agreed. "When I first talked to Gathers he hinted that he thought there might have been a few people who got paid off to forget about the Right to Be Proud, Proud to Be Right get-together. I wonder if the good sheriff was one of those who received a little stipend in return for keeping his lips sealed."

Cobb thought about that. "It's possible. But why the reluctance to talk about the remains — John Bones? Unless there's a connection that he knows about and doesn't care to discuss."

"Yeah, that thought crossed my mind," I said. "Maybe you should take a run at him."

Cobb shook his head. "I doubt that would improve our chances. People like Crombeen often come with a predisposition to hate private investigators." He rubbed his forehead for a while. "Go through it again with me."

I recounted the conversation I'd had with former sheriff Jud Crombeen. Neither of us spoke for a couple of minutes.

I downed the last of my drink. "Why is it when I close my eyes I see Jackie Gleason?"

Cobb grinned. "*Smoky and the Bandit*. Good movie."

His phone rang. He picked up and after "hello" said nothing for long minutes. He nodded a couple of times, glanced at me once, then took out his notebook. Cradling his iPhone between his ear and shoulder, he jotted down a couple of notes that I was unable to decipher upside down. "Thanks," he said and set the phone down.

He looked at the notes he'd made for a moment, then at me.

"Okay, that was Shulsky. The abridged version is this: the cops have confirmed that the blood that was found in Larmer's car was Hugg's."

"Which doesn't really change things all that much. We already knew that there were really only two possibilities —

either Larmer killed Hugg or someone else did and went to a lot of trouble to make it look like it was Larmer."

"You're right. I think Shulsky's worried that even if the right answer is option B, it's getting much harder to prove. Looks like I'm going to be a little busy for a while. Shulsky's called a meeting with the whole legal team in his office tomorrow morning. Then we adjourn to the remand centre for part two with Larmer."

"So what's my next move?"

"I say we stay all-in on the Wyoming angle. You keep working that."

"Without wishing to sound unduly negative, I'm running out of ideas on exactly how to do that."

But, of course, I did have an idea, a pretty clear one, on how to proceed. I leaned forward, my elbows on the table. "Jill told me last night that she's scared, worried that the killer is quite possibly out there and that if we get too close, something nasty could happen."

"I can't argue with her logic." Cobb's voice was quiet, almost subdued.

"She's probably not going to be happy with my heading down to Buffalo to see what I can find."

"You think that's our next step?"

"I think it makes sense. I can get some things done on the ground that I can't with phone calls and emails."

Cobb didn't say anything, at least not at first. Finally he nodded and said, "I doubt that whoever offed John Bones has been hanging around for a decade or so waiting for his next victim to come around."

"Maybe. Maybe not," I said. "But the fact is, there's somebody out there who hasn't been shy about killing people."

"Can't argue that either."

Cobb and I both knew that I'd be going to Buffalo. And we both knew that my objections were window dressing. The truth was, I wanted to go if it would get us closer to a solution to the puzzle. And the third thing we both knew was that despite expressing her concerns the night before, Jill would be onside with my going — for the same reason.

I was on a milk run from Calgary to Denver, then Denver to Cheyenne where I would rent a car and drive to Buffalo for, among other things, a face-to-face with Jud Crombeen, recently retired county sheriff.

I'd packed light — passport, a couple of changes of clothes, shaving kit, laptop, an Ian Rankin paperback (an early Rebus), and the file I'd put together on the Larmer case.

I figured an uninterrupted read-through couldn't do any harm. And besides, there was still something picking away at the back of my mind. I didn't know if was something someone had said or something I'd read, just that there was something that hadn't seemed right. And whether it was significant or not, I knew it would bug me until I figured out what it was.

We were about an hour out of Denver when I had it. One piece of paper, seemingly insignificant, and maybe it was, but it meant I'd be making one more stop during my trip to Wyoming.

The Mint Bar in Sheridan, New York, was instantly one of my three or four favourite places in the U.S. Long and narrow, it ran from the street through to the back alley with dozens, maybe hundreds of rodeo photographs covering the walls. Bar at the front, pool table at the back, booths lining the sides around the pool table. It was in one of those booths where Jud Crombeen and I sat across from each other, our eyes sparring like boxers in the early rounds of a fifteen-rounder.

"You're a persistent SOB, I'll give you that." Crombeen waved a mug of beer roughly in my direction.

"It's one of the traits I like least about me," I said, nodding, "but the thing about a dog with a bone is that the bone is pretty important to that dog."

"And this is important to you."

I nodded again. "Me and my partner."

Crombeen didn't look like Jackie Gleason. More like a bigger, older version of Lanny McDonald, with the same never-ending moustache. Except that whenever you saw Lanny, on TV or around town, he always looked like he was in a good mood. Jud Crombeen looked like decades passed between his good moods, millennia between grins.

He wasn't in a good mood now. And he definitely wasn't grinning.

"I appreciate your agreeing to talk to me," I said. "I know we maybe didn't get off on the right foot when I called."

"I didn't agree to talk to you." Crombeen leaned back in the booth. "I agreed to meet you for a beer. I told you all I had to say on the phone."

"I understand that, but I was hoping I could ask you a couple more questions."

He shrugged. "You can ask."

The implication that he might not answer was not lost on me. I nodded.

"I understand hunters found John Bones?"

Long pause. I hoped this wasn't going to be a childish game that would result in a lot of wasted time for me.

"Uh-huh."

"How did that come about?"

"How did what come about?"

"Did they just stumble across some bones, or were they digging, making a campfire or something?"

"They were tracking a bull elk. Came across some bones — one of the hunters was a doctor, recognized the bones as human — and they poked around and found some more. That's when they came to see me."

"Which is when you began your investigation."

"Uh-huh."

"And that was 2008?"

"Uh-huh. Late summer."

"You said the skull and some of the bones were missing."

Pause. "That's right."

"Would you say most of the skeleton was still there?"

"I'd say maybe seventy percent. But like I said, not enough for an ID. And with no skull, no dental records, we had no luck with Missing Persons."

"Was there any clothing still left intact?"

Up until that moment Crombeen had been relaxed and borderline co-operative. Even helpful. But now we were crossing a line, some barrier, real or imagined. The lines on his face that suddenly became furrows told me that. He looked at his drink, at the tabletop, and at the floor, then finally at me. But his mouth was closed and set.

"Sheriff, there's something I should tell you. We're not on some witch hunt here. Neither my partner nor I are interested in finding fault with the previous investigation or throwing anybody under the bus. We're trying to find information that will help us prove our client innocent. Nothing more, nothing less."

He mulled that over and that's when I decided to try something I wasn't sure Cobb would have approved of. But I thought that if I gave him some information maybe there'd be a quid pro quo without my having to mention it. I told him about the traces of Hugg's blood in Larmer's car. That someone had attempted to clean it up.

"But, of course, it didn't work," Crombeen said. "Just about impossible to get rid of it totally."

"Let me ask you something, Sheriff. It's something I've been thinking about. Is it possible, or plausible, that the real killer planted the blood in Larmer's car as part of the attempt to frame him, then made it look like it was cleaned up, knowing that there would be traces still there for the police forensic people to find? Wouldn't that be a nice part of a frame?"

"Maybe … can't really say, not knowing more about the case, but you asked me about possible or plausible. I'd say yes it's possible. Don't know about plausible."

It was a fair answer and I nodded my appreciation.

"What about the other investigators — the state police and the FBI? They have any theories?"

"The state guys worked it pretty hard, just like I did. We came to the same conclusion. As for the feds, that was bullshit. The kid did more than that FBI clown."

"The kid?"

Crombeen drank beer and looked at me. "Yeah, there was a university kid who spent a couple of months out here doing his own crime-solving exercise — some school-project thing."

I ordered us a couple more beers. Crombeen nodded his thanks.

"Local kid?" I said.

Crombeen shook his head. "Never saw him before. Or since for that matter. He was from the University of Wyoming — some criminology thing they teach out there. I told him book shit will only get you so far — you gotta be out there workin' it on the ground. Looking people in the eye, asking questions, getting dirt under your fingernails. And in a way, I guess, that's what he was trying to do. He 'interviewed' me" — Crombeen made quotation marks with his fingers — "a couple of times. He wanted to talk about the 2003 gathering, too. Just like you. And just like you he got nothing … not on John Bones and nothing on the big secret conference. Finally he just went away, probably back to school."

"You remember his name?"

"No, hell no — too long ago. But I'm not so sure he didn't leave a souvenir behind. A few people saw him hanging around with a local girl — Becky Cardell, she was then; she married later, so her name's Hicks now, but Noah Hicks took off on her, moved south somewhere, Texas maybe. Anyway, she had a baby sometime after that kid was out here. It might be Noah's, but there was gossip — I never paid much attention to that kind of crap, too busy for it — but there was gossip to the effect that her and the university kid might have doin' the dirty and … shazam."

Crombeen laughed at his choice of words and took a long pull on the beer.

"Becky still live around Buffalo?"

"Yeah, in town, last I heard. She works cleaning houses for people. Single mom, you gotta do something, right?"

"Right," I agreed. "So we were talking about John Bones's clothing remnants."

He drank again.

"You were *asking* about clothing remnants. Don't think I'm getting drunk enough to be stupid, boy."

"I wasn't thinking that, Sheriff. I was just hoping you might be able to answer that for me."

He drank again, but a sip this time as if to punctuate what he'd just said, then set the bottle down.

"There wasn't much. Most of it had rotted or been carried off like the skull. There were a few scraps. One piece of a shirt, red I think, with the chest pocket still there. That's where we found the poker chip."

"Poker chip?" I sat up in my chair. "How was that still intact after all that time?"

"That's what I wondered. State forensics figured it was protected by the pocket. I mean, it was pretty damaged and faded and all, but they took it away and went over it like crazy."

"I don't suppose they happened to find the name of a casino or anything like that on it?" Surely I couldn't be that lucky.

"No nothing like that. Just a number."

"Number."

"Yeah, there was a number scratched into the surface of one side. If I remember correctly, the number was fifty-three."

The drive to Buffalo was short and pleasant. Forty-five minutes after I'd left Jud Crombeen with a third beer and a couple of his pals who'd come by, I was at the door of the house that, according to the Buffalo phone directory, was the residence of Becky Hicks.

The house was small but the yard was neat and the smell told me the grass had been mowed in the last day or so. I wondered if Becky did it or if she had a neighbour who helped her out.

When the door opened on the second knock I decided it was the former. Becky wasn't overweight but she wasn't small either. She had the look of a farm-raised girl who didn't shy away from physical effort. She was wearing jeans and a T-shirt that read Daddy of 'Em All, with a bucking horse forming the crest. I knew the caption was the slogan for Cheyenne's Frontier Days — I'd seen it on posters in the airport when I'd flown into Cheyenne that morning.

"Mrs. Hicks?"

"She shook her head. "No *Mrs.* to it. I kept the name, but there isn't a Mr. Hicks. I'm just Becky. And I'm not buying whatever it is you're selling."

I smiled at her, hoping I didn't look like a salesman when I did that.

"Actually, Becky, I'm not selling anything."

A small, shy face peeked out from behind her. It belonged a five- or six-year-old boy. Slender, not built like his mom. Lots of brown hair, eyes to match; a handsome little guy with a baseball glove on his left hand.

I smiled again, this time at him. I thought about chatting with the boy, asking him if he liked baseball, but I knew that was probably exactly what a salesman would do so I looked back to her.

"I'm a journalist. I'm here from Canada. I'm interested in an event that took place in this area back in 2003. A gathering of right-wing folks for a big conference. I'm told that you became friends with a young man, a university student who was here to study that event, as well as a murder that happened around the same time. I'd like to talk to that young man, see if he can maybe shed a little light on some of the areas of the investigation we're struggling with."

"I don't think I —"

I held up my hands. "Listen, Becky, I don't blame you for wanting to shut that door. I'm a stranger to you. I get that. And I'm not asking you to let me come inside. We could talk out here in the yard, or —" I looked again at the boy I guessed was her son — "I noticed an ice cream place on Main Street. I'd be happy to buy both of you an ice cream and we could talk in a place where there are lots of people around. I promise I won't take any more of your time than it takes for your son to eat his ice cream."

I heard a small voice say, "Mom," and I noticed a tug or two at Mom's T-shirt.

"I'm just waiting for a call from my mom in Sacramento." Becky glanced at her watch. "I … we could meet you at Lickety Splits in about twenty minutes."

It was more like half an hour, but the wait was worth it. Even if Becky Hicks had refused to talk to me, the ice cream was as good as ice cream gets.

As we sat outside on the patio, Becky worked something called Moose Moss, which she assured me was a mint flavour, and Bart, who I learned would be six in two months, was enthusiastically licking away at his Cookie Dough, getting most, though not all of it, in his mouth. I'd opted for Huckleberry, and for a few minutes our voices were on mute as we focused on our ice cream.

A couple of kids about Bart's age arrived with their moms and set up not far from us. Bart knew them and asked if he could go sit with them. Becky nodded, then turned to me.

"Tell me again why you want to know about Shane — he's the young man I was … friends with."

I explained in a little more detail my journalistic interest in the Right to Be Proud, Proud to Be Right event. I told her about Larmer and what appeared a well-orchestrated attempt to frame him for a murder he didn't commit. I didn't go into the conspiracy to kill right-wing media types because I didn't want to clutter the conversation, and I knew that to keep my promise about wrapping up before the Cookie Dough was gone meant that I needed to keep my explanation to a minimum.

"Both Mr. Larmer and the murder victim were at that gathering," I finished. "I was hoping that Shane might have learned something during his time here that might help us."

"He didn't tell me very much. Just that he was working on a school project for one of his classes and that conference you were talking about — I can never remember the name — was part of what he was studying."

"What school was he attending?"

"The University of Wyoming. It's in Laramie. I've never been there."

"And what was he taking?"

"Criminal Studies or something like that. I can't remember the exact name. Sorry."

"And what was Shane's last name?"

"Kent. Shane Kent."

"And is he Bart's dad?" Before she could answer I held up a hand and shook my head. "I'm really sorry. That was thoughtless and rude and it's none of my business."

She looked over at her son, who was now exchanging licks of the various ice-cream selections with his two friends. It looked like the object of the exercise was to get as much of the ice cream on your face and T-shirt as possible. If it was a competition I would have given Bart the early lead.

She nodded and a tear appeared at the corner of one eye.

"Have you seen him since that time?"

She shook her head. "He left when I told him I was pregnant."

"Have you heard from him?"

"Every once in a while he sends me some money. It just comes in the mail — nothing with it, no note, no return address. And I really believed he was *the guy*, you know? But after so long I thought he really didn't want to see me ever again." She stopped and both eyes now glistened.

"Thought?" I said. "You don't still think that?"

She shook her head and dabbed a tissue to her eyes. "He phoned a couple of weeks ago."

I didn't say anything, gave her time to say more.

"He said he wondered if we might get back together."

"Did he say where he was?"

She shook her head again. "Uh-uh. And the number didn't come up on my phone."

"What else did he say, Becky?"

"Just that he wanted to see me and maybe we could talk about a life together. And that he would call again in the next few weeks."

"And has he?

"Not yet," she whispered. "Not yet."

"I want to thank you for talking to me, Becky. And if … when Shane comes to see you, if you could give him this —" I handed her a business card — "I'd really appreciate it if he could give me a call."

She took the card as I rose and waved to Bart, who was near the bottom of his cone. I hadn't lied about the time it would take and for some reason I felt good about that.

Becky Hicks was a nice woman, and though I didn't know Shane Kent other than as a guy who'd ditched a pregnant girlfriend, I hoped things would work out for them. And I hoped he'd call me.

I didn't really have an awful lot more to do in Buffalo or the surrounding area, but it was getting late in the afternoon and I was operating on minimum sleep. I decided to put off my drive to Laramie until the next morning, checked into the Occidental Hotel and, after a brief stop at the Jim Gatchell Memorial Museum, headed out for a drive around the area.

It was beautiful country with the Bighorn Mountains off to the west and plenty of woodland between the town and those mountains. I'd asked a volunteer at the museum about the Wagon Box Fight. A small, frail man, he had white hair that provided a stark contrast to one of the reddest faces I'd ever seen. He'd told me his name was Addison Belt and that he was eighty-four years old. He'd seemed very knowledgeable and happy to share that knowledge with anyone who would listen. I'd listened long enough to get a fairly thorough history of the battle. Mr. Belt also knew about the discovery of John Bones and had given me a fairly detailed set of directions to that site, which he figured was about three miles from the battlefield.

Darkness was starting to settle in as the winding, narrow road took me farther into the deeper woods to the west, the sun breaking through the trees only intermittently. I got to the area described by Addison Belt and parked in a small clearing just off the road. I sat in the car for a time looking around the area, trying to imagine some kind of impromptu encampment popping up, then disappearing.

I stepped out of the car and slowly made my way down a meandering path.

I wasn't sure why I was here. Perhaps for the same reason I wanted to get close to the place where Faith Unruh had lost her life — a desire to *feel* the place, to sense what it had been like to be here during the heady Right to Be Proud, Proud to Be Right days and nights. If indeed this was the right place.

But standing there looking at the woods and clearings and paths around and through them, I was certain that this was where the conference had taken place. I walked slowly, venturing off the path a couple of times to poke around areas that looked like good spots for campers to pitch their tents. I knew that there was virtually no chance of my stumbling across something that related to the camp that had been somewhere in the area almost a dozen years before — the knife that had killed Mr. Bones stuck in a tree, a business card with "I'm the murderer" scrawled on the back of it. But I didn't feel I was wasting my time.

Looking around, I was able to get some sense of this place in another time. I stepped through some denser undergrowth into another clearing, larger than the one where I'd left the car. Even in the diminishing light I could see that some of this clearing was man-made — trees cut down and just beginning their re-growth, long grass covering what had once been treed areas. I walked around it, kicking at loose, broken limbs and scuffing dirt-grass lumps here and there. And thinking about political fanatics. Could they kill? *Would* they kill?

The darkness was settling in and I started working my way toward the path that would take me to back to the car. That's when I heard it. Breaking twigs underfoot, branches whipping and snapping against something approaching.

I stopped to listen, my heart beating out its terror-rhythm in my chest. I saw the light next, bobbing toward me. Not some*thing* then. Some*one*. I thought of Jill's words. Whoever had killed four people was still out there.

Out *here?*

He emerged from the deepening shadows, saw me, and stopped. It was Jud Crombeen and he was carrying a rifle. Loosely and not pointed exactly at me, but that was of little comfort. I tried to read his face, but couldn't.

We stood facing each other for a few seconds before he spoke.

"I guessed you might do this," he said. He waved an arm to indicate the woods around us.

Guessed, or followed me here?

"I wanted to see it for myself," I said, "although I'm not sure I'm anywhere near where the camp was. Or where Mr. Bones was found."

Hoping to let him think that I hadn't uncovered any secrets.

He looked around for a few seconds, then shrugged. "Close enough, I guess."

I wasn't sure what that meant. He saw me looking at the rifle.

"If I was here to shoot your ass, you wouldn't have heard me coming, or seen me. There are animals out here. I figured a city boy might not think about that. Bears — a grizzly would be bad, especially a sow with cubs. But it's cats you have to worry about. This area's got lots of them. Cougars. You wouldn't know one was tracking you until it had you."

He moved closer and I saw that he had something in his other hand — a six-pack of beer.

"We better head back to the vehicles before it gets any darker. Even with the flashlight it's hard to get through the denser stuff. Easy to trip and fall — break something."

He turned and started back up the path. He didn't look behind to see if I was following. I decided an ex-sheriff with a 30-30 or something like it and a box of beer was more appealing than a cougar or mama grizzly and fell in behind him.

Neither of us said anything until we were back to the clearing where I'd left the rental car. A white SUV was parked next to my car. Crombeen stopped once we were clear of the path and in this second clearing. He pointed to a fallen log that would work as a place to sit. He leaned the rifle against the log, sat, pulled two Moose Drool out of the box, and handed me one.

"I would have pegged you for a Budweiser man," I said as I sat and twisted the top off the bottle.

"Was for years." He smiled. "Took to drinking these dark ales a couple of years ago."

The night was pleasantly cool. He shut off the flashlight and we sat in the growing darkness, drinking. For a while neither of us spoke. I had the weird thought that if he was planning to kill me, at least I'd go out in fairly pleasing circumstances.

He glanced at me, then looked straight ahead.

"I think the kid figured it out."

"What?" I said.

"That kid from the University of Wyoming."

"Shane Kent?"

"That's the name." He nodded. "I spent the drive out here trying to remember his name. Anyway, I was bullshitting you when I said he got nothing. I think he figured out who John Bones was. And maybe who killed him. Of course he never told me that, but you been around as long as I have, you get so you can read people."

"How do you think he figured it out?"

Crombeen shrugged. "Maybe something in forensics he learned at school that I don't know about, or maybe he had an idea before he got here and found out just enough to confirm it. I don't know. But I'm ninety-five percent certain that he had at least some of it worked out."

"Why didn't you tell me that before?"

"Think about it. I'm a cop. I was a cop all my working life. I worked my ass off on John Bones and I got nothing. Less than nothing. And some book-learned, barely-off-the-tit kid shows up and comes up with the answer. Yeah, that's something I want the world to know."

"But there's never been an arrest — or even a positive ID of the remains. If Shane had some answers, wouldn't he have shared them with someone?"

Crombeen pulled two more beers out of the box and we each took a couple of pulls before he answered. "I've thought about that, too. A lot. And I don't know. Seems to me he'd be letting the world know what he knew, just like you said. Ought to at least get him a damn good mark in whatever class it was he was taking."

I nodded. "That's what I would've thought."

The retired sheriff looked at me. "But what did you say? Four people dead. Someone had to kill them. Maybe it was him. Maybe he did it for revenge. Out here we call that vigilante justice."

"But he'd have to have had a good reason for wanting revenge."

"Like maybe some real personal stake in it," Crombeen said.

"Yeah … like that," I agreed. "Can you remember Shane Kent well enough to describe him?"

"Yeah, I damn sure can."

And he did.

NINETEEN

Judith Eng looked at me over the top of half glasses, which were the only aspect of her appearance that bespoke formal.

She'd given every indication that she was both friendly and helpful, which was counter to my own experience with people in registrar's offices during my academic years. The administration building of the University of Wyoming was part of an attractive campus that sits 7,200 feet above sea level on the Laramie Plain, between the Laramie Range and Snowy Range Mountains. (I'd learned that earlier that morning while reading a brochure and sampling coffee and a pastry at the Night Heron Books and Coffeehouse.) I'd been waiting outside the registrar's office when it opened and been directed to Ms. Eng. I'd spent the past fifteen minutes pleading my case for a look at the records of a former student.

"A murder?" She looked disbelieving, which caused me to rethink my strategy of laying my cards on the table. Maybe I should have lied.

"I'm afraid so, ma'am." I hoped that didn't sound like a bad Joe Friday impersonation.

"And you think a former student might be somehow involved."

"I can't say that for sure, Ms. Eng, and even if he was it may have been strictly on the periphery. In fact, all I know is that he conducted his own investigation into a murder that took place near Buffalo. It was ostensibly for a class he was taking here — I'm guessing as part of your criminal studies program."

"We call it Criminal Justice."

"Right," I said. "So what I'm hoping to learn is whether the school might have an address, perhaps a photo of Shane Kent."

"A murder near Buffalo? Is that a different murder? You mentioned a Mr. Hugg was killed up in Canada."

"Yes, ma'am, two separate but possibly connected murders."

"Nevertheless, the school has strict privacy regulations. We don't divulge details about current or former students except in exceptional circumstances." She wasn't unpleasant about it, but firm. This was someone who knew her job and intended to do it.

"Would the investigation of four murders be exceptional enough?"

"You didn't say anything about four murders. You've only mentioned two."

"We think the Buffalo killing may have been part of a string of murders, Ms. Eng." I was trying to keep it simple. Wasn't sure I was succeeding.

She sat straight-backed now, her lips pressed tightly together, the friendliness not gone but definitely reduced. "But you said this student may not be involved at all, except on the periphery." She seemed happy to repeat my word, which I now realized may have been a bad choice on my part.

"Or he may have been. That's what we need to know. I believe Shane Kent was here for the 2007–08 academic year and maybe more. Could you at least confirm that for me?"

She adjusted the half glasses and swivelled to face her computer. I wasn't sure if she'd just dismissed me or was checking records. I decided to wait it out. After a couple of minutes she swivelled back to me.

"Well, that's that, then," she said.

"That's what, Ms. Eng?"

"Shane Kent was never a student at this school." She looked over her shoulder at her computer. "Landon Kent graduated from UW in 1969. Rory Kent in 1977. And Alicia Kent is a sophomore here now. There have been no other Kents enrolled here."

I stared at her for a long time. That wasn't what I'd expected to hear.

She appeared to sense my discomfort. "Perhaps there's an unusual spelling of the name that I could check?"

I shook my head. "I don't think so."

"I'm sorry I couldn't have been more help."

"There is one more thing," I said. "Do you have a list of people who have taken summer courses here?"

"Of course. Every registered student is listed."

"The summer of 2011. A student named Shawn Beamer. Took a class in screenwriting. I wonder if you could —"

"No, he didn't." She smiled.

"I'm sorry?" I said, not understanding.

"UW does not offer screenwriting, not even as a summer class. We have a creative writing program, but writing for film and television is not part of our offering. It looks like you've been misinformed about both these students."

I stood up. "Thank you, Ms. Eng. I won't take any more of your time. I wonder, though, if you could tell me in what building I'd find the criminal justice program."

She told me and offered directions, as well, not unhappy, I surmised, to be seeing the back of me.

I crossed the campus and found the building. I wasn't sure what I was looking for — maybe a faculty member who might remember a student who conducted research for a class during the summer of 2008.

I wandered the halls for a few minutes, feeling more and more like there was something going on, something I didn't understand … yet. Shawn Beamer had lied about what, if anything, he'd taken, at the University of Wyoming during the summer of 2011. Shane Kent had lied too. Two people, two big lies. There had to be a connection.

I saw a pop machine against a wall on the opposite side of an open common area and strode over, wishing the damn thing also dispensed rye. I settled for a Diet Coke and took a couple of burning gulps. Then I noticed the grad pictures on the wall. I thought, *What the hell. I'll look for Shane Kent's name and picture.* Maybe Ms. Eng had somehow missed it. I started with the 2008 grad group and went as far as 2011. No Shane Kent. Ms. Eng had not been mistaken.

And had there been a larger group of grads I might not have seen it. A couple of rows above the *K*'s, where no picture of Shane Kent existed, there was a photo of someone I recognized.

Shawn Beamer, social media handler at RIGHT TALK 700, had graduated from the University of Wyoming in Criminal Justice in 2011.

I was a little late getting to the terminal at the Cheyenne airport and arrived at my gate just a few minutes before my flight was to board. I called Jill. Kyla answered with a perky "Hi!"

"Hey, kiddo, it's the handsomest man you've ever seen."

"Wow, Leonardo DiCaprio, how you doin'?"

"Jeez, you really know how to hurt a guy, you know?"

She laughed and I could hear her mother in the background calling, "Go, Kyla."

"Do I have any friends there at all?"

"Well, you have two women who love you," Kyla told me. "Does that work for you?"

"You have no idea how much that works for me," I told her. "Do you think I could speak to your mom, or is she holding out for Leonardo?"

"I'll check."

I could hear her handing the phone off with giggling accompaniment.

"Hi, babe." Jill's voice still had an effect on me, roughly akin to looking out at the ocean and the peace those moments brought me.

"I think it's time we talked about reform school for the kid," I said.

"Sore loser." I could hear the laughter in her voice — some of it I guessed might have been relief. I knew she'd been worried, though she'd tried to cover it up when I'd stopped by to let her know I was heading for Wyoming. "Tell me you're on your way back to me."

"We're boarding in a few minutes."

"How about a welcome-back barbecue?"

"Wow, this is forty-eight hours — what do I get if I stay away a week?"

"Replaced," she told me. "We'll see you soon."

My next call was to Cobb.

"Morning," he said. "How's it going in cowboy land?"

"Interesting, to say the least. We're boarding right now, but there's something I think you might want to do," I said.

"Shoot."

"Jud Crombeen checked missing persons when he was investigating John Bones's case. But I doubt if he checked Canadians. I think we need to look at missing persons from 2003."

"Anybody in particular?"

"Yeah, you might want to start with the last name 'Beamer.'"

I heard Cobb's sharp intake of breath. "That's Beamer as in …?"

"Yeah, as in Shawn. Don't get excited just yet. It's just a guess. I'll tell you the rest when I see you."

"Beamer. On it," he said. "Can we meet as soon as you're back here?"

"I arrive at two-twenty, and yes, we can meet, but only if you're buying."

"Okay, there's a pub in Airdrie, the Toad and Turtle, probably fifteen minutes from the terminal. I'll be there. And I won't be buying, but I think your pal Buckley-Rand Larmer could be persuaded to take care of it."

"Even better," I said.

He gave me the directions to the pub and we rang off just as the first call for boarding was made. I was asleep before the flight crew had completed the safety demonstration.

Halfway through our fish and chips, Cobb set his fork down, took a long swallow of Rolling Rock, and sat back in his chair. I'd been doing all the talking up to that point.

"Okay," he said. "So we've got Shawn Beamer getting his degree in Criminal Justice, which no doubt includes forensics. He takes one of his summers and goes off to Wyoming on a research trip using the name Shane Kent. While there, he investigates the discovery of unidentified human remains — John Bones, as he came to be known. The only identifying item on Mr. Bones is a poker chip with a number on it."

He looked at me for confirmation of what he'd summarized to that point.

"Uh-huh." I nodded.

"And you think Mr. Bones might have been designated number fifty-three for the Proud event."

"Larmer told us they got poker chips with numbers on them. John Bones had a poker chip with a number on it in his shirt pocket. I'd say that puts him there, yeah."

"Beamer slash Kent, while in Wyoming, is also keenly interested in the Proud event that took place some years earlier in roughly the same area as the Bones remains were later found."

I nodded. "Right."

"Okay, what else have we got?"

I downed a couple of french fries, chased them with beer. "A few months after Beamer's graduation from UW, the killings start: two in the U.S., then a few months later, the Monday shooting in Canada."

"Okay, so the timing works."

I nodded. "I called Humber College and Beamer wasn't lying about that. He started in January 2012, right after the two killings in the States and right before the first attempt on Dennis Monday's life. Then a couple of years later he's employed at the radio station during the time when another of the organizers of the Proud event, Jasper Hugg, is murdered."

"Okay, so we've got opportunity and a timeframe that fits. What we don't have is concrete evidence, nor do we have a motive, unless the kid's old man happens to be a missing person vintage 2003."

"What about travel records?" I said. "What if we can put Shawn Beamer in San Antonio and Fresno at the time of those incidents?"

"That would help, for sure. Let me go to work on that."

We ate in silence for a while. Cobb pointed his fork at me. "You did damn good down there, Adam."

I grinned at him. "I wasn't so sure of that when I saw Jud Crombeen coming through the woods carrying a rifle."

"Yeah, that would have been a little jarring."

"Just a little. Okay, what do you need me to do next?"

"How about you go enjoy a nice barbecue? You've earned it."

The waitress came by and both of us declined dessert. As she was moving away from our table, Cobb's phone rang. He answered, listened for a while, then pulled out his notebook and a pen and started scribbling notes while firing questions at whoever was on the other end of the line.

"How old was the guy …? Height …? And no sign of him …? Okay, thanks for this."

He hung up and looked at me, then read from his notes. "A missing person from August 2003. Thirty-nine years old, six-two, slim build. He worked for the *Halifax Chronicle-Herald*, disappeared after leaving home to attend a conference in the Western U.S. Was never found or heard from again. Married, two kids, a son and a daughter. His name was Derek Beamer." Cobb paused, then added. "Looks like we might have our motive."

"Does that alter our game plan?"

Cobb shook his head. "I work on travel information tonight, see if I can place Shawn Beamer at crime locations at the right times. Tomorrow morning we have a chat with the young man."

Cobb and I parted in the parking lot, but before I got in the Accord, I opened the trunk and dug through Jasper Hugg's planners until I came up with the one for 2003. I trooped back into the pub, and this time over coffee I went through the planner page by page, day by day. On March 14 I found a notation that he had been asked to co-chair the Right to Be Proud, Proud to Be Right conference. No details.

On April 5 he noted that he had accepted the invitation and written in the dates for the event and that it would be happening in Wyoming. A conference call was scheduled for April 13, but the notation didn't indicate who would be participating in the call.

On the day following that call, I found what I was looking for … or at least hoping for. It was cryptic and would have been easy to miss had I not had some idea what I was looking for. It read:

<u>O.C.</u>
Morrissey — Black
Monday — Green
Swales — Blue
Hugg — Pink

"How fucking junior high can you get?" I hadn't realized I'd said it out loud until I looked up and saw an older couple frowning at me over their glasses of wine. I apologized and went back to the day planner.

What I was pretty sure I was looking at was confirmation that the four members of the organizing committee had been Shawn Beamer's targets.

On May 9 Hugg noted that Larmer had agreed to be one of the guest speakers. There were other less important references to the event, but nothing that shed any further light on what had taken place that August in the woodlands near Buffalo, Wyoming.

But if Derek Beamer had been murdered while attending the Proud conference and his son had rightly or wrongly connected the members of the organizing committee to the killing, then motive was no longer in doubt.

I texted Cobb to tell him about the names/colours notation in Hugg's planner. Then I packed it up, drank the last of my second cup of coffee, and headed for the door. I stopped at the bar on the way out and paid the tab of the elderly couple I had offended. I doubted it would make them feel any differently, but it made me feel better.

The ribs Jill had on the barbecue were some of the best I'd ever had. A fifteen-year-old bottle of Barolo was now almost empty and Kyla was laying out the board for a game of Clue.

"You know, of course, that I am a highly skilled crime investigator and that neither of you has the slightest chance of winning," I told them. "Are you sure you wouldn't like to play something else — something that gives everyone an equal opportunity — Snakes and Ladders maybe?"

My speech was met by derisive laughter to which I shrugged a response and fell to examining the clues I had been given. Forty minutes later Kyla informed us that the killer was Miss Scarlet (that bitch) with the candlestick in the conservatory. I had been certain that Colonel Mustard had committed the act in the billiard room with the rope. And I was also pretty sure the kid had cheated.

"Never trust a nine-year-old, that's my motto from here on," I announced.

"This nine-year-old is going to bed," Jill told her.

"Can I read?'

"Have you ever gone to bed and not read?" Jill asked her.

"Guess not." Kyla shrugged, then leaned over to kiss me on the cheek. "I can let you win next time if you want," she loud-whispered.

"Next time it's Snakes and Ladders," I said.

Kyla laughed and skipped down the hall, savouring the victory and the book she would soon be consuming.

I topped up the wineglasses a final time and Jill and I sat close together on the couch enjoying the peaceful silence of each other's presence.

I spoke first. "I'm no expert, but I'd say the young lady looks great … and seems to be doing pretty well."

Jill nodded. "She's gained back some weight and has an appetite again. So, yes, she's doing well. They're adjusting some of her medication, so we'll see how she does after that. The biggest thing is her attitude. She considers Crohn's to be an inconvenience and nothing more. That's all she's going to allow it to be. And that's exactly the right attitude."

"And I think I know exactly where she got it from."

Jill smiled, kissed me for a long time, then lay her head on my shoulder.

"Adam, I don't want us to be one of those couples where the guy keeps things from his partner so she won't worry."

"Fair enough," I said. "How about we start with what happened in Wyoming?"

I told her everything I'd learned, everything I knew about the case, and everything I thought. It took some time.

"I was worried about you," she said.

"I know you were. The truth is, the only time I thought things might get dicey was when I saw a retired cop coming toward me with a rifle in his hand. But it made no sense for him to shoot me unless he was the killer, and I knew he wasn't."

"But you couldn't have known that, not right then. You might have *thought* he wasn't the killer, but you couldn't have been sure — not yet."

"I guess you're right. But logic told me he wasn't the one. Although I will admit I was starting to rethink my logic out there in the woods, miles from anywhere or anyone, and him with a rifle. I was never so glad to see a box of beer in my life."

We laughed and she sat up and took my hand.

"I will never tell you not to do something you feel you have to do. I know there's danger involved with the kind of work Mike does and that there are times when that danger might touch you. And as much as it scares me, I'm okay with it. I just want you to know that."

"I do know that. And it means a lot to me. *You* mean a lot to me."

She stood up, still holding my hand, and we turned out the lights as she led the way down the hall.

The phone rang at 6:13 a.m. Jill reached across me to answer it. Her voice was low and sleepy. "Hello. Hi, Mike. He's right here." She passed me the phone.

"Yeah," I said.

"Sorry for the bad timing, but we're moving now. I got confirmation late last night that Beamer flew into LAX two nights before the explosion that killed Morrissey. He flew out the morning after. I'm still waiting for word on San Antonio, but we've got enough, and I'm worried that if he calls Becky in Buffalo and she tells him someone's trying to find him, he'll blow town before we can move. I've told the two detectives, Landry and Chisholm, everything you told me, or at least most of it. They've got a search warrant and they're meeting me at Beamer's condo. I'm just letting you know in case you want to be there."

"I want to be there." I was already out of bed and headed for the shower.

"Thirty minutes," Cobb said.

I was five minutes late, and I'm guessing Cobb and the cops might have been early.

The two detectives were sitting in an unmarked car a few doors away from the condo. Cobb was leaning against his car and talking on his cellphone as I pulled in behind him.

I got out of the Accord and approached him. He wrapped up his conversation just as I came alongside. He looked at me and shook his head.

"We're too late," he said. "The cops have been inside. He's gone. That was the station manager on the phone. Beamer didn't show up for work yesterday, didn't phone in. I'd say he got word, likely from the girlfriend, that we were getting close. Now the question is, where has he gone?"

I didn't get to offer a theory as the detectives crossed the street and stopped in front of us.

Detective Landry spoke. "Shawn Beamer crossed the border into the U.S. at Coutts just after midnight two nights ago," she told us. "We've got uniforms on their way to do some canvassing of the neighbours, but we won't likely get much. Somebody might have seen him pack up his car and head out. Probably didn't think anything of it. People go on holidays."

The second detective, Chisholm, looked at me. "Any thoughts as to where he might be headed?"

"One maybe," I said. "He has a girlfriend in Buffalo, Wyoming, Becky Hicks. They had a kid together a few years ago. He contacted her not long ago suggesting maybe they should get back together. I'd say there's at least a chance that's where he was headed."

Landry nodded. "We know about her." She pointed at Cobb. "Your friend told us about her."

"Any other ideas?" Chisholm asked.

I shook my head. "I didn't really know Shawn Beamer. I interviewed him once in the context of the Larmer investigation but that's it."

"What about the school he attended down there? Is that a likely destination?"

I thought about that. "A possible destination maybe. A *likely* one, I don't know. Could have someone in Laramie he could stay with. I just don't know."

Landry looked at Chisholm, then nodded at Cobb and me and turned away. Abruptly she turned back to me.

"If you'd called us from Wyoming when you first learned of this stuff, we might have got him."

I bristled at that and fought to keep my temper. "I didn't have definitive information until after I got back here and we found out that Beamer's father might have been John Bones. And we didn't have confirmation about Beamer's being in California at the time of the radio station bombing until late last night."

"Your attitude's bullshit, Detective, and you know it." Cobb's voice was low and blizzard-cold. "I figured you for better than that, and if you're not you should be. We gave you what we had when we had it and when it wasn't just speculation, which I was a cop long enough to know is not your favourite thing."

Landry's eyes narrowed and she opened her mouth, but closed it again. She looked at Cobb, then at me. Several seconds that felt like minutes passed before she spoke again.

"You're right," she said to Cobb. "I was out of line. Frustrated at being late for the party. Thanks for your help." She turned to me. "Both of you." She reached into a pocket and pulled out a business card. "In case you ever need to get hold of us."

I took the card and nodded. "Any chance we could get inside his place for a look around?"

Landry shook her head "We've got the forensics techies on their way. We need to go over every inch of the place. Can't risk having you contaminate potential evidence."

"I know we can't touch anything, but we might see something that could trigger a thought that might help."

Cobb said, "It's not a bad idea, Detective. He's the only one of us who has actually met Beamer. He might spot something that could prove useful."

Landry looked at her partner, thought about it. "You go with them," she said, nodding in Chisholm's direction. "Fifteen minutes. You touch anything or go anywhere Detective Chisholm tells you not to go, and he has my permission to throw you out of the place. And I don't mean that in the metaphorical sense."

Chisholm looked pleased at the possibility. He led the way to the building's front door, which was propped open, and up the stairs to Beamer's second-floor condo. There was already one band of police tape across the front door. Chisholm unlocked it, ducked under the tape, and stepped inside. He turned to us and nodded, then watched as we moved inside, me first, then Cobb.

I took three or four steps into the apartment, then looked at Chisholm to make sure I was okay to do that.

"That's far enough, he said.

I nodded and looked around. I wasn't sure this would do much good. I doubted Chisholm would let us farther into the apartment, so all we could see was what was right in front of us. We were in the living room, which I guessed was twice the size of mine. It was sparsely furnished but neat, lacking the clutter that defined my own living space. A worn but serviceable couch, a recliner, coffee table, a bookcase along the wall to the left, a hallway that I guessed led to a bedroom, also to the left. The room morphed into an adjoining kitchen to the right.

"Was this place furnished or does this stuff belong to him?" I directed the question to Chisholm.

"Landlord says it was furnished, but some of the stuff belonged to Beamer."

I nodded, looked around the room again. Nothing jumped out at me and I knew Chisholm was hoping for just that — the "not-for-real-investigators" finding nothing.

"Can I get a little closer to the bookcase?"

"Nope."

I leaned forward and willed my eyes to read the titles on the three shelves. The majority were hardcover — thrillers, some non-fiction, mostly political history and biographies.

I peered at the lower shelves, then looked over my shoulder at Cobb. "Can you see that book, middle shelf, third title from the right?"

Cobb leaned forward, Chisholm watching him like an owl watches a field mouse. I pointed at the worn hardcover, the dust cover missing, and read the title aloud: *Nature's Poisons.*

"Any chance we can get a look at that, Detective?" I said over my shoulder.

"Stay right where you are," was the reply, but when I turned to argue, I saw that Chisholm was gloving up and moving toward the bookcase.

He took it from the shelf and carefully set it on the coffee table. "What do you want to see?"

"Is there a table of contents?"

He flipped a few pages. "Yeah, right here."

He held it up and I leaned forward again to look, then read aloud: "'Chapter seven, page 113.' Try that." The chapter was titled "Bitter Homes and Gardens — Home-Grown Poison."

Chisholm finally found the page, the gloves making the task difficult. He seemed interested now and held the book closer for me to see.

"Can you turn the page?"

He did, then again. On page 117 someone had high-lighted a portion of text in yellow. I could see that the high-lighted section focused on the plant monkshood from the *Aconitum* species. It was essentially a step-by-step how-to for extracting the poisonous part of the plant, including the dosage required for exterminating large animals. It even noted that the extract would be tasteless. Next to that section of the text someone had written "Bingo!"

Chisholm moved the book so that he could see what it was we were looking at. I straightened and stepped back.

I looked at Cobb. "Jasmine Swales," I said.

As Chisholm carefully closed the book and placed it in an evidence bag, Cobb said, "Bingo."

TWENTY

Cobb called me three days later. The Stampede had wrapped up for another year and I'd banged out a piece for *Canadian Cowboy Country* magazine. I was at my computer working on the sequel to *The Spoofaloof Rally.* Normally people don't write sequels to books that sell a couple of hundred copies — most to family and friends. But I'd received a call from my Toronto-based publisher the day after we discovered that Shawn Beamer had fled the country.

The call was to inform me that they'd pitched the book at a major book fair in the U.S., and Barnes and Noble had placed an order that had taken *Spoof* from backlist purgatory to a full-page ad in the publisher's next catalogue. And they wanted to talk sequel. Suddenly I was a writer.

"We need to have coffee," Cobb said. And his voice told me that this wasn't so much an invitation as it was a command.

A half-hour later we were sitting at the Starbucks in Bridgeland. Cobb's suggestion. Neither of us was drinking the coffee that sat in front of us.

"Beamer's dead," Cobb said.

I took a couple of breaths while I digested that.

"Wow," I said.

Cobb nodded. "Landry called me this morning. State cops caught up with him just outside Buffalo. He had a gun with him and they shot him. He died instantly. The gun he was holding was a Smith and Wesson 380. It wasn't loaded."

I nodded. "Just outside Buffalo," I repeated. "Not in town. Not at Becky's house?"

Cobb shook his head. "Sounds like there was something of a car chase. He led them to this place. Got out of his car and was waiting for them.'

"With an empty gun in his hand."

"Yeah."

"Pretty much guaranteeing that he would be killed."

"That's how it looks." Cobb took his first sip of coffee. "Landry talked to your friend, the retired sheriff."

"Jud Crombeen?"

"Yeah, he said Beamer died at almost the same spot as John Bones's remains were found."

"His dad."

"Yeah."

I looked around the place. People reading the paper, texting, talking to one another. Probably not many talking about a killer dying in the Wyoming woodlands.

"There's a lot about this I don't understand," I said.

"And a lot we'll never know. Only guy who might have told us is dead."

We drank our coffee for a while, our thoughts far away.

"It had to be revenge for what happened to his dad. It's the only thing that makes sense."

"It's a theory all right." Cobb rubbed a hand over an unshaven jaw. "Hard to say for sure, but I can give you what I think."

"I'd like to hear it."

"I think the kid learned or figured out somehow that his father died in Buffalo while attending the Proud to be Right conference. I don't know how, especially with all the secrecy that surrounded the thing. But if the kid's dad was a journalist, maybe he wasn't part of the cloak-and-dagger stuff. I suspect he found out something he shouldn't have and got himself offed by someone attending the event — maybe one of the organizers. Or more than one.

"Then the kid who by then wasn't a kid anymore read or heard about the discovery of John Bones, and that got him thinking. At some point he made it his life mission to find out what happened to his dad. He even went to school to study forensics to help him with his own personal investigation. He found out enough or at least suspected enough that he narrowed it down to four people. He either discovered that all four were involved or he knew it was one of the four but didn't know which one."

"So he decided to kill them all."

Cobb shrugged. "Like I said, it's a theory."

"But how was he able to figure it out when the cops couldn't?"

"I've thought a lot about that. Two things. First of all, he knew something the cops didn't. He knew who the victim was. And second, it was an obsession. He spent years working it out. Crombeen told you the state cops gave it a half-hearted effort and the feds even less. Crombeen himself tried, maybe even tried hard, but again, he was missing the most important starting piece — the ID of the victim."

"Smart kid." I was having trouble with Cobb's explanation and he could tell.

"Hell, you worked the thing out — I have no doubt the kid either figured it out or thought he had with enough certainty that he could kill four people."

"But we don't know for sure that one or more than one of the conference organizers actually killed Derek Beamer."

"No, we don't and probably never will. What we do know is that Shawn Beamer believed it."

"Yeah," I agreed.

"There might have been something his dad communicated home while he was at the conference — maybe a call to his wife that there was some weird stuff going on or that he was being watched or stalked, and eventually maybe Shawn heard about that from his mother. We just don't know and, like I said, we probably never will."

"There's something else I haven't been able to reconcile in my mind. Shawn Beamer was bent on killing the people he held responsible for his father's death; I get that. And framing Larmer for Hugg's murder, that's just good business. Ultimately you want to get away with the crimes you've committed, so you point the cops to a guy you think is despicable and whom society would be better off without. I get that, too."

Cobb nodded.

"But what about the threats to Larmer before Hugg was killed? What was that about?"

"Good question." Cobb nodded again. "I've thought about that, too. And like you, I'm puzzled. Unless he was trying to set up a motive for Larmer to have killed Hugg. And it worked, sort of. The cops theorized that Larmer found out about the threats and that was part of why he killed Hugg."

"It just seems odd to me. He didn't really need it. The bloodstains in the car provided the physical evidence the cops needed."

"Can't argue that. If this was a TV cop show there'd be a scene where the killer is holding off the cops — or two guys like us — at gunpoint, but before pulling the trigger explains the whole case to them and the TV audience. This isn't TV. I've lost track of the cases that we supposedly solved but had all kinds of unanswered questions at the end. It's bloody frustrating. There's nothing I want more than to talk to Shawn Beamer, but obviously that isn't going to happen."

"I should have had you follow up on my interview with him. That was my screw-up."

Cobb shook his head. "You told me you had some reservations about the kid and it was me who didn't follow up. I would have eventually, but we ran out of time. Sitting here and coming up with all the things we could have and should have done is counterproductive. Our job was to prove our client hadn't killed Jasper Hugg. We did that. End of story."

Of course, it wasn't the end of the story. I knew that, and I was sure Mike Cobb did, too. Both of us would second-guess ourselves for a long time.

"What about Larmer? Guess he's pretty relieved."

"I'm meeting up with him and Shulsky at a news conference later today."

"Celebration time."

"For them maybe. For me — and you — it's payday." He patted the breast pocket of his blazer. "Invoice is right here."

"So he's been released from custody?"

"You'll see it on the news tonight. The Crown dropped the charges and he was released a couple of hours ago."

"News conference," I repeated.

Cobb smiled. "Yeah, it's set for three o'clock this afternoon. Riverfront Stage at Prince's Island."

"That sounds more like a public event than a news conference. I'm guessing Larmer Nation will be out in force."

"And I'm guessing you're right. You going to be among the adoring throngs?"

I started to shake my head but stopped. "Not sure," I said. "Might be an interesting, albeit depressing, way to spend part of an afternoon." I glanced outside. "He's got the perfect day for it. And you can never hear too many rants against the bumbling local constabulary and the corrupt establishment, both of which are trying to quash the voice of the one man who stands up for the little guy."

"Sounds like you could have written his speech."

I laughed, but really I wasn't finding the whole thing all that funny. Now that we had done what we'd set out to do and proved Larmer innocent of the murder, my loathe metre was rising to its maximum once again.

Cobb must've been reading my mind. "Even though he was my client and even though I'm glad we were able to prove his innocence, I will admit the man is a pompous prick. Wouldn't be the worst thing if someone could take him down a peg or two."

"Yeah, that would be nice," I said.

Cobb left for the pre–news conference meeting with Larmer and Shulsky. I placed a call to Martin Gathers at the *Omaha World-Herald*, gave him the story, then stayed on at the Starbucks reading the *Calgary Herald* and taking in more caffeine. I soon tired of that and settled for staring out the window watching people coming and going. I watched them park their cars along the narrow boulevard just metres from where I was sitting.

An eclectic bunch, Starbucks patrons. There were SUVs, compacts, sporty little cars, a couple of pickup trucks, and a handful of the dull, tan-coloured station wagons favoured by hockey parents and the terminally boring. And one Lincoln Navigator. I wondered how similar to Larmer's Navigator this one was. I lingered on that thought.

And there it was at last. The answer to that niggling, annoying feeling that there was something I'd missed. It was right there.

I set my coffee down and raced outside, leaving the other patrons wondering if I was suddenly in a huge hurry for a forgotten appointment, or if I was just weird.

Unlocking the door of the Accord, I reached in and grabbed the file folder containing all my notes and hurried back into the Starbucks, smiling reassuringly at my fellow caffeine consumers as I returned to my seat.

I opened the file folder, skipped past all my handwritten notes and transcriptions of interviews and conversations to the one piece of paper I hadn't really looked at since the first time I'd seen it. It was the list Shawn Beamer had provided for me of the cars driven by RIGHT TALK 700 employees. I remember being grateful at the time for the speedy and thorough job he'd done in putting together the list, grateful because I'd wanted to know if anyone drove a blue Jetta, yet unaware that there was something else on the list, something potentially significant. Something that I had been unaware of until now.

I scanned the page and came to what mattered — the note on Larmer's Lincoln Navigator. The colour, gold, was noted, as was the licence number.

And that's what was wrong. There was no way Beamer could have learned the licence number as the vehicle was already in the police impound lot when I asked him to put the list of employee vehicles together. And Larmer was in the remand centre — incommunicado — so Beamer couldn't have asked him.

While it could be argued that Beamer would have seen the vehicle in a staff parking area and might have recalled the licence number from those occasions, it seemed unlikely. Who remembers the licence numbers of vehicles belonging to colleagues or even friends? Next to nobody. I couldn't recall the licence number on Cobb's Jeep or even Jill's Dodge Caravan, and I'd been a passenger in both countless times.

But what if Beamer had driven Larmer's vehicle the morning of Hugg's murder? He'd have taken it first to the gym, then to the station where he'd stabbed Hugg to death, then back to the gym where he'd cleaned up himself before returning the Navigator to Larmer's garage. He'd have had to park on the street at the gym and at the station, which meant he'd have had to put the licence number into the parking ticket dispensers. Not that any of it mattered now. But perhaps if I'd noticed that before …

I took some comfort from the fact that Beamer hadn't committed any further crimes in the time since I'd completely missed this potentially important piece of evidence. Would it have made a difference to the final outcome? Maybe. It might have led to his arrest rather than his flight and eventual death. But that was hypothetical and not something I could do anything about.

I scanned down the page and noted again the rides of some of the other RIGHT TALK 700 staff, mostly to get my mind off my screw-up. I even managed a smile as I noted again the coma-inducing Bernie McCready's station wagon. "Canary yellow," Shawn Beamer had jotted in the margin.

Bernie, you risk-taking son of a bitch. I looked up and was relieved that nobody was looking at me. Apparently that thought was just that — not something inadvertently verbalized, prompting the stares and glares of other patrons.

I packed up my file folder and decided it was time to take to the streets, not because I had anything to do, but I knew if I didn't move soon, I'd be in danger of full-body atrophy.

I surprised myself by deciding I'd actually take in the Larmer news conference. It would be painful, I knew, but it might be interesting to see the man at work. And to see if any of the media would actually ask tough questions or if Larmer would answer them. I suspected neither would happen and the event would be Larmer doing his rock-star thing without the music.

I'd left it a bit late, but didn't have far to go, so I figured I'd be there for most, if not all, of the fun. I wheeled the Accord through the downtown streets to Eau Clair Market, where I figured I could park and make the short walk to Prince's Island and the Riverfront Stage, home to the Calgary Folk Festival, which would be taking place in just a couple of weeks.

I was almost wrong about the parking. Most of the parking areas in and around the mall proper were jammed.

I cruised for a few minutes and got lucky; a Chrysler 300 piloted by a white-haired gentleman in a suit that had to be hot on a day that I was sure would approach 30-plus degrees eased out of a spot just as I was about to run through most of my profanity vocabulary one more time.

I parked and glanced at my watch — about ten minutes to show time. I climbed out of the Accord, pulled off a sweater I wouldn't need, tossed it in the back seat, and locked the car. I hesitated momentarily, wondering if I really needed to do this to myself, finally deciding that I'd at least check out the setup and decide once I was closer to the stage whether to stay or leave.

I hadn't walked far when I got a surprise, the first of several. A canary-yellow Ford Focus occupied a parking spot not far from mine. Bernie McCready had come to listen to the man he so admired. As I walked past McCready's car, I decided it wasn't that big a surprise, after all. This was a big day for RIGHT TALK 700 and Bernie clearly wanted to be a part of it. I wondered how many more of the station's staff would be on hand.

I was wrong about a few other things, too. The music, for instance. I had underestimated Larmer's ability to mount a medium-scale musical extravaganza on a few hours' notice. As I made my way across the pedestrian bridge onto the island, I could hear — and feel — the high-volume, high-energy blast of one of Calgary's better bands, the Dudes, presumably getting the crowd pumped up for what was to come.

The crowd. Another miscalculation on my part. As I swung left upon entering the park area and looked toward the stage, I stopped dead. A sea of people were dancing, singing, yelling, and drinking beer — all of them between me and the stage I'd hoped to get close to, at least close enough to take in Larmer's performance. That possibility suddenly was in doubt.

With my first glance at the crowd I set the demographic at late teens, early twenties, and I marvelled again at Larmer's appeal to young people — I would have thought that they either didn't know or didn't care about politics. And I wondered about Larmer's audience. Surely this youthful throng wasn't representative of the RIGHT TALK 700 listeners. But it was, I guessed, the group that could be the most quickly mobilized for the show that Larmer was producing. The man was, in addition to being the smoothest orator I had ever met, a brilliant marketer and PR man.

Again I considered turning away, getting back in my car, and finding a quiet lounge somewhere.

But the masochistic side of my psyche won out. Besides, if Bernie McCready could do this, surely I could, too. I began trying to work my way through the bobbing, weaving throng, but after several dirty looks and a couple of shoves, decided to abandon that plan. Instead I decided I'd see if I could ease my way around the crowd and get closer to the stage by following the bank of the Bow River where it looked like there were fewer people.

That worked much better than the barge-through-the-throng approach. The cottonwoods and spruce that bordered the park offered a bit of an escape from the crowd, which appeared to be growing in number. The Canada geese that lived and shit in the park had taken to the edges, clearly thinking, as I did, that there lay the only refuge.

The Dudes wrapped up "American Girl," a single I recalled and liked from a couple of years before. An emcee, big voice, big hair, came to the microphone.

"Hey, how about Dan Vacon and the amazing Calgary band the Dudes!"

The crowd roared for a long time, finally easing off just enough for the emcee's follow-up announcement that there was time for just one or two more songs before "The Man" would be coming out onto the stage, an announcement that was greeted by the kind of cheer that a Flames overtime winner might produce.

I worked my way farther west, ending up even with the stage but still a fair distance away. Curiosity took me to the area behind the stage. I figured Larmer would be camped out in one of the backstage dressing rooms, but I also thought it would be interesting to see who was out back. I might even catch a glimpse of Cobb.

In fact, Buckley-Rand Larmer *was* out there, surrounded by several women, all of them gorgeous, all of them adoring, all of them captivated, as well as a couple of guys who looked like they were helping with the production. What I didn't see was a lot of security. With Shawn Beamer dead, Larmer must have felt that the threat, at least this threat, was over. There would be, I was sure, more in the future as Larmer destroyed more reputations, careers, lives.

I didn't see Cobb and wondered if he had already been relieved of his duties as bodyguard or if Larmer had kept him on the payroll until after today's return to the public eye. Just in case. With the kids and the beer, I could see a few getting overexuberant and maybe out of hand. If I were Larmer, I'd have kept Cobb around at least for today.

I eased my way closer to the stage. The youthful audience obviously liked to be directly in front of the stage, not off to the side. From where I stood, I could survey most of the crowd. The Dudes announced their last tune, appropriately titled "Do the Right Thing."

As I scanned the audience, I noticed Bernie McCready, dead-centre and a short rock throw from the front of the stage, looking slightly out of place in a shirt and tie, sleeves rolled up, jacket draped over his arm. He seemed oblivious to those around him — kids gyrating, singing along, the noise at a decibel level I was pretty sure was foreign to the man who epitomized dreary.

But it was the look on McCready's face that got my attention. This wasn't the adoring gaze of a disciple, a dedicated follower. It was a look I'd seen before. It was the look I'd seen on his face during our interview when he was discussing Larmer's exploits with the ladies. What was it he'd said? "Ladies' man, philanderer, seducer ..."

I'd mistaken the look on his face then, but I didn't now. This was hatred, pure and simple. I thought back to the photo of McCready's gorgeous wife and wondered if McCready knew first-hand about Larmer's talent for attracting women. Hugg's ex-wife had made it clear her times with Larmer had been about only one thing. What if the same scene had played itself out, but with Larmer and ... I tried to recall the name she'd scribbled on the photo. "Tammy," that was it. *To my Bernie. Love you, Sugar. Tammy.*

I tried to edge closer to McCready without his seeing me. But there was no danger of that. His eyes never moved. He stared at the centre of the stage, seeing, hearing nothing else, waiting for the man who would walk to the microphone there and proclaim that he was back; that a badly flawed justice system would not, could not keep him from doing the important work that was his life; that he had overcome the insanity of the liberal, progressive, left-leaning conspirators who had sought to muzzle him and failed.

That Buckley-Rand Larmer was ready to fight harder than he ever had before.

And right in front of him, Bernie McCready wanted to see him fail, to see him fall. McCready's eyes had not flickered or moved even a centimetre in either direction since I'd spotted him.

That's when I knew. Bernie McCready realized, as I did, that Larmer would not fail and he would not fall. There was only one thing that could stop him.

I fumbled for my phone, turned from the stage, keyed in the numbers.

"Answer the goddamn phone!" I hissed into the device in my hand, willing it to reach the man I needed to talk to, praying that the noise from the band didn't drown out the ringing at the other end.

"Yeah?" I heard Cobb's voice.

"It's me!" I shouted. I was moving away from the stage again, thinking foolishly that McCready might overhear me.

"Yeah, where are you?"

"I'm here by the stage. Listen, we don't have much time."

"Time for what?"

"We were wrong all along. The threats to Larmer didn't come from Shawn Beamer. They had nothing to do with the murders. It was a different thing altogether. There's a guy right at the front of the stage, name's Bernie McCready, one of the guys I interviewed. I think he's here to kill Larmer."

No beat. No hesitation. In those few words, in those few seconds, Mike Cobb got it.

"What's he look like?"

"Medium height, build, fortyish, balding, shirt and tie, glasses. He's holding his suit jacket over his arm. I think maybe he's —"

"I'm moving. Stay back." Then he repeated it. "Stay back."

"Do you have your gun with you?"

I didn't get an answer.

I dropped my phone into my pocket and turned back to the stage where the band had just finished the last song and were leaving the stage and waving to the cheering crowd. As the Dudes made their way off, the emcee ran back to centre stage and the microphone.

"You wanna talk about courage? You wanna talk about never-backing-down? You wanna talk about telling it like it is … *every time?* Then this is the man you wanna talk about. Give it up for Buckley-Rand Larmer!"

As he stepped back, Larmer jogged out from the back of the stage and the roar erupted, louder and longer than ever. Larmer shook hands with the emcee, raised his arms over his head. When he brought them down, he pulled the microphone from its stand, brought it to his mouth and yelled, "Calgary, I love you!"

I was weaving my way through the crowd, trying to get to McCready. I'd lost sight of him as the kids pressed forward, wanting to be closer to their hero.

Suddenly I heard a shot, and then things got crazy. Kids panicked, turned, and began running in every direction, including mine. I was knocked flat and quickly lost count of the number of times I was stepped on and had people fall over me and onto me. But finally most of them had fled and were past me.

I struggled to my feet, feeling like I'd lost a fight

with a gravel crusher. I looked toward the stage, expecting to see Larmer lying in a pool of blood. He wasn't there. Either he'd been able to run to safety or people had already pulled his wounded body offstage.

I looked over to where McCready had been standing. He wasn't standing now. He was on the ground, Mike Cobb on top of him, a handgun lying a couple of feet away. I moved to where McCready twisted uselessly in Cobb's grasp. His glasses were broken and he was crying and half-yelling, half-whimpering over and over. "Let me shoot that bastard! Let me shoot that bastard!"

I stepped closer as Cobb pulled McCready to his feet, forced him to the stage, and pinned him against it, his arm behind his back, immobilized.

Cobb turned to me, his face bruised and showing the exertion of what he'd just done. He nodded in my direction. "Good call, partner."

I pulled my phone from my pocket and dialed 9-1-1.

McCready laid out the whole story to the police in the hours after his arrest.

Tammy McCready and Larmer had been having an on-and-off affair for several months, maybe longer, he wasn't sure. McCready had suspected it for quite a while but had only been able to confirm his suspicions a few weeks earlier. That was when he began his campaign of threats against Larmer, hoping that the broadcaster would leave Calgary, making Tammy return to her broken husband. He'd even researched how to disable the kind of alarm system Larmer had in his house and had broken in to add an even scarier element to the threats.

He'd come to realize that Larmer wasn't going to run from Calgary and the threats against him. He'd been overjoyed when Larmer was charged with the murder of Jasper Hugg, reasoning that a conviction putting the man behind bars was even better — and more fitting — than a simple change of locale.

When Larmer was released from custody, there was for this tragic figure of a man only one thing left to do. In his mind there was no choice, no alternative. He had to kill the man who was fucking his wife.

Cobb tried to heap praise on me, but I knew I'd just been lucky. Lucky to recall the look on McCready's face during our interview when he spoke of Larmer, the ladies' man. Lucky to have accidentally walked into McCready's office and seen his wife's picture on his desk. Lucky to have noted the yellow Ford Focus when I was looking for someone driving a blue Jetta. And lucky again to have seen the yellow car again as I was walking to Prince's Island.

Of course, knowing I was lucky didn't keep me from accepting the "hero's dinner" Jill and Kyla prepared and served while wearing cheerleaders' costumes. The dinner was frequently interrupted by the slightly nauseating pom-pom–accompanied cheer:

"Adam, Adam, he's our man,

"He fights crime like no one can!"

I was frankly relieved when the pom-poms were tucked away.

"Kyla's idea." Jill smiled, maybe a little ruefully.

"I'm damn relieved to hear that," I said.

Kyla finally headed off to bed, and I was able to enjoy some much more pleasant hero rewards from my all-time favourite cheerleader.

TWENTY ONE

It was the last game of the season. We were back in High River and the Bobcats were facing the undefeated High River team that had pummelled them into submission some weeks earlier.

The Cobbs, Mike and Lindsay, were seated on either side of me and we had been cheering throughout as Kyla and her teammates had managed to stay close to their much superior opponents. Kyla had two doubles and a single and had made a catch at second base that had both teams' fans applauding.

As Kyla's friend Josie, who had smacked a triple earlier, grounded to third for the last out of the game, the final score of 8–5 was what sports pundits would call a moral victory for our girls. More importantly it was a nice way to finish off the season and to start a day that Mike and I had put together a week earlier.

Jill jogged over to the bleachers where we were gathering jackets and pop cans and getting ready to leave.

"How about those guys?" She grinned at us.

"Amazing!" Mike smiled back at her. "A little different than the last time I saw them. I'm nominating you for Manager of the Year."

"I'll settle for Happiest Manager of the Year."

Lindsay Cobb and I stepped down from the bleachers and high-fived the woman I love.

"Great game," I said as she wrapped her arms around my neck. Are baseball managers allowed to hug fans?"

"Only *certain* fans." Jill's laugh was a welcome contrast to the stress of the past few weeks.

Cobb and I were sitting downstairs in front of the TV drinking Rolling Rocks. Kyla was in the backyard with her pal Josie playing catch. Apparently there's no such thing as too much baseball.

Jill and Lindsay were upstairs looking at some website Jill was hoping to involve Lindsay in.

"What are we watching?" Cobb asked.

We were there at my insistence. "The Pride Parade."

Cobb looked at me. "And we're doing this because?"

"You'll see."

"I didn't even know it was televised. I mean, it's not exactly the Stampede Parade."

"This one might be just as good," I said as I brought up the sound on the remote.

We watched for a few minutes as floats and bands and a couple of classic cars rolled by the camera location. Big smiles, lots of cheering, people waving rainbow flags. The camera zoomed in on some of the walkers. Mayor Nenshi led the group. Behind him I recognized several athletes, a few politicians, entertainers, and throngs of waving, hand-holding men, women, and kids of all ages.

Then the group I most wanted to see appeared. The camera gave us a great view as Buckley-Rand Larmer strode into the shot, a grim neo-smile pasted on his face. He was flanked by two women, both looking markedly happier than the radio star. The women held notebooks and were talking to him, the one nearest the camera jotting down something in her book.

"You did this, didn't you?" Cobb looked over at me.

I nodded and grinned. "The woman on the right is a writer for the *Herald*. Her name's Patsy Bannister. She's interviewed Larmer before. They're not tight."

"And why do I think you know the other woman, too?"

"Ariel Mancuso." I nodded. "Came all the way from Fredericton to walk in the parade. Turns out Ariel was the girl who was there when young Randy Larmer stepped in and saved the gay kid, Jaden Reese, from the bullies. By the way, Ariel was one of the bullies. But it seems Ariel's memory has somehow managed to right itself. She talked with two of the boys who were also part of the incident, including one who got his nose broken, and they decided it was time to tell the real story of what happened that day."

"And that was?"

"Turns out Jaden Reese wasn't the one being bullied. It was Larmer."

"And let me guess … Reese stepped in and did the rescuing."

"Give that man a kewpie doll. And since neither Larmer nor the bullies were all that excited about it becoming public knowledge that the school's fag was tougher than all of them, they hatched a little story that adjusted the facts just slightly.

"Ariel called me the other night to tell me she'd seen Larmer on TV and heard him on radio and the man made her sick. She decided to do something she'd wanted to do for a long time."

"Wanted to cleanse the soul, right a long-standing wrong."

"Or words to that effect," I answered without looking away from the TV. "I thought about it and decided to call her back — suggested we might be able to do better by telling Larmer the group had decided to come clean but might be persuaded to stay quiet about it in return for a concession or two."

"One of them being an appearance in the Pride Parade."

"Correct." I watched as Patsy Bannister leaned in to Larmer with a question. "The other being that he would walk with Patsy and Ariel and submit to an interview as he walked."

Larmer wasn't waving to the crowd. He wasn't smiling anymore, not even the fake smile. But he was talking to his two co-walkers. No doubt explaining how one of the city's most prominent homophobes had come to realize that the parade was a good thing, after all, and that he should be a part of it.

I took a satisfying gulp of Rolling Rock.

Cobb was smiling and shaking his head. He looked at me.

"You don't think using the LGBT community to work your revenge might be a little inappropriate, maybe a tad self-serving?"

I grinned at him. "Guilty as charged. But if it gives that community even a momentary respite from the rantings of a snake like Larmer, I think they'd be okay with it."

Cobb watched for a while before he spoke again. "Well, I'm not sure this is how I would have done it, but

I can't say I'm pained to see that man a little uncomfortable."

"Amen to that."

I was standing in a dark alley. Twenty or thirty steps from where Faith Unruh had lost her life. The garage beside which her body had been found and the house behind it rose up dark and quiet in the still of the midnight hour.

I wasn't alone. Cobb was to my left and on my other side the brooding hulk of the man who called himself Marlon Kennedy, but who'd been known to Cobb and the world as Kendall Mark.

We had met earlier that evening at the Farmer's House, a restaurant in Marda Loop. It was a great place, but none of us did justice to the food or the atmosphere. We'd talked about Faith Unruh and none of us felt hungry.

Cobb had impressed on his former police colleague the need to do things right.

"I'll do them right," Kennedy had said, and despite the warmth of the evening I'd shuddered. I remembered what had happened and what had almost happened the night Kennedy had taken me down in the alley behind my apartment.

"We're willing to do whatever we can to help," Cobb had said, "but for that to happen it has to be legal, and it has to be right. No vigilante shit."

For several seconds they glared at each other and I wondered if either of them would back down ... *could* back down.

"What help is that?"

"I don't know," Cobb answered. "We go back over it again. Maybe Cullen can get the media onside and we ask the public for help. I know it's been done a few times, but maybe this time …"

"And maybe you get nothing just like every other time," Kennedy said.

"That's damn sure possible." Cobb nodded. "And maybe you keep watching the house and the alley for shadows that might never come. And you look at tapes hoping for a glimpse of the guy who killed a little girl. And maybe you get it wrong next time, if there is a next time … just like you did with him." Cobb glanced in my direction, then back at Kennedy. "And maybe next time some homeless person happens to wander into the wrong place or the wrong camera frame and he isn't able to talk you out of it and you waste the wrong guy." Cobb paused then and looked at the ground where Faith Unruh had lain in death.

"Or maybe we try to help each other, and one day — someday — we get it right and we find the guy and we take him down the right way. And put the bastard away forever." He looked back at Kennedy.

Several seconds passed.

"Yeah," Kennedy said. "Yeah."

And the house and the garage and the ground in front of it and the shadows — nothing had shifted … nothing had changed.

And maybe never would.

Or maybe …